The Duchess
of
Hillbilly Dale

By

Jennifer Cadgwith

Copyright

The Duchess of Hillbilly Dale
© 2018 by Jennifer Cadgwith
All Rights Reserved

This is a work of fiction. Any similarities to people, places, events, situations, and/or circumstances is coincidental.

Acknowledgments

Thank you to those of you who have offered encouragement, support, and suggestions for this novel. You know who you are.

Thank you, Lillian Vale, for tirelessly reading the drafts and excerpts I sent you.

A special thank you goes to those of you who purchased and enjoyed my previous novel, *The Face Age*. I appreciate each and every one of you.

Note from Author

To make for an enjoyable tale, some creative license has been taken. This book blends American and British expressions and terminology.

Table of Contents

Copyright
Acknowledgments
Note from Author
Table of Contents
Prologue
Chapter One
Chapter Two
Chapter Three
Chapter Four
Chapter Five
Chapter Six
Chapter Seven
Chapter Eight
Chapter Nine
Chapter Ten
Chapter Eleven
Chapter Twelve
Chapter Thirteen
Chapter Fourteen
Chapter Fifteen
Chapter Sixteen
Chapter Seventeen
Chapter Eighteen
Chapter Nineteen
Chapter Twenty
Chapter Twenty-One

Chapter Twenty-Two
Chapter Twenty-Three
Chapter Twenty-Four
Chapter Twenty-Five
Chapter Twenty-Six
Chapter Twenty-Seven
Chapter Twenty-Eight
Chapter Twenty-Nine
Chapter Thirty
Chapter Thirty-One
Chapter Thirty-Two
Chapter Thirty-Three
Epilogue

I have to see a thing a thousand times before I see it once.
-Thomas Wolfe, *You Can't Go Home Again*

Prologue

1993

My wedding day had arrived. Standing in front of a gold. ornate mirror in my suite at Mayberry Hall, a nineteenth-century Gothic Revival manor house that had been converted to a luxury hotel, I fussed with my bespoke Dior gown of white duchess satin with handsewn real pearls scattered about the bodice.

"Jessie, stop fiddling with your cummerbund," my mother said. That's what she called the wide band encircling my waist that was pinned in front with a small diamond and platinum family crest that my almost-official mother-in-law loaned me this morning.

"I'm not fiddling, Mom," I replied. "I don't want the clasp to fall off when I'm halfway down the aisle."

"It won't," she said, moving my hands away. "I'd be more worried about that heirloom tiara falling off your head if I were you. Are you sure the hairstylist secured it well? We most certainly don't want the thing to slip off, clatter onto the stone floor, and break. We couldn't afford the repairs."

"It's insured, Mom, and it's secure. That's why I have this updo instead of wearing my hair down. Please stop worrying about everything."

"I just don't know why you didn't want to wear a veil. I'd feel better if you had a veil."

I listened to her go on about veils while I gazed in the mirror. I hadn't wanted a veil. The Edwardian-era diamond and aquamarine bandeau tiara was enough. Even in this light, it sparkled against my light brown hair that had been freshly streaked with blonde. The tiara had also been a loan, taken from a vault for me to wear today. I forgot for a moment about the jewels and studied my appearance. I wanted so much to look lovely for Will, and the makeup artist exceeded my expectations with her simple, elegant work. The shadow and liner brought out the emerald-green color of my eyes. The rose lipstick accentuated my full lips, and a touch of pink blush and hint of light bronzer warmed up my naturally fair skin. The only thing I'd balked at were the eyelashes. The makeup artist and my mother insisted I wear fake lashes topped with waterproof mascara.

"For the photos," the artist convinced me. "You're eyes are your best feature. I want them to pop. You don't want to look blank."

After she left, my mother blended a tad more crème blush on my cheeks to give me a rosier glow and added an extra swipe of bronzer. "You don't want to look washed-out on your big day either."

I sighed. Between my mother and Will's mother, this was not the first time since our engagement I'd wished Will and I had eloped, but in his position that was not possible. In his rebellious younger days he'd done just that with his first wife, but that marriage had culminated in a scandalous divorce two years later, leaving him with sole custody of a baby whose paternal parentage was *still* being discreetly questioned by some.

This time Will wanted everything to be right, and his family wanted everything done properly as befitted a duke's son and heir, and that included giving me the ten-carat, square-cut emerald ring surrounded by countless diamonds that had belonged to his great-great grandmother as my engagement ring. This was the first day I'd worn it since our official engagement pictures four months ago. Other than my mother's simple diamond tennis bracelet, nothing I wore represented *my* family.

"The car's here," my father announced walking into my room. "Yours, too, honey," he nodded to my mother who was dressed in a sky-blue silk dress and wearing a Treacy hat. "You look beautiful," he told her and kissed her on the cheek. "See you in a few minutes."

"You two better hurry up. Look at the time. The Prince of Wales is probably already seated by now," she fussed. "I don't understand the need to wear hats. It's silly."

This comment, coming on the heels of her defense of a veil moments earlier, was part and parcel of what had ensued while preparing for the wedding. She and Will's mother had butted heads more than once, but the duchess had won out. After all, Will's parents were paying for the wedding. My parents, though they had some money, could *never* have afforded something this grand, and it wouldn't have crossed their minds that this would even be a possibility in my life. It hadn't crossed mine until six months ago.

"We will be right behind you. I'm ready," I said. But was I ready for this sort of wedding? I'd never felt comfortable being the center of attention; however, a few minutes later my father and I pulled up to the largest church in Hearthstone Vale where I was about to marry into the noble Fielding-Smythe family. I couldn't get out of the car.

***

Will and I did not have one of those meet-cutes that we could tell our children about. We met in a pub not long after I finished school in England. I'd been attending the University of Arkansas for two years but did my junior year's first semester abroad at Cambridge studying English Literature. I'd loved it there and begged my parents to let me complete my studies in England, if I were to get accepted and they could afford it. I did, and they could. But back to my meeting with Will…

After university, I'd gotten a job as a junior copyeditor at a London publishing house. Just a short time later, I'd gone out with my two flatmates for a girls' night. Our usual evenings like this were spent at pubs and clubs in our neighborhood, but this time we decided to splash-out and celebrate my flatmate Elsie's new job and my birthday somewhere different and expensive.

The Crow Flies was in the ritziest part of London, and it was my first and last night there because I met Will Smythe while I was trying to order a glass of red wine. I had just about given up getting the barmaid's attention when I felt a shove. A tall man with dark-brown hair tied in a short ponytail appeared next to me. "Sorry," he said without looking at me.

Like any other twenty-three-year-old, I took in what I could see of him, noticing his strong profile at once. I glanced at what he was wearing, at least the top half, and that was an indigo sweater – jumper I must remember to call it – with a blue-and green plaid collar just visible over the crew neck. His attire seemed out-of-place in the room of expensive suits.

"May I be of some service?" he asked, turning to face me. My God, he was handsome with those wicked-looking hazel eyes gazing down at me. His voice was deep, but not too deep, and his accent was upper crust all the way.

Embarrassed at having been caught staring at him, my voice came out as a grating screech over the pub's din, "I've been trying to order a single glass of red wine for fifteen minutes. I'm not sure what I'm doing wrong."

"North American?"

"Yes," I replied in a more normal tone.

"That's the problem. No one can understand you," he said, laughing. "Allow me." He leaned over the bar and motioned subtly with his glass at one of the barmaids who hurried down. "This young woman would like a glass of red wine. A Cabernet, perhaps?" he asked me.

I nodded. When the woman went to get the wine, I asked him how he did that. "I come here often with my friends. Some of them are good tippers," he replied, shrugging.

"None of my friends have been here before, and neither have I. We're celebrating a friend's new job and my birthday."

"You must join us then. We have a table in the back. There's plenty of room, and from the looks of it, you won't find a seat in here."

"Ummmm, okay." I took the glass from the barmaid and started to hand her the money. The amount was exorbitant.

He waved it away. "On me."

"Thanks! Be right back."

"Are you kidding me, Jess, this guy is inviting us to sit with his fancy friends!" my flatmate Suze exclaimed. "You did agree, right?"

"You said we would, didn't you?" Elsie grabbed my arm. "Please, say you did."

The long and the short of it was that I had. Will and I became friends that night before starting to date a few weeks later. Our evenings were comprised of simple meals, pubs, the cinema, and, uh…you know. He learned I was bookish and quiet, and I learned he was something of a daredevil who enjoyed extreme sports. He was also an Oxford graduate, an architect, and ten years older than I. At thirty-three, he was divorced and had a young son, Alistair, aged six.

A year after Alistair was born, Will's wife left them for an environmental researcher. The last Will had heard they were happily slogging away in Borneo or some other remote place on a quest for something or other. Alistair had seen his mother just twice since the divorce. She sent him the occasional package for birthdays and Christmas, but other than that…nothing. At twenty-three, I was dating a single dad. My friends thought I was daft, to use their expression. I was too young to deal with a guy who had a child, they'd said.

"Do you really want to go to Disney movies on your dates and take a child?" Suze had asked. I didn't mind. I liked Alistair, and he wasn't always with us.

After Will proposed to me just short of a year later, in the romantic, medieval, fortified city of Carcassonne, France, he revealed who he really was. The only son of Arthur Alistair William Fielding-Smythe, The Duke of Hearthe. Will was known as Earl of Ponder, his father's secondary title, which explained why some of his friends had called him 'Pond' when we met.

To say I was shocked was putting it mildly. I'd seen those films and read those novels where the commoner marries into nobility, but this was really happening. When I went to meet the family, I was terrified. The drive through the Lake District, beautiful though it was, frightened me. I was going to the place I'd be spending the rest of my life – Fielding House – where generations of Will's family had lived since the first Elizabeth's time.

The Fielding-Smythes owned an Elizabethan country house just west of Hearthestone Vale, a market town close to the beautiful Lake Pondermere above which Fielding House stood. Will's father I learned also owned a three-hundred-year-old manor house in Cornwall that, due to rock-slides and partial cliff falls, the family feared would one day fall into the sea. They also had a residence in Belgravia they used when in London, and it was the newest. The family had owned it for one-hundred-fifty years. Will had a flat in Chelsea, and I thought *that* was something!

When Will turned into the drive and we approached a gray, two-towered stone gatehouse with an actual portcullis, I was awestruck. "It's part of an old castle that was on this site," Will explained.

As soon as we topped a hill, I saw the E-shaped, reddish-brown stone house with its many mullioned-paned windows waiting for me down a drive lined with shrubbery. Off to one side, I caught a glimpse of the lake beyond the house, and in the distance, hills. "You really grew up here?" I blurted out, immediately feeling foolish. Of course he had grown up in Fielding House. It had been the family home for centuries.

"Yes. I hope you will learn to love it as much as I do."

I hoped so too, because at the moment I was intimidated and felt all those windows were eyes watching an interloper approach. Okay, so I'd seen too many movies set in old mansions, and I'd gone through a Gothic novel phase when I was about thirteen. The moment I entered Fielding House, however, I felt at home, but maybe that was because Will was with me.

I soon learned that Will's favorite place was an early thirteenth-century stone church with a bell tower topped by four short spires. The tower still housed an old iron bell – how old, no one knew. The church stood inside the northwest boundary of Fielding House's property, just fifteen feet from the cliff edge of a peninsula that jutted into Lake Pondermere. The church meant so much to Will that we had a secret wedding there two days ago with just us, my parents as witnesses, and the local vicar.

***

The cries of "Carola, Carola," through the open windows snapped me back to reality. Today, the bookish woman from small-town America, was *officially* becoming part of the Fielding-Smythe family – a family steeped in tradition - in a wedding with all the trappings, including a member of the royal family in attendance.

"Are you sure you're ready for this, sweetheart?" my father asked.

I nodded, finally allowing him to help me out of the vintage, white, Rolls Royce Phantom that was part of the duke's car collection. Cameras went off and people kept calling my name. "Carola, Carola! Look over here," but I looked straight ahead as advised.

My future in-laws felt my first name of Jessica wasn't quite right for a countess and future duchess, so my middle name had been selected. After today, I'd publicly be known as 'Carola, Countess of Ponder,' or more likely, 'Lady Ponder'. Ponder was a small village in the eastern part of the dukedom.

Earl of Ponder was actually an older family title than that of Duke of Hearthe, but for four-hundred-forty-one years there had been a Duke of Hearthe in North West England, thanks to a distant family connection to Elizabeth I and a huge service done for her which shall remain private. It was a small dukedom, but a very wealthy one. If there was one thing the Fielding-Smythes knew how to do, it was increase their wealth through property and investments.

I again heard the calls of "Carola," Carola," mispronounced as 'Corolla' by the locals who had come to watch the wedding procession at the church. Some to see me, but many to see British aristocracy, celebrities, and perhaps royalty in their finery. My father escorted me past the lines of people with their cameras snapping away, and up the steps followed by a procession of giggling little girls and boys as was the custom. I waited until they were all in place, which was no small feat, but somehow accomplished by one child's experienced nanny. I didn't know the children, although I had met their parents who were Will's friends and family.

Much to my disappointment, Alistair wasn't included in the page boys. My mother-in-law wanted younger children in the wedding party. He sat with the family. How I would have liked one of my friends to bring up the rear, but it was Will's sister Lady Aileen who had that honor. My British friends knew about Will's lineage and they were there – sitting in the cheap seats is the way I considered the set-up.

As decided, other than my parents no one from the States attended, not because I didn't want them there, but because my parents and Will's thought it best that who I married in England be kept quiet. It was more for my parents' safety and privacy rather than any embarrassment on Will's family's part. After his first disastrous marriage, they were happy that I was well-brought-up, intelligent, polite, and had an education. If people in my hometown of Hilly Dale, Arkansas found out the Charles and Evelyn Jenson had a daughter who married into a very wealthy, titled family, things could change for my parents, and probably not in a good way. So, it was put about that I was marrying an architect whose last name was Smythe. Hmmmm… they called him Will Smythe. Generic enough.

The string quartet began to play Bach's Prelude in D Major - my cue to start walking - but I stood still. My father whispered, "I love you, my sweet girl," in my ear, and gave me a nudge with his shoulder. "Are you sure about this?" he asked again. "You can still back out and we'll go home to Hilly Dale just as soon as we get you packed up."

I smiled and whispered, "Dad, you know Will and I married two days ago. This is just for appearances. It's nonsense, but it's tradition."

My dad raised an eyebrow and then with love in his eyes replied quietly, "Yeah, I know, but we could still work things out if you don't want all this pomp."

I thanked him and kissed his cheek before walking down the nave barely noticing the guests, many I did not know anyway. As I passed through the crossing, preparing to meet Will and be traditionally married in front of his family, their circle of society, and the Prince of Wales, I wondered if I would ever manage to become a part of this life. Would I fit in? Would I ever stop feeling like Jessie Jenson and become Carola, Countess of Ponder? And then I looked at Will and I knew this was the best decision I'd ever made.

I glanced at the clergy standing before me and smiled. To be on the safe side, we made sure it was known that my name was pronounced 'Carol-ah.' I was, after all, named after my great-grandmother, not a car.

And so my new life began.

Chapter One

Twenty years later…

It was sunny the day of Will's funeral, but a brisk breeze from the west made the air *especially* cold for mid-November in North West England. I shivered in my black wool coat as I made my way, with the help of my stepson Alistair, from Fielding House down the path to where the service was to be held. Just past the graveyard ahead was the stone church with its bell tower. The structure had stood on the Lake Pondermere peninsula since before Fielding House had been conceived.

Alistair and I walked down the gravel path past the old gravestones, many leaning or crumbling, and beneath which were the remains of numerous lesser members of the Fielding and Smythe families. I shuddered thinking there were many other people lying in unmarked graves that dated well before Will's ancestors came into possession of the land. I refused to look at the mausoleum that had been constructed for the dukes and duchesses.

Will and I used to spend hours wandering in the graveyard. He would peer at the dates and tell me the connections of the deceased to the family, enthralled with the colorful history and genealogy. A family tree hanging in the library traced them back to well before William the Conqueror.

I could see the church as we walked along, but the closer we got to it I could hear the lake's wind-driven waves slapping against the low cliff's face. Fitting. Will had loved the water, and it had been his downfall. While this church had stood through gales, landslides, and battles during its eight-hundred-plus years, William, at age fifty-four, had been taken out during a freak storm while participating in a sailing event off Cornwall.

Why he and some others had chosen to take part in such an event in November was beyond me, but that was Will. He loved an element of danger. He and his crew were heading back to port just before the storm hit. They were less than an eighth of a mile away when the sailboat capsized. Will was wearing a life vest, but the waves were towering. I hadn't been there at the time of the accident, but I was haunted by images of my husband floundering and then slamming into the rocks. He wasn't the only one who died that day. Thankfully, some of the other boats made it back to safety and there were less lives lost than would have been expected. I wished Will had been one of the fortunate ones.

I never wanted to visit Cornwall again, although I had always found it beautiful. Prior to the accident I'd enjoyed my time there, except staying at the manor. I'd neither liked the stone house's austerity, nor it's rustic furnishings that had remained through the centuries. What I'd loved was the unobstructed view of the Celtic Sea, but now that was ruined for me.

I probably should have chosen the large church where we publicly married for Will's service, but I had not been thinking clearly and was adamant that the old church was the place. My husband had loved everything about the property - the land, the lake, the view, the house, and especially the church where we had our secret wedding years ago. It was special. That's why I chose it.

He also loved the town of Hearthstone Vale and was loved by the residents. We had opened our property to the public, so the path to the church was lined with locals, most with bowed heads. It wasn't right that the ones who had served and known Will all his life and had known his father before that were relegated to standing outside in the cold, while the upper class were seated, albeit uncomfortably squeezed together in the chilly church. Rank was one of the many things I'd had to learn when I married my husband, and I still wasn't a fan, but in this case the seating situation was my fault. If only I'd considered the townspeople instead of my own selfish desire to have the service in the small church. Perhaps we could have a memorial in town later or have a gathering at Fielding House to celebrate Will's life and include the townspeople.

Peering through my black hat's short, netted veil, I tried to smile at some of the villagers as we passed them. Those who deigned to look back at me viewed me with pity. Some with cameras ignored me but were likely hoping, like at my wedding, to capture a photo of a member of the royal family. I knew one was in attendance. The security detail was there, but discreet. Because of his other commitments scheduled for the day, His Royal Highness had arrived in a helicopter which had landed in our front garden. A black car had whisked the prince to the church. I'd liked to have seen them trying to get the car down the narrow lane on the south end of the property and then hustling the prince up to the back door of the church, but HRH was a good sport, and thoughtfully knew that this was a day for Will's family. It suddenly occurred to me that it might have been easier to lower a ladder from the helicopter and drop HRH at the back of the church. I stifled a laugh at the image. I shouldn't be laughing at my husband's funeral. What was the matter with me? What if someone sees me?

"Is everything all right, Mum?" Alistair whispered.

I nodded. "Just wondering where the security detail was stationed."

Alistair gave me a questioning look. He knew very well I was used to security issues when royalty visited Fielding House. It didn't happen all the time, but I knew the drill.

The vicar, a friend of the family who had assisted at our secret wedding, stood in front of the closed, studded, weathered door, waiting for us to arrive. Alistair took one of his hands and I took the other. I didn't know what Vicar Kester said to me, but I murmured something and he smiled in a gentle way, released his hands from mine and Alistair's, opened the door, and pointed with his arm the way inside.

Alistair and I waited at the back of the chapel until my son Lord William, known as "Liam", and daughter Lady Aisling joined us. Liam was holding on to my mother-in-law, but he needn't have. She stood stony-faced and ramrod-straight for an eighty-two-year-old woman who had recently lost her son. Together with Will's sister Lady Aileen and her family, we walked sedately down the aisle to the front pews. I had none of my American family present. My father had died several years ago, and my mother wasn't able to travel now. I missed them both. I needed them right now. Trying to blink away the tears welling in my eyes, I made my way to the pew.

"Never let them see you cry. You can touch your eyes delicately with a handkerchief, but above all, my dear, keep a stiff upper lip," my mother-in-law had said before we left the house. 'Stiff upper lip' was another thing that I, as an American, never quite understood. I could see not breaking down into loud sobs in front of everyone here, but this was my husband's funeral! It was her son's funeral. It didn't matter to me if he was The Duke of Hearthe. He had been my husband for the past twenty years! He was Alistair, Liam, and Aisling's father.

Alistair sat at the end of the front pew. I sat next to him, with Aisling next to me, then my mother-in-law, and finally Liam. Lady Aileen and her family sat on the other front pew. The Prince of Wales was directly behind Alistair. At least no one was expected to sit by rank at a funeral, at least not in this little church.

My fairy tale romance was over. The death of William Alistair James Fielding-Smythe, The Duke of Hearthe would change everything for me.

***

My stepson's new reality sunk in a few days later. He was now, Alistair, The Duke of Hearthe. He'd always known this would happen and had, more or less, been resigned to it, but he didn't expect it would be when he was almost twenty-seven. No one did. In a small way, though, I understood how Alistair felt. Oddly enough, I had been twenty-eight when Will's father suddenly passed, making us The Duke and Duchess of Hearthe. I'd been Countess of Ponder less than four years and was still learning the ropes of that, but my new title had taken me to a different level. More was expected of me, and now with Will's passing and Alistair unmarried, I was still considered *The* Duchess of Hearthe, meaning I would continue representing the family as such until he wed. After that, I could retire to the background like my mother-in-law. She didn't even live at Fielding House any longer, preferring Ravens' Roost, an early nineteenth-century house on the east side of the property.

Being Will's first-born son and subject to the, in my opinion, antiquated primogeniture, Alistair had inherited everything, but I'd always known that neither the Fielding House properties nor the Fielding-Smythe holdings and possessions had ever been truly mine, unless Will had purchased something specifically for me, but my husband had seen to it that Liam, Aisling, and I were taken care of and would live extremely comfortable lives. Alistair had been raised to be a good, generous man, but he was now surrounded by solicitors and accountants telling him what he had to do and what he should do, all based on tradition and his new position. I had confidence that Alistair would do just fine, if he would think for himself and not be swayed by what I thought of was a pack of hyenas.

I wasn't concerned about finances for myself. I had my own money safe in banks in the States. When the children went off to school, I picked up a hobby I'd had since I was a teenager – writing. I started writing in my spare time and eventually a couple of cozy mystery series I'd created were published. I wrote under the pen name of Jessica Keasden and dealt with a large U.S. Publishing Company.

I had done surprisingly well with the two series - *The Celestial Cat* about a young woman who owned a mysterious B&B, and *Harriet Donovan*, a series about a thirty-something socialite who moved among the British aristocracy, stumbling upon secrets, scandals, and murder in the early 1900s. *Harriet Donovan* was very tongue-in-cheek, but I had to be careful. A few plots came a bit close to friends' family histories, but not close enough to be sued, thankfully.

A fly-in-the-ointment for the Fielding-Smythe accountants and solicitors had always been that I still had my American citizenship. They felt it was problematic for me to keep it, and it was financially-speaking, but I had become a British citizen years ago as they asked. My rationalization was if I didn't have to renounce my American citizenship, why should I? They were there to take care of all the tax issues.

For a year-and-a-half, I drifted along doing my duties, volunteering at and sponsoring charity drives, helping Alistair adjust to being Duke, writing, and making sure Liam and Aisling were all right. Then there were the trips to the States to see my mother and visit with my agent, Dil Daly, but once again November brought change to my life. At beginning of my second year as a widow, I was hit with a couple of blows.

Chapter Two

The call came from one of my mother's close friends, Jackson Barker, retired history professor at Hilly Dale College. He was one of only two my mother had been allowed to tell about my life in England, outside of the fact that I was a successful novelist who had married an architect. Jackson had learned the rest of it when my father died seven years ago. Will and I decided someone should know now that my mother was a widow and the other person she'd told was no longer living.

"Jessica," Jackson said in a somber voice when I returned his call an hour later, "Your mother passed away a little while ago. It was sudden. She was at bridge club – the morning one." He paused for a moment and said, voice breaking, "They called 911, but it was too late…nothing could be done. I'm so sorry."

"I was just there last month," I said. "She was fine, well, as fine as could be expected." Jackson let me ramble on, answering my questions while trying to maintain his composure, and then told me that I needed to make arrangements to come home. "I need to think and talk to the children. Thank you for letting me know." I rang off, closed my eyes, and leaned back in the chair by the fireplace in our Belgravia townhouse.

"Your Grace." I opened my eyes to see Mr. Herren who managed the household along with his wife, standing there. I hadn't heard him knock. "May I bring you tea?"

"Is Lady Aisling home?" I asked. I'd heard him say something, but I had no idea what it was. I couldn't think straight.

"I believe so, Your Grace. Would you like me to…"

"My mother has died, Mr. Herren." Standing up, I said, "We have to leave for the States tonight." I walked stiff-backed from the room, climbed the stairs, reached my bedroom, and collapsed. Never let them see you cry.

Very late that evening, Alistair, Liam, Aisling, and I boarded a family friend's private jet and flew to Arkansas.

***

Another funeral. I had decided to break with the custom of waiting to the last minute before the service and marching down the aisle as a family. Some of my mother's relatives were shocked by the decision and voiced their opinion at my parents' home the day after I'd planned the service. I didn't care. I hated being stared at, and especially at a time like this. I remembered how it was with my father's service, and with Will's, but I had a duty at Will's. I had no duty to perform here.

"Jessica, this is how it's done. What will people think?" my Aunt Jane-Ann said, while squeezing another casserole in the refrigerator. "There, you'll have plenty to eat. I've put numbers on all the dishes and written the names in that book over there, so you'll be able to write your thank you notes and know what people brought, and you'll also need to return these dishes."

My children were fascinated by the array of food that kept arriving, not that they would eat casseroles like this, but I was too polite to tell my aunt that. "I'm afraid we won't be here long enough to enjoy these delicious meals. You are welcome to them, and someone else must deal with the dishes. We are flying home day after tomorrow. Alistair has work to do, Liam has to return to school, and Aisling has other commitments." I wasn't going to explain 'gap year' to my aunt

"Well, I never," Aunt Jane-Ann declared. "Jessica, you are in your hometown. People are going to want to see you. I've told them to come by this house. So many loved your mother. And, you do have fans here, you know. You're a writer and are the biggest thing to come out of Hilly Dale since that man who played for the Razorbacks. You should have planned better for this."

"Aunt Jane-Ann, my mother – *your sister* – died recently. It's been a great shock and this trip was long and tiring. We made the funeral arrangements quickly and are having the service at 11:00 this morning. I apologize for the inconvenience, but I am not here to socialize with everyone. I don't feel like it. I appreciate the kindness of people dropping off food, but I am not staying here to be paraded around or be on display. I'll come back another time to take care of things."

"Don't sass me in that hoity-toity new accent of yours. You're from Hilly Dale, Arkansas. It's tradition to bring food and it's common courtesy to visit with someone after a death in the family. You have relatives who have traveled across the state to see you. You owe it to them. Some are sitting in the living room right now!"

The relatives to which she referred had barely paid me any mind all the years I lived in Hilly Dale, but they were certainly turning out in force now. After this, I wouldn't hear from them again, and that had nothing to do with the fact I lived in England. It's just the way they were.

"Mum," Liam said before I could make a testy retort to a woman I had barely seen in years, "why don't you go upstairs and have a lie-down before we leave for the service. We can handle this for you."

"I'll come with you," Aisling said. We climbed the switchback stairs that led to my old bedroom where Aisling was staying and to my parents' room where I was sleeping. "I like this house, Mum. It's simple and warm."

"So do I," I replied. "I like it very much."

The house, a large white Victorian with front and back wrap-around porches, bay windows, and a turret on one end sat on a hill just north of downtown. From the turret window, a section of the downtown could be seen. As an only child, I had spent countless hours in that room reading. Eventually, I began writing short stories for entertainment. The house provided endless subject matter. My paternal great-great-grandfather had the house built in 1889 and I imagined all sorts of scenarios taking place over the years. My mother, an English professor at the local college, encouraged my creative endeavors. She would read each short story with a practiced eye, giving praise when it was due and offering suggestions when I needed them. She was my editor when I started writing my first series *The Celestial Cat*, and she was still the best editor I'd ever had.

Aisling stopped at my old room and before entering asked if I needed anything. Yes, I needed my mother, but I smiled at her and said, "Thank you, perhaps later. Go text your friends at home."

"I loved her too, Mum," she said giving me a big hug. "I know you miss her. It's all right if you cry. Nan isn't correct. You can let us see you cry."

I hugged Aisling tighter, and we both shed a few tears.

***

We had the grave-side service first with just the family. The memorial service was public and when it was over, we went out a side entrance, stood by the front door and spoke to those who weren't invited to the meal downstairs. "So sorry about your husband and mom, but I just love your books!" a woman I didn't recognize said. "Are you going to be in town long? I'd love to get you to autograph some of them."

I shook my head. "We'll be leaving soon."

"Are these your kids?" she went on.

It was the same with all the others passing through the line. Some were murmuring condolences, some praising my mother, and some asking questions. There I stood, answering people that I didn't know, or at best barely remembered, thanking them for coming, and smiling politely.

"Mrs. Smythe," a scrawny-looking man in a navy-blue suit, said. "I'd like to offer my sincere condolences on the loss of your dear mother."

"Thank you."

"I can see you don't remember me. I'm Gary Minder. I was your mother's lawyer. We must have a meeting about your mother's…"

"Mr. Minder, I don't think this is the time," Alistair interrupted. "Perhaps when she is next here?"

"We really must take care of this, Mrs. Smythe," the lawyer insisted. "When is a good time for you?"

"I, I, I don't know. I live in England and we have to go back day after tomorrow."

"Ah, that does present a problem. We must schedule a meeting right away to go over things. Your mother had quite an estate, if I remember correctly."

Alistair leaned close to the lawyer and said in a very low tone, "THIS IS NOT THE TIME. She will contact you as soon as she can." The lawyer backed off. "We do not live here and this is a sad time for us. We have a copy of the documents. We will look over them and get in touch with you."

More people came through the line. "Will you be selling your home?" a smartly dressed woman I did not know asked. "It's a lovely house on a beautiful lot."

"I have no idea. It's early days, Ms?"

"Jones. Claudia Jones."

She extended her hand as if to shake mine, but instead handed me her business card. I glanced at it and saw *Claudia Jones Realty. If you want to get rid of it, I can sell it.*

"The *nerve*!" Alistair whispered. "Vultures."

By the time the line of mostly well-wishers left, all I wanted was to go back to the house, but my mother's friends and family wanted to have a meal at the church. It was tradition, but it was more for them than my children and me. We were all tired, emotional, and just wanted to be together privately instead of chatting with people. I was asked numerous times if I'd autograph a book. It was flattering to know I had fans, but this was not the place to ask me. Granddaughters of my mother's friends fluttered around Alistair and Liam crying, "Oooooh, I just love your accent. Sounds just like you stepped out of *Downton Abbey*." Aisling stayed near me. This was a different world for her.

"Stiff upper lip," I told myself.

After two hours of introductions, visiting, dodging questions, picking at food, and milling about, Jackson Barker, sensing my exhaustion, intervened and signaled the end of the lunch so that we could go back to the house and rest.

"I think we had a good turn-out for the service," my aunt said, putting a cheese tray in the refrigerator. "I'd hoped for more, what with her being at the college for so long, but you would schedule this on a Friday, Jessica. If it had been Saturday, the Methodist church would have been full."

"I'd like to see the town," Aisling said, successfully stopping my aunt from comparing her sister's service to some sort of macabre social gathering. "Do you think it would be possible to take a tour of the town after you've had another lie-down, Mum? I'd like to see it again. I haven't been here in a long time. Grandfather and Grandmother Jenson most always came to us, and next year we were planning a holiday here with Granny J."

Jackson, bless him, agreed to take my children on a tour of Hilly Dale, and he insisted that my aunt go along to help him, just in case he had the history wrong. I knew he did that to give me some time alone to mourn privately, without my aunt's constant criticism.

As I walked down the oak-planked hallway, I was flooded by memories of my parents and grandparents. I sat down in the upper hall, leaned my back against the wall, and let the tears that had been threatening for three days to spill. The sounds of gut-wrenching soul-sobs filled the upstairs. I hadn't experienced sobs like these since Will died, but I'd let those tears out at the old stone church instead of in the house. Both times, the tears and guttural cries were cathartic. After several minutes, I stood, wiped my eyes on my sleeve, and wandered around the house, taking in the details like the cream walls, clawfoot tubs, pewter chandeliers, and the oak floors with the matching oak trim around the windows and doors. The transom windows fascinated me as a child. My mother kept the one over my door open all the time. I realized now she did that so she could always hear me, but at the time, I felt special because it was the *only* one that was open.

I climbed the stairs to the turret where I'd spent happy hours reading and letting my imagination run wild. Gazing out the window, I could see a small section of The Old Part of Hilly Dale where homes dating prior to the Civil War stood. A bit closer to the downtown, the steeples of the Baptist Church, and the Methodist Church were visible. They rose proudly against the sunset that was beginning.

As I stood there, it occurred to me that for the first time I had something that was truly *mine* – this house and all that it contained. It was a heady feeling for someone who had, for more than two decades, spent her time among museum-quality things that had to be preserved for the next generation and was always aware that she was merely being *allowed* to use them, as long as she was married to Will and part of the family.

I went downstairs, walked out the front door, and sat down on the green porch swing, moving it back and forth, remembering how as a child I'd once gone too high, slid out, and broken my arm. I'd narrowly missed being whacked in the head by the swing on more than one occasion.

For the most part, life in Hilly Dale had been filled with wonderful parents, love, support, and a few friends. It was the life of which many dreamed. Being here in my childhood home was a refreshing change from the opulence of Fielding House and the elegance of the Belgravia townhouse. My childhood home felt simple, safe, warm, and …normal. *That* thought startled me. Had I forgotten what being normal was?

Chapter Three

The second blow came two months later. Alistair texted that I needed to meet him in the library. When I entered the room with its dark paneling above and below the mullioned-windows and its two shelved walls of books - many first-edition classics and some rare works - there stood two of our solicitors and two accountants. The four of them acknowledged me with nods and one asked me to please be seated.

"Your Grace, we are here to discuss some issues that have recently come to our attention during a review," our head accountant Mr. Hartfield said.

"I see. What may I help you with?" I asked, glancing at Alistair who looked worried.

"Your Grace, after considerable thought and much discussion between the family solicitors and accountants, we agree that it would be in your best interest to renounce your American citizenship as soon as it is possible," Mr. Poleduck said, bunching his bushy eyebrows together as he stared at me over his rimless spectacles. "It's been suggested to you before, but now, it may be crucial."

"Mr. Poleduck, please allow Mr. Hartfield to go over this part," Alistair said with an edge to his voice.

"Your Grace, since your husband's death, your dual citizenship has made handling your affairs more complicated than ever in matters of inheritance and taxation." The accountant looked nervous. "The death duties, as you know, were not inconsequential and it is imperative that we preserve…"

"What?" I blurted out in a very un-duchess-like way. "I don't have anything to do with this. Most everything passed to my stepson."

"That is true, but the laws are…unfortunate in your case. It is, however, important that they be followed."

"It can't be too important, since whatever it is has been discovered at this late date. My husband has been gone over two years now."

"I believe that Poleduck & Henstrom and Hartfield & Associates are to blame by not informing Father and you about complications years ago when papers were drawn up giving you certain things upon his death. For that, I am considering whether to continue retaining the firms. It makes me doubt their attention to detail and research."

"Poleduck & Henstrom have been with your family for seventy-five years, Your Grace," the solicitor spluttered, his chubby face turning red and those eyebrows bunching even closer than before.

"As have we," Mr. Hartfield agreed. "My grandfather started the firm and your…"

"Nevertheless, someone years ago failed to inform my parents so that any legality concerns could be rectified at that time. Was it you who failed to follow through?" Alistair looked directly at Thomas Poleduck. "Or you, Mr. Hartfield?"

"I am certain, Your Grace, that this can be handled with ease," Mr. Poleduck said. "There is no need for a hasty decision on your part. No one expected the late duke to die when he did. There were still matters to be sorted."

"Excuse me," I interrupted, "I am in the room. We are talking about things that involve me. Need I remind you that currently I am The Duchess of Hearthe, Mr. Polefu…duck." I reigned myself in. How unseemly to publicly use a vulgar expression in anger, and pulling rank was something I tried never to do, but I had to make a strong statement. "As this appears to concern me, I would like to be informed of what is going on. My husband was killed in an accident. NO ONE expected that!"

"Yes, Your Grace. No need to be upset. It's just a matter of settling things that were left hanging, so to speak, and I'll leave the matter up to Mr. Hartfield to explain what has happened, and he will…" An obsequious Mr. Poleduck began backing away while the accountant came to the forefront again.

"We must discuss the tax and inheritance matters," Mr. Hartfield interrupted, "which is why I need Mr. Poleduck to remain."

"There's some question as to who owns Lilac House - the house the late duke purchased a year before his untimely death and included your name on the deed, along with other items that are now considered yours," the solicitor informed me. "And, of course, your recent acquisitions in the States need to be discussed – the disposal of them will affect your own finances. I assume you have an attorney in your hometown of…what is it again?" He looked at one of the minions who was staring at the ceiling. "Mr. Todd, I asked you a question."

"Oh, sir. Yes."

Mr. Poleduck repeated the question.

"Hilly Dale, Arkansas."

The fact that our family solicitor did not know the name of my hometown was part and parcel for how he viewed me – an outsider of no importance now that my husband was deceased, and that angered me. "Yes, my mother had an attorney. I spoke with him briefly. What do we hire you for? Is it to lollygag about? You should know these things. I've been part of the family for a long time."

"Well, you see, it wasn't important until your mother died and it brought…"

"My mother has nothing to do with the matter we were discussing. I have others to deal with things in America concerning my mother's estate. We are discussing my inheritance here. The Cotswold house issue should have been addressed two years ago. The house is mine now that Will has died."

Lilac House, the pretty eighteenth-century Cotswolds house located in Broadway, Worcestershire had been my writing refuge for the past three years. It was filled with things I had purchased or Will gifted me. I felt at peace there.

"The belongings, Your Grace, that the late duke purchased for it will be part of the Fielding-Smythe…" Mr. Poleduck began. I wished he would stop referring to Will as the 'late duke.' He was my husband. How I wanted to tell the solicitor to shut up.

"Now see here, Poleduck," my stepson cut him off, "that house is hers, and all that is inside is hers. I will not allow it to become part of this estate. I have too much, and Her Grace has purchased things for that house. Her name is on the deed too."

"Our duty is to the family, Your Grace," Mr. Poleduck stated, "but naturally Her Grace may keep the items that she purchased with her own money."

"Her Grace is family," Alistair countered, "and you are not part of our accounting team, so I would like to politely request that you stop talking about finances for the moment."

I was proud of Alistair. He reminded me of Will with his flashing hazel eyes that were giving the solicitor an intimidating look. Chastised, Thomas Poleduck backed up a few paces.

"But she is not your biological family, Your Grace, She is your stepmother, if I may say so," Mr. Hartfield stated.

"No, you may not. She has been my mother since I was a boy. She is the only mother I have known. The belongings are hers and whether my father purchased them is irrelevant, and the same for the property."

"Need I remind you both that she has dual-citizenship. If she retains this property under her name, it and all other items that she inherited will be her sole responsibility in terms of taxes. They will be out of the Fielding-Smythe family. As you know, those with American citizenship living abroad pay taxes in the United States, as well as where they reside and work. America is one of the few countries that require this."

"Alistair, " I interrupted, "if it will make things simple, we can deed the house to Aisling and Liam. It would definitely be 'in the family' that way."

"If it becomes necessary, and you agree," Alistair replied. "I will allow that."

I looked gratefully at my stepson. Turning my head, I smiled sweetly at Mr. Hartfield and Mr. Poleduck, ignoring their useless lackeys who stood gawping at the books on the shelves, and said, "In that way, *you* will not have to deal with me, and it will give my other two children something of their own. I would, of course, like to retrieve my personal items. Will I need to provide receipts for each item?"

"That would be most helpful, but, of course, we will be lenient."

"How *kind* of you to do so. I still do not understand why this is being brought up now. Has there been some sort of misdeed that you have uncovered in your offices?"

"It's because we are reviewing everything for taxes," an affronted Mr. Hartfield stated. "We want to avoid an audit. Our firms are working together."

"We have to make sure the cottage and other property - property the late duke gave you that can be traced back to him – goes into the family trust, Your Grace, as it was not spelled out," Mr. Poleduck, having composed himself, replied.

"To clarify, Your Grace, unless you wish to start paying the taxes on the house and everything you have here to both the British and American government by yourself, it is the most agreeable solution to give these things over to the family estate, unless you rid yourself of your dual-citizenship," Mr. Hartfield added. "When your husband was alive, we were able to include most everything under him, except for your book earnings, of course. We will not do that now."

"Is that a threat?" I asked quietly.

"No, of course not. We have the interest of the Fielding-Smythe family in mind. You are the late duke's wife, and you are not the present duke's mother."

"I am a Fielding-Smythe, as His Grace just told you. Have you forgotten that already?" I rose from my chair, "I am a citizen of the United Kingdom." I'd kept my American citizenship out of a sense of loyalty and duty to the country of my birth as well as to honor my parents, but I hadn't realized what a problem it was. Now, it was hitting me full force of how protected I'd been through Will.

"Only your children are direct Fielding-Smythe family members and they do not hold dual-citizenship. Their well-being is also our concern, so putting the Cotswolds property into the trust would be best. We are trying to help you, Your Grace."

"I'm sure your firms will sort that out under the supervision of my stepson," I gave Mr. Hartfield and Mr. Poleduck a pointed look and continued, "I insist that he monitor both of your firms' work. And I will expect to receive any and ALL copies of everything your firm and Mr. Poleduck's firm has that involves me. If you will excuse me." I left the room, wandered out to the courtyard in the back, and then followed the path through the garden to the old church. After unlocking the door, I walked down the centuries-old stone-floored aisle and took a seat at the front. I sat in silence until an answer came to me.

Chapter Four

The private jet touched down in Little Rock, Arkansas early on a Saturday afternoon in mid-July. After collecting our luggage, Liam, Aisling, and I walked into a wave of heat and humidity. It was probably not that noticeable to those who lived here all the time, but for three people from North West England – and we did experience humidity there – the combination felt miserable.

"Is it always this hot here?" Aisling asked as we got into the hired white SUV.

"No," I said, smiling at my nineteen-year-old daughter. "It can get much worse."

"I'm beginning to re-think my decision," she said, pulling her long blonde hair into a high ponytail.

My daughter was going to attend Hilly Dale College where my mother once taught. Besides Aisling's high marks, her excellent application, and the fact that they had a few slots left, no doubt dreams of *potential* donations from author Jessica Keasden had inspired the college's president Timothy Hayes to expedite matters.

"You can always come back and go to Cambridge with me," Liam suggested, "but I'm not sharing a flat with you."

"What makes you think I'd want to stay with you?" Aisling challenged.

"Mum, You've gone from Hearthestone Vale to Hilly Dale. I know there's got to be a poem, rhyme, or limerick for that! You're the clever, creative one studying English, Aisling. Come up with one," Liam taunted her.

I allowed them to banter and bicker until we drove onto Interstate 40. "I'm exhausted. Neither of you has driven on the 'wrong side of the road' and we have just a tad over a two-hour drive ahead, so please stop talking for a little while. I need to concentrate. And, do not, I repeat DO NOT, let Violet out of her crate, Liam."

Violet was my beloved black Persian cat. She had the most beautiful sea-green eyes. Will gave me Violet, a four-month-old kitten, just a couple of months before the accident. Although my family was a great comfort after Will died, it was Violet who was there for me when I would wake in the middle of the night, shivering from anxiety, alone in a centuries-old bed. She would snuggle up next to me and let me hold her paw. The sound of her purring lulled me to sleep.

"We should have brought Thor with us," Liam said. "He could keep Violet company."

"Thor would not have fit in this SUV, with three of us and our things, and what would I have done with him in the house! I'm sure the owner of the plane Alistair hired would not have appreciated Thor. It's not like we could take him outside for his call of nature." Thor was our Landseer. He had his own fenced doghouse not far from Fielding House. He was definitely not an indoor dog, although we did bring him inside sometimes, but when we did, one of us had to be on "Thor duty" at all times. He was a big baby, but one swipe of his tail, and some priceless object would crash to the ground. At 80 kilograms, or 176 pounds, allowing him on any furniture was forbidden. "Violet is more than enough for me here, thank you very much."

"Are we almost to Hilly Dale?" Aisling asked.

"No," I replied.

"I'm hungry, Mum," Liam announced from the back seat, just like he did as a child. "Are we planning to stop before we get to Hilly Dale? I think her *ladyship* who got to sit in front is hungry too, but she's not going to say anything."

"No," I replied "And remember that you do NOT have titles here. You are not to refer to each other as lord and lady, even jokingly. Is that understood? I will be called Jessica here, or maybe Jessie."

"And you won't find that odd?" Aisling asked, pulling down the mirror and studying her face – my mini-me, except with blonde hair. Mine was blonde when I was a child, but hers had remained so. Any blonde in mine now was compliments of a salon in London.

"I'm trying to remember that to people here, I'm Jessica Jenson aka Jessica Keasden, but to answer your question, yes, it will seem odd, so you may need to remind me if I fail to answer to either of those. I've been Carola, except for my writing, since I married your father."

"You've been 'Your Grace,' for a long time," interjected Liam. 'No one dared to call you 'Carola' except family and close friends."

"That's quite enough. Life is going to change, particularly for Aisling. This is a new adventure for the two of us. Hilly Dale is going to seem like a culture shock." I glanced at my daughter who was still staring in the mirror. "Aisling, what are you looking at?"

"My nose. I think I'm getting a spot."

"Stop fiddling with it," I replied.

"I'm not. I was just looking, but yeah, we visited overnight in H.D., but we didn't stay long at our grandparents' house," Aisling replied, closing the mirror and putting the visor back up. "We always went somewhere else. You dragged us all over the States to see historical sites. We never had much time in Hilly Dale, except after Granny J's funeral. Dr. Barker took us to see the town. Liam and I barely remembered it. The campus was pretty though."

"Yes, it is, and you know why we couldn't stay long in Hilly Dale, Aisling. We all needed to get back home. You are of age now and I expect you to do your best to assimilate here. It's going to be a change for both of us."

"Do you think you can manage it, Mum?" Liam asked. I heard a plaintive mew and the rattling of the crate door.

"I certainly plan to," I replied with forced cheerfulness. It had taken time to adjust when I married Will, so I expected it would take time to readjust to life in the simple, small town of Hilly Dale. Part of me was looking forward to it, but the other part thought I might have made a mistake. "And DO NOT let Violet out of the *crate*, Liam," I warned.

Hilly Dale was, as its name implied, located in a river valley surrounded by undulating hills, with mountains visible in the distance. The downtown, which was located in the center of the valley, had once been attractive with its nineteenth-century buildings, but each time I visited, it seemed shabbier. There were more empty buildings and others in need of restoration. My mother had bemoaned the fact that some city leaders were against restoring anything and wanted everything new, which is why they encouraged industries and companies, along with a couple of chain stores that came to town, to buy land and set up their businesses on the outskirts near the highway that led to the interstate. Locals called that 'The New Part'.

Most of the houses in an area known as 'The Old Part' were situated above a picturesque creek that wound its way along the edge of town before it reached Tarnation River. The town's surrounding forests, creeks, lakes, and wooded areas had been designated as beauty spots in the state. I had *never* been a nature-girl when I lived in Arkansas, but I enjoyed a ramble around Fielding House's many acres. Not long after Will and I married, I braved the long, steep climb to Tintagel Castle while we were staying at the manor in Cornwall, but it was worth the effort when I reached the top. The view was beautiful, and the ruins charming.

At last, I pulled the SUV into the driveway of my childhood home. Sitting in the car for a moment, I stared at the large white house, thinking, not for the first time, how it was mine, free-and-clear. The crabapple and tulip trees and the azaleas were green now, but I knew in the early spring, the flowering trees and shrubs would be beautiful with their varying shades of pink.

"Are we going to sit here forever?" Liam called from the back seat. "I have to take a…"

"Everybody out, and collect at least one bag," I ordered hastily, "and *I'll* take Violet."

Jackson Barker had been overseeing things for the past three months. As soon as we started up the sidewalk, he opened the front door and stood waving from the porch. "I saw you through the window," he cried. "Welcome to your new home, Your Grace!"

"Shhh, Jackson, no one is supposed to know. Remember?" I replied, looking around.

"Oh, I know, I just wanted to call you that one time," he answered, laughing. "Come inside, everything is set up. Alistair didn't join you?"

"No, he had work to do. He *always* has work to do now," Liam answered. "He's no fun anymore."

"Be glad it's him instead of you," I reminded my son. "Being a duke is more than just a title. It may look easy from the outside, but it's not. *You*, dear one, only have to keep your mind on your studies."

"Good to see you all. Let's get you settled-in," Jackson said, changing the subject. "Jessica, would you prefer I stay or go?"

"I'd prefer you give me a hug and then a run-down again on what's been done."

"Gladly," Jackson cried and enveloped me in his arms for a moment. "Welcome to Hilly Dale." He cleared his throat and continued, "Well, you know the security system has been installed for windows and doors. I sent you the temporary code and you can reset that tonight, if you like. The cameras and motion lights are in and working, but the fence will be installed in a couple of weeks. It had to be special ordered. People will wonder about the house having that black iron fence surrounding the property. Your parents never had one."

"I know, but I'll feel better with it," I said, glancing at my daughter.

"Your front, back, and side doors have the grilled security doors," he announced, pointing like Vanna White at the one over the original front door. "The house has been cleaned top-to-bottom by Martha Whitcomb. She does my house. I was here with her the entire time, but she's trustworthy and doesn't ask questions."

"Thank you. I know it was a lot to ask, and I wish you would let me pay you."

"NO! Your mother, despite our twenty-five-year age difference, was one of my dearest friends, and she was a great help to me when we were both teaching at Hilly Dale College. Literature and history coursework sometimes overlap. She taught a course in the backgrounds of both British and American literature, which dealt with what was going on at the time certain works were written. We had great debates when she taught those courses."

"Yes, I know. She loved visiting England for the history, hoping to find something you didn't know. My father just enjoyed playing golf there. Will took him while Mom and I went everywhere. She wanted to see birth places, cemeteries, and homes of the classic British authors and poets. I took her to Ireland, Wales, and Scotland several times too."

"I know, she told me. We always had such wonderful discussions."

"She loved you like a son. Please don't hesitate to ask if there is something I can do for you."

"Well, there is one thing. I'd love to fly to England with you some time, but only if it is convenient for you. I would like to see Fielding House."

"Of course. You are welcome to go any time. I'll be certain to let you know."

"I'm going back in a week," Liam volunteered. "You can come back with me, but I'm flying commercial."

"Liam, what have I told you and Aisling?"

"That we're not to talk about things we can afford," he said, turning bright red, "especially here where people might not understand."

"And..."

"That it is ill-mannered to do so. And now, please...where is the toilet? I have to..."

"Please do not use 'toilet.' It's crass. You've been told that before. It's lavatory, loo, or in the States you may use the word 'restroom' or 'bathroom,' depending. You've been here before. Go on inside. It's down the hall to the left, just past the stairs, and please, Liam, there is no need to tell everyone what you need to do there. You're not three." Turning to Jackson, I added, "I'm sorry. Liam's tired, hungry, and cranky. Three-years-old in a twenty-one-year-old body."

Jackson laughed and walked with us into the house. "I taught kids his age. Believe me, I've heard just about everything."

"Regarding his earlier comment about the plane, Will and I tried very hard to instill good values in our children. We rarely hired a private jet when Will was living. Alistair feels it's safer and easier for us to travel to the States sometimes."

"You don't have to explain a thing," Jackson replied. "Now, the refrigerator is empty, but I'm sure there are a few casseroles left in the freezer. They can be thawed and re-heated if you're hungry."

"Not casseroles," Liam cried, having overheard the dreaded news on his way back from the restroom.

I looked at both of my children who were making 'gag-me' faces like six-year-olds behind Jackson's back. "I think pizza is on the menu tonight. I'll make a run to the market tomorrow."

"I'll take my leave then," Jackson said, bowing to add dramatic flair and making me smile.

"Thank God you're ordering pizza, Mum," Liam cried after Jackson closed the front doors behind him. "If you had agreed to the casseroles that were left over from the last time we were here, I would have walked to that Pizza Hut we passed a mile or two back."

"Even in this heat and humidity?" Aisling asked.

"Even in that. Casseroles are disgusting."

"I've known you to eat your fill of Mrs. Sturge's shepherd's pie, and any of her poultry pies, for that matter" I reminded him.

"That's different. They aren't filled with canned cream soups and gelatinous, processed cheese."

"I'm amazed you knew that."

"You made me try a couple of them years ago that Granny J prepared. I still remember them. Some sort of green bean mess and another noodle-thing."

"The casseroles in the freezer were made by people who loved your Grandmother Jenson. You should be thankful for that."

"I didn't notice you wanting to eat any of them, Mum," Aisling piped up. "Isn't it just a social convention? That's what Aunt Jane-Ann said. Well, she said it was a tradition. Doesn't mean we have to eat them. Who is going to know?"

I had no answer for that, so she continued, "Thank God for the air-con in this place. I see why you said most all had it in the States."

"Most all in the Southern part" I corrected.

"Order the pizza, Mum. Do it in a Hillbilly Dale accent, if you still can," Liam suggested.

"Yes, do it," begged Aisling. "Hillbilly Dale, my new home."

I gave them both the 'disapproving mother' look.

"I read this type of place is referred as 'the sticks,' Mum. You're in the sticks." Aisling teased. "You aren't going to mix in the sticks with your background."

"Sticks? It seems to me that someone named Aisling is going to mix well with that attitude."

Missing the sarcasm, she replied, "I've been reading books from the southern humor genre, just to be prepared."

"Ha, that makes you Lady Aisling Evelyn Rose of Hillbilly Dale," Liam declared.

"Sorry, My Lord, but what about you?" Aisling teased her brother.

"I don't live here. I'm still Lord William Arthur Connor Fielding-Smythe," he replied in a snooty tone.

"Stop!" I cried, "we all know who each other is. If you and Aisling don't want to eat casseroles for dinner, please stop with all this nonsense."

While we ate the pizza, which I did not order in a hillbilly accent, Aisling asked, "Why is this town called Hilly Dale? I know it has some hills, but it's not really a dale, is it. Is 'dale' even used in America?"

"It's not what *I'd* call a dale, Mum," Liam agreed, after wiping a trail of thick, mozzarella cheese from his chin. "This is nothing like the dales at home."

"A man name Ezra Dale led a wagon train to this area from Tennessee and became the settlement's leader. There's a fairly large stone in an old graveyard just outside of town. If you're interested in seeing it. I'll drive you there."

"No thanks," Liam chimed in. "We live near a graveyard. That's enough for me."

"Fair enough. I think the correct term for the town's location is 'hollow,' but I suppose the settlers wanted to honor Ezra Dale, so it became Hilly Dale rather than Hilly Hollow. If you're interested in the town's history, there is the historical society downtown. Interestingly enough, Ezra Dale's family stayed prominent until several years after the Civil War. After that, they went into a decline when two of his surviving sons were hanged as horse thieves and later one of his granddaughters took up prostitution in a Fort Smith brothel. Some of the family remained in the area trying to live down the shame, but most moved away through the years. On a funnier note, the creek that flows around the town is called Dagnabbit Creek "

"Dagnabbit? What does that mean?" Aisling asked, picking up a slice of pizza and twisting the dripping cheese around her finger. "Why didn't you get mushrooms on this, Liam?"

"I only wanted pepperoni, and you weren't in the room when Mum ordered it," he replied as if that settled the matter.

"Mum likes mushrooms," Aisling said. "Why didn't you order them?" She looked at me in annoyance.

Ignoring what would have turned into the 'Great Mushroom Debate,' I chose to respond to her original question. "I'm surprised that with all the southern genre reading you've been doing you would have come across that word. 'Dagnabbit' is a term like 'darn it.' It expresses consternation, annoyance, anger, and maybe frustration, much like I feel about ordering pizza for the two of you at the moment. I suppose before the small levee and low wall were built the creek was a great concern when it rained heavily, and that's how it got its name."

"So it's a swear word?" Liam perked up.

"Yes, I guess it is. Quite a mild one."

"I'm going to use that when I get home."

"I'll find you a book on southern slang. You can impress your friends," I said. "Really, Liam, this isn't a hick town, nor are people in this area considered hillbillies. Remember, this is *just* as much a part of your heritage as the one dating to the early kings and queens. Embrace it."

Chapter Five

It had been years since I'd stepped inside a Walmart, but that's just what I did the next morning while Liam and Aisling were sleeping. I rarely had the need to do marketing except when I was in Broadway. There, I walked to the shops and picked up a few things every other day or so. After plucking a disposable wipe from the dispenser, I selected a large shopping trolley – cart I remembered - wiped it down and entered the store.

Walmart might have been quiet this early in the morning, but the bright lights, enormous space, and array of products were overwhelming. I had no idea where anything was, so I aimlessly pushed the shopping cart down the aisles grabbing items I thought I could prepare, but the thought of eating all those frozen meals after being used to organic produce and meats disgusted me. I shoved that thought aside and picked out some frozen pizzas for Liam and Aisling.

None of us ate beef, so I got poultry and pork chops, scrutinizing each package for expiration dates and any imperfections. At the produce section, I selected a variety of fresh vegetables and fruit, again examining each piece. Meandering up and down the aisles, I got cat food, cat litter, rice, butter, skim milk, non-gelatinous cheese, eggs, orange juice, and had just put a giant package of toilet paper in the bottom of the cart when I heard, "Well, is that little Jessie Jenson the famous writer?"

Good Lord, who would recognize me – a person rarely in Hilly Dale – and a me with no makeup and dressed like a scrub woman in a Walmart at 7:30 on a Monday morning. I looked up and saw a man standing in front of me with an amused look on his face. He looked familiar - tall, trim, with dark hair edged in silver, deep-blue eyes, and dressed in jeans with an untucked pale-blue shirt.

"You don't remember me, Jessie?" He looked hurt and cocked his head to one side, "Jessie-Jess?"

I cringed. It had been *years* since anyone other than my parents had called me Jessie, let alone Jessie-Jess. I didn't even know who the latter was anymore, but that old nickname told me exactly who was speaking to me while looking me up and down. Beckham Hailey, my seventh-grade boyfriend. We'd been considered the golden couple – smart, attractive, witty – until he'd dumped me not long after the start of our sophomore year. He wanted to enter the last three years of high school with a fresh slate, not to mention he was on the fast track to becoming the star football player for our team, the Hilly Dale Hillbillies. From sophomore year on, he barely, if ever, spoke to me. Oh, I moved on from Beck a few months later after I realized what he was like, and I wasn't one of those nostalgics who lived for high school memories, but to have him show up less than twenty-four hours after I'd been back in town…ugh.

"I heard you were moving back here," he said, with an accent not quite Arkansan.

"News travels extremely fast. We just arrived yesterday. I remember you," I said.

"Wow, listen to you. You don't sound the same at all."

"I don't wish to be rude, but I have to finish shopping. My children will want something for breakfast. Lovely to see you again, Beckham."

"Sorry to hear about your mother and your husband. I heard you had kids," he said, leaning on his cart. "I have a daughter."

"Isn't that nice, but the two with me will want breakfast when they wake, so if you will please excuse me." I pushed past him, conscious of his eyes on my back.

"Look, I moved back here years ago," he called out. "I know what it's like to…"

I kept on walking. Cart filled to overflowing, I hurried to the check-out stations. Only three were open and all three had someone ahead of me.

"Hey, I really would like to catch up sometime." I turned and there was Beckham standing behind me in line. "You're pretty famous, I hear."

"Beckham, as I mentioned before, we arrived yesterday. I am tired and have a lot to do."

"I didn't mean *today*. Like I was trying to say before you walked off, I…"

The woman ahead of me left and the checker began scanning my items. I hated that Beckham Hailey could see every purchase I was making. Was this what it was going to be like living in Hilly Dale? No privacy? At least in England, unless I had a function to attend or volunteer work, I was left alone to do my own thing, and work on my books. No one bothered me or made a big deal of me in Hearthestone Vale when I went into town. I finished putting my plastic bags in the cart and started to leave.

"Nice talking to you, Jessie-Jess," he called after me.

I gave him a back-handed wave and headed for the exit.

"Mum, these are *plastic*," moaned Aisling when I carried in the bags.

"We will get cloth ones later. There are a number more in the boot. If you would like to help, go out and bring them in. Where is Liam?"

"Still sleeping." She ran her fingers through her blonde hair and adjusted her tartan pajama bottoms.

"Then, please, go out to the car and get some of the groceries, and get any of the ones with the cold items I might have left first. Check."

"All right," she grumbled.

"I'll help you in a moment. Aisling, remember, things are different here. We don't have people to do, well, things regular people do all the time. Get used to it. If you want to go back and live with Alistair, you can, and you can go to school in England, or wherever you choose."

"No. I apologize, Mum. I wanted this adventure. I'll learn to adjust. I'll go get the rest of the groceries. I'm a bit disoriented, I suppose."

"So am I," I replied and began putting things away.

"Do you even know how to cook?" Liam asked when he joined Aisling and me in the kitchen some time later.

"I cooked before I met your father; I cooked at Lilac House, and I have cooked some at the house in Cornwall, but not much. I'm certainly not like Mrs. Sturge at Fielding House, but I *can* prepare simple meals. I bought potatoes and vegetables, and my mother has one of those George Foreman grills somewhere, so I can put poultry and chops on. We won't starve." I set out boxes of cereal and a plastic jug of milk before filling two glasses with orange juice. "Start with this until I have the rest of it ready," I said turning to the cooker where bacon was sizzling in a skillet. Cracking some eggs, I broke them in another skillet and began scrambling. The toaster dinged and Aisling got up, grabbed the slices, and placed them on the plates next to the cooker.

"I'd like to begin by marking items to keep, items to store, and items to sell. Our own things, Aisling, should arrive in a few days and we have to make room for them. It's best to do this while Liam's here to help." I put the plates of food on the table.

"Can't we hire people to do that?" Aisling mumbled, picking at her bacon. "I'm not used to the time difference yet."

"We could, but we are not. You wanted an adventure. This is part of it."

"Come on, old girl, I'm here to help," Liam punched Aisling in the arm before taking a bite of scrambled eggs. "Not bad, Mum. Where's the fried bread? Where's the real bacon?"

"It's toast, and you'll get streaky bacon here."

"I was hoping for a full English. Nothing like one of *those* to get you going," he said, flexing his arms.

"I'm sorry to disappoint you. You are getting a mini American version with just bacon, eggs, and toast, plus cereal. Take your pick, but I don't recall either of you *ever* eating a full English, Liam, and I'm not going to stand here frying up everything that goes into one. None of us likes blood sausage, and Aisling and I can't stand baked beans. You're already getting more than you have at home."

"Dad liked one sometimes," Aisling spoke up, taking a bite of cereal sans milk.

"You're father also liked fish for breakfast which is something I abhor. I never noticed you wanting fish either, Aisling."

"Can we go somewhere for lunch or dinner today?" she asked, still eyeing the food on her plate with suspicion.

"The food's edible," I told my daughter. "Most places are closed on Sundays and Mondays, if I remember correctly. We'll try somewhere tomorrow."

"You're serious. Nothing on Sundays or Mondays?" Liam complained.

"Just fast-food restaurants that I know of."

"Least there's that. Where are the cups? You forgot to put them on the table."

"In the cabinet next to the sink."

"Which side?"

"The right side. There is a box of tea bags on the counter and the water in the kettle is hot. Pour a cup for each of us, please. Your grandmother didn't have tea leaves and a strainer."

"Even the pubs in Hearthestone Vale are open those days," Liam said, setting a cup each of tea in front of Aisling and me. "I'd rather have a coffee," he mumbled.

"There's a jar in the cabinet next to the cooker. Since when did you start drinking coffee?" I replied.

"Since tea isn't strong enough for all-night study sessions." Liam reached into the cabinet and grabbed the jar, grimacing at the instant coffee.

"And how much time are you spending in the Hearthestone Vale pubs, or any pub, Liam?" I teased. "And there aren't any pubs in Hilly Dale. It's in a dry county, believe it or not. You can drink, I think, in some places now. My mother told me that a few years ago. It was a big deal to some people, and still is."

"Come on, Mum," he laughed, "Quit taking the piss. Dry county?"

"Language, Liam. We'll have lunch or dinner out tomorrow. How about barbecue? I remember a cute place not far from downtown. Piggie-Pen or something like that. They serve fried okra and fried pies."

"Piggie-Pen? Sounds disgusting. Fried okra?" Aisling asked.

"Yes, and it's delicious. If you would try it, you might like it."
"No thanks."
"But since there's no pubs and you aren't of age, anyway," my son said to his sister, "you can stuff yourself with fried foods." Liam reached down to pick up Violet who was begging for a bite of something I knew she wouldn't eat. She was always that way.

"No alcohol is correct, but about stuffing oneself with fried food, I'd re-think that," I replied. "Please don't feed Violet the streaky bacon, Liam."

Violet, sitting in Liam's lap, looked at me and slowly blinked her sea-green eyes. She'd adjusted well to the change in location. As long as she got her meals, and she'd had a big breakfast when I fed her at 6:00 a.m., she was happy.

***

"Mum," Aisling said as we were tagging things in the house, "could I have the room in the turret?"

"For what? You had a tower at Fielding House you never used," Liam remarked while he dragged a box across the rug in the dining room.

"Careful," I cried. "That may be some of my great-great grand's china."

"I don't know, maybe for studying. And, Liam, the tower at home isn't attached to the house," Aisling continued, "and I didn't like it. You know that!"

"That is the original Keep from the old castle. We are fortunate it hasn't fallen into complete ruin," I reminded her. "Tourists love it."

"Yeah. I know our history," Aisling groaned. "It's also a creepy place. I don't like going there."

"It was the last bastion when the castle was overrun. People died there, in gruesome fashion I might add," Liam gleefully volunteered. "The old castle part of our house, the ruins, the Keep, and the legends surrounding the family estate - all those rivalries going way back - remind me of *Game of Thrones*, but without the dragons and the White Walkers."

"Liam, that's enough," I cried, exasperated. "It's hardly like that at all, but most castles and extremely old country houses still standing have had, shall we say, 'unfortunate occurrences,' and there are, of course, legends." Changing the subject, I asked Aisling if she had been in the turret room yet.

"Yes, I think it will suit my purpose."

"Playing Rapunzel? One of those big ole country boys can climb up your hair if you let it grow long enough," Liam said using an appallingly-bad American 'hillbilly' accent followed by a knee-slap and snort of laughter.

"Tosser," Aisling replied.

"Aisling, what have I told you about saying that?"

"I shouldn't say it, but it's not as bad as some things I could have said," she argued.

"Don't say any of them, especially in my presence." Looking at my son, I chided, "Making fun of others shows a distinct lack of class, and it's beneath you to do that," I admonished. "You know better than that." I turned back to Aisling and said, "the room in the turret has usually been a reading room, but at Christmas we always had a lighted tree up there. I spent a lot of time in that room."

"I'd like it as a study room," my daughter said. "I wish you would let me live on campus."

I had argued with the college's Dean of Students about that. I couldn't say I wanted her at home was because she was from one of the wealthiest families in the United Kingdom, was titled, and the family was concerned about security, even in a small town like Hilly Dale. What I'd said was that I knew they had housing issues and this would leave room for someone who didn't have a place to stay. How Aisling was going to get to the campus was still an issue. She and I had U.K. driving licenses and international driving permits, and I had kept my Arkansas license renewed under my parents' address. Aisling, however, had never driven in the States, so the orders of business this week and next were buy two cars and teach Aisling American driving skills.

"You can use it for a study room. I'm taking my father's ground-floor office," I replied. "We can…" I was interrupted by the doorbell. "Go on upstairs, both of you, and look through the closets while I see who is here. I'm not expecting anyone."

"Well, nice of you to call when you arrived," Aunt Jane-Ann declared when I opened the door. She brushed past me into the foyer. "I had to hear it from a woman who saw you at Walmart this morning. She said you walked right past her." My aunt fluffed her silver hair and peered at me through silver, wire-frame spectacles that made her blue-gray eyes look huge in her small face.

"Good afternoon to you, too, Aunt Jane-Ann," I said. "Come in."

"I'm already in. Jessica, that woman was Betsy Franklin, well, she was Betsy Potter. You remember her. She was in your class, and you were childhood friends."

"The name is familiar, but I wouldn't know her if I saw her. I've not lived in Hilly Dale for twenty-nine years." I lied. I knew the name of Betsy Potter extremely well. What I remembered about Betsy when we got to high school was that she and her circle of friends had picked on me and others mercilessly, but I wasn't going to admit that to my aunt.

"You need to pay better attention. She said you were talking to Beckham Hailey. You sure did remember *him*, and yet you snubbed Betsy. That's not a good way to begin in this town, Jessica. Betsy has THE gift shop. She knows absolutely everyone, is on the City Council, and her husband Peter Franklin is very well-connected here. He owns the *Hilly Dale Gazette* now, and her ex-husband John Knoss owns that factory outside of town that makes parts for farm equipment. Don't offend Betsy." She smoothed down her floral skirt. "Aren't you going to ask me to sit down? Manners, Jessica."

"I didn't remember Beckham on sight. People change," I told her. Pointing to the archway through which was the living room, I addressed my aunt, "By all means, please, have a seat where you can." The room had boxes piled in the center.

"This is just a friendly reminder that you don't live in a big city now." My aunt sat on the mahogany, Empire-style sofa with its butter-colored cushions. In order to see her while we spoke, I had to sit next to her.

"I didn't really live in a big city before."

"You don't call London a big city?"

"Oh, yes. I have other things on my mind." I was going to have to be careful. Hearthstone Vale wasn't as small as Hilly Dale, but it wasn't big either. While I did stay in London some, it was not my primary residence.

"And some people were wondering when they were going to get their casserole dishes back. It's been eight months since Evelyn passed. At least you sent your thank you notes out promptly and I didn't have to cover for you."

Eight months since my mother died. I felt I'd barely had time to grieve and here sat my aunt berating me about casserole dishes! "I just arrived in Hilly Dale yesterday afternoon! Casserole dishes are not my priority at the moment. If you would like to collect them, they're still in the freezer."

"You didn't even eat them!" she exclaimed as if I'd committed a terrible sin.

"How was that going to happen when we weren't in the country? I tried to tell you. You should have taken them home with you."

"Someone might have seen them at my house during a meeting."

It was on the tip of my tongue to ask who would go to someone's home and snoop through the refrigerator and freezer, but I resisted the urge.

"Well, the children ate the Coca-Cola chocolate cake. They loved it. Jackson baked it and he has *his* cake-pan back. They also ate the fruit and cheese from the deli trays. I'll wash the dishes and let you return them. You know most of the people who brought things. Why didn't you tell everyone we weren't going to be in town long enough to need meals?"

"It would have been impolite."

"If you had, we wouldn't be discussing the return of eight-month-old uneaten frozen casseroles. Aunt Jane-Ann, if you have come to help, you are welcome to do so. We are sorting things to keep, sell, or store. The children are upstairs now. My furniture and other items from England are arriving later this week. I have a lot to do, so if you are not here to help…"

"You're getting rid of family things? I can't believe it! Are you even going to let me see what I might want of my sister's?" She stood and walked over to pick up a small, etched crystal basket that I'd placed on the back of the baby grand. I hadn't made a decision about the pretty piece. "This was part of our grandmother's crystal. It's a wedding basket. It was used at my wedding!"

"We are merely sorting. When we have finished deciding what we want, you may look at what is set aside for the sale."

"I have to buy my own sister's leftovers?" She clutched the crystal basket to her chest as if I planned on snatching it from her.

Dear Lord, grant me patience with this woman. Her nagging and interference drove my mother to distraction, and now I'd inherited her. "Remember that she's seventy-nine. Remember that she's seventy-nine," I silently chanted.

"Don't be ridiculous. No, you don't have to buy things. By all means, take the basket with you. It's yours. I simply do not have time for a discussion about each item in the house right now." I stood up, indicating the conversation was at an end, and thankfully she got the message.

"You had better make time for people, Jessica Carola Smith or Smythe or whatever your late husband's name was. You're living in this town now, and I wonder why. You seemed to have a very nice life in England, although I was never invited. You didn't invite anyone to your wedding, and don't think that didn't ruffle feathers around here. Your own aunt, and I was not invited."

Here we go. I'd been waiting for this. She went on about it every time I visited until I finally asked my mother not to tell her I was in town. "You wouldn't have been able to afford the airfare, Aunt Jane-Ann. You said so yourself. You said I was marrying a 'foreigner' and you wanted no part of it even if you could afford it. And then, at the last minute, you said that my parents should pay for you and your husband to attend just so you could go and wouldn't be embarrassed. No one knew what to think."

"You should have sent an invitation. Your wedding announcement wasn't even in the *Hilly Dale Gazette*. It was like you just wanted to disappear from Hilly Dale."

"Perhaps my husband and I felt it was no one's business in Hilly Dale, Arkansas. My life was in England. My parents understood that. Why couldn't you?"

"Well, you're back here now, aren't you, and you're going to have to fit in. I don't know all that you were up to in England, but that hoity-toity accent and your successful career aren't going to endear you to people if you aren't friendly, and you can stop ignoring people you run into at Walmart. It's part of life here. You'll have to make sure your children, Aisling – and that's a name no one around here will be able to pronounce by the spelling – and Liam, don't act like they expect things to be done for them. I don't know how they were raised, but it's…"

The duchess in me came to the forefront. "Aunt Jane-Ann, perhaps you will find this hard to believe, but I don't particularly care about Betsy Potter, or her husband, whatever his name is. I have not kept up with everyone from Hilly Dale High. Contrary to your way of thinking, I don't know her anymore, and I was never friends with her after elementary school. I've been away for twenty-nine years. How many times must I say that? She, like others you may think I should recognize, are complete strangers. As I said, if you wish to help us sort, then please do, but I will not be lectured in my own home about how to act in Hilly Dale, nor will I allow you to criticize my children. And you can tell people that A-I-S-L-I-N-G is pronounced "Ashling." It's Irish, in honor of her paternal grandmother who is half-Irish." *And from an old, well-connected Irish family at that!* I wanted to say.

"Well, I never."

I was sure she had "nevered" a lot.

Chapter Six

The truck with our things arrived a few days later. "Liam," I called from the front porch, "please make sure everything has been removed." After double-checking, thanking, and generously tipping the two men, my son and I went into the house. Aisling was sitting in the living room on my treasured carved-oak, seventeenth-century throne chair that had been in my beloved Lilac House.

"Aisling," I said, looking at the mess of cardboard and wraps on the Persian rug, "what are you doing?"

"Sitting." Ask a ridiculous question…

"I see that. Why this box?"

"I just saw it was marked 'CHAIR' on the side and thought, 'why not', so I opened the box.'" Teenage logic, but at least she got started.

With Liam leaving in a couple of days, we needed to get as many of the big items in place as soon as possible. "It's really crowded with all this," he said. "When are you going to have the sale?"

"I'm not sure. Perhaps when it's cooler."

"When is that?"

"Maybe late in October," I replied. "In the meantime, I suppose I'll have to hire someone to move the sale items to the storage room out back or to the basement."

"The storage room is full of boxes, some furniture, and other things," Liam declared. "I was out there looking around. Might I have great-great grand's old golf clubs? The hickory ones?"

"Yes, but I'll have them shipped. I don't want you taking them on the plane."

"Thanks, Mum." He kissed my cheek.

***

The next day, the first stop was the main bank in Hilly Dale. My father had been the bank's president for years, as had my grandfather, great-grandfather and great-great-grandfather. I'd joked with Will, that although I couldn't trace my lineage back to before William the Conqueror, this was *my* family's line of succession.

"Ms. Jenson, or is it Keasden now," bank president Terrence Leaf greeted me.

"Hello, Mr. Leaf. The last name is Smythe. My children, Aisling and Liam."

"Please, call me Terry. Come with me." Terrence Leaf's office space was right where my father's had been, but his looked cold and out-of-place in the late 1800s building that my family had owned. My mother sold it after my father died.

Mr. Leaf noticed me looking around. "We remodeled this space a year ago. Got to keep up with the times. The rest of the bank will be done next year. Please sit down." After taking a seat behind a lacquered black desk, he asked in a folksy voice, "Now, what can I do for you today?"

"We are buying cars, Mr...Terry. I wanted to let you know in advance. The money will come from my Jessica Jenson Smythe account – the one I shared with my mother. Aisling and I will need a joint account. I'll have money wired from my bank in England for that, and of course, I have my own account, under Jessica J. F. Smythe where my royalties and such go."

"None of that will be a problem," he said, checking the account on his computer screen. How much do you need?"

I estimated the amount, based on the cars we wanted. Terrence Leaf cringed.

"Is something wrong? Do I not have enough to cover that amount in the accounts? According to my statements..."

"Oh no...I mean, yes, you have *more* than enough to cover that. In fact you have..." his eyes widened, "plenty in both accounts."

"Wonderful. I'm sure you will be receiving a call. I trust there will be no problem. I'm taking my son to Little Rock tomorrow and will make the purchase then. The decision of what cars we want has been made."

"No, no problem. I'll make sure my employees are aware you will be using this account. We do have some car dealerships in Hilly Dale, you know."

"Yes, but they do not have what we both want. Thank you for your time, Terry."

As we were leaving, a petite girl with straight, medium-length brown hair and big brown eyes asked, "Aren't you Jessica Keasden?"

"Yes," I replied.

"I'm a big fan," she exclaimed.

"Thank you."

"My mom said you were good friends in school."

"Oh, who is that?"

"Betsy Franklin, well, she was Potter back then. She said you were so close."

"Did she?" I smiled and said nothing more.

"Will you autograph my book? I love *The Celestial Cat* series." She pulled one of the books from her handbag. "See, I have your latest one, *The Moon over Butterfield*. I like paperbacks better than digital."

That was a surprise. Most her age loved digital and audio books. I signed my name on the title page.

"Could you put 'To Allison,' please?" She handed the book back to me. "Are you her kids?" Allison asked Aisling and Liam.

"Yes. I'm Aisling and this is my brother Liam. He's leaving tomorrow."

Allison looked wistfully at my handsome son. "Oh, that's too bad. Are you leaving too?" She turned to my daughter.

"No, I will be attending Hilly Dale College this term."

"Oh, I'm going there. I hope we'll become friends." Looking back at the book and then at me, Allison asked, "Ms. Keasden, don't you have a message for my mother? I mean seeing as how you were so close in school."

I certainly did. Close friends? Betsy Potter had treated me like dirt.

"Yes, you may tell her thank you for letting my aunt know I arrived safely in Hilly Dale," I replied in a pleasant voice. "Please excuse us, Allison. We've things to do."

"Lovely to meet you," Liam said, smiling at the blushing girl.

A man opened the front door, stepping aside to let us pass. I looked up to thank him and found myself looking into Beckham Hailey's dark-blue eyes. "Hey," he said. "Fancy meeting you here."

"Trite, Beck. First Walmart and now the bank. What a small world," I replied, awkwardly.

"Mum?" Aisling gave me a funny look.

"Aisling, Liam, this is Beckham Hailey. We were in school together."

"Oh, like with Allison's mother?" Aisling asked.

"Something like that, yes." I turned back to Beck. "We just met Betsy's daughter."

"Allison Knoss. She and my daughter are friends. Allison works part-time at the bank."

"So nice to see you again, Beck." I hurried Aisling and Liam along.

My daughter peppered me with questions all the way back to the SUV, while Liam remained quiet. "Aisling," I finally said. "this may be an adventure for *you*, but I grew up in this town. It's small and many people know my family. They remember me, but I have been gone for quite some time and *cannot* give you the information on everyone we see. I barely recognize people. Please remember that I've been living the same life you have. This is a big change for me too. Please stop asking so many questions. You're only going to get an 'I don't know' most of the time." *That was certainly an over-explanation.*

"You could have stayed in England, Mum. You didn't have to move back here," Liam joined in.

"Focus on tomorrow. Tomorrow, Liam, you will be on a plane back to England, and you will be selecting a car, Aisling. In the next day or so, we will be going back to Little Rock to turn in this rental and pick up our new cars. Jackson's going with us. He'll ride back with you, so you can practice driving in the States."

"Oh, I'd like to stay to see Aisling driving on the wrong side of the road."

"That's enough, Liam. Have you packed your things?"

Silence.

"I thought not."

At the stoplight just before we left downtown, Aisling suddenly cried out, "Look, Mum," pointing to a new red Mercedes parked in front of a white brick building. "Isn't that the name of Granny J's lawyer – the one Alistair wanted to punch at the funeral?"

"Oh my God!" Liam said and started laughing. "Look what he did to that car!"

I looked. A sign was attached to the car door that read:

Gary Minder Law Firm.
We mind your business, so you don't have to.

Two phone numbers were listed below.

"I have to call that obnoxious man this week and settle your grandmother's estate soon. I couldn't believe he had the audacity to say something to me right after her service! Unlike back home, I shouldn't have any difficulties, but let's focus on getting the cars. I don't want to drive this giant SUV everywhere."

"Don't forget that estate agent who wanted to sell the house," Aisling reminded me. "You aren't going to sell it, are you?"

"I don't know."

***

I ran my fingers over my great-great-grandfather's mahogany desk - a desk which had been in the bank's office and been passed down in the family through the years. I marveled that it was mine now. There was no one to tell me I couldn't have it. On the desk, my laptop sat open to the most recent draft of *Shadows and Stones*, the first in my new series *Secrets of Snowdonia*. I'd devised a story about a young woman who ran an antiques store in Wales and discovered she was a witch. It was a cozy paranormal mystery, but with a time-travel twist. The main character was able to travel back in time to learn the provenance of items she had in her shop, most pointing to age-old crimes that still had relevance in the present. The plot still wasn't right, but the past two weeks had been so busy that the only time I had a chance to work was in the evening when I was tired and unfocused.

I sat down in the old banker's chair and started to type a sentence, but I couldn't make myself continue. The feeling wasn't right. I suddenly missed Lilac House with its honey-colored limestone, slate roof with chimneyed gables, white framed windows and welcoming front door with its transom above, and cozy feel. My place of solitude. I looked back at Chapter Two of my manuscript and then stood up. I couldn't concentrate. The short time I'd been in Hilly Dale had been occupied with taking care of my family's interests and trying to cope with the loss of my mother. The family interests were small potatoes considering what Alistair had inherited, but as an only child, it was my responsibility, and I certainly did NOT want the Fielding-Smythe solicitors involved.

One of my biggest challenges was deciding on a date for the estate sale. My aunt had informed me that I would have to work the weekend event around the Arkansas Razorbacks' schedule, which made anything in the autumn months a challenge.

"It's important that you don't schedule a sale for an 'at home' game day. For the games that are held away, you must choose a date where the game is held in the evening, or you won't have any people showing up that Saturday. EVERYONE watches the games. Those who are fortunate enough get to go. You should pick a date when there is no game."

Good grief! I'd forgotten how nuts people were about this!

What I remembered about Hilly Dale was pleasant, for the most part. I was privileged for the town and had little responsibilities except school and homework. I had a car at sixteen, went on family vacations, went to university, joined a sorority, and briefly dated a couple of frat guys. It was all normal to me, but I wasn't truly happy until I left for England for school.

Living in the United Kingdom was an adjustment when I arrived, just as moving back to Hilly Dale had become, but I felt excitement in England, even before meeting Will, that was unexpectedly missing here. After just over two weeks of living in Hilly Dale, I already felt smothered by the past, which concerned me, particularly since I wasn't surrounded by centuries-old things and living in a four-hundred-forty-one-year-old house in a country rich in ancient history everywhere you went.

Here, it was my past that confronted me, and it had started the minute I saw Beckham and then Betsy Potter's daughter, but it was more than that. Aunt Jane-Ann was already telling me what to do. She criticized the way I lived my life, offered unsolicited advice, and she interfered. Remembering our recent encounter, I sighed.

"Margo's having our book club and wants you to do a reading, Jessica," Aunt Jane-Ann said three days ago when she unexpectedly dropped by.

"Margo?" I asked.

"You know Margo. Margo Hunter. She was Margo Johnson. She was a few grades ahead of you."

"I apologize for not knowing people, but I do not remember Margo."

"Well, she knows you! And you shouldn't refuse her invitation."

"I've yet to receive an invitation. I'll consider it if I do."

"I am your invitation. I'm extending it for her. I'm in the club, so she asked me to. Now, Hilly Dale Book Club meets this Thursday night at Margo's house. She lives in that big, red-brick house on the next block. It used to be the Samuel Shuckenbammer house, but after he died, his children didn't want it and sold it to Margo. She used to live…"

"I know which house. I remember the Shuckenbammer name. Who could forget that? I do not remember Margo Johnson Hunter. If I receive a formal invitation from Ms. Hunter, I will consider it, but I simply will not show up at a stranger's home to give a book reading. In fact, I don't do book readings as a rule."

That Jessica Keasden was Jessica Jenson made no difference to me. It was putting them together with my other identity – my real one – that I was trying to prevent. It was easier to go unrecognized when I married Will, and for several years after that. I was a nobody and blended in. If a picture appeared of The Duchess of Hearthe, I was be-hatted with perfect hair and makeup and dressed in an elegant suit at some charity function, just like others in my position. When social media, camera phones, and viral videos became more popular with each passing year, I had to be more careful, particularly after becoming a successful author. I had to protect my parents from who knows what, and now, in Hilly Dale, I needed to protect my daughter.

"You'll certainly have to do book readings here. EVERYONE wants to see you, and there's talk they want you to emcee the Pumpkin Festival along with Lucky Fine."

I knew I was going to regret this, but I asked.

"You don't know Lucky Fine? He played for the Razorbacks. Oh, I know he's younger than you, but surely your parents told you about him. His parents are Richard and Jean Fine. Richard played golf with your father. He had the Chevrolet place until he sold it a few years ago. Lucky's a local hero."

"No, they did not tell me. I did not follow the Razorbacks in England. I'm not a sports fan."

"You're just going to have to become one. EVERYONE loves the Razorbacks here. You won't be liked if you don't. You'll be ostracized. It's tradition to love the Hogs."

Oh, God, not another tradition. I'd had so many of those with Will's family that I looked forward to the move and not having to pretend I liked something. "That's ridiculous. Whether I like or don't like a sports team should not make a bit of difference. I did not follow football in England after Alistair and Liam stopped playing. They still follow it madly, however."

"That's not the kind of football I'm talking about. The Razorbacks are important here. And have you scheduled the estate sale? You need to get on that before someone else schedules something. Everyone rushes to pick dates that don't interfere with the games. There's a lot of competition for those Saturdays."

"I never understood the team name," I tossed out. "It's a wild boar or a feral pig."

"It's a wild hog. That makes it dangerous. My grandmother found one in the kitchen of a cabin the family rented at Low Gap. It was a frightening experience, according to her."

"And yet they have those odd plastic hats."

"They're clever and cute, Jessica. I'll get you one."

My first thought was 'please don't', but then I remembered I could get Liam one for Christmas as part of our joke gifts. He'd flip. Since I couldn't win the argument, and really didn't care to try, I gave up. "Is there something else you wanted. I need to work on my book."

Of course there was. Aunt Jane-Ann always had something to say. "Why have you got that God-awful black iron fence surrounding your property now. Your parents never felt the need for a fence, and your father was a bank president! If the gate wasn't unlocked, I wouldn't have been able to get to the door."

What a shame that would be!

When I didn't audibly reply, she continued, "That's not a very friendly welcome to people. What are you hiding that you need a fence like that? In the back, no one could even climb over it, if they needed to."

"That would be trespassing. Why would anyone need to do that?"

"You just never know. And you don't have a mailbox out front. That's unfriendly to the mailman. EVERYONE has a mailbox. You have a street address; you need a mailbox. Where is the one your parents had?"

"It's next to the front door where it always was. With the fence, I have a box at the post office, and I use my address only for deliveries for when I know I'll be home. I'm accustomed to that, and that is how it's going to be. I really do need to work on my manuscript."

"And you don't even go by your married name to people here or your maiden name. You're going by your pen name. That's strange."

"I didn't select the last name used here. The citizens of Hilly Dale and all those fans you mentioned use it, and that's fine with me."

"I'll let Margo know that you'll do a reading but require an invitation. Perhaps she can just toss it over the fence to you," my aunt retorted before stalking down the sidewalk and out the gate which she left standing open – to be friendly, I'm sure.

After she drove off, I went out and locked it. The gate and the front fence were only four-feet high. It wasn't like they were eight feet and topped by razor wire.

Chapter Seven

"Ms. Keasden, we absolutely must have you for our book club meeting Thursday night. We've been reading your *Harriet Donovan* series this year," Margo Hunter exuded enthusiasm when she rang me, thanks to my helpful aunt handing out my number. "We're on book seven now. The one where Harriet infiltrates the Tsar's circle. She and Lord Shellsea are getting cozier. Are they going to marry later on?"

"Ms. Hunter, I normally do not do readings, nor do I attend book club meetings. I…"

"I promise there will be no cameras. We won't even have anything on social media or in the paper," Margo Hunter explained. "It will just be us club members. We understand that you're *shy*. Your aunt said you were always shy."

I hated that word. It had such a negative connotation and could have lasting effects, which I'd learned when I'd worked with a mental health organization in Hearthestone Vale. Some people did not feel the need to be the center of attention, or else despised being so. I was both, but I'd given my fair share of speeches at county fairs, charity events, and even given a tour or two of Fielding House in a pinch when it was opened several times a year to tourists.

"Ms. Hunter, I appreciate that you like the books, but…"

"You have to come. I've told everyone already. We have a full house for Thursday night. I'm sure you want to get off on the right foot here in Hilly Dale. Your mother was part of Hilly Dale Book Club, but she never brought you up, and we never read your books for discussion before. You have a fan base here. I will not take NO for an answer. Besides, we're neighbors," she added, as if that was a valid reason and solved everything.

It was just like the time Mrs. Harpy – yes, that was her name - back in Hearthestone Vale had pushed me into chairing a flower show at a most inopportune time. Liam, at age thirteen, was leaving for Eton – not my idea, tradition – and I was on deadline for my second book in *The Celestial Cat* series. All at the same time, Will was rock-climbing in the Highlands. "But you simply must," Mrs. Harpy had pleaded. I did it but was far from pleased. It was, however, my duty to do those things in the town, according to my mother-in-law, so I couldn't refuse. This I could, but should I?

"We'll have so much fun," Ms. Hunter said. "And we are so honored to have the great Jessica Keasden join us. Of course, some of us have known you since you were little Jessie Jenson, and we just loved your mother."

Bloody Hell! This woman was determined, and she'd just played the 'we just loved your mother' card. "Of course, Ms. Hunter, I'd be delighted, but there will be no videos and no photographs. You understand? I'll have a paper for you all to sign." So, I fibbed. I didn't have a paper, but I did have an agreement with the publisher about not doing public promotions, and I could draw up something and print it.

After the call and the mention of photographs, I went to the attic and dragged out several boxes of family pictures. For a couple of hours, Aisling and I sorted through them. There were portraits of my great-great-grandparents, staring straight ahead and unsmiling, into the camera, my great-grands dressed in elegant clothes for Hilly Dale, and lots of pictures of my parents and grandparents attending various functions, along with church directory photos, studio portraits and the like. "Is that Aunt Jane-Ann?" Aisling asked, pointing to a studio portrait of an extremely attractive woman with dark-brown hair.

"Yes. That was taken when she was about twenty-years old."

"She was beautiful," Aisling said, and then added, "what happened?"

"Life," I replied. Her husband drained her emotionally and financially."

"Oh my God! These are of you!" Aisling had picked up a couple of photo albums. "What a chubby baby you were!"

"Just like you were," I reminded her, while deciding which of the family photos spread out in front of me to keep and which ones to toss. I didn't need all these party, club, and organization photos they had kept, and I certainly didn't need duplicates and triplicates. *Pick the best ones or ones you love*, I remembered. It's what I'd done with Will's personal photos, and I'd let the children go through the rest afterwards. What wasn't wanted was destroyed.

"And you had really blonde hair. What happened?"

"Age. You are fortunate yours is still blonde."

Aisling began laughing as she went through the second album marked *JESSICA 7th-12th grades*. "Who is this?" she asked pointing to a boy with unruly dark-brown hair and big, dark-blue eyes. He was sitting next to me on a cart full of hay. He's a bit familiar."

"A friend," I answered.

"He looks like that man we met at the bank."

"Mr. Leaf?" I replied, knowing full-well who it was.

"No, the man we met on the way out."

"Oh, Beckham Hailey," I said. "We were friends. After we finish going through these pictures, I'd like to start on Granny J's jewelry. She had some nice costume pieces, but her diamonds and such are in the safe deposit box at the bank. I should have gone through that box the day we were there."

"Is it difficult going through everything, Mum? You didn't do so much of that after Father died."

"It's hard. This was my life; it's my heritage. I have to make the decisions. When your father died, I didn't have to do much of anything. Everything went directly to Alistair, other than my personal belongings or gifts your father gave me. I didn't have to sort through things other than photographs." I only lost Lilac House, and that hurt, but Liam and Aisling didn't know about that yet.

"That doesn't seem fair that Alistair inherited everything. If he wasn't such a nice person, he could kick us all out. That happened to a school friend's family. They weren't living rough, but they were all cut-off when some male cousin inherited because her parents had only girls."

"I know, but times are changing. Maybe when you have children, estates will be split equally among the spouse and all the children – male and female."

***

"I'm on my way to pick you up," Jackson Barker's voice came over my phone. "In fact, I'm standing at your front gate right now."

I opened the front door and looked through the grilled door. At the end of the sidewalk I saw the short, thin, sandy-haired, bespectacled man who looked every inch the professor peering at me through the gate's bars. Because the new buzzer and electronic opener were not working properly, I hurried to let him in. "Pick me up for what?" I asked, closing *and* locking the gate behind him.

"Why, the book club reading," he replied. "I'm saving you."

"Saving me? I was going to walk over there in a few minutes."

"I *know*, but Jane-Ann was going to make sure you showed up and planned to personally deliver you – her words - until I said you were going with me."

"Thank you. I didn't know you were part of the Hilly Dale Book Club."

"Oh, I'm not, but since your book deals with Russian history, they invited me to comment on things."

"I took considerable creative license, Jackson, in writing that book. It's fiction with some historical facts."

"You know that and I know that, but will they?"

"How much time do we have?" I asked, after I'd ushered him into the living room.

"Oh, let's make a dramatic entrance about seven minutes late. Let them wonder," he said, looking around the room. "I haven't seen the house since you did some furniture swaps. Love that chair! Seventeenth century?" he asked, pointing to the carved throne chair that was next to an occasional table.

"Yes. I love it too."

"Did you bring it from Fielding House?" he asked excitedly.

"Alas, it came from an early eighteenth-century Cotswolds house."

"Did you buy the chair in the Cotswolds?"

"No, at an antique shop in London, but it was perfect for the house."

"Wonderful!"

"Yes, it was wonderful there." Before he could ask, I added, "Long story. Will bought the house for my use, put my name on with his and intended for it to be mine eventually, but…"

"But it went back to the estate when he died?"

"Extenuating circumstances." I smiled. "Aisling's in the turret, reading and texting her friends at home. Let me tell her we're leaving." After I did, Jackson and I sauntered down the sidewalk and through the neighborhood to my doom.

"You look wonderful, Ms. Keasden," said the bony, blonde woman who opened the wide, white front door of the red-brick Georgian-style home. "I'm Margo Hunter. Please come in."

"Why thank you, Margo," Jackson, who had been completely ignored at the door, said.

We entered a short hall and were led to a charming room in back with a glass-paned wall overlooking a patio and swimming pool. Seated around the room were a number of women and a couple of men. They all looked me up and down. Did I look "authory" enough in my black ankle pants, untucked long white shirt and high-heeled nude-tone sandals? Just in case, I'd fluffed my light brown hair with its sun-kissed highlights and brought my black Chanel readers.

"Jessica, you're late," Aunt Jane-Ann announced in front of everyone. I studied her for a moment the way she was studying me. I took in her light-blue slacks and white knit top under a lightweight navy-blue jacket. Her silver hair had a recent perm. Her blue-gray eyes stared at me from behind wire-rimmed spectacles; her lips, currently painted a bright rose, were pursed in annoyance.

"Don't you know the star performer always makes an entrance!" Jackson exclaimed. "For goodness' sake, Jane-Ann, don't make a fuss." Now everyone looked at my aunt.

"Please, please, have a seat, Ms. Keasden. Oh, may I call you Jessica?"

"I...I suppose so." Although it had been happening since I moved to Hilly Dale, being called Jessica still felt strange.

"Let me introduce you to everyone, although I'm sure you aren't so famous that you don't remember all of us here!" Margo cried. "I guess we could play a guessing game. An ice-breaker?" She looked at me hopefully and seeing my confusion, added, "Well, we do have some recent transplants to Hilly Dale here tonight." She pointed to a couple of women who sat in a corner looking at me so intently that I wondered what they'd been told.

"Perhaps you had better make the introductions," I said graciously.

Margo went around the room rattling off names. Some were familiar and some were not. She stopped at the last woman in the group. "And of course you remember Betsy Franklin. Well, she was Knoss, but before that, she was Potter. She married Peter Franklin a few years ago, but I suspect you knew that, since you were always such close friends in school. I'm sure your mother kept you up-to-date on her every move."

She certainly had not! What planet were these people on? I thought, borrowing one of Liam's expressions. *And where did they get the idea that Betsy and I were close friends.* I soon had my answer.

A short, squat woman with a dark-brown bob, big brown eyes, and too much makeup rushed up to me, exuding excitement. "Jessie, it's so wonderful to see you again. I've missed you *so* much. I'm so sorry we lost touch some time ago. We had *such* fun together in school."

"Look at them. Betsy and Jessie back together," Margo cried, clapping her hands.

This was Betsy Potter? My high school nemesis. The pert, cute little head cheerleader who ridiculed my friends and me daily about something or other? The same Betsy Potter who taunted me over the loss of Beck when I was in tenth grade? I'd gotten over him a few months later, but Betsy had continued to throw the fact that her best friend Bianca Callahan had caught him. Bianca either ignored me or made snide comments to and about me. I never understood their animosity.

"A pleasure to see you, Betsy," I said. "We really must..." I let it trail off, hoping people would think I was about to say, "have lunch soon." Leaving Betsy in the middle of the room, I joined Margo beside a comfortable-looking chair placed next to a candle-filled fireplace. The hostess indicated this was where I was to sit.

"Margo," I said quietly, after I had settled back in the chair, "if you will please collect the papers, I asked everyone to sign, I will begin." I was enjoying this a tad. I perused the papers and made sure everyone had signed and dated them, especially Betsy. I did not trust her. Opening a hardback copy, I began reading a section of the book, *Harriet Donovan and the Faberge Egg*. I reminded myself that this was just like when I was doing my own proofing and editing before I sent it to my real editor. I always read my manuscripts aloud several times to see if the flow was right. When I finished reading, applause rang out, with Jackson egging everyone on.

After refreshments, the members spent two hours discussing what each character was thinking, the themes in the book, and speculating on what *my* motivations were. I found it crazy that people were reading into the story all manner of things. They were disappointed that I didn't have a story board and didn't know what each character was thinking or what their motivation was. I just let the story flow. After that, I went back and edited, reading it at least ten times until it was what I wanted before sending it on.

"So, have you met anyone famous?" a woman I didn't know asked.

"Yes, have you met the Queen?" Betsy threw out with a smirk.

Best friends, indeed! Still the same old cow she always was. How I would like to wipe that smirk off her face and say, "Why, yes. I have. In fact, my late husband associated with some of the family members from time-to-time." One didn't boast of these associations in the circle in which I had traveled. Instead, I ignored her question and that of the other woman, choosing to take a book-related one. I delighted in telling the group about my new series and how I'd learned a bit of Welsh for authenticity, just as I'd learned a bit of Scottish Gaelic for the second book in the *Harriet Donovan* series that was set in the Highlands.

"Well, what was that all about?" Jackson asked as we walked back to my house.

"What do you mean?"

"You and that Betsy Franklin? Were you really close friends?"

"In elementary school, but in high school, absolutely not. I haven't the slightest what she's up to now, but that routine in there was fake, and it's not the first time I've heard how we are supposedly so close." I told him about the encounter with her daughter at the bank, and how she'd seen me in Walmart where I'd supposedly ignored her. "I didn't even notice her, and I don't think I'd have recognized her anyway. Betsy felt slighted enough to call my aunt to tell her I was in town, before I even had a chance. I don't understand how anyone can think I would recognize them after all these years, especially if we were never close to begin with."

"Betsy *could* have spoken first and introduced herself. Perhaps she's forgotten how she acted in high school and is only remembering your time in earlier years. Some people have short memories. She owns *Betsy Gifts*. It's not far from the bank. I'm surprised you didn't see it. It's in one of the old drugstores. You know, they've torn down some old buildings in the past few years and let others deteriorate without offering any sort of real assistance to the property owners who end up getting blamed for the 'blight' downtown."

"That's pathetic. I think I saw a building with a colorful awning out front not far from the bank. It *was* an old pharmacy, if I remember correctly."

"That's it. Betsy and her ex-husband John Knoss bought that old drugstore several years after they married. She turned it into a gift shop, and it does well. They renovated the small upstairs into an apartment that's rented out. I'm guessing it's eventually for their daughter Allison if she decides to stay in Hilly Dale. Betsy got the building in the divorce, I understand. I take it you and your mother didn't venture downtown much in later years when you were here. She never mentioned it, and the times we all went to lunch, it was always out-of-town."

"We didn't spend much time in Hilly Dale. My parents enjoyed showing the children America. Then after my father died, my mother stayed with us at Fielding House for a few months. The children hadn't been here for ten years until she died. And, of course, you know the rest."

"She enjoyed seeing her grandchildren. So did your father. I'll leave you here at your gate. My dog will want a romp before bed," Jackson said, bowing. Seeing my surprise, he added, "My bow can be our private joke."

"Thanks, Jackson, " I said, hugging him, "For everything," I whispered in his ear.

After watching him drive away, I entered the house, climbed the switchback staircase to the second floor and then up a narrow staircase to the turret where I found Aisling curled up on my grandmother's Victorian love seat, scrolling through phone messages. "How was your evening?" she asked, looking up.

"Different. Aunt Jane-Ann was there, and a bunch of people I was supposed to know."

"Did you know any of them?"

"Allison's mother," I replied. "She put on a good show of us being such close friends."

"Were you? You wouldn't say when we saw that girl at the bank."

"Not in later grades. She was like Lady Alexandra Fairmount-Borringer."

"God! Not like her! She was awful to me at school."

Aisling had attended a boarding school in Switzerland for nearly three years beginning at age thirteen. It was another of those family traditions I despised. My sister-in-law, the Lady Aileen, had gone there. Alexandra Fairmount-Borringer was the daughter of a Marquess, and until Aisling's arrival she had the top ranking in peerage, appearance, and in grades, but my daughter knocked her from the top in all ways, which did not set well with Alexandra. Aisling was barely sixteen when Will died, and I immediately pulled her from that school and sent her to one in London. much to the dismay of Will's mother and sister. "The *shame*" they had both said. Will and I wanted our children to be happy and Aisling wasn't in Switzerland.

After kissing her goodnight, I went to my room and found Violet lying right in the middle of my fluffy cream-colored duvet instead of on the blanket I'd provided at the foot for her. She was giving me evil looks. I'd been neglecting her with everything going on. Sitting down beside her, I stroked her thick, soft fur, watching the long black strands and bits of fluff float and land among the others that were all over the cover. The bed itself had been in my family for over one-hundred years. I didn't like it, but I hadn't brought one with me. It was strange to be sleeping in my parents' bedroom, not to mention their bed. I hadn't considered remodeling yet, but if I planned to stay here, I'd need to. There were just too many memories.

As if sensing my emotions, Violet climbed in my lap and started purring, thankfully interrupting the maudlin path down which my thoughts were starting to travel. I picked up the cat, resting her head on my shoulder. Despite Aisling's presence, I still felt lonely. I missed Will, and I missed my mother. I missed my home in England, but I didn't miss my life there without Will in it. That fairy tale had ended, and now I was trying to start a new life back in Hillbilly Dale. Wasn't that what Liam and Aisling called it?

Chapter Eight

"Jessica," my aunt's voice came clearly across the speakerphone a week later, "I'd like to take you and Aisling to lunch today. You need to meet more people. Meet me at The Old House restaurant located on Calder Street. It's in The Old Part in that house where the Carter family lived."

"Aisling and I have a meeting at the college this morning. If you had checked with me earlier…"

"What time is your meeting?"

"10:00," I replied. It was 9:30 now, and I had just finished my makeup. Aisling had overslept and was hurriedly dressing.

"You'll be done by noon, and you won't be far away. I'll expect you then." I thought I'd escaped being ordered about by imperious old women when I'd left my mother-in-law back in Hearthestone Vale. Aunt Jane-Ann could give the dowager duchess - antiquated term - a run for her money. I didn't mind Josephine…much. When her husband died and Will became the new duke, she retreated to the background, if only a bit at first. I didn't defer to her as much as the years went on. She was a little older than my aunt, but I had an image of them having a cage-fight – a gilded cage, of course. Stifling a laugh at the thought, I agreed to meet her at noon.

Hilly Dale College was situated on forty landscaped, gently-rolling acres north of The Old Part. The buildings were either faded-red or whitewashed brick, with two of them dating back to 1870 when the college had been established. Most of the buildings, however, were later 1800s-1940s. All had been renovated and were well-maintained. The only eyesores were the more modern dormitories that had been built on the west edge of the property in the 1980s. I could understand adding more dormitories, but why make them stand out with their modern shapes and sliding-glass windows. The dormitories on the east side were from the 1940s and had undergone modernizing, yet still retained charm of the era in which they were built.

Aisling and I were seated in surprisingly uncomfortable chairs outside Timothy Hayes's office in a lovely building that dated from around 1900. His administrative assistant was extremely solicitous, offering us coffee - no thank you - and apologizing several times for the delay. "He's been on the phone all morning, Ms. Keasden," she kept saying.

"It's quite all right," I replied, shifting on the faux-leather seat and stretching my back. I looked at my daughter. "Aisling, put the phone away. You know the rules. No texting at engagements."

"This isn't an engagement; it's a meeting," she said. "I'll put it away when we go in."

"And turn down the volume, please. No ringing; no pinging; That's our motto for engagements and meetings."

"I always turn it down," she said, not looking up. "I'm chatting with Gemma." Gemma Tattersdown was one of her closest friends. Her mother, Elsie, was mine. She'd been one of my flatmates who was with me when I met Will. Elsie married one of his friends and was now Viscountess Toddle. Elsie hated her first name and had always said her parents who had owned a large dairy business named her after their first cow. When Gemma was born, Elsie declared she was naming her daughter something that sounded less bovine.

A door opened and a short, balding man, clad in rolled-up shirtsleeves and a pair of khakis approached us. "Ms. Keasden, an honor to meet you. I'm Timothy Hayes." He stuck out his hand for me to shake. Aisling cut her eyes at me. In my wildest imagination, I'd never have thought the president of a college would dress in such a casual manner to meet a new student and her parent. It was a far cry from what we were both accustomed.

"I've been working with the planning department all morning," he said, looking down at his rumpled attire. I watched as he turned to Aisling and gave her a quick once over. "And you must be our new student, Aisling." He pronounced it as 'Ayzling.' "I'm so sorry you had to wait. Please come in the office."

"It's pronounced 'Ashling,' Mr. Hayes," I replied as I brushed past him.

"Oh, yes, I think I knew that. I'm sorry, Ms. Keasden."

I'd visited my mother's office in one of the 1920s buildings and found it charming, but Timothy Hayes's office was unexpected. It was minimalist, like the one at the bank, and did not fit the style of the older building. Aisling and I took the two black leather chairs across from his glass and steel desk. Mr. Hayes sat down and, like the bank president, folded his hands before inquiring after our health and how we were liking Hilly Dale.

"Ms. Keasden, I understand you are a native to Hilly Dale. We are so glad you chose this school for your daughter," he said in a reedy voice. "Your records are impressive, Miss Smythe." Turning to me he, said, "Now about this not living on campus. It is a requirement for first year students and we do have a room for her. It's a nice one in our best dormitory." Timothy Hayes looked at his computer screen and back at me.

"I went over this with Sidna Primrose the Dean of Students and she assured me that Aisling could live at home. That was part of the reason I decided this was the school for her. She doesn't have to attend Hilly Dale College."

Timothy Hayes visibly blanched. "Well, you see, it's policy and Mrs. Primrose shouldn't have…"

"Nevertheless, she did, and as a result of that, I shall hold you all to it."

"Mum, I might…"

"No. Not your first semester at a new school in a new country," I said, throwing her a warning look. I trusted Aisling, but she was only nineteen. "If the school is to your taste, we will revisit your living on campus for next term." I sat up straighter and fixed Mr. Hayes with a look to imply this was it or nothing.

"Oh, well, I suppose we could make an exception. We do have first-semester students from other countries staying here though."

"Yes, but their parents are most likely not here with them. I've done my research, Mr. Hayes."

"Very well, but…"

A knock on the door interrupted whatever he was going to say. A striking, dark-haired woman dressed in jeans and a white blouse walked in the room.

"Ah, Miss di Santi, I'd like to introduce Jessica Keasden and her daughter Aisling. Aisling will be one of yours. Patrizia di Santi coordinates our International Students' Program."

"I understand you are from England" she said in Italian-accented English. "Are you familiar with our program, Aisling?"

"Sì, Signorina di Santi. Piacere."

"You speak Italian?" Miss di Santi asked, with more than a hint of skepticism.

"Sì, signorina. Sono fluente," replied Aisling and went on to tell Miss di Santi in Italian how she also spoke French, along with some Spanish and German, but was not fluent in the last two. I haltingly translated to Mr. Hayes before finally asking Aisling to speak English so he could join in the discussion.

"Aisling has a flare for languages," I told him.

"She was explaining that she spent a summer teaching English to children in Italy," Miss di Santi said. "The children were from the poorer areas. It is admirable. She attended school in Switzerland where she was exposed to different languages."

"Perhaps, Aisling, you would like to assist Miss di Santi with the international students, if that is agreeable with Miss di Santi, of course."

"Most of our international students speak Spanish, although there a few who speak French. I would be happy to work with you, Aisling," she said. "I can arrange a small payment for work I ask you to do. A form of work-study, it could be called."

"Is that all right, Mum?'

"It's up to you. I have no objections."

"I see you plan to major in English, Aisling," Mr. Hayes stated after looking at his computer screen again.

"My mother and Grandmother Jenson studied English literature," my daughter said proudly.

"I remember your grandmother. She was, of course, not teaching here when I started, but I met her at some college functions in her later years. She was well-loved." He glanced at Patrizia di Santi before addressing Aisling, "You might be able to assist the international students with their English assignments. You could set yourself up as a tutor."

"Well, I suppose I might could," Aisling said, but I sensed hesitancy in her voice.

"Aisling, you don't have to do this," I told her. "It's not a school requirement." I looked at Timothy Hayes and then at Patrizia di Santi.

"No, I'm sure it will be fine, except I was hoping to have a bit more freedom to enjoy my time here and not be responsible for anything but my own studies. If it won't take up a great deal of time, I am willing to help a little."

"We can work that out," Miss di Santi said. "There is no need to decide this now."

**

Aisling pulled her bright-blue Mini-Cooper into the lot just across from the restaurant. The Old House was in a fair-sized, rock pre-Civil War structure that sat on a wooded, low hill above Dagnabbit Creek that ran through The Old Part. I remembered the house well. As children, we'd all thought it was haunted, and we probably drove poor old Mrs. Carter, the owner, crazy. I'd heard from my mother that after the old woman died, her heir had difficulty caring for the place. After some time, it had been purchased and restoration begun. Now, it was a restaurant.

Aisling and I crossed the narrow two-lane road and began walking toward the white-painted rock footbridge that spanned the creek. A back entrance provided an easier access to the place, but it was nice to see the bridge entrance was still there and people were using it.

"Excellent driving and parking," I complimented my daughter as we stepped onto the bridge.

"Jackson's a great teacher, and it's easy enough."

I took a deep breath, exhaled, and said, "Let's get this over with."

"Mum, do you not care for Aunt Jane-Ann?"

I stopped in the middle of the bridge and looked over the edge at the water. With little rain, the level was low. "Why on earth would you say that? She's my mother's sister."

"It seems you don't want much to do with her."

Seeing no one in the vicinity, I looked over at my daughter and replied, "My aunt and I have different personalities, but she made things difficult for your grandmother. My father was a wonderful, successful man. Aunt Jane-Ann's husband was neither, but she pretended everything was all right. Uncle Ed squandered and gambled their earnings away, leaving Aunt Jane-Ann, a librarian, nothing except the house when he died, and it had a second mortgage she didn't know about. My father, your father, and I all put money in her account when Uncle Ed died. It was specifically made to appear as if she had inherited something from a secret account Ed had set up. Your father and I paid off the second mortgage on the house. Aunt Jane-Ann never knew. She was told it had been taken care of with funds her husband had set aside for that. She never questioned anything."

"That's really nice, Mum, but she's a bossy-bum to you," Aisling said as we stepped off the bridge and started up the sloping sidewalk to the house.

"I know. She treated my mother the same way, although Aunt Jane-Ann was the younger of the two. I help out of a sense of duty, but that doesn't mean that I truly like being around her, Aisling. Just because you're related doesn't automatically guarantee that you will like someone or even have to like them. Uncle Ed may have had an addiction, but my mother said her sister drove him to it with her demands for a better lifestyle. She wanted the same as her sister."

I stopped talking and stepped onto the grass, pulling Aisling with me, and nodded to the two women who passed by. One turned around and gave us the once-over before catching up with her companion.

When we reached the front porch, Aisling opened the white, scrolled screen door and then the simple white wooden door with its four-paned window. Wide, unpolished oak plank floors, white plastered walls with watercolors depicting Hilly Dale and the surrounding areas, and a narrow oak staircase just several feet back from the door met our eyes as we entered. The new owner had at least tried to maintain the house's character. A hostess who looked like a college student led us to a room on the left. Aunt Jane-Ann, in a lavender summer dress with a white cardigan thrown over her shoulders, was sitting at a table with three other women, all dressed in similar summer dresses and cardigans.

"Jessica, Aisling, come join us," Aunt Jane-Ann called in her syrupy voice that was reserved for times she wanted to make a good impression. She waved her hand in case we hadn't heard her or we couldn't see her sitting across the room. All the patrons had heard her and some blatantly watched us make our way to the little party by the window.

Aisling and I pulled out mismatched white chairs and seated ourselves at the rectangular table that was covered by a white tablecloth. A bunch of wildflowers stood in a crystal vase in the center. The hostess handed us black-edged menus. After she left, Aunt Jane-Ann introduced us to the three women with her, giving part of their family history with each introduction. Knowing I would never keep all of that straight, much less remember their names after the genealogy lesson, and since they were members of the local garden club, I mentally named them. Lady Daffodil wore a yellow dress with a dark-green cardigan. Lady Begonia was dressed in bright pink with a pale-pink cardigan tied over her shoulders. Lady Cornflower's dress was a deep blue under a light-blue cardigan.

"I like this," Aisling said, looking around at the comfortable room with its old paintings on the walls. "It's quaint. I mean not like the house in…"

"Yes, it is," I interrupted her. "It would be a cozy spot in the winter." I took in the fireplace and the barrister bookcase filled with old books and imagined that instead of tables and wooden chairs, there would be a comfortable sofa with a table and lamp nearby. "What an unusual place for a picture." I said, looking at a woman's portrait hanging over a swinging door I thought probably led to the kitchen. "It looks old."

"It's of the original owner's wife. I thought you might like this place. It has that old style you seem to admire," my aunt said. "There are other reasons, too."

"It's charming," I replied, and then noticed something odd. We had entered into a room with at ceiling of at least fourteen feet, but toward the back where the painting was located, the room was closer to eight feet in height. It didn't slope, just dropped. I wondered if the new owner had designed it that way to give a more modern feel to the space.

Before I had a chance to comment, a server with a black apron over a navy tee and light-blue capris appeared with glasses of water for Aisling and me. As I was deciding between the lunch specials, a man's voice asked, "How are you ladies today?"

"Oh, Beckham, you're here today," Aunt Jane-Ann said. "Beckham owns The Old House, Jessica. I thought you would find that interesting."

Beck leaned down and said to me, "Everything's good, but I'm biased," and then he turned to Aisling. "Nice to see you, again."

"You own the restaurant?" Aisling asked.

"Yep. Bought it a couple of years ago from Mrs. Carter's niece and fixed it up. The restaurant just opened six months ago."

"And it's doing very well," Lady Begonia declared.

"We're holding our own," Beck answered, looking at me. "I've got a good manager, but it's early days, of course."

"How's Jordan?" Lady Daffodil asked.

"She's fine. She starts back at Hilly Dale College soon."

"Oh, I start there this term," Aisling cried. "Has she picked a subject to study?"

"She wants to be a teacher. How about you?"

"English. I'm uncertain as to what I'll do with it but look at my mother and my grandmother. They studied English, and so did my great-grandmother, but she didn't do anything with it."

"Then you'll be part of an impressive group of women. Even your great-grandmother was an interesting woman. I remember my mother saying that your great-grandmother used to have *Jocelyn's Corner* at the library where she read books to children every Saturday afternoon," Beck told her and smiled. "I'll tell Jordan about you."

"How is Bianca these days?" Lady Daffodil spoke up.

"Uh, fine…I have to get back to work. Enjoy your meal. Jessie, a pleasure to see you. Stop by any time. There's always a table for the famous Jessica Keasden. Aisling, you and Jordan will have to meet," he said before walking away.

And then the gossip began.

"You know Bianca really did him dirty," Lady Daffodil shared.

"Bianca? Bianca Callahan?" I asked.

"Of course, Jessica. You remember her. She was in your class. She and Betsy were good friends," Aunt Jane-Ann informed me. "And the three of you were friends in elementary school."

Elementary school was pretty hazy after all these years, but I remembered a blonde with big blue eyes who strutted around the high school as if she owned the place, and she did own Beck.

"Well, they were good friends," Lady Cornflower confided. "Bianca's been dating Betsy's ex-husband. John Knoss."

"How long have they been dating again?" my aunt asked.

"Oh, I don't know. Betsy and John divorced years ago, but Beckham and Bianca's divorce isn't final yet. They separated nearly two years back, so you figure it out," Lady Daffodil hinted.

So Beck had married Bianca. That was surprising news. The server brought our food. As soon as she left, the women were back talking about so-and-so, and didn't I remember them. Questions about my books abounded too. Poor Aisling sat there glumly eating her chicken sandwich and chips. I hoped her life here wasn't going to be boring. She was used to friends, society events, diversity, and travel.

Chapter Nine

In the short time that I'd lived in Hilly Dale, it seemed my new life was a series of trips to Walmart, visits with a lawyer and an accountant, and attempts to avoid my aunt's interference in just about everything I did. She even despaired of my new car, a red and black Mini Cooper. "It's too small," she'd complained. "You won't be able to take people around in it. No one will be able to fit."

The rest of the time had been spent coping with the loss of my mother, getting Aisling used to this new life, trying to work on my book, and committing the ultimate sin, according to my aunt, of driving to a salon in Little Rock *once* to have my hair highlighted. At least the cleaning woman Jackson had suggested was working out well, or I'd have to contend with all the housework too. When things began to settle down a bit, boredom took over.

Because my daughter's classes had started, she was out of the house during the day and sometimes attended an evening event. To combat the loneliness I felt, most of my time was now spent on *Shadows and Stones*, but I needed out of the house, and a trip to Walmart wasn't the answer. Jackson and I occasionally got together when he was in town, but other than that, it was my aunt inviting me somewhere with *her* friends. "To meet people, Jessica," she always said. Each time I joined them, though, they talked about my mother when they weren't gossiping, and they asked nosy questions. When another opportunity presented itself, I was delighted.

"Hello," I said on the fourth ring of the landline phone, not bothering to check Caller ID, because I fully expected it to be my aunt who refused to use my new mobile number.

"Ummm, is this Jessica?" asked a woman in a locally-accented voice.

"May I ask who is calling, please?"

"Ummm, this is Heather James. I used to be Heather Dale," she said, haltingly. "Jessica and I went to school together."

"Yes, this is Jessica speaking. Heather Dale?" Having recently explained about the 'Dale' part of Hilly Dale to my children, I knew she was a member of that family, and her name was extremely familiar.

"Yeah. Kids called me Heather *Hilly* Dale through school. Do you remember?" she replied, trying to jog my memory. "I heard through the grapevine you were back in town. You *do* sound different. Everyone I've talked to said you did, but of course, you've been away."

Heather Dale! She had been one of my friends through school. Poor Heather! She'd developed early, and a lot, so the boys made crude comments about her figure. Because her last name was Dale and she was busty, they added the 'Hilly' part. It made sense to them, I supposed, but Heather hated it.

"Yes, I remember you, Heather. How nice of you to ring me."

"I...uh...wondered if you would like to have lunch sometime. You know, so we could catch up a little. That is if you aren't too busy with your writing or anything. I thought you might not know anyone here."

"How thoughtful. I'd love that. When did you have in mind?"

"You would?" she sounded surprised.

"Certainly. Would tomorrow be good for you?" I asked, trying not to convey complete excitement that I was having lunch with someone other than my aunt, and Jackson was on an extended trip to visit his family in Massachusetts.

"Oh, yes! It's Saturday and I'm off-work that day. We can go to The Old House. Have you been there? It's the nicest place in town."

"I went a few weeks ago with my daughter, aunt, and some of my aunt's friends. Would 12:30 be a good time?"

"Okay. I'll meet you there."

"I'm looking forward to it, Heather. Thank you for the invitation." I resisted doing a happy dance after we disconnected. I genuinely looked forward to meeting an old friend.

***

Standing in my bedroom's walk-in closet, which my parents created from an attached nursery, I studied my wardrobe. While I didn't run around in fancy clothes everyday back in England, I also didn't wear much of what was trendy in Hilly Dale, so my style pegged me as an outsider at once. I chose my idea of casual: a pair of black skinny jeans paired with a fitted, boat-neck, black-and-white Breton top, and a pair of red Jimmy Choo kitten heels. An hour later, I was ready to meet my old friend. I set my fifteen-year-old, black Hermes handbag on the Victorian hall chair while I studied myself in the tall pier mirror that had stood in the foyer since the house was built. My hair looked neat and my makeup fresh. Of course the facials I received in the London salon helped, but I decided I looked pretty good for a forty-seven-year-old woman with three children. That thought gave me a much-needed boost of confidence.

I recognized Heather as soon as I saw her standing on The Old House's front porch. She was tall, auburn-haired, and had an enviable hour-glass figure encased in faded jeans and an emerald-green tee. "Jessie?" she asked, ducking her head, her blue eyes peering out from under long shiny bangs.

"Hi, Heather," I replied, reaching to take her hand. "It's lovely to see you. It's been a long time."

"Since graduation," she answered. "Wow! You look incredible Jessie…oh, Jessica."

"You look so pretty, Heather. You always did."

She tossed her long, straight hair and smiled. "I don't know about that. You remember what people used to call me."

"You reminded me on the phone. I'm sure they don't call you that now."

"I hope not," she said, laughing. "I'd hate for my kids to hear it."

"How many children do you have?"

"Lots." Seeing my puzzled look, she continued, "I teach first grade. That's why I didn't make it to your mother's funeral. I'm sorry about that."

"No one would have better understood your reason than my mother. She taught for years."

"Yeah, she was my English professor at Hilly Dale College. I have two sons and a daughter," she said, changing the subject. "My older son doesn't live here anymore, but my younger son is at U. of A., and my daughter's in high school. Let's go inside." She stopped with her hand on the screen door and gave me a worried look. "You do know Beckham Hailey's the owner, right?"

"Yes, I've seen him around, and as I said, I had lunch here with my aunt. I've spoken to him."

"And you're okay with that? I mean you two were so close…"

"When we were barely in our teens."

"I know, but people talk, and they remember, especially those who never left Hilly Dale, like Betsy Potter – well, she's Franklin now, but I'm sure you remember her."

"I've seen her."

The restaurant was almost full. We followed the hostess into a dining room to the right of the entrance. It was similar to the one where I'd dined before, including having the odd drop in ceiling height. This side, however, had a better view. Through the trees, I glimpsed the white footbridge just below the rise. It was a lovely, peaceful scene.

Heather and I were quiet while studying the menu, until I broke the silence. "It was so nice of you to invite me today. I didn't know you were still in Hilly Dale. My aunt never mentioned it to me."

"I never left. I married a *professor* a year-and-a-half ago. David James. He's the one who took Jackson Barker's place after he retired. I…uh…was married before to Steve Taylor. You remember him?"

"I'm so sorry, I don't."

"That's okay, he was a few years behind us. He wasn't that memorable at anything…believe me," she laughed. "The younger two kids are his. Steve and I try to get along for their sakes, but it isn't easy. I don't care for his wife. My other son's by another guy, but the boy's been in trouble. Raising kids is hard. I've got a grandson, too. He's nine. He and his mother live in Fort Smith."

Grandchildren! I'd never given that much of a thought. Alistair was nearing thirty, but he was my stepson. Children were the last things on the minds of Liam and Aisling. They were focused on school and having fun. "I have three children," I finally said. "My eldest, my stepson, is in…uh…real estate management. Aisling is at the college here, and my other son is at Cambridge."

"So, your daughter's at Hilly Dale. Does that mean you're planning to stay then? Everyone said you were going to sell up and go back to England. They said you were too sophisticated for our small town, and I've got to admit that your clothes and accent…well, they're not exactly Hilly Dale. Hermes? Jimmy Choo?"

"Brilliant observation. They're not new. I'd forgotten you wanted to be a fashion designer when you were in school. Why the switch to education?"

"No opportunity to do the other. You had more options. Hilly Dale College is different from when I attended. It was more affordable for us locals back then." She took a sip of water. "Steve went there too, and, surprise, surprise, we got together at a dance, got married, and then *our* kids came quickly. In fact, I was pregnant when I graduated. I stayed home with the kids until they were all school age. Steve and I divorced a few years after that, and then I got a job at the elementary school. Mr. Land, the school superintendent, helped me. I've been there ever since. When I met David, it was like a dream come true, and such a change from Steve. I know David would love to meet you," she rambled. "He and Jackson are friends…not close friends, but they get together with some of the college staff, past and present. I remember your mother was one of Jackson's good friends."

"Yes, she was, and he's been a great friend to me since I moved here. I'd love to meet your husband," I said when Heather paused for breath. I'd forgotten how much she loved to talk.

The server placed our food on the table. I'd ordered a grilled salmon salad and Heather had the turkey and bacon club sandwich. "Is this a good place for dinner?" I asked, looking around at the room.

"Oh, yes! It's elegant at night. There's a candle on each table and Beck lights candles in the fireplace, but there's a fire when it's colder. He draws those heavy red-velvet drapes too. It's very intimate. The menu is more upscale, at least for Hilly Dale. It's probably nothing like what you had in London. That is where you were living, right?"

While I thought about my answer, I took a bite of my salad, finding the salmon delicious. "Yes. There is a place in London, and a house in the Cotswolds," I decided to say. No sense lying about *that* house. It was in my author bio.

"Wow, two homes! I heard your husband was wealthy…oh, I'm so sorry. Gossip in town, you know." She took a small bite of her sandwich.

"I'm sure there will always be gossip in Hilly Dale, just like *every* small town," I said without thinking.

We ate our meals in silence and then she asked, "Do you want to live here, Jessie? All those memories and such, and you alone."

"I'm not alone. My daughter's with me," I replied. "It's different, Heather. I needed a change. I can't explain it. Please excuse me if I seem rude or aloof. I've been living abroad, and this is another way of life to me."

"Culture shock after the big city? Is Aisling adjusting well?"

"I think so. She's helping Patrizia di Santi with the international students. Aisling has an interest in languages."

Heather made a face. "Be careful of Patrizia. She's, well, as you might put it, different. On another subject, our class reunion is coming up. I know, it's just twenty-nine years and we should wait until next year for a blow-out, but it's only when a couple of people decide to get off their butts and organize something that we have one. Do it when we can is what I say. We're having it during Homecoming, and you know our Homecoming is pretty early. It's the third Friday night in September this year. That's right around the corner. I hope you'll come. You're the most famous one of us. Lots of people show up. We have food and dancing at the Hilly Dale Country Club! Please say you'll come."

I couldn't think of anything less I wanted to do, and I was surprised Heather was excited about it, but when I looked at the eagerness in her eyes,

I couldn't refuse right away. "I'll consider it, thank you." I hoped I had a meeting with my agent in New York then.

"Oh, it would be wonderful if you could come. It would be a feather in *my* cap. You know, Betsy Potter Franklin is in charge of it this time, but I'm on the committee. If Betsy hadn't decided to do it, no one else would. So, you see we can't just wait around for the big decade ones. There's a good chance nobody would bother."

"As I said earlier, I've seen Betsy since I've been here. She's been saying she and I were best friends in high school. Heather, you know how she, Bianca, and their little group treated you, me, and others in school. Where on earth would she get the idea she and I were best friends?"

"Because you're famous in Hilly Dale and we were all friends in elementary school. You moved away to England and became a well-known author. You know she wants to be friends with the most *popular* people. It makes her look important. Besides, you weren't here to correct her. I bet she's wetting her pants right now for fear you'll expose her as the liar she is."

"No, I wouldn't do that. It's unimportant, but I'm not popular. I barely know anyone here. I've moved on from her teasing, insults, and snide remarks, but it doesn't mean I want to be her friend NOW. I still remember how she treated not only me, but others, and the same for Bianca. They *led* that group."

"Shhhhh. Bianca's daughter Jordan works here sometimes. I don't see her but she's probably around. You know Beck is Bianca's ex, well, soon-to-be ex."

"I heard. I was surprised they married. Beck didn't strike me as someone who would marry his high school girlfriend and live in Hilly Dale."

"Oh, I don't think he planned on it. After university, he moved to New York. Personally, I think she tracked him down after he made a lot of money. The whole town's talking about Bianca and John Knoss. John's *Betsy's* ex-husband, and he's rich." Heather took a sip of water and then added in a gleeful voice, "Betsy and Bianca hate each other now. It's been an *ugly* situation. The whole thing's been dubbed *Hilly Dale Wives*." She started laughing. "Seriously, a network should film one of those reality shows here."

I didn't know what to say, so, I focused on the meal in front of me. Despite how Beck had acted towards me after we broke up, I felt sorry for him and his daughter if what Heather said was true. It had to be embarrassing. We finished our lunch and began our goodbyes on the porch.

"Let's do this again, Jessie. It was fun."

I enjoyed seeing Heather, but I wasn't sure 'fun' was the right word. It was certainly an informative get-together, but somehow things didn't feel the same. Maybe I had changed more than I realized.

"Promise me you'll think about the reunion," she encouraged. "Like I said, I'm on the committee, and what else do you have to do here. It'll be a hoot. I can't wait to see how everyone will react when you arrive."

"Trust me, I saw how Betsy reacted at my aunt's book club meeting Margo Hunter hosted."

"You went to that?"

"My aunt arranged it."

Heather hugged me - another thing I was going to have to get used to – and said goodbye again. I'd wanted to get out, and I'd wanted a diversion. Heather's call had provided me with both. She'd parked in the back lot which connected to a road that wound around behind the wooded side of the property before merging with Calder Street via a modern bridge a mile south. Because of the meandering Dagnabbit Creek, Hilly Dale had several bridges of varying ages and types. In *The Bridges of Cassiopeia*, the first in my *Celestial Cat* series, I'd based the story on that set-up.

As I was crossing the little footbridge, I saw a now-familiar figure approaching quickly from the sidewalk leading to the road and front parking area. He stepped onto the bridge.

"Hey, you just leaving?" Beck asked, giving me a sheepish grin. "Did you enjoy your lunch?"

I stared at his still-handsome face. Although I knew his first name was his mother's maiden name, I wondered what he'd say if he knew I'd met David Beckham. Stifling a laugh, I replied, "It was lovely. I had lunch with Heather James."

"Heather James? She's a good teacher, I hear. I'm not friends with her."

"You never were, and you didn't treat her so well in school. You ignored her like you did…" I stopped. Why was I, a middle-aged, successful woman going there. It was beneath me. This town dredged up too many memories I thought were buried.

"I know. I was stupid, but listen, why don't you stop by for dinner one night. I've been trying to tell you that I moved back here years ago from New York. I know how strange it seems moving from a big city to Hilly Dale, and I wasn't gone as long as you were."

"That's kind of you, but I'm busy with work and my daughter, and speaking of both…"

He stood aside, leaning against the bridge's rock wall. I had just stepped off the bridge when I heard him call: "Our daughters are friends at school."

I turned. Aisling hadn't mentioned that. "Isn't that nice," I replied brightly and headed for my car.

Chapter Ten

"Are you making a lot of new friends?" I asked Aisling over a dinner of grilled pork chops, roasted potatoes, and steamed asparagus. I had been perfecting my cooking.

"A few. Everyone's been extremely nice to me, but I'd rather not assist Signorina di Santi."

"Why is that?" I asked. "Has she been unkind to you? Or has she discovered something about you? You are being careful? Remember what I told you."

"Yes," Aisling replied, rolling her eyes. "I'd prefer not to be considered an *international* student though. Oh, I know I'm technically one, but my first language is English. I want to experience the American side of my heritage, and I can't with Signorina di Santi pushing tutoring and stressing the international part all the time. I'd rather find my own friends. Her language skills aren't what I thought, either."

"I understand. Miss di Santi probably thinks she's helping you adjust. You don't have to continue, but I'm quite serious about being cautious. You cannot let it slip who you are. If that happens, you have to leave. The family and I would insist on it."

"Oh, Mum! Stop worrying about me. Would it be such a bad thing for you if you had to leave with me? You don't seem happy here. All you do is write, read, eat, and sleep, take care of crap, and you go out of your way to avoid people."

"I do?" I took a bite of pork chop. The George Foreman Grill did a pretty good job in a pinch. "I had lunch with a former classmate today."

"Did you? Proud of you, but take Aunt Jane-Ann, for example." She held up her hand to stop me from replying. "Oh, I understand how you feel about her and her treatment of Granny J, but she's an old woman, and Granny J is gone. You're all Aunt Jane-Ann has. And there's Jordan's dad. Jordan says he's tried to be nice to you, but you barely speak to him."

"I've spoken with Jordan's father. I saw him today when I was leaving the restaurant. He said you and Jordan were friends. Are any of your friends at home attending Cambridge? Elsie told me the last time she called that Gemma was going to St. Andrews this term. What about Penelope? Amaranthia?"

"Pen is at St. Andrews with Gemma, and Thia didn't plan on going to uni. She's pretty serious with Liam's friend, Zac."

"The Earl of Lawton's son? When did this happen?"

"During a house party. They fell madly in love, according to Thia, the moment they laid eyes on each other. I imagine the idea of someday becoming Countess of Lawton played a role. Thia is only an Honorable. It's a step-up, and she's always been class-conscious."

"An unattractive trait, Aisling. A good education is not a waste. Young women of your class are going to university and making something of themselves. It's not the nineteenth century where a good marriage was what you looked forward to all your life. Look at the Duchess of Cambridge. She has a university degree. I have one in English Literature."

"I know, and she married a prince and you married a duke." My daughter looked at me, shrugged, and took a giant sip of water. "I'm staying here for the term, at least, but we're talking about you, Mum. Are you going to stay in Hilly Dale?"

"I'm here now. As for your Aunt Jane-Ann and Jordan's father, there's a lot of water under the bridge with those two."

"Jordan told me the two of you dated."

I stopped, the fork with its small piece of meat halfway to my mouth. "If you wish to call it that, but it started when we were in seventh grade. We were barely thirteen." I placed the fork on my plate. "We broke up at the beginning of our sophomore year. Aunt Jane-Ann is another matter. I'm trying with her. She tends to be a busybody and can't be trusted. That's the reason she was never invited to the wedding or to visit. Unfortunately, her husband's gambling addiction played a part in the decision, too. If Uncle Ed had known about the Fielding-Smythes, he would have privately tried to borrow money from Will's father and later Will, putting my parents and me in an awkward position."

"As I said, Granny J isn't with us any longer and Aunt Jane-Ann hasn't anyone but you."

I was painfully aware my mother was no longer here. I was reminded of it daily just living in the house. I *should* make some decisions– either sell the house and move or remodel. I got up, carried the plates to the sink and began the washing-up. Aisling joined me and put the rinsed dishes in the dishwasher. "I apologize. Jordan's unhappy that her parents are getting a divorce, and her mother's been seen everywhere with another man for some time. She wants her dad to be happy, and I want you to be happy. We just thought…"

"Let's finish with this and watch a film."

"Sorry. I have studying to do. I wish I'd been allowed to stay on the college campus. Jordan's there and they have so much fun in the dormitories. I feel left out."

"I'm sorry, but until you adjust to the culture and lifestyle, it's better you live here. Your friends are welcome to come over, and you're free to join them places. You're free to date but be careful you don't get so close you share our business."

"I don't know about dating," she said and walked out of the kitchen. I flopped on the plush, brown, overstuffed sofa in the den, a room just off the kitchen. The blinds were open over the glass windows that lined the east-facing wall. Violet was standing on a side table staring at whatever cats see in a dark back garden. The motion lights didn't go off, but I closed the blinds anyway and settled in to watch reruns of *The Big Bang Theory*. A few minutes later, Violet landed in my lap where she proceeded to turn around three times before settling down.

***

I woke to the ringing of my phone. Sleepily, I reached over on the nightstand, flipped on the lamp, and grabbed the offending electronic. It was 6:00 a.m., but when I looked at the name, I was instantly awake.

"Alistair, what's wrong? Why are you calling so early?" I cried.

"Early? Oh, sorry. I forgot about the time difference. Nothing's wrong. I have some news."

"What's that?" I sat up, moving the pillow behind my back.

"Ceci and I are getting married!" he cried happily. "I asked her last night and she said 'yes.' I couldn't wait to tell you. We're planning…"

"Wait a moment." I shifted the pillow to a more comfortable position. "You and Cecilia? Congratulations! I wondered if you would ever decide to do this."

"I had a talk with Mr. Poleduck and…"

"Alistair, Mr. Poleduck does not have a say in your romantic life," I warned. "I don't trust him. He neglected to give your father and me the proper advice about Lilac House when we purchased it. Romance matters are out-of-bounds, as far as he is concerned."

"Your situation is fine. I'm having them take another look, but I do agree that renouncing your American citizenship is the best solution, for the most part."

"I've never liked that pompous man, but that's neither here nor there. Tell me all about the engagement. Where were you?"

Alistair launched into a brief description. Cecilia – Ceci – Alistair's longtime girlfriend had come to Fielding House for a mini-break from her job at an art gallery in London. They walked around the property and ended up at the old church. Alistair had proposed to her outside while they were watching the sunset.

"It sounds very romantic. I'm happy for you both."

"It's a special place, Mum. I wanted to do it there, and I gave her the ring Father gave you. I hope you don't mind."

"No, I left it behind for you. It's tradition. That ring has been in the family for well over a century and is given to the duke's wife." I'd never loved the emerald and diamond ring. It was large and unwieldy. I only wore it for special occasions, but I'd worn the diamond wedding band Will had given me, and I still did. It was on my right third finger as of last year.

"Ceci's parents are over-the-moon about this. They've been hoping for a long time."

I bet they have. Alistair was a catch – handsome, titled, intelligent, and rich. The second thing would appeal to Cecilia's socialite mother and the last to her banker father, but I liked Cecilia. The fact that she seemed so grounded was probably due to having had excellent nannies.

"We're planning a wedding around Christmas," he said.

"So soon. It's two weeks gone September. What about the plans? Cecilia's gown?" I cried, remembering how Will's parents thought six months was too short of an engagement for us.

"We've been talking about this for some time. I hadn't made it official by a proper proposal and ring. Ceci's going to wear a simple gown. She loved the picture of you in yours. And, I think she's going to wear great-grand's tiara - the ruby and diamond one – since it's the holidays. We're going to marry at Hearthestone Vale's largest church, of course. Her parents wanted it to be at a cathedral, but then that wouldn't be in Hearthstone Vale. The church will be decorated for Christmas. Then we thought to have the reception at Fielding House. It always looks so beautiful at that time of year, and then…"

I started laughing. "Alistair, you're as giddy as a bride."

"I guess I am. Even if old Poleduck thought it was a good idea that I have a wife, I'm so happy to be marrying Ceci. I've loved her for years, even before we started dating."

"I remember. You met at school and she was dating your best friend."

"That's right. He and I are still mates, but not best ones. I'm inviting him and his wife to the wedding. When will you be able to come? I'll hire a private jet, of course."

"You don't need to do that. Commercial is fine. When do you need me? It sounds as if you've got everything under control."

"The wedding will be on December 27th, and we're planning a reception in the Long Gallery. We'll have a big party for special guests in the Great Hall, if Ceci stops thinking of people to invite, and we will use the formal dining room that night. The wedding meal for invited townspeople will be on the lawn after the wedding, as is the family tradition."

"But it's December, Alistair. It's too cold for anything outdoors, and the weather can be unpredictable. What was your Nan's opinion?"

"Haven't told her yet. We're hiring heated marquees, and I'm getting the kind with a floor that can be added. If you could come a week or so before that would be best, and you're welcome to stay after we leave."

"Is it impertinent to ask if I can bring a friend?"

"Who? Are you seeing someone? Aisling didn't mention that."

I shifted the phone to my other ear. "No. I want to bring Jackson. He's been so good to us, and he loves England. I promised I'd bring him the next time I visited."

"You absolutely have to bring him. "I'll hire a jet. It's the holidays and I want you to get here. I don't want any delays."

I finally got him to agree that we would go commercial and to arrange the reservations right now.

***

Aisling was excited to hear the news from Alistair, but not quite as much as Jackson when I told him. That man was ecstatic!

"Oh my God! I'm going to England for Alistair's wedding? To a duke's wedding? For Christmas? I can't believe it!" he cried and did a happy dance. "I'll start checking the places I want to see in your area."

It was heartwarming to see how excited the retired professor was. He'd been to England several times, but this time he would be sharing in something tourists would not. "I'm glad you want to attend," I said, smiling.

"I am beyond glad, Jessica. I'm thrilled! Do I call you 'Your Grace' or 'Duchess' while I'm there, or do I call you Jessica or what?'

"We have time to go over protocol. It's antiquated and very silly. I had a difficult time getting used to it when I joined the family."

"Are you getting used to being called 'Jessica' in Hilly Dale?"

"A little. My nickname 'Jessie' is foreign to me. I don't even remember who that part of me is."

"Well, you've moved on in life a good deal more than most. You know at some point your secret is going to get out. I'm surprised it hasn't already. There's so much technology out there that privacy is a thing of the past."

"I know. When I married, my photo might show up in U.K. newspapers, but it wasn't posted all over the internet. And, now with search engines I could be found, but I'm not that interesting."

"As an author, though…"

"Jessica Keasden was born Jessica Jenson in Arkansas to Charles and Evelyn Jenson. She attended the University of Arkansas and graduated from Cambridge University with a degree in English Literature," I replied, quoting author bio sites. "The other information says I divide my time between a house in the Cotswolds and Arkansas. Now if someone was to search for 'The Duke of Hearthe,' that would be a different story, but even so, I'm Alistair's stepmother. I'd be listed as his siblings' mother, but as Carola. I don't even think there's much posted about me. I'm in the red print on most web encyclopedia sites."

***

I'd managed to complete another draft of *Shadows and Stones* and had just started proof-reading when my phone rang. It was Heather James. I should have ignored it and let the call go to voicemail, but the ringing had already disrupted my concentration.

"Jessie, the reunion is this Friday. Have you decided to join us?" she asked in an excited voice.

"I'm afraid…" I began

"Please say 'yes,' because so many people know the famous Jessica Keasden is back in town and want to see you. Don't be angry, but I put it in the email blast I sent out reminding people of the reunion, and I posted it on social media. Did you get your email blast?"

I had received something from 'Class of '87' but hadn't opened it. The email address I'd given her was for my Jessica Keasden business account. "I'm not sure that this will work for me, Heather."

"Jessie, please. I spent my high school years as a laughingstock." She played the Heather Hilly Dale card. "I want to redeem myself instead of being thought of as a ditzy nobody with big boobs."

"You are most definitely not a ditz. You teach school. Ditzy people don't do that, Heather."

"You're right, but please," she pleaded. "David and I'll pick you up for the game, so you won't have to go alone. Please. It can only help your books' popularity, you know. Make new fans. Think of it as a meet-and-greet without the book-signing part."

I'd rather do the polar plunge than go to a football game and reunion, but she was right, and she wasn't the first to remind me of the importance of local fans. Both my aunt and my agent Dil Daly had said the same when I'd balked at doing readings and signings here. "All right," I agreed. "What time?"

"David and I will pick you up at 6:30. The game starts at 7:00. My daughter's in the Homecoming Court as Junior maid. Can you believe it? Heather Nobody has a daughter who's in the *Court*! I'm so ecstatic! Krista will be Queen next year, mark my words!"

"I'm sure your daughter is thrilled," I replied, not knowing what else to say.

"Steve will be there to escort her, and it's always such a joy to see him," Heather said sarcastically. "I'm sure his wife Shauna will be there. You know, she's just thirty-five. They were having an affair. I caught them in our house. They were doing it on the dining room table," she shared. "I made Steve take that table outside and put a sign on it with 'Free' written in big letters. That table had been in his family for one-hundred years and was his pride-and-joy, but he desecrated it. Someone going by in a truck full of junk got out with a woman and together they forced that table in with the other trash they'd picked up by the side of the road. I made Steve watch, just like I watched him and Shauna going at it. After I shouted at them and Steve leaped off, her big butt was staring me in the face. Who wants to serve family holiday meals off a table that's had her sprawled half across it, and…"

"So," I interrupted, "you'll pick me up at 6:30? What should I wear?" Anything to keep from hearing more about what she saw when Steve and Shauna were making use of the dining room table. Having lived in centuries-old buildings, I knew scenes like that had most likely been played out on various pieces of furniture that remained – Will and I had contributed a bit to that ourselves – but in the cases of Fielding House and the Cornish manor, I imagined that sort of activity was the least of what had occurred in those places. A family legend had it that in the seventeenth century, two people had been poisoned at the formal dining table in Fielding House, but we still used it for holidays and special occasions.

"Oh, yes. 6:30. It's casual. No one dresses up around here anymore. Pretty disgusting what some wear. No taste at all. Shauna dresses like trash."

"Fine, I'll see you then." *What had I gotten myself into?*

Chapter Eleven

"Aisling, I'm going to the football game and then the reunion afterwards. I shouldn't be late," I called up the stairs. "Are you and Jordan planning anything?"

"Yes," she said, coming down to meet me. "We're going to a movie with some friends. You look beautiful, Mum!"

I looked in the hall's pier mirror. I'd straightened my hair and put on classic makeup, playing up my green eyes. I'd chosen to wear my black skinny jeans tucked into black high-heeled boots, and a fitted, pale-gray cashmere sweater. Jewelry was simple – thick, white-gold hoops. I'd grabbed a dark-gray pashmina in case I got chilly. Instead of my usual black Hermes bag, I'd selected a bright-pink Mulberry one for a splash of color. "Thank you," I replied. "This should be…interesting."

"Have a good time. We'll talk tomorrow."

"Don't forget to set the alarm and lock the gate when you leave," I reminded her.

She waved as she started toward the stairs. Aisling was a beautiful young woman, I thought as I watched her trot back up the steps, her shiny blonde ponytail swinging side-to-side. She had a wide-open future, and not for the first time did I think it was a mistake allowing her to come to the States with me. Although I never mentioned it to her, I knew part of her decision to move was a young man named Ian Daniels. She, like her friend Amaranthia, had fallen for one of Liam's friends. Aisling had met Ian when he visited Fielding House one weekend. He came from a good family, but Ian had a tendency, according to Liam, to love 'em and leave 'em. After a couple of months dating, Ian had moved on with someone else, breaking Aisling's heart.

I walked out on the porch and sat down on the swing to wait for Heather and David. A few minutes later, a silver Lexus pulled into the drive. David, a tall, thin man with graying light-brown hair and wearing a red-and-white shirt with his jeans greeted me at the gate. I settled into the back seat and off we went to the football game, something I hadn't done since the start of tenth grade.

"Our group's sitting over there," Heather said, pointing to one area of the bleachers.

I followed her finger and saw about fifty people, most wearing the school colors of red and white. An attractive bleached-blonde in tight white jeans and a filled-out, long-sleeved, red tee, shouted, "Well, I can't believe it! Little Jessie Jenson the famous author is here. We were taking bets you wouldn't show."

"Bianca," Heather whispered. "Betsy's about three rows above. See she's waving at you."

"Please, let's choose a seat away from them," I said, trying to ignore Betsy's waving arm. Graciousness won out, however, and I raised a hand in greeting. Betsy looked around and smirked at the ones nearest her as if to say, "See, I told you we were friends," before she whispered something to the person next to her. That person looked at me in surprise.

"Beckham's not here yet," Heather volunteered, "but he's coming. It'll be awkward, seeing as how Bianca's here with John, and here you are."

I glanced at Bianca's boyfriend who was standing up after letting someone pass. He was an average-height, plain-looking man with gray hair and wearing a red shirt and khaki trousers. Other than hearing he was wealthy, I couldn't see Bianca leaving Beck for him, especially if the rumor mill – Heather and Aunt Jane-Ann - was to be believed, Beck hadn't done too shabbily in the finances department.

"And there's Shauna going up the bleachers," Heather hissed in my ear. "See, look at her butt. Let me tell you it's riddled with cellulite. You could put quarters in those dimples all those years ago. Imagine what it looks like now."

Shauna's aforementioned butt was safely encased in indigo jeans and she wore a white, fitted tee under a red-and-white striped denim jacket. Her hair fell in soft black waves halfway down her back. She was pretty, and I didn't find her behind particularly large, but I hadn't seen it without covering, so I'd have to take Heather's word for it.

We sat next to a couple I didn't recognize and I was scrunched against the woman. "Hi, I'm Dee Dee. You're that author, aren't you? Before I could answer, she rushed on, "I didn't go to school here, so you don't have to try to figure out who I am, but my husband was a Hillbilly." She nudged the ribs of a balding man who was sitting on the other side of her. "Jason, this is that Jessica-woman you went to school with. You know, the one who writes the books I read. Heather said she was bringing her."

Jason glanced at me, grunted a "Hi," and went back to watching the cheerleaders trying to rev up the crowd before the game started.

"He's really into sports. I'm sorry. You're from England now, right?"

"Yes, she is," Heather spoke over me. "We are so lucky she decided to join us tonight. I had to practically push her."

I smiled apologetically at Dee Dee who muttered, "I was pushed into coming too."

"You don't live in Hilly Dale?" I asked.

"No, I'm from Oregon originally. Met Jason in Omaha when we both worked there. We live in Little Rock now," she said, switching her gaze to the cheerleaders and then Jason. Turning back to me, she sighed and continued speaking. "Jason loves to come to these reunions. You know they have them just whenever. No rhyme or reason like my school. We have decade reunions. I mean in Hilly Dale it can be the next year or five years later. No organization at all with the planning, but Jason still wants to come and hang out with his old buddies who are still around. He and Beckham Hailey are friends. Do you know Beck?"

"Does she *know* Beck?" Heather chimed in. "They dated for over two years."

"Jason, did you know this famous author dated Beck?" Dee Dee poked her husband in the side to divert his attention from the cheerleaders.

Jason looked at me. "Who are you again? You sure aren't Bianca. Jason dated her all through high school."

"No, this is Jessie Jenson. She dated him from seventh to the beginning of tenth," Heather shared.

"That doesn't count…if you get my drift," he said, snickering. This time Dee Dee gave *me* the apologetic look.

Doing the unthinkable in public, I reached into my handbag, pulled out my phone and was scrolling through my emails when I heard Jason say, "Hey, Beck, glad you made it, dude. Come on over and have a seat. Looks like a good game tonight."

Beck was standing at the end of the row. David, Heather, Dee Dee, Jason, and I stood up to let him pass. "Nice to see you here, Jessie. Figured you wouldn't come," he said, squeezing past us to sit on the other side of Jason.

"So, are you okay, Jessie," whispered Heather anxiously.

"What?"

"Because Beck's here. I know it must be difficult with your history with him. Bianca's here too, so that must hurt. We can go if you want. You've made an appearance, and you spoke to him. We'll drive you home and come back."

"Heather," I said softly, "I am quite tired of this nonsense. We are talking about a very long time ago. This silly teenage business is ridiculous, and if it continues…"

"I'm sorry, Jessie. I didn't want you to be hurt or embarrassed. I'm just so happy you're here. You were my good friend in school. I'm so proud of you and want tonight to be *perfect* for you, but if the sight of Beck spoils it for you, I would never forgive myself!"

Oh, brother! She pushed me into coming and now that I was here, she worried I'd be so upset I'd want to leave?

"Please don't concern yourself. We're all adults, Heather."

"Oh! Listen, the band's playing!" she cried and jumped up. "It's starting! Look, the Homecoming Court is being escorted out! There's my Krista. She's so beautiful. Inherited my figure, but no one's teasing *her*. They're all jealous because *that's* her boyfriend with her on one side. He's the quarterback, you know," she added, eyes shining. "Oh, and there's Steve." In a matter of seconds, her tone went from excitement to disgust.

Steve, an attractive man, looked very happy being one of his daughter's escorts, but I wasn't going to tell Heather that.

***

After what seemed like an eternity, the game finally concluded. The Hilly Dale Hillbillies won by a moderate margin. Jason had yelled and complained about the refs the whole time, much to his wife's embarrassment. After being subjected to the man's obnoxious behavior, I finally remembered him. He hadn't changed much…in attitude, that is.

"Man, that was a great game, Beck!" I heard him say. "Reminds me of that one game where we played this team as seniors and won, except by a bigger margin. We were great back then and we really kicked the..." the rest of his comment faded away as I followed Heather and David down the bleachers and out to the car.

"Are you going to the country club?" Beck asked, catching up to us.

"I'm at the mercy of Heather and David," I replied, pulling my pashmina tighter around me, "so I suppose I am."

"See you there."

"I guess they'll all be there."

"Who?" I asked.

"The Three Bs," Heather said, laughing. "Remember?"

The Three Bs was a name I'd bestowed on Bianca, Betsy, and Beck in the tenth grade after Beck dumped me for Bianca. It stood for 'Two Bitches and a Bastard.' It fitted the way my group of friends thought of them and was our private joke.

Hilly Dale Country Club was several miles out of town and had a breathtaking view of the mountains. The tan brick building with white shutters overlooked the nine-hole golf course on one side and a swimming pool on the other. I'd spent many happy times lying in the sun by that pool while my father played golf. Bon Jovi's *Livin' on a Prayer* could be heard as we opened the door to the clubhouse. It was an emotional moment for me when I stepped inside, but the nostalgia I felt had nothing to do with the reunion. I pictured my parents having drinks at the bar and my family enjoying our Sunday dinners in the dining room off to one side.

A woman with 'Mary Blake (Barley)' on her badge asked us to sign in and find our own name badges. I was horrified to see they had each person's senior photograph attached. It wasn't the best photo I'd ever had, and I'd definitely changed – upgraded my appearance, Aisling would have said. The idea, I imagined, was that we laughed about the photos, and it made people easier to recognize.

The clubhouse was decorated with 'Hilly Dale Hillbillies 1987' banners. Standing in a corner next to a table covered in a cheap checkered tablecloth was our old mascot - a large scarecrow dressed in overalls that had 'Hilly Dale' printed on them over a red-and-white flannel shirt. Instead of a straw hat, the mascot was wearing one of the team's football helmets. Scattered on the table were our Senior Yearbook, old game-day ribbons, and school newspapers for anyone interested in perusing them.

Above the table, on a wall that had seen too many nails, hung color blow-up posters of the football and basketball teams, cheerleaders, and the band. Hanging directly on either side of the football team poster were blown-up yearbook photos of Beck and Jason, each player decked out in full uniform and posing on one knee while holding a football. There was another of Beck in his basketball uniform slam-dunking. All the posters had been autographed.

"We're raffling off a football and basketball signed by the teams. Well, the guys who are here," a woman whose name badge read 'Susan Patterson (Hallmore)' informed us, edging me aside to place the balls on the table next to a red box. "Only $1 a ticket or $7 for ten." She smiled at me, looked at my name tag, and said, "Oh, you're that author. I haven't read any of your books, but I heard they were good. Glad you're here."

"Thank you," I said, before walking away. I was uninterested in purchasing raffle tickets, but I noticed Heather bought a few.

For someone who had been a shrinking violet in school and felt ridiculed for her figure, Heather had certainly overcome that and was running her mouth full force. She dragged me around the room, introducing me as, "Jessie Jenson, but now she's an author called Jessica Keasden who used to live in England." Those to whom I was introduced did one of three things: stare at me, ignore me, or gush over me.

Betsy was a gusher, and a hugger. "Excuse me, *Heather*, don't monopolize our guest of honor! Jessie, I'm so happy you came! We really need to catch up. Let me finish the introductions. There are some people I *know* you want to see." She grabbed my arm before I could make a polite excuse and steered me to a table full of people who looked vaguely familiar but with whom I had never associated.

"You all remember Jessie Jenson. We were just talking about her. She's been in England almost ever since she left Hilly Dale. England! And she's an author. I know several of you read her novels. They're those cute, little cozy mysteries. She spoke at my book club a while back."

Some of the women in the group had big smiles on their faces, while the men in the group gawped at me. I was clearly overdressed. "Hello," I said. "It certainly appears you have a nice turn-out for this."

"Just listen to her," Betsy cried. "Such a long way from our Hilly Dale accents."

"Jessie, do you remember when Betsy, me, and the rest of us girls sent those *other* girls joke messages that we were coming after them?" a dark-haired woman with the name badge of 'Harmony Hughes (Green)' on her Hillbillies Forever white sweatshirt asked, looking at me. "We were just laughing about their reactions before you and Betsy came over. Some of them were so scared! It was hilarious!"

Now I knew why they looked familiar, and I was not going to let *this* moment pass without a comment. "Why, yes, I *do* remember that," I said smiling. "I was one of those 'other girls'. Isn't it interesting how people can view the same thing or certain events in different ways."

There was silence at the table until Betsy spoke, "Oh, uh, I forgot. Didn't you think it was funny?"

"No. I thought it was cruel. I showed it to my father and he was ready to contact law enforcement."

"Oh, ha ha. It was meant to be a joke. Everyone thought it was hilarious," Betsy said, looking uncomfortably at the rest of the people at the table, all of whom were staring at me.

"I'm glad it provided amusement for all of *you*." I looked around for Heather and David. They were filling their plates from the buffet. "If you will please excuse me." I walked away, hearing "Did you ever?" and "Stuck up," and I heard Betsy chime in with "She's so *different* now."

Damned right I am. I don't have to put up with that sort of behavior any longer.

While I was deciding what to have from the limited selection of heavy appetizers, I felt someone slide up beside me and reach across to get a plate. "Please, go ahead," I said, looking askance at the person.

"Still the same Jessie, with that touch of sarcasm," a man with black hair, beautiful gray-green eyes, and caramel skin, said.

I looked at his name badge. "Tommy Fitzpatrick," I cried. Tommy had run around with Heather, me, and a few others all through school. "I should have known without looking at your name badge. I remember those gorgeous eyes."

"It's Tom now," he replied while helping himself to a pig-in-a-blanket, or two. "I know you've been doing well. I've kept up with your career."

"You have?" I asked cautiously.

"Yeah, you've made quite a name for yourself with those series books. You were always writing stories in school and reading, so I'm not surprised. My wife loved your books."

I relaxed a little. "What are you doing now, Tom?"

"Took over my dad's automotive business. I built it up to two shops and had hopes of expanding, but, well life happens, you know."

"I do know," I agreed, and picked up a plate with the club's logo stamped on it and began to follow him down the line.

"Yeah, but what can I say. *Your* plans…boy, did they change! I remember you wanted to be a professor like your mother, but off you went to Cambridge, married an architect, and became a successful author. You've had it all, Jessie, and you deserve it. I always knew you were someone special."

"Thank you."

"Your aunt said you're a widow. I'm so sorry. Was it recent?"

"It will be three years in November." I skipped the pigs-in-blankets and took a couple of tiny quiches and made my way down to the eggrolls. Tom was piling his plate with everything.

Seeing me glance at it, he said, "Missed dinner. My wife died a couple of years ago."

"Oh, I truly am sorry. How are you doing?"

"You know."

"I do. Indeed I do. It can be hard."

"Yeah. She was sick for a long time. I tried the dating scene recently, thinking it might help, but this is Hilly Dale and rural Arkansas. Not much choice or opportunity. If Beckham Hailey lost his wife to someone like John Knoss, old Betsy's cast-off, what chance does someone like me have here?"

"I suppose we have to move on eventually," I said, giving him a slight smile. "So you still live in Hilly Dale. I thought you would have moved to Dallas. Isn't that where you always wanted to live?"

"Yeah. Almost wished I'd moved away after my wife died, but…anyway, it's the same-old, same-old with this crowd." He eyed the table with Betsy and her friends, and I noticed Beckham with Jason and Dee Dee had joined them.

"Do you keep up with anyone from our old group?" I asked, reaching for an eggroll.

"Heather's around, and I see Kismet. You remember her. She was Kismet Carter, cute, brown hair. She worked in the school library some."

"You used to date her. I liked her. How is she?"

"Yeah, that's her. Kismet's had a tough time personally and financially. Her husband left her with a couple of kids. She works at the factory John Knoss bought. Until Beck bought her aunt's house, she lived there. I don't think she got a huge amount for the house, although I heard Beck gave her a better price than the place deserved."

"I'm sorry to hear about Kismet. Is she here tonight?"

"No. She doesn't come to these things. She didn't like the way she was treated in school, and she's embarrassed about her life. Most of the time she's working. She pulls double-shifts when she can."

"I hate to hear that. I hope I get to see her. It's been nice talking to you, Tom, but I'd better join Heather and David."

"Maybe I'll give you a call and you, Heather, and I can get together sometime."

"Of course. I'd like that."

Someone I didn't recognize dinged a glass for attention. "Let's all stand and sing the alma mater, followed by the Hillbillies' fight song, and if there are any cheerleaders here, and I'm looking at you, Betsy, Harmony, and Susan, and I see Annie Booker hiding behind Jason and his wife, come on up and give us a cheer!"

After *that* spectacle, I sat down and began to nibble at my now-cold appetizers and listen to Heather ramble on about this one and that one. I finally had enough and excused myself. Beck was leaning against one side of the hallway when I walked out of the restroom. "You want to go outside and talk for a minute?" he asked.

"Stalking me, Beck?"

"No, but the truth is I'm hiding for a few minutes. Bianca's arrived with John. I don't want to get caught up in any drama."

"I'm sure you knew she would be here. She was at the football game. Is there drama?" I gave him a sardonic look.

"With Bianca, there always is."

"You dated her. Didn't you know what you were getting into when you married her?" I attempted to move past him, but he blocked my way.

"Just hold on for a second," he said sharply. "You and I were kids when we dated, and for the record, after you left town, Bianca and I broke up for several years. I moved to New York after university. Bianca and I ran into each other at a Broadway play and started dating again. We married quickly. Things weren't easy for us in New York, so we moved back here."

"Jordan seems well-adjusted. She and Aisling are becoming friends."

"Hey buddy, I need to take a piss. You think you can move it somewhere else?" Jason said, pushing himself between Beck and me.

I made a move to leave the hallway. "He's right; we're blocking the hallway to the restrooms and the way some of the people are starting to drink out there, we really should move," I said.

I think it's nice our daughters are friends. You and I were…"

I turned at the end of the hall and looked back. "Yes, it's lovely the girls are friends, but, Beck, I can't go through the other stuff with you. Heather has driven me nuts with all this nostalgia. Before that, Betsy and someone named Harmony had momentary lapses of memory regarding an ugly incident involving your group of friends and my group of friends. They have it straight now."

"Jessie, I knew you were in there behind that perfect façade." His eyes crinkled at the corner as he smiled at me.

"What do you mean?"

"You can be a little spitfire, if I remember correctly."

"Tommy remembers me as sarcastic and you remember a spitfire. I don't remember being either. I'm going to call Aisling and ask her if she will pick me up. I've had about as much high school 'fun' as I care to experience."

"I can take you. I've been ready to leave since I arrived, which hasn't been all that long ago. It's not my thing, and people are whispering about John, Bianca, Betsy, and me all here together. I came because Jason was my best friend in high school, but he lives for nostalgia. All he wants to talk about are the 'old days.' I swear we've driven past every old haunt, listened to the music of 'our time,' and talked about the same old things. We do it every time there's a reunion. I'm more than ready to leave."

I hesitated. The music started again and people were getting up to dance. I saw Heather and David on the floor. Crowded House's *Don't Dream It's Over* was playing. David looked relaxed and Heather so happy that I didn't want to interrupt them. "All right. Let's go."

As we walked onto the floor, Beck put his arm around my waist. "One dance, and the music's almost over, so it's okay."

I let him twirl me around the floor on the way to the door. Heather raised an eyebrow as we went past. I just shook my head and waved as we stepped through the doorway. Outside, I texted her:

Everything is all right. Beck's driving me home. I'm tired.

You and David enjoy your evening together.

"Whew, I'm glad to get out of there," Beck said when we stepped off the porch into the cooler air.

"So am I. Thanks for the rescue."

"Thanks for mine. I knew Bianca would be gunning for me after she started drinking. For Jordan's sake, I try to keep things civil, but Bianca's another story. She…"

"Beck, I don't need to know the details. This is your business."

We were both silent until he pulled his truck into my driveway. "Everyone's talking about this fence you put in. Your parents never had one. What's up with that?"

"I'm not my parents, and I like it," I replied. "Thank you for driving me home."

Beck eased his truck to the back gate that stretched across the driveway and killed the engine.

"What are you doing?" I asked, reaching for the door handle.

"Walking you to the door," he replied, hopping out of the truck. "Wait."

I didn't. I was already out of the truck by the time he reached the passenger side. "Hey, I was trying to be polite," he said. "I'll walk you to the kitchen door. It's late."

Seeing as how he wasn't going to take no for an answer, I clicked the remote and the gates slid open. When we reached the back door, I turned and thanked him again. Standing on the patio in the bright light from the motion detector, he said "You remember how we used to sit out here and look at the stars when we were kids?"

"Yes. It's a bit difficult now that these lights come on automatically. If you sit for a few minutes without moving, they go off though."

"Do you mind if we sit and talk for a moment?" He walked over to the white iron chairs that had belonged to my great-grandparents, dragged two into the center of the back garden, and took a seat in one. "I always liked these chairs. No one in town had anything like them. They look like cane until you touch them. The design is so *cool*. Look how they bounce. If you decide to sell them, let me know. They'd look great on the restaurant's front porch."

I smiled. "They're from the '30s. I researched them once. They're Howell Cane Bouncers or Springers. An interesting history about the design. A Bauhaus…" I stopped. Beck was giving me a puzzled look, and who could blame him. What sort of person would stand there after a class reunion and begin to give a detailed description of vintage chairs? Me, that's who - someone who had no idea what to say to him.

"Sit down. Let's talk a bit."

"Ummm, all right." I took a seat next to him.

"So, what did you think about the reunion?"

"What did *you* think? The crowd was mostly your old friends, and your picture was plastered everywhere."

"Huh? Oh, yeah. *That*. I don't know why they made those posters. It's embarrassing. I can't even count how many times over the years of reunions that people have come up to me and asked about that game where I led the team to seven touchdowns in the state championship. If people didn't keep reminding me, I would have forgotten about it by now. Like *that's* the biggest accomplishment in my life. I don't want to be another one like Lucky Fine."

"My aunt mentioned Lucky, but she glorified him."

"He's a local hero."

"Do you think so?"

"NO," Beck answered emphatically. "Hey, the motion lights went off. Don't move too much but look up."

I did, seeing the spattering of stars. Beck started naming the few constellations we could view from our location. "Remember how Katie Peters' dad would take us on hayrides around his farm when we were kids? We'd all lean back in the hay and look at the stars while Mr. Peters walked off to smoke or pretend to check for wild animals?"

"Yes," I replied a tad too dreamily.

"Wasn't Jasmine Hall one of your friends?"

"Uh-huh," I murmured, while looking at a constellation I recognized. "What happened to her?"

"She moved to Hawaii years ago. Has a degree in astrophysics."

"She loved stargazing. When our group started getting driving licenses, we'd drive into the country, take blankets, and lie there for hours looking at the constellations. Jasmine knew all of them, and she would tell stories about how they got their names. That's how I came up with *The Celestial Cat* series," I shared. "One night, she told us the story of the constellation *Felis*. It was deemed obsolete in the early twentieth century. She hoped that one day the brightest star in the constellation would at least be remembered and named for the lost cat. Years later, I wrote a short story about an unwanted starry cat and submitted it for a class I was taking at uni."

"And you got an 'A', am I right?" Beck said, softly.

"As a matter of fact, I did. I still have that story. It's called *The Lost Celestial Cat*."

"You always had an active imagination," he said, standing up. The motion lights effectively ended the stargazing. "I'd better get going."

"Thanks for the ride home." I watched him pass through the open gates and get into his truck, before I walked back to the kitchen door.

***

"So, what happened?" Heather asked when she called at 10:00 the next morning.

"I texted you that I was tired and Beck was driving me home," I replied, somehow knowing where this line of questioning was heading.

"Everyone saw you on the dance floor and watched you leave together, and that song...*Don't Dream It's Over*! Was that some sort of clue about what's happening between you two?"

"What? No. It was just a song that was playing when we left. It might as well have been another by Bon Jovi, Whitesnake, or Def Leppard. They were playing '80s music all night. We were simply leaving at that time."

"You were dancing and looked so cozy."

"Cozy?"

"He twirled you."

"When is twirling someone to the door at the end of a song considered cozy? We weren't even dancing. He wanted to leave as much as I did."

"I imagine he did. Let me tell you that Bianca saw you leave and was absolutely livid. She and John got into a fight, with him telling her that she was still in love with Beck, and her telling him he was cheating, which, by the way, he denied. And Betsy sat there, with her group soaking it all in. You know her husband Jack didn't attend. A lot of spouses don't, and that's when trouble starts. Old memories, drinks, dancing, well, you get the idea, but Beck's spouse WAS there."

"With her boyfriend," I reminded her. "I'm sure it was embarrassing for Beck and others there, but I can't account for what happened after we left." The toaster oven dinged and I removed a slice of cheese toast.

"It was something. Everyone was so stunned," Heather exclaimed loudly.

I held the phone away from my ear and rolled my eyes. If 'everyone' was like Heather, they were looking for the popcorn and settling in to watch the action unfold.

"So, did Beck spend the night?"

"What?"

"Did you and Beck … you know?"

"Heather, you and I may have been friends," I replied in the best upper crust accent I could muster, "*years ago*, but that doesn't give you license to ask me such personal questions now. However, in the interest of quelling any salacious gossip, the answer is no. I also have a daughter at home." Violet jumped in my lap and I stroked her thick, soft fur and listened to her purr for a moment, before I continued. "I'm sorry to disappoint everyone, but Beck drove me home and left." I was not about to tell her we'd talked for nearly an hour outside. Before I could take a bite of toast, cat hair floated and stuck to the cheese. I set Violet on the floor, got up, and dumped the toast into the rubbish bin.

"Oh, okay." Heather sounded skeptical. "Well, Bianca never liked you, and Betsy's group was saying what a snob you were."

"I have no interest in what anyone had to say about me last night. I also don't like participating in gossip."

"Are we still friends?" she said, her voice wavering. "Tommy and I are having lunch at Piggie-Pen next Saturday at 12:30. Will you join us? He really wanted to call you, but you didn't give him your number."

"Yes, we're friends, but if you are asking if I'm annoyed with you, I'm not, and I'm glad to meet both of you at Piggie-Pen. Thank you. I'd enjoy getting reacquainted with Tom."

Heather sighed audibly. "I'm so glad. I really want us to be close again, and Tommy's so nice. I just wanted to warn you that people are going to start talking about you and Beck."

And you were being nosy. I politely rang off and prepared another slice of cheese toast. Cat-hair free this time.

Chapter Twelve

"Now, we have you down to help emcee the Miss Pretty Pumpkin Pageant, Ms. Keasden," the local Chamber of Commerce president told me when he phoned a few days later. "The Pumpkin Festival Committee approved it, and the mayor is just thrilled."

"Pumpkin Festival?" I knew Hilly Dale had one every year, but this was the first I'd heard about emceeing it. "When is this? And who again was it that told you to put me down as an emcee? The Pumpkin Festival Committee? I've never talked to anyone on that." I looked at my calendar, there was nothing there but deadlines for certain chapters I wanted done, and a few last-minute things with my mother's estate.

"Jane-Ann Simmons, your aunt. She said you agreed to it. The mayor and I were going to invite you to lunch and discuss it with you, but she said she'd talk to you about it."

"I don't believe my aunt told me anything about this," I replied, confused. And then a snippet of a conversation I'd had with her flitted across my memory. I recalled we had been discussing book readings and she mentioned briefly that some people would like me to emcee during the local festival; however, I didn't remember agreeing to anything but a reading at Margo Hunter's house. After that, I'd done a private reading at the library for the staff and volunteers and given one talk to a creative writing class at the local college, but I'd been personally approached by the librarian and one of the English professors. Talking about my books was one thing; emceeing a beauty pageant was quite another.

"Mr...? I'm sorry, but I've forgotten your name."

"Oh, I forgot to tell you. I figured your aunt would let you know I'd be calling. I'm Jim, Jim Tooney."

"Mr. Tooney, she may have mentioned something about the festival, but I was never asked to do it. Unfortunately, this is something...Violet, get down please." She stayed put.

"Pardon?"

"I was talking to my cat. Mr. Tooney, I can't do this."

"But we have the flyers ready to go! Don't you get the *Hilly Dale Gazette* each Thursday?"

"No, I don't, and my aunt did not confirm any of this with me." I set Violet on the floor where she flopped on the Persian rug, before rolling around. "You have plenty of food in the kitchen," I told the beautiful black cat. Violet gave me a baleful look, got up, waved her fluffy tail, and walked away. "I apologize, Mr. Tooney. Pets, you know."

"Of course, I have several dogs. Now, if you don't agree to do this, and I'm sorry Jane-Ann did not discuss this with you, we're put in a bind, Ms. Keasden. We've already lined up Lucky Fine, and you were to be our female celebrity."

"I'm afraid you will have to find someone else. I have deadlines to meet."

"We can't at this late date. Your aunt told us you had agreed. It shouldn't take too much of your time."

"Didn't you think of ringing me and confirming it?"

"Uh…no, your aunt's on the festival committee like she's been for thirty years. We took her word for it."

"I suppose I needn't say you should not have done that. She spoke in haste."

"Well, no I shouldn't have, but we're stuck, and I'm begging you, Ms. Keasden. Lucky Fine can't do it alone." My thoughts drifted to what Beck had said about Mr. Fine.

"Very well, but I don't want to be emceeing swimsuit competitions. I find that degrading to women."

"We don't do swimsuits now. Some of the young ladies' choices were quite controversial over the past few years. It's evening gown, street clothes, talent, and a question. It's tasteful. And you'll only be doing the Miss Pretty Pumpkin part with Lucky. He's," Jim Tooney paused for a moment before going on, "got, uh, an eye for the ladies. We need you to temper his comments. We have out-of-town judges, so everything is impartial. A radio announcer and an elementary school principal, Carol Kendall, are doing the children's pageants. There are several of them to get through, but they're the night before."

Several? There had only been The Miss Pretty Pumpkin and Little Miss Pretty Pumpkin when I was a child. My parents had pushed me at age six into the latter – I didn't win. It wasn't my idea of a good time. Bianca had won and Betsy had been first runner-up, but we had been friends back then and no one had cared. We were all excited just to ride on a float in the parade.

I caved. "All right, I will do this, but please, if my aunt volunteers me for other things, contact me and ask before you announce it."

Thanks to my aunt, I was stuck. I could do this; Will had judged cattle. I only had to announce contestants not judge them on their merits. If I turned this down, I would be alienating a number of people. If I chose to remain in Hilly Dale, I couldn't afford to do that, especially for Aisling's sake

***

"Why couldn't it be pumpkin carving rather than calling out the names of women parading around a stage," I told Liam when I rang him.

My son burst into laughter. "I wish I could be there. Hillbilly Dale has a Miss Pretty Pumpkin! Brilliant! Is there a Mr. Hayseed of Hillbilly Dale too?"

"Liam, that's unkind," I chided, "but I am annoyed with my aunt for volunteering me and not saying anything. She put me in an embarrassing position. Emceeing is something I couldn't decline without appearing anti-community, anti-social, and ill-mannered. It's apparently an honor to be asked."

Liam struggled to regain his composure. "Sorry, Mum, but if anyone at home hears about this, Nan will collapse from mortification," he started to laugh again. "I can see her face!"

"On to more important things," I said. How are your studies?"

My son suddenly stopped laughing. "Going well, at least I think so."

"Good. Are Alistair and Cecilia getting on with the wedding plans? I haven't talked with him in a couple of weeks. I don't want to interfere."

"Like Nan did when you married? Yeah, Alistair told us that! He wanted to be a page boy and she wouldn't let him. Ceci is keeping Alsy busy. I've got plans in a few minutes. Love you."

"I love you too."

Alsy? I didn't think any of us called him that anymore. Cecilia probably revived that as her pet name for him. After our chat, I'd just returned to my writing when the landline phone rang. I detested phone calls, unless they were from my children. This call was from my aunt, and her calls were disruptive. Apparently, she'd just learned about the class reunion – the gossip mill must be running slower these days.

"You're new here. You have to preserve your reputation, Jessica. You can't be causing scenes and creating gossip."

"Causing scenes? To whom have you been talking?"

"Agnes Dunston. Her daughter was there."

"Are you accusing me of things after listening to second-hand gossip from someone I don't know."

"You've met Agnes. We had lunch with her. She's in my garden club. She was wearing the yellow dress with a green cardigan that day you and Aisling joined us."

Ah...Lady Daffodil. "I barely met her, and I certainly don't know her daughter."

"You do. She was Lindsey Dunston. She was in your class. She's Lindsey Canton, now. Petite, short brown hair, freckles. Lindsey works at Dunston's Dolled-Up. I'm sure you remember that place. It's been here for years. It was started by Lindsey's great-grandmother in the '30s. Your mother used to shop there until you started getting her those fancy things in Europe. Well, Lindsey said..."

I let her drone on while I revised a paragraph in my manuscript, until I heard: "just because you're somewhat famous now doesn't mean you can be rude to people, and it certainly doesn't mean you can entertain other women's husbands overnight."

I couldn't believe I was hearing this! "And you really think I'm someone who would do that? You believe someone else? Aunt Jane-Ann, Beck drove me home from the reunion. We both wanted to leave for different reasons. Heather and David were having a lovely time. Beck offered me a ride. I accepted. For goodness' sake, Aisling lives here, and Aisling and Beck's daughter Jordan are friends."

"Well, Agnes is my dear friend," she spluttered, "and she was shocked when Lindsey told her."

"And I am your niece," I reminded her.

"Yes, you are, and you are a niece I have barely seen since you left Hilly Dale. Decent people from good families don't do those things in Hilly Dale. He's *married*, Jessica."

"Aunt Jane-Ann," I began, but she kept right on talking.

"How do I know what you're like now? I know this, though, you're associating with Heather Dale James and that says a lot. She is not the right sort. The Dale family has fallen far since old Ezra started this town. Oh, I know you were friends in school, and I'm a big proponent of staying in touch with old classmates, but her oldest son is..." she lowered her voice, "*illegitimate*. After you left for U of A, Heather turned up pregnant by Nick Nethermeyer. You remember the Nethermeyers who owned that junk shop just outside of town. They had several children. None of them amounted to a hill of beans!"

"Aunt Jane-Ann!"

"Well, they didn't. Anyway, Heather got pregnant and proudly walked around Hilly Dale big as all get-out. I know these days this happens a lot, but I tell you her parents were so embarrassed. They tried to get her to put the baby up for adoption, but Heather said that everyone knew and she was keeping it. The Dales kept the child for her while she went to work and then when she went to Hilly Dale College a few years later. She met Steve Taylor there, he's from a good family, but Heather messed up with him. Married him too quickly. I'm sure she told you how *that* marriage ended. What a scandal! The Taylors were humiliated, and that girl caused them the loss of their beautiful dining room table. It was a family heirloom," she said vehemently, as if the loss of the table was the most important thing that had happened. "And Heather's son with that Nethermeyer fellow got into some trouble after high school. No one talks about it."

"She has a good man in David James, now," I said.

"Yes, " my aunt replied, "but he, like Jackson Barker, is from…up north. You know they are different from those of us in Hilly Dale."

Grant me the strength to stay silent on that matter. I chose a different subject. "While you are on the phone with me, I'd like to know why you told the Chamber of Commerce president that I would be happy to be the emcee for The Miss Pretty Pumpkin Pageant?"

"I told you about it some time ago. It's an honor to be considered."

"You may have mentioned that they wanted me to do it while you told me about book readings, but I certainly do not recall agreeing to anything other than the book club meeting at Margo Hunter's house. Jim Tooney and I were both embarrassed that I did not know about it. He is the one who told me you said I had agreed. I'm stuck doing this silly pageant because the flyers are done and it's been announced in the local paper. I'm surprised they found an open weekend, seeing as how you told me they were in short supply during football season."

"Don't be impertinent!"

Why did you not tell me you volunteered me?"

"I assumed you being such a reader, read the newspaper," she snipped. "You would have seen it then."

"I do not. I get my news online."

"Well, you need to get a subscription to the local paper. I'll get you one, so you won't be out of the loop."

"That is not the point, and you know it. NEVER volunteer me for anything again, Aunt Jane-Ann. You are my family, but that does not give you license to decide what I should or shouldn't do here. I have a career and a daughter. I have responsibilities and commitments."

"If you are going to live here, you need to fit in. And I'm thinking of Aisling. She needs to fit in too. Do you know I've had to explain her name to everyone?" my aunt complained.

"I'd really like to know who this 'everyone' is people talk about. They seem to be the ones whose opinion is the most valued in this town," I snapped, peeved at her bringing my daughter into the conversation.

"Don't be smart with me, Jessica. Your mother would have been troubled by the way you're acting. You may have been married to a wealthy foreigner, but don't you forget where you came from. You're just a girl from Hilly Dale, Arkansas, no matter the fancy accent, expensive clothes, and your high-and-mighty attitude. People think you're a rich snob, and that can't be good for your career, or your personal life, and it can't help Aisling here at all. Children are the reflections of their parents."

My career wouldn't be hurt, and I wasn't looking for a 'personal life' at this point. Considering how an innocent ride home from a class reunion generated such accusations of 'entertaining another woman's husband overnight', I wasn't sure I would want a personal life here. My mother would have been proud of me for standing up for myself, and my father would have been thrilled. Aisling couldn't care less. She was having an adventure in my hometown.

"Aunt Jane-Ann," I said, while walking into the kitchen to get a cup of tea, "I know you are coming from a place of love and concern, but I'm new here. I don't know people, but the townspeople think they know me. They remember the teenage me; they do not know the forty-seven-year-old woman I am today. We've had different life experiences. I'm a novelty, that's all. It will wear off, much like it did with those I met when I moved to England. Keep in mind that I'm re-learning life in Hilly Dale. This is a change for me, and it's a completely different world for Aisling. And if you have to keep explaining her name, then stop. It isn't necessary. I assure you, that Aisling won't care if it is mispronounced." I plugged in the kettle and sat down at the kitchen table waiting for the water to boil.

"I'm only trying to help you get involved and fit in."

"I know, and I appreciate it, but please give me the chance to accept or not, and please do not volunteer me. I may not have a traditional job, but I do work and I have deadlines to meet."

"Whatever you say, Jessica. It's always all about you!" she sniped.

You've got to be kidding me!

Chapter Thirteen

It was mid-October and the Pumpkin Festival had begun. Times had certainly changed. When I drove through town on my way to a meeting that Thursday, the town square was full of vendors selling carnival-style trinkets, and there were food trucks everywhere. Where were the locals selling their homemade jams, pumpkin pies, quilts, hand-carved canes and toys, cast-iron items, and handmade crafts? Where was the biggest pumpkin contest? Where was the family offering hayrides? Where were the local musicians performing on the courthouse steps? Where were the children playing games? If this was any indication of what the Pumpkin Festival was now, the small-town charm had been lost. Even the venue had changed from the fairgrounds to Peters' Pumpkin Patch which was several miles outside of town. According to the itinerary I was given, pageants were still held on Friday and Saturday nights, so the winners and contestants could ride on pumpkin-themed floats through the middle of downtown on Sunday afternoon. I was glad that hadn't been changed.

I drove into the parking lot of the early 1900s Presbyterian Church which now housed The Chamber of Commerce, among other offices. Glancing up at the gorgeous stained-glass windows, I felt happy knowing the building had been purchased by the city and was being used, unlike others I'd noticed. The meeting was with Jim Tooney, Aunt Jane-Ann, and the rest of the Pumpkin Festival committee to go over last-minute details. The second week of October had already been filled with meetings about who was going to do what. I couldn't imagine there was anything else that needed to be discussed. I soon discovered that it was nothing. We went over the same things we'd discussed last week.

"So, we're all clear?" Sassy Freemont, the head of the committee asked.

There was a chorus of 'yesses,' and I stood up to leave. I had lunch plans with Jackson.

"Ms. Keasden, Jessica," Mr. Tooney stopped me at the door, "You do know that you will want to stay after the pageant. I don't think Sassy told you that. If you look on the itinerary, you'll see that the street dance that used to be held after the pageant on Saturday night is now held at Peters' Pumpkin Patch. You may remember it as Peters' Farm," he said, as if I couldn't read the itinerary in my hand, and we hadn't spent two weeks talking about the location. "I'm sure you're confused about things. We relocated all the usual activities out there years ago. It made sense. Freed up the town for more commercial use. The fairground isn't what it used to be. The move was good for the town's economy, good for the Peters, and good for our over-all image to blend the old with the new."

"Thank you for clearing up any questions I might have had, Mr. Tooney," I replied, trying not to sound sarcastic.

"Jim," he reminded me.

"Jim," I repeated. "You mentioned the fairgrounds. I noticed there wasn't a county fair in September?"

"That's right. We decided not to have those a few years ago. Too much crime for our little town, and a couple of children were hurt on the rides. Instead, we hold an event in early June at the Hilly Dale Community Center where locals can bring their crafts and homemade pies, jams, and whatnot for judging, and of course we have a Farmer's Market on the square. I'm sure you've seen it." I had, but Jackson kept me supplied in seasonal vegetables from his garden. He told me it was because he had watched me try to select produce on one of our Walmart trips and found it odd.

The loss of the county fair saddened me. Even after all these years, I could almost smell the 'Fair Scent'– popcorn, wieners turning on a spit, cotton candy, and caramel apples mixed with that of barnyard animals. I remembered walking down the colorful, lighted midway with its music blaring and barkers hawking games. I recalled stopping at booths along the way and being badgered into playing one of those games in the hope of winning a giant, blue teddy bear. Beck won a stuffed penguin for me instead. I'd named it 'Paddy the Penguin.' The toy was packed away somewhere in the attic, probably moth-eaten by now. I'd never like the rides; they always looked rickety to me. When Beck finally coaxed me on the small Ferris Wheel, it had gotten stuck about halfway.

I'd enjoyed seeing the people selling homemade goodies, toys, and quilts, and I loved looking at the prize ribbons, imagining how happy the winners were. My mother had won a quilt ten years ago and her first comment to me when she called to tell me was, "I was only trying to help that society raise money. What am I going to do with another quilt, and one that is newly made? I have so many of your great-great grandmother's. They wouldn't take it back and let someone else win." I'd seen the new quilt on a shelf in one of the upstairs closets. It was nice, but I saw her point.

"Are you going somewhere, Jessica?" My aunt's voice startled me back to the present.

"I was planning to meet Jackson for lunch."

"Jackson Barker?" Jim Tooney chimed in. "We were hoping he'd do a reading for the children this year, but he declined. We've been trying to get more children's activities out at Peters' Pumpkin Patch."

"I remember the readings. They used to be held on the library's front lawn, but I'm glad to know some traditions are still being kept, even if they are out at Peters' Pumpkin Patch. With all the things on the square, it's nice to know some things are still continuing."

"Well, the committee decided years ago that we needed to attract more downtown attention and the old traditions just weren't bringing much traffic. The food trucks and vendors supply that. It's been good for the town," he said, rather defensively.

I wasn't challenging him, but perhaps others had over the years, although I wondered how outside vendors and food services benefitted the shops and few restaurants in Hilly Dale. The cute, quaint town I'd known – the one I'd described to close friends and my English family - had once been more of the Hallmark film-set type, but it was developing a sad, neglected look to it, despite attempts to modernize by tearing down old buildings and replacing them with new ones that looked out-of-place in the historic area.

"How…innovative?" I replied, searching for a word that didn't convey my own thoughts on the matter, thus avoiding a 'scene' as my aunt would have put it.

"Oh, I was hoping you would have lunch with the members of my garden club. I've proposed you for membership," my aunt interrupted us.

"Aunt Jane-Ann, may I speak with you privately, please."

She put on her brown coat and followed me into the Chamber's hall that was lined with doors, their stained-glass windows memorials to long-ago church members. I closed the door to our meeting room after us. "How many times have I asked you to consult with me before you volunteer me for things? I'm in this situation because you did."

"I didn't volunteer you. I proposed you for membership in a fine organization in town. You need to get involved in this community and stop staying by yourself." She arched her eyebrows and stared at me over her spectacles. "It isn't normal to not want to get involved here."

What was the point of going over things again with her. Instead, I said I wasn't interested. I was not a gardener.

"You don't have to be a gardener to join."

I knew this was a stupid question, but I asked anyway. "Why would anyone want to join a garden club unless they enjoyed gardening?"

"To be part of the community. I've been approached by several organizations wanting you to join. I selected Hilly Dale Garden Club for you, for the first one. Your mother was a member. So far, you have only done two readings, and one was at the college for some creative writing class, and that's not going to get you involved where you will meet people. You only associate with Jackson Barker, Heather James and that Beckham Hailey. He may have a popular restaurant, but he's not a good man for you. He's married, and he lets his wife run around. I think they might be," she lowered her voice, *swingers*."

I wasn't even going there. "I'm doing the Miss Pretty Pumpkin Pageant. Isn't that enough?"

"It's a start. You don't want to be considered a snob. I'm looking out for your best interests."

"I understand and thank you, but I've mention numerous times, please let me decide."

"That's just it. You have been here since July and you've haven't…"

"I apologize for cutting this short, but I'm meeting Jackson."

I left her and drove north past The Old Part to Cajun Daisy's, a restaurant housed in an old log cabin on the edge of a forest. From the front porch, one of the local lakes, Troutwood, could be seen in the distance. Jackson was waiting at one of the several empty tables in the small front room that was decorated with old farm implements and spinning wheels. Fairy lights were draped over the fireplace mantle and along a bar at the back of the room. I'd eaten here with Heather once. The food was a blend of Creole and Cajun, and it was good. The owner, Daisy Lafayette, claimed she was from Louisiana's Cajun Country, but Jackson said she landed there via Atlanta, Georgia. It had been a while since Jackson and I'd had a good chat, and we filled each other in over bowls of gumbo and a loaf of crusty bread with a spicy butter-blend on the side.

"Honestly, how can people believe you left that party and let Beckham Hailey waltz in and spend the night with you. Your own daughter lives there! Your aunt, God love her, and the Hilly Dale Garden Club bunch are the nosiest people in town. Just pay no attention. I've learned to do that."

"Why did you decide not to do the reading for the children this year?"

"I have company this weekend. My brother and his family are going to be in town. For once, I'd like to enjoy Peters' Pumpkin Patch and the festival before Jim Tooney and his cronies change it to something even more commercial. John Knoss is part of the push for commercialism, but his ex-wife is a different story. She's against it, as are a number of other people in town. It's a divisive issue."

"This place *is* empty today," I observed.

"See what I'm talking about. People are down on the courthouse square eating. I guess Saturday night's your night to shine."

***

Scattered along each side of the private, paved-road leading to Peters' Pumpkin Patch were old-fashion black lamp posts with their iron lanterns' fake flames helping illuminate the short drive. The road dead-ended at a parking lot, light spilling from the open doors of the enormous stone barn ahead that had been in the Peters' family for at least one-hundred-fifty years. I parked, exited the car, and headed toward the main entrance.

"Ticket?" the woman I remembered as Harmony from the reunion asked. She was sitting on a high-backed chair behind a small wooden table with a slotted cardboard box and a giant Styrofoam drink container from one of the local mini-marts next to her.

I held out my pass. "Oh, it's you," she said, a tad surly. "Go on." She took a long sip of whatever it was through the clear, plastic straw and stared at me.

"Thank you," I replied, and entered the barn. I hadn't been in the Peters' barn since I was a teenager. It was nothing like this then. They'd grown pumpkins, but it was also a working farm when I was growing up. Animals lived in this barn. Mr. Peters used to sponsor hayrides during the Pumpkin Festival.

I learned from attending festival committee meetings, none of which Lucky Fine participated in, that the Peters turned the place into a venue twenty years before the trend of barn and rustic weddings caught on. Heather, Tommy, Kismet, and I used to come out here and play with Katie Peters. She had animals galore. I'd gotten my first kitten from her – a fluffy little black and gray tabby with white feet and chest. Fluff was his name; I wasn't very creative with names at eight. Fluff had been mine until ten years later when I went off to the University of Arkansas. He had died while I was attending Cambridge.

The remodeled inside of the barn held rows of straight-backed, uncomfortable-looking chairs facing a stage with a short runway. Jim Tooney was waving his arms at me from the back of the huge space. I made my way across the slate floor to him, dodging a few children who were darting around the chairs, screaming and laughing. The room was already filling up with people who were bringing in drinks and snacks with them.

"Sassy's running around somewhere taking care of last-minute details, but here's your spot," he said, pointing at the podium on one side of the stage. "The list of contestants is right there. There's just ten this year. All you have to do is announce their names and read a short bio about them, and later, you'll ask the question. It's the same question for all of them. They'll do the rest. Your accent is going to class up the pageant."

"Thank you." I looked at his blue sweater and jeans as I removed my black puffy jacket. Was I overdressed for this event? I'd worn a black cashmere sweater with black trousers and black high-heeled boots. My hair was slicked back in a chignon and I wore a single statement piece - a large square-cut ruby set in a thick, burnished 18-karat gold medieval-style necklace. My lipstick was almost the color of the gem. I had told myself that I looked appropriate when I left the house, but now I was uncertain.

An hour later, the pageant began. A local band played classic country tunes to capture the audience's attention. After a short set, the mayor, a man who looked like he would rather be anywhere but here, hopped up the two steps and was suddenly beaming and welcoming the crowd sitting on chairs, on hay bales around the edges, and in the loft. The latter is where I spotted Aisling. She stood out in any crowd. Jordan was no slouch either. The two complemented each other. Jordan had dark hair like her father's but had sky-blue eyes. Both girls were swinging their legs off the edge of the loft. Two boys in Hilly Dale College sweatshirts were sitting on either side of them.

"And our emcees for the evening are: Lucky Fine," said the mayor, stopping while the crowd went wild. Lucky appeared wearing a Razorback cap, red sweater, boot-cut blue jeans, and cowboy boots. Lucky was at least 6'3," but obviously hadn't kept up his football physique. He heartily shook the mayor's hand and waved to the crowd, eliciting another round of whoops and applause, and finally the famous 'Calling of the Hogs' three times. "Now, settle down," the mayor yelled over the excited voices. "We have another emcee tonight. She's not new to Hilly Dale, but she's been away for years as you will be able to tell the minute she starts speaking. Many of you may know her as the well-known author Jessica Keasden, or as little Jessie Jenson, Charles and Evelyn Jenson's daughter. Let's give her a real Hilly Dale welcome!"

There was polite applause. I was clearly not as big a draw as Lucky Fine. After taking the two steps to the stage, I reached for the mayor's hand, but instead of shaking it, he bent and bestowed a kiss to the back. Lucky Fine drew me to him in a hug. "Let's welcome the lady!" he cried, after holding me a few seconds too long. The audience cheered. He may have been a washed-up athlete, but to the folks in Hilly Dale, he was a sports legend. I thanked him and smiled at the crowd.

Lucky and I took turns reading out the ten contestants' names as they took part in the street clothes' competition. I had the first card. "Contestant Number One is Duluth Hammond. Duluth is nineteen years old, enjoys all forms of hunting, and it's noted here that she is *particularly* fond of using a bow-and-arrow. Duluth enjoys watching reality television shows, playing video games, and crochet. Duluth Hammond, ladies and gentlemen!" Duluth was dressed in a pair of faded jeans, over-the-knee, high-heeled boots, and a white long-sleeved top. She had completed her ensemble with a black crocheted vest. Strutting her thin body with her overly made-up face, and poofed, long brown hair along the short runway, she nodded and duck-pouted all the way down, and all the way back let her behind perform an exaggerated sway.

"Now that's my kind of woman going right there," Lucky leaned down to whisper in my ear. He was too close to the microphone. The crowd heard him and laughed.

Oh my.

"Contestant Number Two," Lucky snickered, "Yeah, Number Two," he continued is "Allison Maisie Knoss. Allison is nineteen and likes nothing I do. She likes to read, sing, cook – well, I like that – quilt, and she's going to Hilly Dale College to get a degree in music. I don't know what she's going to do with that, but let's give her a round of applause." Allison, whom I'd met at the bank, was attractively made-up and was wearing a pair of dark trousers with a cream sweater. She walked very well in her four-inch stilettos. And on it went, with Lucky often making inappropriate asides, and the pageant-goers clapping, catcalling, whistling, and cheering for their favorite contestants. One woman yelled, "Take another walk, Carly Jean! Show 'em what you got!"

We were finally at the talent competition. My, *that* was an eye-opening and ear-splitting event, and also proved to be a dangerous one. Some had wonderful talents, and some I felt had been roped into participating in the Miss Pretty Pumpkin Pageant because there hadn't been enough contestants. Those young women were simply doing the best they could to get through their performances. I felt for them.

"And now we have Contestant Number Seven, Vancy Copperfield," I announced. "She is a skilled baton twirler."

Vancy, in a very short costume, walked on the stage twirling her batons – fire batons – to The Marshall Tucker Band's *Fire on the Mountain*. The crowd enjoyed her performance, clapping along to the music. At one point during her performance, she tossed one of her two twirling batons and missed the catch, which caused her to lean to the side and grab it before it hit the floor. Unfortunately, the baton came close enough to one of the decorative bales of hay on the stage, igniting it. I noticed that Beck was the one who grabbed a fire extinguisher and rushed to put out the small fire. The contestant continued twirling her batons on the other side of the stage, while he sprayed the bale until the song finished. The show must go on.

"Well, that was something!" Lucky cried. "Let's get this cleared up and we'll return to the pageant in a few minutes, folks." The band began playing.

Someone opened the barn doors so the smell of burned hay and chemicals could air out, bringing in the chilly night air, which I found to be a welcome relief. Finally, the pageant continued with the last three contestants' talent presentations, followed by the evening gown competition and question. Babies cried and children squealed, making it difficult to hear the contestants' answers. While the judges voted and the band played, Lucky and I took a seat until we were handed the winners. This was the part I dreaded. All the contestants looked caught up in the moment, even if some had originally not wanted to be a part of the pageant.

We announced the winner together. "This year's Miss Pretty Pumpkin is," we paused for dramatic effect, "Allison Maisie Knoss."

The crowd began cheering as last year's Miss Pretty Pumpkin draped a sash with the title around the new winner and then placed a rhinestone tiara, complete with a pumpkin-shaped orange jewel in the center, atop Allison's head, fiddling with the tiara until she gave up and shoved the thing down until it stayed in place. Although that must have hurt, Allison kept smiling. The mayor presented her with a bouquet of fall flowers. Betsy stood up clapping and cheering as her daughter waved and smiled as she walked the runway a couple of times. I could see John and Bianca sitting a few rows back from Betsy. John was beaming, but Bianca glared at her boyfriend's ex-wife.

With the pageant finished, the band took over, the chairs were moved, and the runway was detached. The dance was about to begin. Aisling and Jordan rushed over to me as I was gathering my things. "I'm glad Allison won," my daughter said. "She's really nice, and she won that small scholarship to Hilly Dale College. She goes there with us."

"She has a lovely singing voice. I didn't know she went to school with you. You've never mentioned her."

"I remembered what you told me about her mother."

"I shouldn't have done that, Aisling," I said, pulling her aside, "Your friends are *your* friends. Who their parents are or what sort of relationship I had or have with them has little bearing on their children. Allison is welcome at the house anytime. Do you understand me? Jordan's welcome too. My past here is mine; it should not affect your present."

"All right. Thank you, Mum."

"Now, what about those two boys?" I teased.

"Mother!" she cried, blushing. She only called me 'Mother' when embarrassed or guests were present. "We're going on the hayride," she added quickly.

"Have fun, girls." I laughed as they swiftly walked away from me and out the main entrance where I saw the boys catch up with them.

I was gathering my things when I heard, "Wanna go on a hayride?"

Beck!

"Hey," he said when I turned around.

"Hello." I slipped on my puffy jacket.

"Remember when we went on that hayride during a Pumpkin Festival? We were like fourteen or fifteen," he reminded me.

"Actually, I do. That's the night before you took up with Bianca. Am I right?"

I'd never seen Beck flush, but there's a first time for everything, and he was glowing red under the lights. "Uh…I guess we remember things differently. I thought you didn't want to go out with me anymore?"

"Come off it, Beck," I said, reverting to my American way of phrasing things. "You sat right there on that wagon and told me you weren't going to have time for me now that you were playing football, and that you had an image to keep up. 'Free Agent' I believe you called yourself." Despite having moved on from that, I still remembered it.

"Jessie…I, uh…"

"You don't have to say anything, Beck. That was a very long time ago."

"Bianca told me the night before we went on the hayride that you were dumping me for Tommy Fitzpatrick. He always liked you, but then you started dating Josh Billings, the Math Club Guy." I could hear the disdain in his voice. "I couldn't understand what she meant and asked her about it. She said she was confused and that Tommy and Josh were about the same to her."

"Bianca told you that? Tommy was a friend. He introduced me to Josh. I was sorry to hear Josh was in that plane crash several years ago."

Beck ran his hands through his hair before he said, "Yeah, that was a bad deal. His wife Molly moved back to North Dakota to be with her family. Look, I'm sorry. We have different versions to this story. Are you leaving?"

"It's nothing, Beck. It was years ago. Why does it seem that people are stuck in the past and try to drag me back into it?"

"Small town? Lots of people remained here? I don't know. It was like that when Bianca and I moved back. People talked about us, but it wasn't that hard to settle in. It looks like you're having a hard time."

As we walked out of the barn, I could see the hay wagon pulling away. "Looks like we missed our chance for another hayride," I said. "I hope Aisling is enjoying herself."

"Of course she is. It's fun. You know that. We talked about it the night of the reunion. Maybe we could get the girls and have a private dinner at the restaurant one night. I close on Sundays and Mondays."

"I don't know about that. I'm busy with the final touches for my new book, and I have a wedding to attend in England."

"You do? Whose?"

"My stepson's. By the way, that was quick thinking when the hay bale caught fire. You saved the pageant."

"I was closest to the extinguisher," he said modestly. "You remember my dad was a firefighter. They should never have allowed that fire baton routine in the barn, especially with hay bales all around."

"Why did they?"

"The twirler was the mayor's stepdaughter. Like I said, maybe we can get together with the girls, but when you get back."

"We'll see." I got in my car and drove off.

***

It was 7:00 p.m. and Aisling was on her way to a Halloween party with her friends. Because of the gate, I was not expecting trick-or-treaters. To those in Hilly Dale, it was unfriendly. To someone like the me I was now, it was what I knew, but I wanted to watch the children going door-to-door. I turned off the lights downstairs and carried my laptop up to the lit-up turret. For fun, I stuck a witch's hat Aisling had discarded on my head, dragged the spinet desk to the front window, and watched for the trick-or-treaters to walk by. About that time, Violet came in and jumped on the windowsill. It amused me at all the looks we got from children and their parents as they passed down the street. Next thing I knew, someone would say I was a witch, and that would make the gossip rounds. Sipping a glass of wine, I began the final revisions on *Shadows and Stones*.

***

November contained the third anniversary of Will's death, along with my mother's first. I was not looking forward to this month at all, but I had to move forward and that meant giving Aisling an American Thanksgiving. My go-to idea was that we attend a popular Thanksgiving lunch held annually at the Episcopal church in a nearby town.

Aunt Jane-Ann did not like this idea. "We always have Thanksgiving at your house. Your mother and I cooked the most wonderful meals together, and we invited the less fortunate of our friends to join us. Now that you're back, why can't we continue this… for Evelyn and Aisling. Your daughter deserves to have a traditional American Thanksgiving with friends and family. I don't know what you do over there at this time."

"We have a harvest festival, but it's not at the same time as America's Thanksgiving. I'm not the cook my mother was, and it's just the three of us. Heather told me many people go to the Episcopal church's holiday meals. I'm not a big fan of holiday food and we certainly don't want all those leftovers for just the three of us. Let's try something different this year, but if you don't want to, maybe one of your friends will invite you to dinner at her house."

Aunt Jane-Ann fussed for a few days and then joined us at the Episcopal church's gathering. It appeared that several of her club friends were there. Lady Begonia and Lady Cornflower wearing their signature colors joined us. Aisling's reaction was that the whole thing was "meh" and that Jordan was having her Thanksgiving with her mother. That meant Beck was on his own this year.

I took a tour of the church while Aisling and my aunt talked to people they knew. Two of the clergy invited me to attend services and were very interested that I was Church of England. They'd visited England on numerous occasions and spent a good half-hour telling me about the visits to various cathedrals and churches. I enjoyed talking with them.

Chapter Fourteen

Time passed quickly after Thanksgiving. Aisling and I were preparing for our trip to England the following week. My daughter had packed way too much. "I don't know what I'll need," she said. "I plan to see some of my friends. I don't have to spend all my time at Fielding House, do I?"

"No, you can spend a couple of days in London if you want and see your friends."

Although we'd be spending the week of Christmas abroad, I still wanted to keep a couple of Jenson family Christmas traditions alive. With the help of Jackson and Aisling, we brought down the Christmas tree and set it upstairs in the turret's window. Aisling and I decorated it and I told her about all the family ornaments. She delighted in the sterling silver Santa that had 'Baby's First Christmas' etched on it. "It was your grandmother's."

"I love it," Aisling said. "What else should we put on the tree?"

By the end of the day, the tree was decorated, the timer set, and the wreaths up on all the exterior doors. A few days later, we left for the wedding.

***

We arrived in London at noon. The car was waiting for us as we stepped out into the dreary, gray day.

"Mr. Herren, so good to see you," I said, greeting our driver. I never called him by his last name. It seemed antiquated and disrespectful.

"Your Grace. I trust you had a good flight?"

From the corner of my eye, I saw Jackson's startled look. I'd warned him enroute that things were different and that this was how my life was here."

"We did indeed," I replied as our chauffeur opened the door to the black Bentley, a recent model that Alistair had purchased for use in London. Jackson will sit in the back with me, and Lady Aisling will ride in front." Mr. Herren raised an eyebrow but didn't question my decision.

"My God!" exclaimed Jackson after we arrived at the London residence. "I feel like I'm stepping into a PBS series." Standing stock-still, he gazed up at the tall townhouse the Fielding-Smythes had owned for one-hundred-fifty years, until he was brought back to reality when the black front door was opened by Mrs. Herren.

"Good afternoon, Mrs. Herren," I said leading the way into the marble-floored foyer. "May I present Dr. Barker. He will be our guest while in London. Is my son at home?"

"Yes, Your Grace. I believe his Lordship is in the library."

"Thank you. We shall see ourselves to our rooms." I knew I sounded extremely formal, but this was the way my mother-in-law taught me, but I broke the rules sometimes, especially if she wasn't around. "Jackson, please come with me. Aisling." Up the mahogany staircase we went. Remembering how I was once stuck in the cage-lift that was installed decades ago. I wasn't about to set foot in it. I had been given a guest room instead of the old room I'd shared with Will. It was just as well. Jackson had a room down the hall.

"How is your room?" I asked when I met him in the foyer a half-hour later.

"Perfect. Thank you. Jessica, it gives me a start each time I hear you called 'Your Grace.' I know you're a duchess, but it didn't sink in until the driver referred to you that way. And you have a different way of addressing people, I noticed."

"That's true, and you will hear me addressed as 'Duchess.'" I blew out my cheeks and exhaled, "You will also hear my children addressed by their titles. It's silly, and I don't think every household does it with as much formality, but I'm used to it now. Mr. Herren is a modern butler who wears several hats. We aren't at this house all the time, so it doesn't make sense to keep a full staff. Mrs. Herron, his wife, is the house manager. We have an agency send cleaners as needed."

"Well, I'm loving it," Jackson cried, following me into the library where Liam, with eyes closed, was leaning back in a chair, his jeans-clad legs resting on an antique leather-topped desk. Music was blaring.

Grasping one of his ear buds, I pulled it out. He straightened up immediately and tried to smooth his messy dark hair.

"William Arthur Connor Fielding-Smythe," I cried over the music. "How many times have I told you not to play that thing so loud in your ears? Your grandfather was nearly deaf and you're on your way. Besides, you know you are not to lean back in chairs."

Liam turned off the music, stood up, and kissed me on my cheek. "Sorry, Mummy. Welcome home." Seeing our guest he went over and shook Jackson's hand. "Good to see you, Dr. Barker. Enjoy your flight?"

"Oh, yes. I'm happy to be here," Jackson replied. Glancing at me, he asked, "Do I need to add anything to that?"

I shook my head. "No. You're family to us." Turning to Liam, I said, "Do you have plans?"

"I have a date. New girl. Catriona Casdole. I met her at uni."

"Well, then, it's Jackson, Aisling, and me for dinner tonight."

"Don't count on it. Aisling texted me before the flight that she's planning to meet Gemma, Pen, and Thia later. It's the holidays, and they're in town for a few days, and Ceci's Hen Do is tomorrow night."

"I assumed Cecilia and her friends would go away for a weekend."

"No, they're keeping it simple. Going to a restaurant and then out dancing or something. Alistair just wanted to go to a pub in Hearthestone Vale."

After giving Jackson a tour of the house, the four of us had a snack in the dining room. Following that, Jackson took a walk. While Liam and Aisling were catching up, I phoned my best friend Elsie who was excited about the upcoming wedding, and also wanted to know more about my life in the States. What could I say except it was not quite what I expected. Elsie laughed about the Pumpkin pageant. "Someone actually thought it was a smart idea to twirl fire batons in a hay-filled barn? My father always warned us children not to play with fire, particularly in our barns. I *have* to see Hilly Dale for myself."

***

"What a marvelous night!" Jackson said, helping himself to a bowl of cereal the next morning. "Dinner at Rules! The history, Jessica! The people who have been there. Just incredible! Thank you! I felt like I was a character in *Downton Abbey*."

"It was my pleasure."

"And the meal was delicious. How did you even get reservations for last night?"

"Alistair made them when I told him when we would be in town. I'm sorry it was a late seating. We'd better hurry if we want to make the train."

"How long before we reach Fielding House?" he asked on the way to the station.

"Almost four hours, depending. There will be one change along the way. Someone will meet us at the station in Hearthstone Vale and drive us back to the house. The town is north east of us. Fielding House sits above Lake Pondermere. The mountains should be snow-capped by now. Beautiful to behold. It's somewhat like Hilly Dale's geography, only more so because it's farther north."

Jackson crowed with happiness as we traveled through the countryside. He traced our trip on a map, often recognizing the names of villages and towns, regaling me with the history of some of them. When we stopped to change trains, I texted Alistair with an arrival time and added:

Your sister and brother will be home tomorrow. Probably late.

Evening out and Hen Do? he texted.

Of course, I shot back.

Sometime later, a driver from Fielding House met us at the station and we began the twenty-five-minute trip home. The roads became narrower and edged by low rock walls the closer we got. We wound through the charming village of Ponder with its small church, shops and cottages surrounding a tiny village green that displayed a large Christmas tree. Just outside of the village we crossed over a wide stream via an arched bridge that had been there for centuries, before turning left a couple of miles later. We stopped in front of two round towers standing guard on either side of a portcullis, all remnants of the castle that had been built during the early thirteenth century.

"I feel like I'm time-traveling. I'm going from century-to-century. Look at those arrow slits in the towers. They're in the form of crosses," Jackson said, an awestruck look on his face.

While our driver pushed a code into the modern keypad and we waited until the portcullis raised, I told Jackson, "Will's father wanted a more modern gate installed - one that matches the iron fence around the property, but the rest of us vetoed that. Will argued that if it became necessary to open the place year-round to the public, the gatehouse and portcullis would be draws."

"Do you think that's going to happen?" Jackson asked, with a horrified look. "I figured the Fielding-Smythes were…"

"Loaded?" I switched to an Americanism.

"Well, yes."

"At some point, if our finances drop, the death duties are going to get to us like they have so many old families. These estates, while gorgeous, are terribly expensive to maintain. There is always something to be done and updates to be made. It's Grade I, so we have certain restrictions, but, over the years, sometimes things have to be improved. For example, iron had to replace the traditional wood on the gate. That entailed a lot of work to ensure the structure wasn't damaged. Heat was put in the family and staff areas of the house many years ago, but because the house is draughty, fireplaces are still used to help take the chill off. The side open to the public, which is where Alistair and Cecilia's friends will stay, *requires* that the fireplaces be used round-the-clock at this time of year. There is electricity, so portable heaters will be placed in the rooms as well. Most of our guests live in old houses, so they understand the joys and the inconveniences, such as poor heating and shared bathrooms."

We drove under the gate and it slowly closed behind us. "I'd hate for that thing to come down quickly," Jackson shivered. "The points on the bottom of the gate are scary. Is there a dungeon?" he asked excitedly.

"I'm sorry to burst your bubble, but not that I know of. There are a couple of secret passages. Liam will be delighted to show them to you."

"How *does* a girl from Hilly Dale, Arkansas end up a duchess?" Jackson mused.

"You know the story," I said.

"Oh yes, I know all that, but it's strange, isn't it. Your mother said as a child and teenager, you were fascinated by English history. You read gothic stories about governesses and cliff houses, and all the Jean Plaidy historical novels you could by the time you were sixteen. She also told me you watched the re-runs of British television series on PBS and were completely besotted by the Tudor and Elizabethan times. And now, you're living in an Elizabethan country house and a member of an old family."

"Synchronicity? I've had an affinity for England for as long as I can remember, and I was obsessed with castles and medieval décor. Being able to play in my home's turret probably fostered some of that, but from the moment I arrived in England for my semester abroad, I felt I was home. I was so grateful I could continue my studies at Cambridge."

"Don't let anyone in Hilly Dale hear you say that," Jackson teased. "I grew up in Boston and developed an interest in the American Revolutionary War. That's what made me want to become a history professor, and then I started studying European history, and I was hooked."

"If you loved Boston, why didn't you move back after you retired?" I asked.

"Too big. I don't like the traffic, or the winters," he replied, gazing out the window as we drove over another rock bridge, before we reached the main drive to the house.

When we topped the hill, Jackson sat up straight and stared ahead. Fielding House came into view down a short drive edged by evergreen shrubs. I remembered how nervous I'd been when I saw the country house the first time as a young woman coming to meet my soon-to-be in-laws. How grand it seemed, and it was, but knowing I was going to live there was terrifying. I wasn't afraid of ghosts in the old house, but I *was* afraid of those living inside and measuring up to their expectations. The house had the opposite effect on Jackson. If he hadn't been wearing a seat belt, he would have been bouncing up-and-down with joy.

The driver parked in front and opened the door for me. Jackson hopped out on the passenger side and walked around to my side. As we crossed the drive to the entrance, two men in black suits with white shirts, rushed out, while Jackson and I stepped under the portico – a later addition- and then entered the first hall before passing into the Great Hall.

Christmas at Fielding House was always beautiful. In the Great Hall, an enormous tree covered in traditional ornaments stood between two arched doorways at the rear of the room. Both were topped by wreaths suspended from the minstrels' gallery above. I watched Jackson gaze around the room, looking first at the black-and-white marble-tiled floor and dark, square paneling, and then at the elaborately carved ceiling beams fifteen feet above us. A large, eighteenth-century chandelier that had been refurbished with electric lights, hung above a trestle table lined down the center with greenery and holly berries. A fire burned in the walk-in stone fireplace above which was a decorated mantle below a large mirror, its glass showing the patina of age.

Jackson eyed the portraits of Queen Elizabeth I, Anne Boleyn, and Henry VIII hanging in a row along one wall. "You are immersed in history," he cried. "The furniture, the portraits, the… well, I just can't take it all in."

Drowning in history, more like, I thought.

"You have a week to explore, but I warn you it took me a couple of years. Of course, I don't have a PhD in history." It was nice to see Fielding House through the eyes of someone who had never seen it before and truly appreciated it. I'd grown so accustomed to the elegance, the history, and the life here, that I hadn't given much thought to the physical trappings, or the family history. Having been brought up here, Alistair, Liam, and Aisling knew nothing else. This was simply their family home, just as the house in Hilly Dale was mine.

Alistair was destined to remain here, along with the history and all the trappings, whereas the other two had options. My stepson told me long ago that he envied his half-siblings for their freedom to choose their lot in life, but tradition and duty ran deep in the Fielding-Smythes. My husband had rebelled on occasion and done reckless things; however, he, like Alistair, knew this was his lot in life. There had been a duke in residence since before this house was built.

"Where is your staff, Your Grace?" Jackson teased, looking around. "Are they scurrying about readying the house for your arrival."

I smiled. "It does take a staff to run this place, but it isn't like the old days. We operate with a low level of employees most of the time, but I'm sure Alistair has more hired for the wedding. In the family-wing, where you will be staying, we have a casual style. There's a small kitchen, a living room, several bedrooms, what we call The Duke's Study, and an informal dining room.

The south wing has reception rooms, a formal dining room, and more bedrooms. It's longer because it also contains a small segment of the old castle. That wing is mostly for the tourists, or for events that are held here, but it is livable too, and it will be used for the wedding celebration because the dining room is much larger. You will find most of the history you seek in that wing. The library is located there, and I think you will find it interesting. Along with rare books, it also houses Medieval manuscripts and Fielding-Smythe ancestral works, but the latter two are under lock & key. Alistair should be fine with you having a look-see. The furniture in many rooms is original to the house. If you prefer to stay in that wing, it's fine, but as I indicated, it doesn't have the same amenities as the family wing."

"No, I like the atmosphere, but prefer my creature comforts," he said. "Who are the additional guests?"

"We'll have to wait and see." Taking his arm, I guided him to the door on the tree's right.

"You're being cryptic, Carola. See, I got the name right."

"You may call me Jessica, if you're more comfortable with that, but not in front of the staff. Close friends know me as 'Carola.' This way, Jackson," I replied, opening the door.

We were in the middle wing of the 'E.' The paneling was a mix of carved and plain, dark-wood squares. The staircase that rose in the middle of the room split into two separate ones, leading to each wing. This was the result of a remodel in the eighteenth century to make access easier to the wings. Jackson paused on the way up to look at the tapestries hanging on either side of the landing's walls. "What's the view from the windows," he asked, staring into the fading light. "I glimpsed a lake when we topped the hill."

"The back garden. It was designed by an opponent of Capability Brown's style. It's more natural-looking and is lovely in the warmer months. At least there are some evergreens or else it would look drab now."

"Well, Hilly Dale Garden Club would go nuts seeing it, but I shall as well."

"The back of the property gently slopes until it stops at a low cliff edge. If you walk due west and turn north, you'll see a very old stone church. Perhaps tomorrow you would like to take a stroll through the property. I'm not sure what my plans will be, but you are welcome to explore at will. If you don't want to walk, we have golf carts, but when you reach the wooded area where the Keep is, you will have to go on-foot."

"I'm excited, but right now, I'd like a rest before dinner. This has been so much to take in."

"We will eat in the family dining room at 8:00, but let me show you to your room, so you can get settled. You'll be on the first floor near me," I said, as I climbed the stairs.

"Second floor to me, Jessica."

"Yes. Sometimes, I forget to whom I'm speaking." Opening a dark-wood door, I said, "This is your room, Jackson."

Crossing the room, he sat on the seventeenth-century bed that faced a stone fireplace with a thick mantle. He declared the fire pleasant and the bed comfortable. "At least I know you don't have the original mattress!"

"Now that *would* be something if it had survived. The stories it could tell if it was able to talk!" I pointed to the floral draperies. "Tomorrow you will have a view of the side garden, and if it's clear, you may see the bell tower on the old church I told you about. The bath is tiny, but it's behind that door, and your clothes go there," I said, pointing to a giant mirrored wardrobe.

"Just lovely."

"My room is at the end of the hall. It's traditionally called The Duchess's Bedchamber."

"Because men and women of certain classes did not share bedrooms in the past and it made it easier for…assignations?"

"I suppose so, though I think many couples need their own room in which to retreat. Will and I did not subscribe to the separate bedrooms idea, however, and The Duchess's Bedchamber is used as a guest room. My mother-in-law, Josephine, stays there when she visits, but she prefers staying in Ravens' Roost, a smaller home on the eastern edge of the property. You couldn't see it on the drive up."

"I can't say I blame her. This is a wonderful house, but without your husband, and with a new duke in place, it must not feel like it's your home any longer. Ravens' Roost sounds like an ominous name for a house and conjures up all sorts of images."

"It's a pretty, early nineteenth-century house with a lovely view."

I left Jackson to admire his room and went to The Duchess's Bedchamber at the end of the hall. My bags were not in the room. Mrs. Thomas, the house manager, responded to my text, informing me that my bags were in The Duke's Bedchamber that I used to share with my husband. I was surprised Alistair hadn't taken it over, especially now that he was marrying.

I crossed the hall and entered the room opposite. It had only been a few months since I'd stayed there, and it was emotional to return. The centuries-old dark-wood tester bed with its heavy draperies stood proudly between two windows on the east side of the room. The plump duvet was the same rose-red brocade that had been there when I left. In fact, everything in the room remained the same.

Sitting down on the cream-colored velvet sofa that was placed in front of the fireplace, I pulled off my boots, rested my feet on the small table in front, and toasted my toes. I'd spent many an evening in here reading next to the fire. Memories of Will and me were everywhere, even this long after his death. I alternated between feeling comforted and oppressed. I hadn't realized until now that this was how I'd felt the entire time staying in this room and this house after Will died. I *should* have insisted on staying in the other bedroom and would have moved back, but I'd already asked Mrs. Thomas to put Jackson in The Duchess's Bedchamber. It was much nicer than the room I'd shown him.

On Christmas Eve, we opened gifts and attended a service in the town's beautifully-decorated church. I'd forgotten how magnificent the choir was. Alistair hosted our traditional Christmas breakfast at 9:00 and then we went to the small church on the lake as a family, Jackson included, to say a prayer for those who were no longer with us.

Following that, despite the cold, we showed Jackson, who had spent all his time indoors going through manuscripts and family history since he'd arrived, around the property. Thor, our Landseer, took to Jackson right away and walked alongside him. Jackson patted him and referred to him as a 'magnificent dog.' When we reached the path to the Keep, Aisling hung back.

"Wait here with Thor or go on back with him to the house, Aisling." After she and the dog left, I turned to Jackson and explained, "When she was little, the boys told her the Keep was haunted. When she finally got up the nerve to go inside, they scared her by making spooky sounds."

"I'm glad to see this place," he said, as Alistair unlocked the heavy wooden door. It was rather dark inside, the only light coming from the open door, arrowslits, and our phones. "So. Much. History. I don't need to climb those stone steps to the top. I agree with Aisling. This place is haun*ted*," Jackson declared, shuddering.

"Well, it *was* the last bastion for those who lived in the castle, so I suppose it might well be," I replied. "It's kept locked so the tourists can't enter. The steps are steep and narrow, and, as you can see, it's poorly lit these days. You can just make out where the sconces are for torches."

***

That night, I was awakened by a loud clap of thunder, and then another. I lay in the tester bed, hugging my pillow and watching the lightning through the gaps in the draperies. There was no cat to comfort me this time. Someone knocked on my door. "Come," I called. Into the room hurried Aisling.

"Mum, can I stay in here with you?"

My daughter had, as a child, been afraid of storms. Nodding, I pulled back the covers. "I need to tell you something," she said, climbing in with me, and pulling the covers up to her chin.

"All right. You've not re-developed a fear of storms, have you?"

"No, it's not that. It's just, I…I…I'm not going back to Hilly Dale with you. I'm staying here. I don't mean with Alistair, at least not for long. I want to go to university in Scotland with Gemma and Pen. I'm sorry, Mum. I truly am. I don't want to live in Hilly Dale anymore. And Thia has a flat in London now, so I could stay with her until the following term."

Stunned, I asked, "Why didn't you tell me this? When did you get accepted? You've been in the States since July."

"I applied a while ago. I didn't want to tell you."

"Why not? I told you several times if you didn't want to stay it was all right."

"I made such a big deal about living there being an adventure that I felt foolish. I didn't want to let you down. Alistair thought it was a good idea to move back, and he encouraged me to tell you, but I just couldn't. Hilly Dale isn't me. I hope you understand. I'll come visit, but I can't live there. I don't belong."

I sighed. "Believe it or not, I do understand. I wished you would have told me before now. We could have shipped your things and they would already be here. How many times did I tell you that you didn't have to stay? You could have said something then. I hoped you would give it a year, but if you're not happy, and you're sure you want to be here, I'm not going to stop you. You'll be twenty soon. You have your own life, and you need to get started with it."

"The thing is, Mum, you don't seem happy there either, and Aunt Jane-Ann is riding you all the time about something." I almost laughed out loud at her use of 'riding.' She'd picked that up from one of her new friends.

"It's not that, Aisling. It's different for me, too. I have to remain and take care of family business. I still haven't gotten the estate sale done."

"You could hire someone to do it."

"I don't want a stranger picking through my family's things. You may have few memories of Hilly Dale, but I have many. Not all of them good, but not all bad, and I want time to process all of this. Your grandmother has been gone a little over a year, and I'm still trying to work through that."

"Please don't be annoyed with me."

"I'm a little sad at the prospect of not seeing you often." I pulled her close to me. "I'm not used to that, but I'm not annoyed with you."

"Except when I went to Switzerland to school for a few years."

"Except for that, and I hated that you went. Tradition and all, but I wasn't annoyed with you."

"I know, and I made it okay there for three years, but I was so happy you insisted I come back to England to finish. I'm proud of you, Mum, and I love you."

"I love you, too, and I always will."

We were interrupted by another knock at the door. Instead of waiting for me to answer, the door swung open and Liam and Alistair came in.

"To what do I owe the pleasure of my children all in my bedchamber at once," I said, like a queen.

"The storm woke me and I went to the kitchen to get something to eat and found Liam down there. On the way up we heard voices, and we knew it wasn't the Blue Lady wandering the halls, so we listened and it was coming from in here."

"Ouch," Aisling cried. "You sat on my foot, Liam. Move."

Another knock on the door. "Come," we said in unison.

"What's going on. I was awakened by the storm. Someone knocked on my door, but when I got up to answer and no one was there. Then I heard voices coming from across the hall."

"Which one of you knocked on Jackson's door?" I asked. "That's not nice."

All three of my children claimed they had not. "It has to be the Blue Lady. It's nights like this she does that. I'm surprised you never heard her, Mum," Liam said, getting off the bed and pulling open the draperies.

"The Blue Lady?" queried Jackson.

"The Blue Lady is one of the family legends. She was Agna, the first Duke's first wife who fell off…" Alistair began.

"Or jumped," Liam interrupted in a serious tone.

Alistair gave his brother a sour look. "I'm telling the story. The Blue Lady fell or jumped off the balcony that used to be at the end of this hall. The balcony was eventually removed and the wall sealed three-hundred years ago. Someone was either pushed or fell in the eighteenth century. I don't remember who it was. There's a portrait of Agna in the south wing. According to legend, she always dressed in blue."

"On stormy nights, she's said to walk the halls, particularly this one, and she stops at The Duke's Bedchamber, knocks on the door, and if there is no greeting in answer, sadly moves on to her own – the one where you're staying, Jackson," Liam said with relish.

"I always answer a knock on my door," I replied, "and I've yet to see anyone but my family or staff."

"Well, YOU are the duchess now and if you responded, she wouldn't have appeared. You are in The Duke's Bedchamber with or without the duke." Liam hypothesized.

"You mean I might have met a woman from the sixteenth-century?" He looked disappointed. "That would have been a coup for me! I could have asked so many questions."

"But she doesn't knock on her own door," I sensibly reminded them. "So, which one of you knocked on Jackson's door?"

Silence.

"Alistair, I just learned Aisling is not coming back with me."

He opened his mouth to say something, but Aisling interrupted. "Mum, let's just sit here and watch the storm through the windows. I want to make a memory of us all together in this room." Ah, another expression my daughter had learned from her American friends.

"You, too, Jackson," I invited.

Alistair stirred up the fire, and Liam and Jackson dragged chairs over and opened the draperies. We spent the rest of the night talking and watching the lightning strikes over the lake. To me, it was perfect.

Chapter Fifteen

Except for it being the holiday season, Alistair and Cecilia's wedding was much like mine and Will's special day - full of tradition. Wearing a dark-green wool dress with matching coat and a simple dark-green fascinator, I sat beside Aisling on the first row, an empty chair on the other side of me was reserved for Will. My mother-in-law and sister-in-law with her family completed the front row. Various friends of the groom and mine, including Jackson Barker, Elsie, and her husband, were seated on the other rows. Prince Harry was behind the empty chair. Cecilia's family and friends had their places across the aisle. There were scores of friends and 'lesser' family members seated in the nave. I couldn't wait to hear Jackson's reaction to the guests when we returned to Fielding House.

Alistair, and Liam stood at the front of the chapel, handsome in their dark-gray three-piece suits, crisp white shirts, and dark ties– no morning suits for my sons. Both men reminded me so much of Will – tall, dark-haired, and with those gorgeous hazel eyes.

We all stood as Cecilia walked down the aisle with her father. My soon-to-be daughter-in-law wore a simple, white velvet gown with a sweetheart neckline, and diamond drop necklace my mother-in-law had loaned her. Atop her sheer veil was the ruby and diamond tiara that had belonged to Alistair's great-grandmother. On her finger, the emerald and diamond ring sparkled. I looked down at my left third finger devoid of rings. I twisted the diamond wedding band now on my right third finger. Memories. Too many.

Cecilia carried a bouquet of red roses and greenery. Following her down the aisle were the pages and bridesmaids. The little girls wore white dresses with circlets of greenery and red roses in their hair. The boys wore green ties with their small suits. Cecilia's sister brought up the rear in a long, winter-white wool gown with bell sleeves, and also wore the same circlet as the little bridesmaids.

It was a lovely ceremony, and afterwards, we had a reception in the Long Gallery on the top floor of Fielding House. The huge stone fireplaces at either end burned brightly, providing much-needed warmth in a room lined with windows on two sides. A quartet in one corner played Baroque music as servers passed trays of hors d'oeuvres and champagne. Below us on the lawn under heated marquees, a wedding meal was being held for those invited from the village. Alistair and Cecilia had been down to speak with them and share a drink, as was the custom for the Dukes of Hearthe going back two-hundred years.

"I spoke to Prince Harry!" Jackson cried, grabbing my arm as I passed him on the way to speak with Bissonette, The Comtesse de Beaupoume whose husband had been one of Will's good friends - kindred spirits who enjoyed extreme sports.

"His Royal Highness was so personable; he was so real. Told me about some of his charity work. Admirable fellow! You should have told me royalty was going to be here. I would have dressed better, but I *am* remembering to properly refer to you. Why didn't you tell me the prince would be here?"

"Then it wouldn't have been a surprise," I replied. "He's one of Alistair's friends, and his father one of Will's circle. Will was interested in preserving historical sites, and he was a fan of organic farming, so he and the Prince of Wales had some interests in common. It's the same with Alistair and Harry. They met doing charity work a few years ago. I'm glad you enjoyed meeting him. He had to leave for another engagement, or he might have stayed for the party tonight. And you look elegant, Jackson. I told you that this morning when you were deciding on black or gray. The gray was right for the ceremony, and it blends with Alistair's and Liam's suits. Tonight, you will want to wear black-tie."

"So that's why you told me to bring a tux. By the way, what did you tell your aunt?" he asked. "About your trip to England? Does she know I went with you?"

"I told her that I was going to Alistair's wedding with you, but because I did not offer to pay her fare, she did not make a fuss. Besides, as she put it, this was only my stepson's wedding. Can you believe she said that? I am the only mother he's known. Andrea rarely contacts him, but she got in touch with him after Will died and wanted to be a part of his life."

"Wonder why," Jackson said with a sneer.

"He did not invite her to the wedding."

A woman in a navy silk dress and matching hat, tugged at my arm. "Elsie," I cried happily. This is my dearest friend, Vicountess Toddle, Jackson. And Elsie, you have heard me speak of my dear friend Jackson Barker. Here he is." They exchanged brief pleasantries.

"Damaris is making a spectacle of herself," Elsie said, nodding toward a woman with short dark hair, a bit too much makeup for daytime, and dressed in a deep-purple silk dress and black stilettos. The purple feather on her hat bounced as she talked animatedly with the Countess of Lawton. "Beverly looks like she needs a rescue. You know she loathes Damaris. I'm sure Damaris is lording it over her that Cecilia outranks her. Carola, I don't know how you're going to stand that woman being part of your family."

"Cecilia more than makes up for her," I replied. We talked for a few minutes. Jackson and Elsie were laughing together over Elsie's memories of me. I whispered, 'bovine' in her ear, reminding her of why her name was Elsie, winked, and walked over to rescue the countess.

***

That evening, the main party for close family and friends was held in a large reception room in the south wing, rather than the Great Hall as planned. There were too many people to fit comfortably, thanks to all the invitations extended by Cecilia and her mother. The affair was black-tie, which is what Cecilia, or more likely her mother, wanted. I was attired in an indigo velvet gown and wearing the aquamarine and diamond bandeau tiara I'd worn at my wedding. As hostess, I spent much of the time making small talk. Jackson and I took a few turns around the room to music from the band Alistair hired, before passing through an open doorway into the formal dining room. I nodded to the guests who were seated in chairs along the perimeter.

"I wish Heather could have been here," I said, laughing.

"Why? David said they were going to his family in New Hampshire for the holidays."

I told Jackson the history of Fielding House's infamous dining table.

"Poisoned?" he gasped, eying the huge array of food now filling the table.

"Yes, but do you know what happened on Steve Taylor's dining table?"

"Oh, God, yes! The whole town knows about that," he exclaimed while we filled our plates. Taking them over to a couple of chairs, we sat down and ate the delicious food in silence and listened to the chatter as guests wandered in and out. This was my last hurrah at Fielding House. I was now the 'Old Duchess.' The torch had been passed at the wedding, and Cecilia's mother let everyone know. The joke was on Damaris. While I was no longer *the* duchess, I was still a duchess. Damaris was snapping photos with her phone right and left and taking embarrassing selfies. At midnight, I excused myself and went to bed. The party continued until the wee hours of the morning.

Chapter Sixteen

After a late breakfast, a tired-looking Alistair and Cecilia left for Barbados while Jackson and I began the journey back to Arkansas. All said and done, with a London overnight, the layover, the plane change, and the drive from Little Rock, we arrived in Hilly Dale late afternoon on the thirtieth of December. I was jet-lagged, and tired from all the Christmas and wedding festivities. Violet alternated between happy to see me and miffed because she'd been at the vet's for over a week. She swatted my leg as I wearily began mounting the stairs. "You've been fed. Come on. I'm going to bed," I told her. I'd climbed no more than five steps when the landline phone rang. I trudged back down, hesitated for a moment when I saw the caller's name, and then picked up the phone in the foyer.

"Hello," I said, cautiously.

"Well, I see you're back," my aunt said sourly. "You could have told me the date you were returning. I would have had the house ready for you, but, of course, I don't have a key to it. My own sister's house, and I don't have a key! I've been driving past several times a day since yesterday."

"Lovely to hear from you," I said as sweetly as I could. There was a reason she didn't have a key. My mother had not trusted her with one, preferring Jackson had it. Aunt Jane-Ann had been caught snooping through the desk drawers on more than one occasion when my mother walked in from an errand. My father had a fit when he found out, demanding the key be returned and the locks changed. He'd had his own share of run-ins with the formidable Jane-Ann Simmons. There was just so much 'feeling sorry' for her he could take at times.

"I just got home not too long ago. I haven't had a chance to let anyone know I'm back."

"And you didn't call from England? And you didn't send a photo of Alistair and his bride. The wedding was three days ago. You could have emailed one to me."

Now she was interested in Alistair? I thought he was only a stepson in her view.

"I've been very busy. I have photos on my phone, but I took a few with a camera and will send you one of those when I transfer them to my computer. Did you have a happy Christmas?"

"I spent it with my husband's niece – the one who lives in Fayetteville – and her family. She invited me to join them. Their daughter came to Hilly

Dale to pick me up and bring me home. I spent Christmas Eve AND Christmas with them."

At times, I wished we had told Aunt Jane-Ann about my life in England, but at others, I was glad we had not. I thought about telling her now, but I was exhausted and knew there would be questions and upsets. I wasn't ready for that.

"I'm glad you had a nice time," I replied, setting the bag I'd been carrying upstairs back down.

"And how is Aisling?"

"She's well." I dreaded saying the next thing, but I knew there was no way I could avoid it. "Aisling decided to stay in England and attend university at St. Andrews with her friends."

"What?"

I held the phone away from my ear.

"Yes, she…"

"Hilly Dale College wasn't good enough for her? Jessica, you've raised a little snob, and you've become one too!"

I couldn't quite grasp why my aunt was having this reaction. I knew I should be more understanding because she was older and I knew her history, but I was tired and now I was extremely annoyed with her. Good manners be damned! "Aunt Jane-Ann, I expect you to remember that you are talking about MY daughter, and refrain from insulting her. Aisling enjoyed her stay here, but she was only here for a few months. She was born and raised in England. She is ENGLISH! She is a citizen of the United Kingdom. Instead of being offended, you should be pleased she wanted to come to Hilly Dale and learn about her American side. She did not dislike it here. She had friends. However, Hilly Dale is not her life; she has one at home. Now, I'm tired and need to get some sleep. I apologize. Goodbye." And with that, I hung up on her.

A little while later, I was curled in bed with Violet on the pillow next to me. The house seemed empty without Aisling, but I'd get used to it. I remembered when we sent her off to that fancy school in Switzerland. I cried and cried on the flight home, and I was angry at Will for agreeing with his mother that she should attend it, but it was another of those pesky traditions. I turned off the light and went to sleep.

***

I awoke the next morning to Violet gently pawing my face, her long black fur tickling my nose. "I see we are on different times, my lady." I sat up and placed her on my lap. The cat slowly blinked her sea-green eyes at me and kneaded the comforter. "It's just you and me, now." I got up, threw on my plush black bathrobe and fuzzy boot slippers. "Just a minute, Violet. Let me use the restroom please. You aren't starving." Unashamed, the cat rested on her haunches and stared at me as I sat on the toilet. She meowed plaintively while I washed my hands and then wove in between my feet as we walked down the hall. I paused for a moment at Aisling's room and looked inside. There was my old bed with the new duvet looking back at me.

Crossing the room, I opened the closet, and then looked in the bureau and desk drawers. Not much left to ship. Aisling hadn't brought a great deal with her and she'd taken all her favorite belongings home. That answered why I had to pay extra for luggage. What was left could wait. I sighed. "Okay, kitty, let's get you fed." Violet galloped, for her, down the stairs, leading the way to the kitchen.

After serving the cat her breakfast of canned tuna – her return from more than a week's boarding was a special occasion – I put the kettle on and stuck two pieces of bread into the toaster oven. While I waited for them, I went to the front hall to retrieve my handbag I'd left on a table after my aunt's call. Through the etched glass oval set in the front door, I saw the wreath hanging on the exterior security door. Oh no! The Christmas decorations!

At the Fielding-Smythe residences, trees and decorations remained up until January 2nd. At the Jenson house, everything came down on December 26th or thereabout. My mother did not want to look at holiday decorations past that because they went up on the first or second. The holiday parties she had hosted each year began early.

After I ate, I went to the turret and began lovingly packing up the ornaments my family had collected since the late 1800s, along with the ones I'd bought in antique shops over the years. There was one especially beautiful ornament I brought to Hilly Dale with me. Made of porcelain, and about six inches high, the 1920s St. Nicholas figurine had a hand-painted face and was clad in a red velvet coat covered in tiny glittering stones. He was holding a staff with a crystal ball, rather than a sack of toys. Will had given it to me the first Christmas after we married, making it very special. Following a few minutes of debating whether to place it in the barrister bookcase downstairs and enjoy it all year, I reached for the soft wrap and carefully packed it in its velvet box, then placed it in with the other ornaments I'd brought with me.

Altogether, there were three medium-sized boxes of ornaments to return to the attic.

After I'd managed to finagle the boxes up the narrow attic stairs and set them in the designated 'Christmas' space, I went back and stared at the eight-foot tree. It had taken Aisling, Jackson, and me to move it down those stairs. I was pretty sure the tree came apart, but my mother had never done that. It stood as it was in the attic until it was time to bring it down. The other tree, which until this year dominated the living room, definitely came apart. It was ten feet in height when assembled, not counting the star on top.

Around noon, discovering I had very little in the house to eat – another reason Violet was having canned tuna - I showered and dressed in an oversized white sweater and stuffed my jeans into tall, soft-brown Ugg boots. After pulling my hair into a ponytail, I threw on my puffy jacket. It was cold, but not quite like it had been in the Hearthestone Vale area. I drove to the only other place to do the marketing in Hilly Dale besides Walmart.

Cobbles' Market was on the other side of town. I spent part of the time inside filling my cart and the other part stopping to chat with people – one unfamiliar-to-me woman carried on a conversation for ten minutes about the lack of olive oil variety at Cobbles'. I was able to escape her only to run into Lady Cornflower on the next aisle.

"Jessica, dear. I heard you spent Christmas in England. How wonderful. I was there one spring and was fortunate enough to view the gardens at Sissinghurst Castle. Have you been there?"

I searched my memory. Had I visited there years ago with my mother? I knew the place of course. "Yes, I believe so, but it was some time ago."

"The Rose Garden is glorious. You do know the history of the place?"

"It was used as a prison at one time centuries ago," I replied.

"What? No, I'm talking about the poet and novelist Vita Sackville-West and her husband – what's-his-name. Rather scandalous she was, and him too, but they created the garden there. I really would think the daughter of an English professor would know about that, especially since you visited the place."

"I do know of them. I'd really love to stay and chat, but I need to get on with the marketing. I only just arrived in Hilly Dale late yesterday afternoon."

"Oh, I understand. Jane-Ann told me."

I'd gone two feet with my cart when Lady Cornflower, and I really must learn her real name, called after me, "Have you decided when you want to attend your first meeting?"

That got my attention. "Meeting?" I asked, turning around.

"Yes, at our garden club."

"I explained to my aunt that I had no interest in gardening and so would not be joining." Clearly, my aunt did not understand when I told her I was not accepting the invitation, or she didn't tell her club members.

"Oh, not everyone likes gardening. It's really just a social time. We sit around, talking, someone does a little something about flowers, and then we talk some more and have cake. Sometimes we even have," she stepped closer, and lowered her voice…"*wine*."

"Well, I really must get on with my shopping."

"I'm sure you have a lot of information about English gardens to impart. Your mother told us the two of you attended some flower shows in small villages. She showed us photos of gardens you had both visited, but not Sissinghurst. I did a program on my visit there."

"Oh. Was the discussion about Vita and her female lovers an occasion for wine?" I asked with a straight face. "You know her most famous one was Virginia Woolf."

"It was the *roses* we discussed."

Backing the cart down the aisle, I slowly drifted away while she continued to talk about roses.

"Must get home," I called from the end of the aisle. After grabbing a box of pasta from a shelf, I hurried to the check-out area.

***

That evening, I sat on the living room sofa with a glass of wine and an open laptop looking at photos Liam had sent of the wedding, reception, and after-party, deciding which ones taken after the wedding I could send to my aunt. There weren't many, but I emailed her a couple of shots in the Long Gallery that didn't reveal too much. If anything, she might think they were taken at a wedding venue.

As I continued going through the photos, I focused on one of Aisling at the evening party. She was dressed in an age-appropriate ice-blue silk evening dress and dancing with James Walkstone, the Earl of Cradleburn's youngest son. Aisling was laughing up at him in the photo as they danced. She was where she belonged. I could see it in her eyes. I already missed her presence here. The house seemed so lonely, and full of memories. I barely remembered my great-grandparents on either side, but everywhere I looked, everywhere I went in the house, there was a memory or a story. The sofa I was sitting on belonged to my great-grandmother Jenson; the coffee table had been in my mother's family, the Whitleys. The comfortable leather chairs in the den had been in my Grandfather Jenson's bank. Other than the things I brought from England, everything in this house belonged to someone from my family's past, except if I didn't want something or like something here, I could sell it. I really must get around to doing that.

While I was studying pictures, smiling at the looks on my children's faces and those of the guests, the gate's new doorbell chimed. I looked at my watch. 9:30. Who would be ringing the gate's bell now? I looked down at my white plush pajamas with the blue Tardis from *Doctor Who* printed all over them, and then at my fuzzy house shoes. The bell chimed again. The motion light came on and flooded the yard. I switched off the living room light and went to the window. Peering through a gap in the blue velvet curtains, I saw a man standing at the gate waving an arm to set off the motion lights. He was balancing something on his right hand. It looked like a pizza box. I hadn't ordered pizza. My landline phone rang.

"Are you going to open the gate or not?" Beckham Hailey asked. "It's damned cold out here."

I looked down at myself. Oh my God! I wasn't expecting company, let alone Beck.

After a moment's hesitation, I said, "I'll buzz you in."

When he came through the front door, Beck looked handsome and polished, making me very aware of my own attire and lack of makeup.

"Happy New Year's Eve!" he said, thrusting the pizza at me. "Better put it in the oven to get it warm. I stood outside for a while, waiting on you to answer the bell."

New Year's Eve? I'd been so mixed-up on the days since the wedding and the flight home, I had not realized. "What are you doing here?" I asked. And more importantly, *why* was he here on New Year's Eve?

"My assistant manager is taking over the later shift. I wasn't in the mood for our New Year's Eve menu, so this is what I got." He paused and then pointed to the pizza I now held in my hands and continued, "I was headed back home from Pizza Hut with this and drove down your street to see if you were back from England." He took in my attire with an amused look on his face, "Nice jammies. I never knew you liked *Doctor Who*."

"There's a lot you don't know about me," I said. "My sons and my late husband were fans. Aisling and I got caught up in it with them. I mean, what can I say? Liam gave me these pajamas for Christmas this year."

"Didn't you love *Tooth and Claw*" he said, referring to an older episode with David Tennant which dealt with Queen Victoria, a werewolf, and aliens.

"It's one of my favorites!" I cried. "I love the ones that blend history with aliens. Remember the one with Charles Dickens and the zombie-like people when Christopher Eccleston was the Doctor?"

"Yeah, it was a great idea for a story."

"This house hasn't changed since I was a kid," Beck exclaimed, leaving the foyer and wandering toward the kitchen. "Still the same white walls everywhere, and this kitchen is the same too." He took in the pale-yellow cabinetry and white-tile floor while leaning against one of the light-colored butcher block counters.

I put the pizza on a pan and placed it in the oven on the lowest setting. "I've noticed that." I grimaced as I looked around. "And the walls are cream, not white."

"You don't like the house? I've always thought it was beautiful."

"Oh, it is. It's just that…"

"It reminds you of your family."

I nodded.

"I get that. I don't think I could have lived in my parents' house after I left and returned. My parents sold the place and moved to Michigan. Mom's with my sister and her family, but Dad's been in a nursing home for nearly three years."

"Oh, I'm so sorry. I didn't know."

"Well, you wouldn't. We haven't exactly been in touch for nearly thirty years."

"I would have thought my mother would have said something to me."

"I think it was just after your husband…" Beck sat down on a stool and leaned his elbows on the counter.

"It's all right to say it, Beck. Will died. He was killed in an accident off the coast of North Cornwall."

"I knew it was an accident. I'm sorry, Jessie. That must have been really hard for you and your kids."

"It was. It is. I had my husband's family with me. My mother couldn't come then. She wasn't well. I think the past two, or is it three by now, years have gone by in a blur for me." I couldn't say I'd been both angry and sad when Will died. He'd done it to himself, going out on that sailboat. He just *had* to be a part of that stupid event – an event that should have been canceled. Everyone knew weather on the coast could be dicey, and this had even been predicted to happen two days later!

"So, what were your plans for New Year's Eve? Big party?" He eyed my pajamas again and smiled.

"Certainly, I always wear something like this for parties. It's all the fashion. Haven't you seen the young people wearing pajama bottoms everywhere these days? It helps to stay on-trend," I replied, grateful he diverted my thoughts to the present.

"You know, Jordan misses Aisling, but she has Allison. It's a little tough, though, what with Bianca dating Allison's father."

"That must be hard on all of you." I looked at Beck and had a thought. "Listen, while the pizza's warming would you please help me move a Christmas tree back to the attic. I think we can get it up there. It took Aisling, Jackson, and me to bring it down, but we can do it if you take the heavy end." I shrunk back in embarrassment.

"Anything for a woman in *Doctor Who* pajamas," he said, standing up and grinning like he was thirteen again.

Beck lifted the tree with ease and carried it, heavy end first, up the stairs with me bringing up the rear. In all of ten minutes we had the tree in the attic and were back down in the kitchen. The oven dinged and I motioned for him to hand me the potholders that were on the counter. "If you will get a couple of plates, please." I nodded toward one of the cabinets next to the sink. While he was doing that, I reached into the opposite cabinet and grabbed a wine glass. Beck set the plates on the counter and placed a couple of pieces on each one.

"Black olive and mushroom," I cried. "Yummy!"

"That's right. You liked that combination, too. Where should we take these?"

"The living room. It's my favorite room, next to the one in the turret. There's a fire and comfortable chairs," I told him, but instead he joined me on the sofa.

"Whatcha looking at?" he said in a teasing voice, and then suddenly cried, "Whoa! Is that who I *think* that is?"

I looked at the screen. Damn! Before I could say a thing, Beck asked in a puzzled-sounding voice, "*Prince Harry* talking to Jackson Barker?"

And then I uttered a very unladylike word.

Chapter Seventeen

"Jessie?" Beck stared at me, eyes narrowed and brow furrowed. "What's going on here? How does Jackson Barker know a member of the Royal Family?"

"I, ummm…"

"Jessie?"

"Beck, until the day we met in Walmart right after I moved to Hilly Dale, you and I hadn't spoken since we were teenagers. There's a lot about me you don't know."

"Jessie," he said, looking straight into my eyes. "What's going on? Jackson and royalty? I know he's really into history, so did you photoshop this as a joke for him?" Before I could answer, he said softly, "I can ask Jackson, you know."

I made a decision I hoped I wouldn't regret. My private life was about to come out, and it was coming out to *Beckham Hailey*, of all people. He just *had* to show up at my house when I was looking at photos. Why hadn't I shut the laptop before I opened the front door. "That photo was taken at my stepson's wedding reception on the twenty-seventh of December."

Beck sat there staring at the photo. "It's a joke, right? Come on. Tell the truth. Someone photoshopped Jackson into a picture for you."

"It's no joke." I took a sip of wine, and scrolled through the photos, stopping at one of me with a group of people in the Long Gallery.

"That's you, and there's Jackson and Aisling. Who are all these people? Where is this?"

I took a deep breath. "Guests at Alistair's wedding. This photo was taken at my house, well, the main one, in England. Fielding House, to be precise. We were at the reception following the wedding. I suppose someone took a photo. Liam, probably, since he sent these."

I clicked on a few more photos of the reception and then the after-party. There was one of me chatting with the Comtesse de Beaupoume.

" You're wearing a…"

"Tiara," I said. "It belongs to my husband's family."

"Who are you?" he asked, his voice flat.

"Carola, Duchess of Hearthe. Will was the duke, and now it's Alistair."

Looks of disbelief and shock skimmed across Beck's face. "*You're* a duchess? I don't believe it."

"It's true."

"Seriously?" He started laughing. "And Carola? Your middle name? You don't even go by your real name?"

"That *is* my real name. Just because it's a middle name doesn't mean it's fake!"

"Does anyone besides Barker know all of this…this nonsense."

"No, and it's not nonsense. I *am* Carola, Duchess of Hearthe and have been since I was twenty-eight. When I married Will, I became Countess of Ponder. Will was Earl of Ponder, his father's secondary title. My parents only told one person, Millie Bosser, my mother's best friend, but when my father died, my mother brought Jackson into the circle. Millie's gone now, so tag, you're it." *Not by choice.*

He stopped laughing. "Your own aunt doesn't know?"

"Beck, you know what she's like. She'd tell everyone."

"And you're so ashamed of Hilly Dale that you don't want to let your royal friends know where you're from, is that it?" Beck sounded annoyed and looked away from me for a moment.

"It's not like that at all," I replied. "The family thought it best for my parents that no one knew my husband's identity. He was Will Smythe to everyone here, an architect, and clearly it got around that he was a wealthy one."

"Was your husband royalty?"

"No. You don't have to be royal to have a title. You're nobility, but not royalty."

"Well, no, I wouldn't know that for certain. I don't run in those circles." He downed his glass in one drink and reached for the bottle. "I don't believe this. You're kidding me, right? To get back at me after all these years? I told you, it was a misunderstanding. I regret losing our friendship, but this is crazy stuff."

He actually believed our little relationship was so important that I'd carry a grudge and prank him? After all these years? I wouldn't have told him if he hadn't seen the photos. I closed the pictures and typed 'Fielding House' into the search engine and showed him the photos online. "Look, *this* is my house." A gorgeous springtime photograph of Fielding House caught just at sunset appeared on the screen. I read aloud:

Fielding House is a privately-owned, Grade I listed, large Elizabethan country house constructed on and around the ruins of a medieval castle. The gardens are designed in the Picturesque style. Fielding House sits above Lake Pondermere just outside Hearthestone Vale in North West England. It has been the seat of the Dukes of Hearthe since 1575. There has been a structure on the site since the twelfth century, and ruins of a thirteen-century castle can still be seen.

Before Beck could say a word, I typed in 'Duke of Hearthe.' There on the page was a photo of Alistair, and I read the part that was most important:

The present holder of the title is Alistair Alexander James Fielding-Smythe*, son of the late duke, William Alistair Thomas Fielding-Smythe and first wife, Andrea Hughes. He is half-brother to Lord William Arthur Connor Fielding-Smythe and Lady Aisling Evelyn Rose Fielding-Smythe by his father's second wife, Carola Jenson.
*On December 27th 2016, he married Cecilia Elizabeth Hempstead, daughter of Everton and Damaris Hempstead of London.

"*No*w, do you believe me?" I asked.
"I don't know what to say."
"I am a duchess, but I'm no longer *the* duchess. Cecilia took that title. I'm like my mother-in-law."
"So, you're the Lady Violet from *Downton Abbey* I take it?"
"Not quite, she was a countess. My mother-in-law Josephine would be a closer match to her in many ways, other than title."
He laughed, and I knew I had him. "So Aisling?"
"Lady Aisling. *Now* do you see why I didn't tell anyone. Can you imagine if people knew? Aisling could have been the target of, well, anything. I've not intentionally been reclusive, snobbish, or unfriendly to people. I was protecting my daughter, and I was protecting my parents when they were living."
"Oh, Jessie. I wish we had been closer through the years. That's a terrible burden. You've been living a double life of a sort, especially here. How have you managed keeping it quiet this long?"
"It was easy when Will and I married, and it's not that hard in England. It's a minor dukedom, in the scheme of it all. The main house is a bit isolated, but most of all, the children haven't ended up in the tabloids. They don't even have social media. We didn't encourage it. As far as my career goes, I don't have a photo shown. It's always Violet, my cat."
"The cat thing is pretty clever."
"People know Jessica Keasden is Jessica Jenson. That's not an issue. Few would make a connection to Carola, Duchess of Hearthe, unless they

started searching, but I'm not that interesting. Of course there are some who need to know, but they aren't saying anything out of professional confidentiality or close friendships."

"I wouldn't say you were exactly *uninteresting*, but I get what you're saying. Thanks for telling me. Wow!" He took a bite of pizza and stared at me thoughtfully, while chewing longer than necessary.

"So, you see why moving here has been a really big change and why I couldn't discuss it?"

"I do," he said after finally swallowing. "So, why did Aisling stay in England?"

"She learned her 'adventure' was not quite what she thought it would be; however, I didn't expect to learn her decision over Christmas while we were away. Because she didn't want to leave me here alone, she was afraid to tell me."

"Yeah, Jordan knew, you know. About the change in schools, not the other stuff. She told me that a few days ago. That's another reason I stopped by when I saw your lights on. I figured you would be alone and missing her. Jordan misses their friendship. Aisling was someone who didn't know the stories about Bianca and me."

I leaned back on the sofa. The wine, the pizza, or the opening up to Beck had relaxed me. I listened to him tell me about his life with Bianca. He'd had a row with her last week at the restaurant because she wanted to host a private New Year's Eve Party for her and her friends, including John, even though the place was booked. "Bianca thought that because she was on the deed, she could simply waltz in and take over the place any time she wanted. She gave no thought to the people who had made reservations."

From what I could glean, Bianca was a self-absorbed woman. I remembered that in high school she strutted around like she was Queen Bee, thought she was entitled to everything, and was mean-spirited to boot. I had no idea what had happened to the little girl with whom I'd played Barbie dolls.

"I never knew what you saw in her, Beck," I said.

"She plays a good game. Things were going pretty well for a time when I was working on Wall Street, but when Jordan was a child, we decided it was best to move back here. Bianca wasn't happy about that idea at first, but eventually she realized the city wasn't a place to raise a child, and by that time, it hadn't become a good place for Bianca *or* me. Too many distractions for both of us."

"My children went to boarding school, but before that we sent them to Hearthestone Vale's schools. I think it kept them grounded a bit. Will and I thought living in London might be the answer and we tried that for a while, but the city was not what we wanted for the children either."

"Andrea Hughes was Will's..."

"First wife." I explained about her running off.

"Poor Alistair. Glad you came into the picture."

"Me too, So, when are you getting your divorce?" I blurted. "Sorry, that was tactless."

"It's okay. I've signed the papers. Bianca's balking. She still thinks she's the most popular, most beautiful woman in Hilly Dale, and she's under an illusion that she has the option to choose – me or John Knoss. She doesn't."

"Poor John. First Betsy and now Bianca. He doesn't have much luck picking women."

"Oh, I wouldn't say that. Money talks where he's concerned, and some women go for that. He's not all he's cracked up to be, but I can't say anything. I haven't always been the best husband. I wish Bianca and I had divorced sixteen years ago when we were in New York. Bianca was hanging out with some wannabe socialites and partying too much. She's easily...distracted. This isn't her first affair. It's just one where she got caught and it became public."

"Oh, Beck. I hate to hear that."

"I'm no saint, Jessie. I was focused on my career and worked long hours. I ended up dating a co-worker for several months before Bianca, Jordan, and I moved back. Bianca and I hoped this move would save our marriage, and it did for a while until she had a fling with Lucky Fine several years ago, but it was kept quiet."

"That disgusting man!" I immediately covered my mouth. "I'm sorry, but from my only experience with him, I found him crass! Why did you stay with her after that?" I asked, appalled.

"For Jordan. I might have gotten full custody in New York, based on Bianca's partying behavior. No one knew us there, but not here. Her uncle was a judge for years."

"I'd forgotten that. My father said Benjamin Callahan wielded a lot of power."

Beck and I sat without speaking for a while and stared at the fire, eating the remains of the pizza, and sipping wine, until he asked, "What was it like living the way you did in England?"

"It was strange at first. I had a lot to learn, much like here, but I felt free there. I finished school and got a job. I had friends from uni, flatmates, and friends from work, most of whom found my differences either humorous or charming. And then I met Will and everything changed. I knew he was well-off; I knew he had an upper-class accent. He didn't keep me hidden away from his friends though titles were never mentioned. He told me he was born in Hearthestone Vale, went to Eton College, and then Oxford. He was divorced, had a young son, and lived in Chelsea."

"So, he lied about his real identity, like you've been doing," Beck stated.

"I wouldn't say it was lying. It was protection. If he'd told me right off who he was, how could he be certain I'd love him for himself or for his title and money. He was Earl of Ponder, for goodness' sake. Women flocked to him. He was handsome." Beck winced at that. "And how could I be sure *I* wouldn't run away from *him* if he had told me straight-off? If *you* and Jackson were shocked, imagine what it would have felt like for me to meet someone and after a couple of dates he said, 'Oh, by the way, I'm an earl and heir to a dukedom'. I'd probably have thought he was lying and just out for one thing."

"Didn't you find it weird you never went to his house? Did you ever even see his apartment?"

"Of course I saw his flat. Many times, I might add. And no, I didn't think it strange that I didn't go to his hometown and 'meet the folks'. I met his son after a few months. Beck, I had a job and couldn't take off every whipstitch. He had a job, too, by the way. Do you think all titled people sit around these days being waited on and watching the money roll in from who knows where?"

"I have no idea how people like that live, and you probably didn't either."

"I did. I *was* at Cambridge. There were titled students. Most I knew didn't flaunt it, and they wanted a career, particularly those who were not set to inherit a lot. Times have changed."

"How are you doing since your mother died?" Beck leaned back on the sofa and laid his arm along the wooden edge.

"I had a difficult time at first – the grieving part. I didn't want Aisling to see too much of that, so I cried in the shower or when she wasn't home. I miss my mother. I see her, my father, and my grandparents everywhere I look in this house. I'm surrounded by their things. It's comforting in a way, but in another, it's holding me back. It's much the same as it was after Will died. I thought I was escaping memories when I left England, but I've run full force into those of *my* family here, and I ran back into the ones with Will when I went back for the wedding. I have to find a way to deal with both."

"I'm really sorry. When we moved back, I worked for a national financial planning company that has a small office here, you probably know the one. Jacob Kane? I worked there for years. Bianca was a stay-at-home mom and very interested in the social life. She spent most of her time, hanging out at Hilly Dale Country Club though and furnishing the house we own outside of town. It has a great view of the river and the mountains in the distance. She and Betsy were thick-as-thieves again, until…"

"Well, it seems your fairy tale came to an end too."

"It was never a fairy tale with Bianca. She's too much of a drama queen. You're the one that lived a fairy tale." Beck stood up and reached for his jacket. "I'd better get going."

I picked up my phone. It was 3:00 a.m.!

"Happy New Year, Jessie," he said at the door, planting a kiss on my cheek. "Thanks for spending it with me."

"Happy New Year, Beck," I said, and watched as he walked down the sidewalk. "Hey Beck, wait," I called.

He turned around. In the light from the motion detector, I saw anticipation on his face, "Please close the gate."

Chapter Eighteen

"Happy New Year and welcome back!" Heather James screeched in my ear at 9:30 when I answered the phone. "Did you have a *good* New Year's Eve?" Her voice went from high-pitched to a sly, whispery tone.

Rolling over in bed, I collided with Violet who was under the covers. I raised up on an elbow and answered in a sleepy voice, "Happy New Year to you, Heather. Why are you calling so early?"

"It's not that early. Is he still there?" she asked anxiously.

"Who?"

"*Beck*! Who do you think?"

I sat bolt upright. "Beck?" I rubbed an eye with the side of my right hand. "Why would he be here?"

"Oh, so he's already gone home?"

"I'm too tired to play back-and-forth. Say what you have to say," I said, stifling a yawn. Usually I was an early riser, but a late night and the remnants of jet lag had taken a toll.

"Beck spent the night, right?"

"What? No. Why would you say that?" Violet crawled into my lap and began batting at my hand that was holding the phone.

"Well, David and I went to a party at the country club, and you know we live two blocks behind you. We took the route along your street and drove past your house about 1:30 this morning. Unless you bought a white extended-cab truck, Beck's was parked in your driveway."

"Heather…"

"Come on, you can tell me," she wheedled.

"Just a moment." I moved the cat, crawled out of bed, slipped into my house shoes, and put on my robe. Violet, the ever hungry, sensing her late breakfast was in the *immediate* future, leaped off the bed and ran towards the bathroom, which was where I usually headed before going downstairs. Her confusion was short-lived as she saw me head to the open bedroom door instead. With her fluffy tail in the air, she led the way down the hall, looking back at me several times to make sure I was following.

"Beck did *not* spend the night with me. He stopped by on his way home from Pizza Hut and saw the lights. We ate pizza and talked. That's it."

"Why wasn't he at the restaurant? Didn't he have to take care of all his customers?" she quizzed me.

"He took the early shift and his assistant manager was taking the late one, but in case you're still interested in our exciting night, he helped me move the Christmas tree back to the attic. Is there anything else you want to know?" I said, padding down the stairs to the kitchen.

"What did you talk about?" she asked excitedly.

"How was your evening?" I ignored her question and put the kettle on, and then reached in a cabinet for the cat food.

"Oh, like I said, we went to a party at the club. Bianca helped host it."

"I thought you and Bianca weren't friends, " I said, placing canned chunky chicken in gravy on Violet's plate and setting it on the floor.

"Well, John and David play golf together so, uh, well, you know. I *tolerate* her. She doesn't really like me though. I've tried to be nice to her, but, well, it's Bianca and she's still the same old member of 'The Two Bitches and a Bastard Club,' if you know what I mean," Heather said, chuckling. "Tommy brought Kismet to the party! That shocked everyone. Kismet doesn't go anywhere, and she can't stand Bianca, John, and the rest of the bunch, and Tommy hates John!"

I let her ramble on about who was there and what everyone wore while I sat sipping my tea. Every now and then, I'd make the appropriate murmur. When she paused to take a breath, I asked, "Was Betsy there?"

"Didn't you hear me just say she and Bianca had a fight? Are you even listening to me?"

"Sorry, I was distracted by the cat." As if she knew I was disparaging her, Violet looked up from her meal and gave me a nasty look.

"Oh, well, they did. Bianca looked stunning in her red satin dress, but she would. She's had enough plastic surgery. Her boobs were spilling out of that low-cut number. I mean, I'm no slouch in the boob department but at least mine are real! Did you know she's had her lips and eyes done, and I think a butt-lift?"

"No, I didn't." I felt sorry for Jordan. What an example Bianca was setting!

"Well, she has. It started when they lived in New York. I heard she ran with a fast crowd up there. Anyway, Betsy can't keep up with her. You've seen dumpy Betsy. Oh, she's made her mark on the town, don't get me wrong, but she can't hold a candle to Bianca, and she never has. Anyway, in the Ladies' Room, Betsy called her, well, I can't even say it." But she did anyway.

"Were you in the *restroom* with them?"

"Yes, I was in a stall. I heard *everything*. Bianca was kind of drunk and ridiculed Betsy and then said that if she'd been smart years ago, Betsy could have hung onto John and she wouldn't be married to that bore Peter Franklin. "And, worse," Heather blabbed, "Bianca *knew* Peter was a bore because she'd slept with him too! This is just like one of those reality shows!"

"Oh my," I said. "I'm sure that was quite a performance."

"Oh it was," Heather exclaimed. "Catching Steve with Shauna like that was bad, but he married her, and I got David. Well, at least we know why Beck wasn't at the party," she said, giggling. "He was having his own *private* party with YOU! Tommy Fitzpatrick was looking for you last night. He told me while Kismet went outside to call her youngest kid that he wants to ask you out. I told him you would probably be okay with that."

"He had a date with Kismet last night! I can't believe he would even *mention* something like that to you. Please don't become like my aunt who volunteers me for things without asking."

"You like Tommy and he was Josh's best friend. We used to hang out together all the time. He had a big crush on you."

"When we were teenagers, maybe."

"Tommy lost his wife and I thought…"

"Yes, I know his wife died, but that doesn't mean I want to date him, and I certainly wouldn't want to hurt Kismet!"

"I guess I should tell him you're seeing Beck again. You know, he saw you leave with him at the reunion."

"Heather, we had lunch with Tommy at Piggie-Pen a week after the reunion. It was quite platonic. You saw that yourself! I haven't heard from him since. I don't want to hurt his feelings. I like Tommy, and I feel sad for him. I know what he's going through, but that does not mean I want to *date* him. I'm not sure I want to *date* anyone at this point." *Why wouldn't she let this drop. She was just like my aunt!*

"Well, he covered it up. He's crazy about you. I just know it. I'm willing to bet he brought Kismet because he thought you were going to be there with or without Beck. You know, he doesn't like Beck and *never* has."

She was wrong about Tommy's feelings, and I should have said something else, but I'd learned that the more times you tried to explain something the deeper the hole you dug, so I ended the call with the excuse of having things to do. God forbid, that Tommy and I would be dragged into the goings-on in Hilly Dale simply because we had both lost our spouses.

Although it was New Year's Day, my only plan was to do the final read of *Shadows and Stones* before sending it off to the editor tomorrow. The first book in a series was difficult for me to write, and with this series, between not having spent much time in Wales, the paranormal aspect, and the time-travel twist, I had to do more research than usual. The series was more intense, and I wanted people to see the shadowy things that lurked in a few villages I'd created in Wales, and to feel as if they were really there when the main character visited the past. I'd kept some humor, but the overall tone was darker than my other two series. Maybe it was because of my own tragedies over the past three years.

The phones, constant sources of interference in my life, rang and pinged several more times with Happy New Year's calls and texts from Alistair and Cecilia, Liam, and Aisling, Jackson, Elsie, and a couple of London friends. I'd managed to somehow, amidst all of this, ready the manuscript to be sent and was just shutting down my computer, when the landline rang.

"Happy New Year, Aunt Jane-Ann," I said in greeting.

"And to you, Jessica. I understand you had a busy New Year's Eve."

"Busy? I stayed at home. You know I haven't been back in Hilly Dale but a couple of days."

"You may have stayed at home, but I heard you had company, and it's not welcome news."

"*How* does this news spread so quickly in such a short time, Aunt Jane-Ann?"

"People pay attention. You're *relatively* famous in Hilly Dale, and you're still new here. People want to know about you. When you weren't at the New Year's Eve party at Hilly Dale Country Club where so many of your high school classmates and friends were, word gets out. And anyone who is anyone in Hilly Dale was there."

I resisted the urge to ask if she attended, although I knew the answer. Most of the 'Country Club Set' were a decade or four younger than my aunt.

"I wasn't invited, Aunt Jane-Ann, and besides, I'd just returned from England. I can't imagine why anyone would have expected me to be at a party." Half the town probably knew I'd been in England over Christmas.

"Jessica," my aunt said in a serious, but oddly-caring voice, "in case you've forgotten, Hilly Dale is a small town. A number of your classmates remained here. Oh, I know not all of your close friends stayed, but a few did. Don't forget some of your parents' friends are still living, and I'm here. It's your reputation I'm thinking about."

"Thank you for your concern, but there's really nothing to talk about."

"I'm not immune from gossip. Your uncle had a secret that I tried very hard to keep from everyone. I struggled to protect our reputation, and I succeeded."

With my father's help.

"I don't want that to happen to you. People talk here. And Beckham Hailey spending another night with you is just fodder for the gossips," she added in a low voice.

Like you and your Hilly Dale Garden Club and Book Club friends, I wanted to say.

"He has NEVER spent the night with me. Yes, he drove me home from the class reunion. Yes, he stopped by last night. We visited for a long while, but he did not spend the night. We did not have sex, and even if we did, that would not be anyone's business but Beck's and mine. This is a distasteful conversation,"

"I'm just warning you, Jessica. People talk."

***

How right my aunt had been. The next morning, when I opened my laptop and clicked on the U.K. version of my preferred newsfeed, there in the lineup of news was a picture of Alistair and Cecilia in their wedding finery, not unexpected, but with the headline:

Socialite's Daughter Steals Eligible Duke (See the Wedding)

Clicking on the article, I began to read:

Alistair, The Duke of Hearthe, married Cecilia Elizabeth Hempstead, daughter of banker Everton Hempstead and his socialite wife Damaris, on December 27th at 11:00 a.m. in Hearthstone Vale. A reception and a later private after-party were held at Fielding House, the seat of the Dukes of Hearthe since 1575. The Duke is the son of the late William Alistair Thomas Fielding-Smythe and his first wife, Andrea Hughes.

The Duke has a half-brother, Lord William, and half-sister, Lady Aisling, by his late father's second-wife, Carola Jensen, an American who also goes by the name of Jessica Keasden, well-known mystery author. Prince Harry was present, but did not attend the after-party, due to a prior engagement. It should be remembered that his father the Prince of Wales was a friend of the present duke's father.

There were other details of the wedding that an anonymous source had provided, including what everyone wore, as well as the food and drink. Five photos were attached. The first was of Alistair and Cecilia at the private after-party. Another was of me standing in the Great Hall in my indigo velvet dress and the aquamarine and diamond bandeau tiara, while Jackson Barker could be seen in the background talking to the Comte de Beaupoume. I clicked on the three other photos. One was of Fielding House, and the other two were portrait shots – one of Cecilia in her wedding dress gazing adoringly at Alistair, and the other of the family.

I gasped. Oh my God! WHO wrote this and WHO provided the photos? I looked at the by-line. 'Isabel Allensworth.' She was a noted gossip columnist for one of the tabloids, and a friend of Cecilia's mother. A lightbulb came on. Damaris Hempstead, with a huge smile on her face, was in that family photo. To be honest, the correct name for her was 'social climber' instead of 'socialite', and this had her handiwork all over it. Although he was on his honeymoon, I picked up the phone and rang Alistair at the resort in Barbados.

"We saw it. Ceci's been looking for a write-up of our wedding ever since we married, but this isn't what we expected."

"Isabel Allensworth is known to enjoy revealing things to her readers, and she's one of Damaris's friends. Your grandmother, aunt, and I tried to tell you about Damaris."

"I know. Look, Mum, this puts me in rather a bind. Ceci wasn't thinking. Damaris picked up a copy of your book and she accidentally let it slip that you were Jessica Keasden. Ceci's gutted. She knows how much you wanted to keep your private life, well, private. Unfortunately, Damaris has no qualms when it comes to privacy – hers or anyone's. If you remember, she wanted to put her family on a reality show once. Thank God her husband stopped that, or…"

"Or you wouldn't have married Cecilia."

"I'm afraid you are right. I love Cecilia, but had Damaris gone ahead that would have been a deal breaker for me. It would have put our family in a crass light."

I paced around my office thinking for a moment about the situation. To a woman like Damaris Hempstead, Alistair was a stepping-stone, even if it was through her daughter.

"Are you still there?" Mum?"

"Yes. I was considering something. With your Grandparents Jenson gone and Aisling back home, there's no one to protect any longer. I don't *like* that my identity was outed without my permission. and especially by someone like Isabel Allensworth, but it was inevitable. I'm surprised it didn't come out when your father died. Information is readily available on the Internet, if someone cares enough to do research."

"All right. As long as you're not angry with Ceci."

"I'm not. She didn't mean to say anything, and even if she did, it's her mother who is the problem. If you don't want to be tabloid fodder, be careful what you reveal in Damaris's presence."

"Understood. Ring me if you need anything…anything at all. We'll be at the resort for a while."

For a few minutes, I sat at my desk and buried my face in my hands. Then I sat up, smoothed my hair, and made two quick phone calls.

Chapter Nineteen

Jackson Barker and Beckham Hailey sat in matching navy-velvet wing chairs on either side of the fireplace staring at each other. After serving them wine, I stood poking at the logs, wondering how to start the conversation.

"Jessica," Jackson began, "you're going to burn down the house if you keep stirring up the fire. Look at the sparks flying. Let's get down to why you called this little wine klatch tonight, not that I mind spending time with you…or you, Beckham, but you made it sound urgent on the phone."

"Yeah, Jessie. I never expected to hear from you this soon."

I looked at Beck before speaking, "I thought you would have changed your mind about talking to me after last night."

Jackson swung his head between the two of us so quickly I was afraid he might sprain his neck.

"Something came to light today and you two are the only ones in Hilly Dale who know. It has to do with England…" I trailed off.

"Does he know?" Jackson looked at Beck in surprise. "I understood you were not exactly friends."

"It's okay, Jackson. Jessie and I made our peace."

"Oh?" Jackson looked at me and raised an eyebrow.

"I told him last night, and I'm glad I did. Take a look at this." I showed them the article, along with others that had appeared because the prince had attended.

"Are you suggesting I did this?" Jackson asked. "The very idea."

"No, not at all. I imagine Damaris Hempstead is the source. My daughter-in-law's mother," I explained to Beck. "Jackson met her. She had access to everything. It would be just like her to announce her daughter's title at the start of the new year. I'm not bothered about it when it comes to back home. Her antics are fairly well-known there. Unfortunately, I might need a game plan to counter this in Hilly Dale, and maybe in Arkansas. I highly doubt the rest of the States are interested," I said, taking a seat on the sofa.

"So the story is out. What do you mean by 'game plan'?" Jackson asked. Before I could answer, he continued, "I look pretty good in that photo. I wonder if anyone will notice me. The Comte de Beaupoume was an interesting fellow. He told me all about his ice-climbing exploits, and then there was that photo of me with the prince…."

"Hey, Jackson," Beck said, "Jessie…um…Jessica is worried about the ramifications here in Hilly Dale. No one knew any of this. I think she might be concerned how the good citizens will perceive her when they find out."

"Oh, yes, I see. I'm sorry. I was just reliving the time at Jessica's country estate and that glorious time I spent among history and…"

"Yeah, I get it. You had fun at Jessie's house," Beck cut off the professor's reminiscing.

"Houses," Jackson replied. "Yes, I did. I'm still on cloud nine."

"Try to come down to earth. I don't think Jessie meant this to be a social call."

"Gentlemen," I interrupted. "I told you both that when I married Will, our families agreed it was in my parents' best interest to keep the details of my new husband quiet to protect my parents' interests and not negatively change their lives."

"I hate to break it to you, but when this gets around here - and it will - *your* life is going to change. People are proud of you because you're an author but look how that's gone since you've been here. You're damned if you do; you're damned if you don't. Your writing career is small potatoes compared to this! You never lied about your writing career," Beck said, twirling the red wine in his glass before taking a sip.

"I didn't lie. I didn't live here, and my parents did."

"Lie by omission," Jackson said, "Look, some already feel you're different because you lived overseas for many years and that would, of course, change you. There's an air about you, and people will notice it more now." He raised a hand before I could object. "Let me go on. It's not just your voice and accent that's different, but your mannerisms, your expressions, the way you carry yourself, and your style. There's nothing wrong with it. It's who you are… now, but in the eyes of this small town, you're still little Jessie Jenson. It's not your fault you're out-of-touch with Hilly Dale. You've been gone a long time."

"It's not their fault either," Beck added. "They have no concept of what life as a duchess entails, other than what they read or see on television. I know I don't."

"What can I do about it? It's who I am."

"Nothing much you can do, I'm afraid," Jackson pointed out. "It's a perception. You'll have to face the music, and you'll have to start with your aunt. She'll lead the pack if you don't tell her this before it gets out, and you know it will."

I sighed. "I guess so. I hate this."

"Don't you think you're overreacting, Jessie?" Beck asked.

"Perhaps. I've been so conditioned to protecting my parents all these years, it's all I know how to do here."

"But they're gone," Jackson said gently. "There's no one to protect. I've got to get going." he announced and headed for the front door. "Start with your aunt."

***

I called Aunt Jane-Ann the next morning and asked to stop by her house around 11:00. She lived on the west side of town in a small, yellow Craftsman house. Although it looked well-maintained at a glance, as I got closer, I could see it was in need of a new roof, gutters, and a touch of paint on the white trim. I made a mental note to have that done for her. After ringing the bell and standing in the cold for several minutes, Aunt Jane-Ann answered the door. She was dressed in a burgundy cardigan, layered over a gray sweater and a long, gray skirt. Her hair looked freshly done. My mother's pearls hung around her neck.

"Come in, Jessica." She held the door open and I entered her small, tidy living room. No fire burned in the hearth and the room was chilly.

Ashamed I hadn't visited her at her home before this, I commented on how lovely the room looked.

"I try," she said, looking around before taking a seat on an old padded rocker I remembered. "Well, have a seat and tell me why you needed to see me. Neither you nor your mother made much of an effort to do that. I just got home from the salon and I have a luncheon at the church at 12:30," she said. "I hope this won't take too long." And then she added: "You're welcome to come with me. You need a church home. I don't know where you went *over there*."

Well, there it was. The church-issue. And I might not have visited her house, but I knew my mother attended church with her sister each Sunday and picked her up to boot. Seating myself on a floral loveseat which served as the sofa in the room, I looked at Aunt Jane-Ann sitting across from me. "This shouldn't take long." I said, hoping that would be the case. "And, we are Church of England."

Aunt Jane-Ann nodded, but made no reply.

"I'm not here to argue with you about anything. I'm actually here because I need to talk to you about something private. Well, something that *was* private between my parents, my in-laws, my late husband, and me," I said politely.

The rocker creaked as my aunt leaned forward in anticipation. "I *knew* there was something strange going on," she said importantly, "Your parents going to England all the time, but when you came here, you stayed a couple of days – no time for me or anyone else - and then took those children on vacations around America with your parents. And that husband of yours rarely showed his face when you came to town, *if* he even bothered to come to Hilly Dale at all. No one could be sure. Of course, NO ONE from here was invited to your wedding in England," she reminded me for the umpteenth time.

I could understand her bitterness about not being invited, but it had been for the best. Today, I was here to protect *her* reputation.

"Would you like coffee?" my aunt asked, starting to rise from her rocker. "Or is it tea with you now?"

"No, thank you. I need your promise that you will not share any of what I'm going to tell you. It's important that you keep this to yourself."

"I don't gossip," she said a little too quickly.

"I'm serious, Aunt Jane-Ann. Unless I receive a promise, you will find out with everyone else. I'm giving you the courtesy of telling you first, so you can be prepared."

"Beckham Hailey," she said, shaking her head. "Is this what all this is about? You've been furtive about him ever since you moved back. The man may be going through a divorce, but he's still *married*!"

"Why would you even assume something like that? NO, this has nothing to do with Beck. This has to do with my late husband!" I said, fighting to retain my composure. "If you will please be quiet, I will tell you. If you cannot do that, then I have nothing else to say."

I had just reached the door when I heard a quiet voice: "I promise, Jessica. I'll get the family Bible if you want me to."

"That won't be necessary, but you cannot tell *anyone,* including those in our family. Do you understand me?"

"Yes. I promise."

I sat back down and began my tale, starting with meeting Will and not learning about his family until we were engaged, and ending with Alistair's wedding and the media reports. When I finished, Aunt Jane-Ann folded her hands and said, "Well, at least I know before the rest of the town." If she'd been sucking a lemon just a moment before, her face couldn't have had a sourer expression. "I don't like this one bit, but at least you have preserved my dignity. How awful for *me* to have people coming up with questions and I'd have to stand there. How embarrassing for people to learn that I, your own *aunt*, didn't know! I'd have been the laughingstock of the town!"

Stunned that she could make this about her, it took me a moment to compose myself before I finally said, "I can understand your disappointment and shock, but it was never meant to hurt you. It was to protect my parents – *your* sister - and perhaps even you and Uncle Ed. Once the local and state media got hold of a story about a Hilly Dale, Arkansas girl marrying into a duke's family, you might have been *besieged* by people digging into *your* life," I said, exaggerating just a little.

"Well, I suppose so," she said slowly, no doubt thinking about her husband's gambling problem coming to light. "Who are you now? What do I call you? Do I, your own relative, have to call you by your title?"

"Of course not! I'm Jessica Carola Jenson Fielding-Smythe. I am a duchess. That's who I am." There, I'd said it!

Chapter Twenty

"Jessie," Beck's voice came through my phone two days later, "look online. Do it now, while I'm on the phone with you."

"Not even a 'good morning'?"

"Good morning, just please do it. Look through the headlines."

"All right. I was outlining the plot for the second book in the *Secrets of Snowdonia* series. I'm already behind. Let me switch screens." Puzzled, I scanned the headlines, not seeing anything unusual, and I said so.

"Scroll down the page and pay attention to the headlines."

Oh. My. God. There it was. The other news had been pretty basic, but there, next to a professional photo taken of Will and me at our wedding and another of Alistair and Cecilia at their reception, was the headline:

Late Duke's Wife Now Known as 'Duchess of Hillbilly Dale, Arkansas.' Talk About a Comedown!

Is an old-fashioned hillbilly feud brewing? Carola Fielding-Smythe, stepmother of Alistair, The Duke of Hearthe, has been revealed to have small-town roots in Arkansas. Born Jessica Carola Jenson to Charles and Evelyn Jenson, she graduated from Cambridge University and went on to snag eligible widower William Alistair Thomas who was Earl of Ponder. Upon the death of his father, he became The Duke of Hearthe, making her a duchess.

Sources say that Carola has now returned to her Arkansas hometown since her stepson married. Could it be there is bad blood between the old duchess and her replacement, the former Cecilia Elizabeth Hempstead? Was Carola sent packing? Guess she's going to forfeit her private jet jaunts between the U. K. and the States now. She reportedly flew commercial back to the United States immediately following the wedding celebrations. She was accompanied by an unidentified male. It should be noted that Carola Fielding-Smythe is behind the popular Jessica Keasden mystery novels.

And there was another article,

Author Jessica Keasden is A DUCHESS AND LIVES IN ARKANSAS!

Jessica Keasden (real name Jessica Jenson), author of two successful series, The Celestial Cat *cozy mysteries and* Harriet Donovan *nobility spy novels has more in common with the latter series than anyone realized. There's a reason those books are so good. The reclusive Ms. Keasden is an actual duchess!*

The article went over everything from my birth to my marriage and children, and on to the deaths of my husband and parents. There were photos of me at my wedding and at Alistair's wedding.

And still another article:

From Dale to Vale to Dale: The Story of an Arkansas Duchess

There was the same information about my life along with photos of Fielding House, the London townhouse, and the Cornish manor, comparing them with a photo of my 'humble beginnings' in my great-great grandfather's not-too-shabby, large, white Victorian. There were photos of Hilly Dale and photos of Hearthestone Vale, noting how the two areas had geographical similarities, but there was also a silly comment about how the two names rhymed.

"Jessie, are you there?" Beck's voice came through loud and clear. "Jessie? What are you thinking? Answer me."

"I...I...I..." I stammered, "I don't know. The first article is absurd. Feud? God, I loathe that term that's bandied about these days. The references to 'hillbilly' concern me. The last two articles are pretty straightforward."

"Yeah, I don't get that hillbilly stuff. That's not even the name of your hometown. I just wanted you to be aware of them. It's not like it's big-time news, but in Arkansas you might see this on the news channels or in the papers. Small-town girl makes good, and all."

"That's not the point." I dug around in my desk drawer until I found what I was looking for. "Listen to this, Beck."

I read him the poem my daughter wrote that was inspired by Liam's comments not long after we moved here. She'd given it to me as a joke Christmas gift, but I didn't think anyone would know about it, except the family. Jackson hadn't even heard it. Aisling had slipped it under my door on Christmas morning.

The Duchess of Hillbilly Dale

There once was a duchess who lived in a Vale,
But across the sea she decided to sail.
What did she find when she arrived in the sticks?
She found that she didn't know how to mix.
She tried and she tried but her efforts did pale,
And now she's called Duchess of Hillbilly Dale.

-Lady Aisling 2016

"Shit!" Beck cried. "How'd they know that's what you had called it?"

"*I* never called it that. Liam and Aisling did, but I'm willing to bet that one of them told Alistair and he may have told Cecilia who…"

"…told her parents, thinking it was a *family* joke," finished Beck. "You said that Cecilia's mother liked the limelight."

"Do you think anyone's seen these articles, other than you, me, and probably Jackson who keeps up with all things English."

"I don't know. You told your aunt, didn't you? "

"Yes, the day after we talked."

"How did that go?"

"I'm not sure. She was shocked, I suppose, and then made it all about herself. I had to remind her of some things."

"You mean Ed Simmons's gambling and how your father covered for him?"

I was surprised. "How did you know about that?"

"Small town, Jessie. I'm sure a lot of people figured it out. Ed owed just about every business in town, and then one day the bills were paid-in-full, and in cash."

"My parents didn't want to see Aunt Jane-Ann go down with Uncle Ed, and *I* don't want to see her embarrassed either. She annoys me with her interference, but this town is her life. Ever since my father died, I've put a stipend in her account every month. My aunt thinks it's from an investment Ed made."

"*That,* I didn't know. Very kind of you."

"It's nothing. She needs the money, and I think there's going to be a bonus check or two. Her house needs work. She's too proud to say anything. I wonder if anyone will pay attention to this article-nonsense?"

"I guess you're going to have to wait and see. At least they didn't publish the poem. Hey, I have to get downstairs. The wait staff's arriving, but if you have any trouble, call me…or you can call Jackson. He's probably not that good in a fight, though," he said, laughing. "We'll talk later. Maybe we can go to Cajun Daisy's. Jordan's working here tonight. She knows what to do."

My landline phone rang. "It's Jackson calling. Cajun Daisy's it is. Thank you for letting me know about the articles. "I switched off my mobile and grabbed the cordless. Had the news already spread?

"Good morning, Jackson," I said cheerfully.

"Unidentified male? Sounds like a body in the morgue. Who writes these things?"

"Isabel Allensworth, the one who wrote about the wedding, was the author of the first one. Someone named Coral Cloud wrote the second piece, and Gaz Appleton, the last one. More importantly, who was the source."

"Well, it can't be anyone close to refer to me in that way, and what's with the Hillbilly Dale bit?"

"It *is* someone close, I'm afraid."

"But you just posed the question…"

"It was rhetorical. I think it's Cecilia's mother. I guess all party gloves are off now that Alistair and Cecilia are married."

"I met Damaris, so she would know I'm not an unidentified male. She could have at least put my name in there," Jackson complained, offended by the slight

"She's trying to get her fifteen minutes of fame by making me look bad and propelling her daughter to stardom," I said. "She's only interested in those who can help her achieve it. Be glad you can't. Cecilia knows how her mother is, but I do believe she knew her mother was going to have one of her friends write an article. Now that Cecilia's a duchess, Damaris is certain to use that to gain fame. I've never understood why her husband hasn't divorced her, but he's somewhat mercenary, so I suspect he's interested in the Fielding-Smythe fortune."

"Look who's gossiping," Jackson teased.

"Beck let me know about these latest pieces. Since Arkansas was mentioned, he thinks at least one will hit the state news."

"Likely. It's big news, for here, and you *are* Jessica Keasden. I can see a blurb about that being the case, but not any of that feud nonsense."

Following my talk with Jackson, I got in touch with my children. After inquiring about their studies and social lives, I broached the subject of Hillbilly Dale. As I suspected, Liam and Aisling both admitted they'd told Alistair, and Aisling said she recited her poem at the pre-wedding Hen Party held in London. "I'm sure Ceci thought nothing about telling her parents, since it is rather a family joke. Her parents are part of the family now."

Don't remind me. "I don't want to bother Alistair again on his honeymoon, but if you do speak with him, please tell him to phone me," I said.

"Mum, I'm sorry," Aisling said. "It might not have been Ceci who said anything. Her sister was there and so were her friends. They all thought my poem was funny. Is everything all right in H.D.?"

"Of course. It's just been a bit hectic with this news. It's nothing for you to worry about."

"So, Jordan says you and her dad have made up…"

***

Sometime later, I got up from the desk, stretched, reached for my phone, and headed to the kitchen to find a snack. Violet who had been hopping up and down on my lap and walking on my desk for the past hour while I was researching seventeenth-century England, followed me. While walking, I swiped the phone's dark screen and up popped three voicemails, four emails, and two texts. Now, why hadn't I heard the phone ring? It was right there on the desk, and then it hit me. Violet had been in there after I spoke with Beck and been doing her morning desk cruise. She must have stepped on the mute button. It had been blissfully peaceful without any ringing, dinging, or pinging for a few hours.

The calls were from my agent, Dil, and the CEO of the publishing company. I never heard from Joe Fornot, so something was up. The emails were from my editor, and the texts were from my social media manager. Rushing back to my office, I opened my laptop and accessed my social media and fan pages. The articles were on every site. I scanned a few comments on my fan page:

'Harriet Forever 54 ' had written, "Wow! Now we know why *Harriet Donovan* novels seem so realistic."

A Mary Henderfall had posted on a social media site that she thought the story was 'fantastic' and 'would make a good plot for a new series.'

"I knew she wasn't a cat," Toby Tysdale-Green posted. "Why all the secrecy?" He was referring to Violet's photo I used everywhere.

Why hide it? Interesting! Big deal! Who cares? On it went – shock, disbelief, anger by a few, but mostly positive, with some asking questions about my life as a duchess, and several, like Mary Henderfall, wanting me to write a book about it. However, one poster called 'Krazy for Keasden' had been the one who shared the articles on my fan page and had prefaced them each time with the phrase, *What a liar!*

I read the texts and emails, and then played the voicemails. My agent was shocked that I didn't tell her. Joe Fornot, who knew about me, was wanting to figure out a way to put a spin on it to generate more sales for the *Harriet Donovan* series. He wanted me to start working on a new book right away. "Written by a real-life duchess," he'd said. My social media manager wanted to know what she should do about 'Krazy for Keasden.' I texted back to do nothing.

Violet jumped on the desk and stared at me. "Looks like the cat is out of the bag. No more using you as the face of Jessica Keasden, mystery writer." Violet blinked at me, and I blinked back. She was a comforting presence in my changing world.

I went upstairs, showered, and dressed for my date – no, it wasn't a date – with Beck, and then drove to Cajun Daisy's. Beck stood waiting on the front porch. When we walked in, Heather and David were there and waved us over to their table.

"I saw those articles," Heather said after Beck and I sat down. "You're really a duchess? I'm best friends with a *duchess*!"

I simply nodded and took one of the single page menus from the old napkin holder in the center of the rough wood table. Cajun Daisy's wasn't fancy.

"It seems you have led a fascinating life, Jessica, or is it..." David trailed off, looking confused.

"Jessica is fine. I don't know if I'd call it fascinating, but it is certainly different than the life I led growing up."

"You can say that again! It must be just glorious living in that lovely old country house," Heather sighed.

How I wished I could tell her that it was drafty, smelled sometimes of damp, frequently in need of repairs, and there were the times of the year when tourists traipsed through part of it, but seeing her dreamy-eyed look, I didn't want to shatter her image. "Yes, It's quite an experience," I said.

"I read up on the house's history, and that of your family. Lots of interesting facts. Did someone really push a person from the top of the Keep that remains on the property?" David asked.

"I believe so, but you must remember that the Keep is from the early thirteenth century, as are the castle ruins and the church on the lake. Given the age, there are probably lots of gruesome stories going back that far." Liam would have been proud of that answer.

"And the poisonings?" he asked.

"Well, yes. There were at least a couple at our dining room table that I know about."

"You still *use* that table?" Heather gasped. "I couldn't even use the Taylor table after catching…"

Thank goodness David stopped her from telling that lewd tale again by asking a question about Fielding House's location. For the next few minutes we talked about the similarities between Hilly Dale and Hearthestone Vale's geography. "It can be colder, and there's less daylight in the winter months than here."

"I think it's time for us to order," Beck interrupted, ending further questions by signaling the server, but that didn't prevent others in the restaurant stopping by the table, mostly to speak briefly to Beck, teasing him about checking out the competition at Cajun Daisy's or taking a night off. They barely addressed Heather and David, but they certainly gave me a good look.

We ate our blackened chicken and dirty rice, while trying to talk about anything but my title and life in England. Each time I looked up or around at something in the room Heather pointed out, the other diners would suddenly look at their plates. The word was out, and I suspected that it wasn't just because they knew I was a duchess. Beckham Hailey was having dinner in the quaint, cozy restaurant with a woman – and not just any woman. He was dining with The Duchess of Hillbilly Dale.

Chapter Twenty-One

"I'm certainly glad you thought to share your life with me," Aunt Jane-Ann declared as she walked into my house a couple of days later. "I've been absolutely beset with calls about you."

"Weren't you before?" I closed the front door, locking it after securing the grilled door. The inquisitive minds and verbal attacks had been online, but it had been oddly quiet in Hilly Dale and I was about to find out why.

"It's been so tiresome," my aunt complained, drawing her hand across her brow. "Let me sit down, and might I have a cup of coffee while you're up?"

A short time later, I brought a tray with a silver coffee service, a china cup and a matching plate of cookies – I'd stopped calling them tea biscuits after I'd asked at a bakery for a box to give Heather James for her birthday and received petite, fluffy, white Southern biscuits with a side of honey butter. Rather than explain, I gave them to Heather anyway. She was delighted. I poured my aunt a cup of coffee and waited for her to add sugar, take a bite of cookie, and a sip of coffee.

"I'm telling you, Jessica, It's been non-stop since you told me who you were. I've had interviews with the local paper and the historical society. I've been asked to speak at various organizations. Me! I haven't had a moment's peace, and now these other articles have come out." Her eyes sparkled behind her spectacles, and her cheeks were flushed with what could only be excitement. "But that one article where this town is called 'Hillbilly Dale' is just terrible! How could you say that about your hometown? It's humiliating."

"I didn't. I understand everyone knowing about the articles, but you just said, 'since you told me'. I saw the blurbs and the articles, but I follow the nobility and the U.K. version of my news, so…"

"Well, I suppose others read that stuff, Jessica," she interrupted, looking uncomfortable.

"You told someone, didn't you." I stated.

My aunt squirmed ever-so-slightly. "Well, only Margo Hunter. We were talking about the next meeting of the book club and I said that since you were a duchess you might be able to give us insight on…"

"What?" I cried.

"It slipped out. We were talking about how *Harriet Donovan* seemed to know exactly what all those upper-class ladies and gentlemen were doing, so I said that you should know very well because you were part of that."

"Oh, Aunt Jane-Ann," I groaned. "You promised me."

"Well, it's out and a good thing, now that those other articles have appeared. You couldn't have kept something like that quiet forever, you know."

I took a deep breath, blowing it out slowly, hoping the tension and annoyance I felt would go with it. "I'm curious why you are being asked about my life. Why am I not the one handling this? Don't you think that is something I should be doing?"

"I've told them you don't wish to be bothered. As a duchess, you are used to certain…precautions. I'm screening for you." She helped herself to another cookie. "Gatsby Gregson wants to run a column about you in the Hilly Dale Gazette. He's asked for my input."

"What? Did it not occur to you to ask me about this first? What have you been saying?"

"Oh, I'm just playing up your life. The romantic meeting, the beautiful wedding, the children, and the tragic loss of your husband which left you a grieving widow roaming about your ancient manor until you decided to come back to your hometown," she dramatized. "And, of course, taking private jets hither and yon, socializing with royalty, and attending glorious parties wearing gorgeous jewels, and things of that nature when you were married."

"First of all, I don't live in an *ancient* manor, and I certainly didn't have time to roam aimlessly about my home after Will died. Second, I don't travel by private jet…much. Third, please do not talk about jewels. Why invite a criminal element to consider I have them here!"

"Hmmmph. I'm just trying to help. From the looks of the latest news articles, you could use that. Hillbilly Dale indeed! How could you call Hilly Dale by that ridiculous name? It's how we get a…a reputation," she sniffed. "It's bad enough the local sports teams are known as 'Hillbillies.' Unfortunately, you've made our town seem like we are a bunch of hicks with that stupid 'Hillbilly Dale.' One of my friends phoned and said something about memes – and yes, I know what that is. One Arkansas town is sponsoring a contest for the best one. See what your little play on the town's good name is costing us. It's cost us our dignity, Jessica!"

My aunt acted as if this was the end of the world for Hilly Dale. Most likely, it would put the town on the map, at least in Arkansas. "Perhaps it was a misspelling. The local high school sports teams, as you pointed out, are known as 'The Hilly Dale Hillbillies,' and they have been since the teams began."

"Then why was there a mention of an 'old-fashioned hillbilly feud' between you and the new duchess?" She took a sip of coffee, set it down, and glared at me.

"I've no idea. Creative license by the writer? A play on the silly term 'feud? Cecilia is a lovely young woman. I'm proud to have her as a daughter-in-law." I grabbed a cookie and stuck it in my mouth before I added something about Cecilia's mother.

"Have you talked to the children? Perhaps they know." My aunt was fishing, but I wasn't taking the bait.

"I have spoken with them about the articles. I'll address any others that may appear the next time I speak with them. Liam is back at university. Alistair and Cecilia have been on their honeymoon for over three weeks but will be home soon. Aisling is on holiday in Spain. Besides, it's probably just someone's idea of a joke, given my hometown's name and location," I said, although I did not think that for one minute.

"Are you saying where you live is a joke? That it's so rural that it's full of hicks and hillbillies? You're a writer, perhaps you should enter the meme contest," she said in a snarky tone.

"I'm not saying that at all. Where I lived in England is somewhat similar to Arkansas with its lakes, mountains, and valleys. It's beautiful, and popular with tourists. I believe a couple of articles mention that."

"I thought you lived in London. You didn't mention where you actually lived. Oh, I know Hearthestone Vale, but not its proximity. See how little I know?"

You could have looked it up like everyone else has probably done!

"We have a townhouse in London and our country house is the family seat. This is precisely why you should direct people to me."

"Of course. So fancy and wealthy you've become," she said. "Socializing with royalty, I suppose, and traipsing around on a private jet, and having more than one residence. It must be wonderful to have that kind of money while the rest of us pick our teeth with sticks and chomp on corncob pipes back in your hometown."

Thank goodness I'd omitted Lilac House in the Cotswolds and the house in Cornwall. That private jet must really stick in her craw since she mentioned it before. "Don't be ridiculous. No one thinks that about Hilly Dale. There's a college here for goodness' sake! From now on, direct the people to the landline phone, and please stop embellishing about royalty, jets, and things about which you know nothing."

"Well, I think you are going to have to step up and apologize to the people of Hilly Dale for the Hillbilly Dale comment."

"I'll do no such thing! I did not write the article, nor did I refer to this place by that name."

Aunt Jane-Ann stood up, and with a look of disgust on her face, said, "Fine. I'll abide by your decision and let you take charge of everything. The local paper wants another interview to fill in the gaps, since I wasn't privy to your life. I only gave them the basics."

Yes, like me wandering around an ancient manor house wearing jewels and hobnobbing with royalty.

"On to something else I heard about you. I understand you had dinner with Beckham Hailey. That's something else people are talking about. He's *married*, Jessica," she reminded me.

"Don't people have anything else to talk about besides me? We were at Cajun Daisy's having dinner with Heather and David. It's not all that clandestine a place if people saw us. And he's getting a divorce. Bianca has been dating John Knoss for I don't know how long."

"Nevertheless, you don't want to be a slut like Bianca Hailey, and you certainly don't need any negative publicity after referring to Hilly Dale as Hillbilly Dale!" She marched into the foyer and opened the front door, all without my suggestion. Standing there in the doorway, her hand on the knob of the security door, she looked me straight in the eyes, and added, "Mark my words, Jessica, this is not over." She turned the doorknob. "Am I trapped in this place now!"

"No," I replied, turning the key that was still in the lock and then holding the door open for her. "And I didn't refer to the town that way," I cried, shutting the doors behind her with more force than usual.

Chapter Twenty-Two

I wasn't sure what was the biggest scandal: the town being referred to as Hillbilly Dale in the media, me keeping my title a secret from Hilly Dale all those years, or Beck and I having dinner together at Cajun Daisy's. All three had been causing problems for me all week, but the worst of it had been my dratted phones ringing with people requesting money. Tim Hayes, the college president, had finally decided to contact me. Jessica Keasden was one thing; Carola, Duchess of Hearthe was quite another in terms of potential donations.

"We are saddened that your daughter, Lady Aisling, is not returning to Hilly Dale, but we hope that you will find it in your heart to continue supporting the college. We have all sorts of plans for expansion, and we can establish an endowment in whatever name you choose. Your money would be put to good use. We plan to buy a few lots nearby and..."

"Don't you realize that you have places that could be renovated and repurposed downtown?" I asked, thinking of historic empty buildings that would work. "I'd be interested in *that*."

"Well, uh..." he stumbled, "It's been determined that, I mean we don't..."

"...want to bother," I finished for him. "I thought not. I will consider your...suggestion, Mr. Hayes. Thank you for calling."

Besides other requests for donations, there were calls from people wanting me to speak at this or that club, organization, and even at the schools. "Having a member of royalty speak would be a thrill!" one of my aunt's club friends said.

"I am *not* a member of the royal family. My late husband was *not* a royal duke." I started to explain the difference but gave up.

"Your aunt said that you had judged flower shows. That explains how your mother knew so much about English roses and had such lovely pictures. We hope you will be the judge at ours," the woman persisted.

"It would depend when it is," I said, eyeing Violet who had jumped on the bannister and, balancing perfectly, was carefully making her way up. After agreeing to have a think about it, I made the excuse that my cat was getting into mischief and disconnected. "Thank you, Violet, for the rescue," I told the furry lovebug as I lifted her from the bannister.

Had it not been for the fence around my property, I'd probably have had people coming to my door. My aunt had certainly done her part in creating drama when she'd told stories about my life, or at least the life she thought I led. I was now the very wealthy duchess who wasn't willing to help out her hometown, had a bad attitude, and offended people, but at least I was able to handle things myself. Changing my phone numbers crossed my mind.

My agent, Dil Daly, emailed me the good news that the *Harriet Donovan* books were selling 'like wildfire.' My agent and publisher wanted me to do a book tour, something I'd never done. My publisher wanted me to play up the duchess angle and 'look the part' at the readings. I wasn't clear on what that meant. Part? I wasn't acting a role. As for looking like a duchess, I was sitting at my desk in my plush Tardis-printed pajamas that I'd worn on New Year's Eve and sipping Irish Breakfast tea. Perhaps my publisher would like an at-home photo of me, complete with my hair in a ponytail, no makeup, and stuffing my face with homemade pancakes while I worked. I suppose he was thinking more along the lines of what he saw in the wedding photos: tiara, evening attire, expensive cars in the drive, and so forth, but that was *not* how I lived my day-to-day life, and I didn't know anyone who did. Most of the time, I was in jeans or trousers and a sweater.

Looking at my calendar, I noted a couple of area book club readings, including one at the local library that were coming up. I had also accepted an interview with the *Hilly Dale Gazette* this afternoon. Peter Franklin, Betsy's husband and newspaper owner, had personally called me. His best journalist Gatsby Gregson was coming to the house because I wasn't comfortable going to his office, or anywhere the public might be at the moment.

Heather called to tell me people were commenting on my assumed relationship with Beck. According to her, some were saying that Bianca was angry about that. "Here she is, the former Homecoming Queen, and she *is* dating John Knoss, and here's that nerdy little Jessie Jenson who became a duchess, and now caught Beckham Hailey, *her husband*! And then Betsy Potter Franklin's going around saying you are best friends again, just to annoy Bianca. And Tommy Fitzpatrick *was* upset after we had lunch at Piggie-Pen before all this came out," she told me again. "He *did* want to ask you out. I asked him."

"Why would you do that? Please don't stir the pot. I don't know why he would be upset. We were never more than friends."

"He told me he thought you both had bonded due to the loss of your spouses, and you said you would be open to another lunch."

"I meant with the three of us, and any others who still live here who were part of our group. A lunch does not a relationship make."

"But a dinner might," she concluded. "Look at you and Beck. You had a good time with him at Cajun Daisy's."

"Heather, I have a job, although it seems people think a writer can take all the time she needs, but I have deadlines to meet."

"I just think you and Tommy would be so good for each other. I feel bad for him."

"He's dating Kismet again," I reminded her. "I feel sorry for Jordan Hailey and Allison Knoss. They are the ones who are suffering the actions of their parents, and I do not want to contribute to that by getting involved in some brouhaha with Bianca over Beck. I'd say that I was not having a relationship with him, but who would believe me."

"Well, you can't fart in this town without everyone knowing it," Heather replied, giggling.

"*Everyone* must have great retention. My aunt believes *everyone* knows everything. I heard John Knoss was a catch and Bianca was fortunate to have landed him, so I can't imagine why she would care who her soon-to-be ex-husband sees."

"Oh, he is, I suppose. He's not real handsome or anything, but he's wealthy and from Los Angeles."

"How did he end up in Hilly Dale?"

"He has relatives here. Do you remember Jody Knossbacher?"

"From the old bakery?"

"Yeah. Her grandparents owned Knossbacher Bakery. Anyway, John is her first cousin. He was born in Hilly Dale, but his parents moved out west when he was two or three. He came back after his uncle died and helped Jody cut a deal to sell the place, of course he got his portion of it. I don't think John does anything without making sure he comes out well, I can *tell* you. Anyway, John invests in things around here. He owns a lot of property around town."

"The downtown?" I asked.

"Not now. He gave Betsy the building where *Betsy Gifts* is in their divorce, but he owns LAND! Lots of it. He was a realtor for celebrities in L.A. at one time. He has a nose for real estate. He's been buying up land around here. Betsy caught herself a big fish when she married him, and he's really big in this little pond! Too bad she couldn't keep him happy, but you remember how Betsy acted."

"Going back to John's property investments…" I interrupted, thinking I might like to speak with him about a project I'd been considering.

"Oh yeah. He's into buying cheap-cheap and selling high. He's popular with some of the movers and shakers in town because he gets things done. He nitpicks properties and points out all the flaws making them seem bigger than they really are, so the seller thinks he's their only option. He did that to Tommy, and he hates him for it. I understand he tried that with Kismet, but she didn't fall for his act. John and Tim Hayes are buddies too."

"Hmmmm, that makes sense," I said, walking to the kitchen in search of something to eat. I'd become a better cook now that my only other choice was to repeatedly visit the local restaurants.

"What?"

"Oh, nothing. You seem to know a lot about him. Is he that popular?"

"Oh, yeah, but like I said, not with everyone. Women mainly. What are you doing? I can hear shuffling sounds."

"I'm rummaging through the refrigerator looking for the peanut butter. I have an interview with the newspaper in…" I looked at the clock. "In an hour! I'll speak with you another time."

I hurried upstairs to get cleaned-up, paying special attention to my hair and makeup, fairly certain Gatsby Gregson would bring a photographer.

An hour later, I was sitting in one of the navy wing back chairs across from a casually-dressed man in his early 30s. Gatsby, as he'd asked me to call him, looked me up and down before signaling to his photographer. I was dressed in a v-neck camel-colored sweater, indigo skinny jeans, and brown pointy-toe leather boots. My streaked, light-brown hair was straight, thanks to a quick run-through with the ceramic straightener Aisling left behind, and I was wearing very polished makeup with a soft rose-tone lipstick. Since my aunt had indicated that I wore such gorgeous jewels all the time, I kept the jewelry simple with a short, thick gold necklace and small, gold earrings.

"Perfect," the photographer, a tall, thin woman who looked in her early 20s, said. "Just act natural and pretend I'm not here. I'll take a few shots while you're being interviewed, if that's okay, I mean."

"Of course," I replied, slanting my legs to the left.

"Shall we begin?" Gatsby asked. "May I record this?"

"Yes," I said with trepidation.

The interview started with general questions about me, my writing, and then swiftly moved on to questions comparing my life in Hilly Dale with that of my life in England. I gave brief, cautious answers, despite his attempts at probing deeper. And then came the zinger: "So, why did you cover up where you were from?" he blurted, "Are you ashamed of your hometown?" He stared intensely at me through a pair of black-framed spectacles.

I hesitated for just a moment and then said, "It was right there online for anyone who was interested and determined enough to locate it and put it all together. I'm surprised you didn't find it, Gatsby. As for being ashamed, no, I'm not. This is where I grew up. It's where my parents all the way back to my great-great grandparents, all who were well-known in this town and who contributed a *good deal* to the community, lived. If you recall my paternal great-grandfather saved this town during the depression and set up..."

"Yes, we're all aware how *prominent* your family's been in Hilly Dale, and that brings me to another question. If you are so proud of your hometown why did you refer to it as Hillbilly Dale. You are aware of the jokes and memes that are going around on social media, right?"

"I understand that *I'm* the butt of the joke, not the town. I am the one called 'The Duchess of Hillbilly Dale,' which is not particularly flattering when used in that context, and a few local friends have sent me a couple of memes with me dressed in overalls and wearing a tiara, in a sort of *Green Acres* style, and comparing me to that program's character, Lisa Douglas, but I don't follow social media, as a rule. I don't even have my own account."

"You have a few for Jessica Keasden, your *nom de plume*." He reminded me, making me sound deceptive.

"Those are business accounts. I'm a writer, as you are fully aware. I have a fan page, too, but I'm sure you know that. I also have a manager for those sites."

"There have been mixed reactions to the revelation that you're actually a duchess."

"Well, we all have to be something, don't we. And there *would* be mixed reactions. I don't control my readers' thoughts and opinions."

"And how's your daughter," he looked at his notes, "Lady Aisling? She attended Hilly Dale College for one semester. Why did she leave?"

"My daughter is not the subject of this interview."

Undaunted, he continued, "There's a rumor that you're feuding with your new stepdaughter-in-law. She's the new Duchess of Hearthe. Is that why you came back to Hilly Dale? Any truth to that article?"

"No," I replied, with a curt enough tone for him to realize he would get nothing further from me on the subject of my family. "I understand you plan to publish a column about me each week."

"Yes! You're big news around here. People are curious. Even the state papers have expressed interest. Are you willing to do a question-and-answer series?"

"No." I knew he'd go full steam ahead anyway.

"Oh, that's too bad," he said, feigning sadness. "So, is there anything you wish to say to the good people of Hilly Dale?"

Knowing he was angling for the apology Aunt Jane-Ann had encouraged me to give, I paused for dramatic effect, smiled sweetly and said, "Just that it's nice to be back in such a *lovely* town filled with *so* many memories." The photographer kept clicking away, even as I walked them both to the door. Now to deal with my publisher and agent, and I was glad it went well. They were rushing the book tour and scheduled it for the fourth week in February, possibly going into the first week of March.

On reflection, I wondered why I'd ever worried anyone would find out who I was, now that my parents were gone and Aisling was back in England. It seemed unimportant, but when Alistair called later, he pointed out that I'd still need to be careful.

"Mum, the same reasons it was agreed not to say anything are the same ones that now apply to you. Don't you remember?"

I did and told him I could handle it. I had already experienced the requests for donations, interviews, favors, and engagements, as well as the hangers-on, and security concerns. The latter was due to my aunt running her mouth about private jets and jewelry, but so far, I'd been pleasantly surprised things weren't worse.

"I can't stay in the house forever, Alistair. I live in this town and other than the cleaner who comes twice -a-month, I don't have additional help to run errands, so that I can work. I also don't have the anonymity in Hilly Dale – I didn't have that even before all the duchess business came out. I go to Little Rock to have my hair done. It's one of my few private outings, although I don't know how it will go the next time I visit her."

"Done? You're acquiring a more varied vocabulary style."

"I'm versatile. What can I say?"

"Reverting?"

"I'm trying to fit in. Things should settle down soon." I scanned the calendar on my computer as we talked. My next appointment at the salon was right before Valentine's Day.

"A solution would be for you to move back home," Alistair said wistfully. "You're missed here. You've always got a home, and you know what Poleduck said about your citizenship. It would be easier on you financially."

"I understand all of that. It's something to consider. I need time away to make decisions, and I'm still taking care of my parents' estate."

"Promise me if you need help, you will let me know."

I promised. "Now, how was the honeymoon?" I asked.

Chapter Twenty-Three

A few evenings later, I stood behind a podium in the local library's main room reading excerpts from *The Moon over Butterfield*, the latest in *The Celestial Cat* series.

"Bravo," Jackson Barker cried when I finished "Bravo, Jessica!"

During the applause that followed Jackson's cheer, I saw Beck standing near a back corner, away from the crowd. He nodded slightly. Careful not to look again in his direction, I asked the crowd if they wanted a preview of my new series, *Secrets of Snowdonia*.

"We want to hear more about your life as a duchess," my aunt's garden club friend that I'd dubbed Lady Daffodil called out. There were murmurs of agreement.

"You're more famous than Lucky Fine," a man cried, "and better-looking too," he laughed. "That's why I came to this reading."

"My life is quite unremarkable," I told the crowd. "I'm not royal, as some people have said. There's a difference between…"

Margo Hunter raised her hand, "We've simply got to get you to read at the next meeting of our book club."

"Hey, tell us about your life," a woman's voice rang out.

"Leave her alone," Betsy Potter Franklin said, standing up to look at the woman. "Let her read from her new book."

"Yes, let her," Heather chimed in and turned to give Betsy a big smile. Betsy looked away from her.

I reached for the proof-copy. "The first book in the series is called *Shadows and Stones*. Now, shall I read an excerpt?"

"Are there ghosts in your house?" a teenaged girl asked. "Did anyone die horribly?"

"The house is around four-hundred-forty-one-years old - older in some parts - so I'd say that people have died there. As to horrible? Perhaps. There are legends," I replied. "I've not seen any ghosts, but my children say they have." I told them about The Blue Lady and the Haunted Keep.

"I went to college with Aisling," another girl said. "We were in the same classes. I liked her. Is she going to come back?"

"Thank you. Aisling enjoyed her time here." I looked over to see Jordan Hailey and Allison Knoss sitting together. "She made good friends in that short time, but she will be attending St. Andrews in Scotland. Let me share the opening to *Shadows and Stones*."

After I finished reading, refreshments were served. The local bakery had tried to recreate a High Tea served at 8:00 p.m. They'd done an admirable job and I thanked them. Betsy came rushing up to me just as I was about to take a bite of a small scone.

"What a treat to hear you read. Everything sounds better with your accent," she gushed.

"Thank you, Betsy. My accent is rather mixed, much like my vocabulary."

"Well, it's just *gorgeous* to me. Listen, I know about you and Beck," she whispered. "I know he's here. I saw him earlier. Why are you keeping it a secret? The whole town knows about Bianca and *my* ex. If you two want to hook up, why should anyone care? There's a bunch of nosy people around here who like to start things," she said, looking around at the crowd. "I hate that Allison and Jordan are caught up in it. Be glad *your* daughter isn't here. I mean, that she doesn't have to put up with the gossip, not that she's not here with you or anything. I'm sure you miss her."

"I do. I saw Allison tonight with Jordan. Aisling keeps in touch with both, I believe. There's no reason for them not to, especially since things are out in the open now."

"My daughter, friends with a real lady, and you're a duchess. That's funny. You know back in high school, people barely paid you any mind. Well, I know *I* didn't, but I *was* best friends with that piece of trash Bianca. She didn't like you, and all because she thought Beck was still crazy about you. Look at you now. You got the last laugh on all of us. Titled husband, well-known author, fabulous lifestyle. Had I paid attention to you, the nerdy, quiet thing that you were, and stayed your friend like in elementary, *I* could have had a friend who was destined to be a duchess, but instead I got screwed over by that back-stabbing Bianca! I knew she had her eyes on John way back. You have it made, honey. I was such a bitch back then."

Was that supposed to be an apology?

"You're forgetting that my 'wealthy, titled husband' was killed in an accident three years ago, Betsy. I don't think my life has been all that fabulous," I responded with an edge. *Nerdy, quiet thing, indeed*!

"Well, uh..." she stammered, "except for that, but you still lead a more exciting life than those of us here. All those parties, and you've met royalty, and you travel on private jets," she went on. "Had I been nice to you, I might have gotten to be part of that."

Doubtful. Unsure of how to politely respond, I looked around for an escape. "If you'll excuse me, I need to speak with the librarian. She and her staff went to a lot of trouble."

"Your mother was just the sweetest woman," the librarian said when I caught up to her. "I hope you'll be stepping into her shoes and joining the same organizations and taking part in the Methodist Church."

It was on the tip of my tongue to say my mother and I wore different-sized shoes, but I demurred and told her that I hadn't lived in Hilly Dale long enough to make any sort of commitments, and then I thanked her again and went to grab my coat. On the way, I was waylaid by Heather who bent my ear for fifteen minutes about Betsy. She managed to work in a tale of Bianca and John at the Pumpkin Pageant before launching into something about how her ex-husband's wife Shauna had once hooked-up with Lucky Fine in public.

Is that all people did around Hilly Dale? Gossip and have affairs? Surely not, but it made me wonder what Hilly Dale Garden Club and Hilly Dale Book Club got up to in the privacy of their homes, or in Shauna and Lucky's case, the public park's swing set. One thing was for sure, Hilly Dale was providing fodder should I ever wish to write a steamy romance novel.

"Glad you finally decided to leave," I heard Beck say as soon as the library's front doors closed behind me. Stepping out of the shadows, he added, "Is there anyone left in there?"

"Just the librarian and her staff. What are you doing skulking about in the cold?"

"Waiting to talk with you about something."

"You should have waited near the loos like you did at the class reunion. I'm certain there's a broom closet nearby. We could have gone in there."

"Someone might have seen us and gotten the wrong idea. I don't want anything going wrong now."

"People have already seen us and are talking about it, or haven't you noticed. You must be freezing out here, " I said, turning up the collar of my vintage camel-hair coat. "How long *have* you been standing in the cold?"

"Not long. I was inside behind the rows of books. I didn't want Betsy to see me."

"I hate to inform you, but not only did she see you, she gave us permission to 'hook-up.' Oh, I doubt it was out of genuine caring, but more along the lines of annoying Bianca. I'm cold and I'm tired of talking. I really just want to go home. Can it wait?"

"Hey, I waited for you all night," he said, pulling me next to the building. "Bianca's going to sign the papers. I've got the restaurant free and clear! She says John's so wealthy she doesn't need anything from me. I must admit I was surprised by that confession today. The papers are being signed, if you can believe it, on Valentine's Day. I was hoping you would celebrate with me that night."

"You wanted to speak with me in the cold after my book reading to invite me out for Valentine's evening?"

"In a manner of speaking. Hey, it's a gesture." By the lamplights' dim glow, I saw him shuffle his feet and run his fingers through his hair just like he did when he was thirteen.

"How can I refuse," I said, laughing. "All right. Where and what time?"

"The restaurant."

"Don't you have to work that night?"

"Part of being the owner is that I can delegate. As long as I make a couple of appearances, it's fine. Besides, my manager is there. Come by at 8:00."

"IF the papers are signed that day, I'll come. You and Bianca are still married, and, according to Aunt Jane-Ann, 'still' is what makes the difference."

Beck uttered a four-letter word.

"I was teasing," I said. "Yes, I'll be there."

"Bianca left me two years ago. We haven't been truly *married* for over four years. Why should anyone care? Come to the back and ring the buzzer next to the small back door. It rings in the apartment. I'll unlock it. "Or," he said in a low voice, "you *could* take the old iron bridge and go along the trail to the restaurant. The city put lights along the way. Remember that bridge? We used to sit and dangle our legs over the edge, talk, and then sneak up to Mrs. Carter's house. We were a daring pair back then, weren't we?"

I nodded, remembering sitting on the black iron bridge. It was the first time Beck had kissed me. We were thirteen and felt so grown-up. I hadn't thought about that in many years.

"Just don't come through the front and up the stairs. No sense courting trouble."

"Isn't plotting to sneak around at night a bit clandestine, Beck?"

"Maybe, but you have to admit it's a bit exciting too. You're a duchess sneaking off to meet the riff-raff." I couldn't see his face well, but I knew he was smiling by his voice. "I assumed you might not like everyone knowing our business. They know enough about you already. Why add fuel to it."

"Fair enough, If anyone notices me, I'll say I'm giving a reading for a private group. How about that?"

"Not as exciting, but deal. You *could* do a private reading for me. I'm sure Jordan's got one of your books in the apartment."

"All right. That's enough. I'll see you at 8:00 on the 14th. Right now, I need to get out of the cold. I'm surprised it hasn't started snowing."

"Wouldn't stick. Ground's not cold enough, yet. The weather prediction indicates rain followed by an Arctic Blast. If it snows or ices, I'll pick you up," Beck replied. "Surprised people aren't keeping you informed of the weather. Talking about the weather is a great pastime around here. Wait until tornado season."

"I remember from when I was growing up in Hilly Dale. All people talked about was how the weather changed. It's the same at home. Having a house not too far from the coast, and another right *on* the coast, we worry about gales, but the structures have been weathering storms for centuries. Fielding House and the Cornish manor have very thick walls, not like here."

As we walked to my car, I told him a family story about a gale in Cornwall many years ago. The waves rolling in were so tall that when they crashed against the cliff the spray rose as high as the second story of the manor. The fishing village nearby was flooded and Will's great-great-great grandparents, who were in residence at the time, opened the manor to the needy villagers. "The cliff edge is getting closer to the house due to erosion." I shivered thinking about the house one day falling into the sea and pulled my coat tighter around me.

"Here's your car," Beck stated.

"Aren't you afraid the Hilly Dale spies will see you with me? Betsy already did."

Beck gave me a quick hug and opened my door. I looked at him before he closed it. I had accepted a date on Valentine's. I hadn't been looking for romance. After Will died, I never thought I would again, but now I wasn't so sure.

Chapter Twenty-Four

The weather predictions had been correct: a heavy cold rain for two days, then a dry day, followed by an Arctic Blast. There was a chance of snow tonight, but I decided to drive to The Old House Restaurant. I didn't want to be dependent on Beck. I had no idea how the evening would go and wanted my escape pod, even if it was a small car.

It was nearly 8:00 p.m. when I pulled into a parking space across the street from the restaurant. I wasn't surprised that there were only a few cars in the lot. With the threat of snow, most who had kept their reservations appeared to have parked in back. Pulling the collar of my black coat up around my ears, I twisted the turquoise scarf around my neck and tucked my gloved hands into the coat's deep pockets before heading across the road. My boots made a scuffing sound as I walked across the sanded footbridge and up the sidewalk to the restaurant. Turning right, just before I reached the front porch and guided by the light coming from lampposts, I walked briskly down the sanded sidewalk until I reached the narrow wooden door Beck mentioned.

I pressed the buzzer and turned the knob. Finding the door wouldn't budge, I pushed the buzzer again, waited a few seconds, and tried the knob. Still locked. God, it was cold. The wind had picked up, and I could hear limbs creaking. I was just about to text Beck when he finally appeared.

"Get in here and get warm," he said, standing aside to let me enter.

"I feared you had forgotten. I was just about to text you. I buzzed and tried the door a couple of times."

"No, don't be silly. I was, er…in the bathroom, so it took me a couple of minutes to get down here. I should have explained it's not like the gate at your house. I have to let you in the old-fashioned way."

"All right. You're excused this once. One needs to urinate, I suppose," I teased.

"My, how formal. Come on upstairs. Dinner's keeping warm on the stove."

"I don't use these stairs often," Beck said as we climbed narrow, steep steps. This way, Duchess," he added with a hint of laughter in his voice. "Here we are."

I walked past Beck into a welcoming kitchen from which emanated a mouth-watering smell. "Lovely," I commented, looking around the small kitchen with its white walls, exposed rock, and cabinets made from mahogany-stained bead board. In the center of the room was a beige stone counter with a stainless-steel bar-style cooker on which rested a cast-iron Dutch-oven over a low flame. Nearby, was a built-in stainless oven with a broiler drawer. Through the oven's glass panel, I could see a pan of rolls.

"The appliances," he said, pointing to the stove and oven, "are from a 1950s renovation when the apartment was put in. At first, it was for old Mrs. Carter's son who went to Hilly Dale College, but after that, she rented the place for extra income. Old houses like this need lots of work. This is where her niece Kismet was living when I bought the place. The old appliances work great. They knew how to make them back then."

Beck helped me off with my heavy coat and turquoise scarf, hanging them in a small kitchen closet. "This wasn't originally a closet," he said. "During the '50s renovation, Mrs. Carter wanted to create one to block off the stairs that went to the attic."

"Do you need any help with the meal?" I offered.

"No, thanks. I just have to plate everything. Make yourself at home in the living room. It's straight through there." He pointed to an open doorway. "You look beautiful, Jessie," he said, his eyes sweeping over my white fisherman's sweater, black wool trousers, and black riding boots. I'd worn my hair up to showcase a pair of ruby and diamond drop earrings, but I wished on the walk from the car to the building that I'd worn my hair down, or at least a knit cap. My ears were still cold.

"Thank you. You look nice, too." Beck was wearing a black sweater over faded jeans, making me feel overdressed, but that was the norm for me in Hilly Dale.

"There's a bottle of wine on the coffee table. Help yourself to a glass."

Within a couple of minutes I had shoved my gloves into my handbag, tossed it onto a battered-looking beige sofa, and stood warming my hands before a blazing fire. Beck had tried to create a romantic atmosphere in the small living room. There wasn't much light except that from two dim lamps on either end of the sofa, the fire, and one lone candle in the middle of a card table covered by a white cloth. I recognized the signature glassware and flatware from the restaurant. Picking up a glass, I walked over to the coffee table, poured Cabernet from the bottle he'd placed on a wooden tray, and took a seat on the sofa. The only thing spoiling the scene was the big screen television hanging on the wall across from a reclining chair. Just as I leaned over to take a closer look at one of Jordan's photos on an end table, Beck joined me carrying two soup plates.

"Well?" he asked. "Is this okay?"

"Yes, of course." I stood up and joined him at the table.

"Then let's eat." He set the soup plates down and pulled out a metal kitchen chair. "Also, from the '50s," he said, taking a seat in a matching chair opposite me. While the diners downstairs enjoyed a wonderful Valentine's dinner, Beck and I had a private one upstairs in his apartment.

"Are you certain you don't need to check on things downstairs?" I asked before taking a second bite of the delicious coq au vin that had been prepared for The Old House Restaurant's Valentine's Day menu.

"The manager will text me if there's a problem. How's the meal?"

I took another bite. "Fabulous. Was this the only choice for your guests tonight?"

"No, we have filet mignon with a salad, homemade rolls, roast potatoes, asparagus, and a dessert, but I figured a simple meal for us would be better."

I picked up a roll and spread a generous amount of butter on it. "This is beyond my expectations, Beck. Thank you."

"Anything for the Duchess of Hillbilly Dale," he teased and took a sip of wine.

"I can't believe I've been given that name, but I am surprised the fall-out wasn't worse." At some point, though, I assumed people would move on and find something else about which to gossip.

"It hasn't been easy, I imagine, turning down people seeking money," Beck said before slathering his own roll with butter.

"No, it hasn't. I'm not turning down so much as putting people off while I research the programs and projects, and some are worthy ones. I don't have much time to bother with it though, so I've been working with a woman named Debbie Doolittle who is in charge of Community Projects. What an unfortunate name for a woman who does so much."

"Yeah, I know her. She works with organizations to get funding, and she works with the local charities. I know she prefers to help those who are overshadowed by the obvious choices for donations, but sometimes she doesn't have a choice. She's been pushing for donations to overhaul the downtown."

"Hilly Dale's downtown does need some help. It's certainly changed since I lived here. I understand a need for modernization - London and other cities have certainly mingled the *very* old with the modern – but there's something special when a town utilizes what they already have and retains the small-town feel. I'm glad you kept the character of the Carter place."

"It's all about image, money, and quick profit for most. I didn't want to build a modern place. It wasn't cheap to renovate this house and outfit it for a restaurant, but it's worth it when I look around and see the transformation. It *will* take a while to make a profit though. Kismet was asking a reasonable price, given the location and history, but it had been sitting here for years and had no takers. She had to keep dropping the price. If I hadn't bought it, I suppose she would have had to let it fall to ruin when she could no longer afford basic care. Some townspeople and leaders would then complain about it being an eyesore and yet do nothing to help her. It's a shame. Hilly Dale is located in a beautiful area of the state and that means the opportunity to have a town that, with some motivation, inspiration, and help, might attract tourists."

"I agree, and wish I could do more, but I've started back on the next book in the *Celestial Cat* series, *Stars and Spikes Forever*, and I've also been working on the second in the *Snowdonia* series. I don't like working on multiple books at once, and now my agent says the publisher is wanting to postpone those two books and capitalize on *Harriet Donovan* instead. Usually, I do one book at a time about every six months. I just submitted the first book in my new series for publication too, so all of this is more than I can handle. Prolific is the new norm these days, but I don't crank them out. It takes time for me to craft the story."

"It shows, too. I read a couple of those *Harriet Donovans*."

"That surprises me. You're not my target audience."

"Why? You wrote the series and there were a couple around here that Jordan had. I figured you knew a little about the subject matter."

"Some of it, but I still had to do my own research about the era. I wasn't living in the early twentieth century. What did you think of them?"

"Easy read and pretty light-weight," he admitted. "I read the action-adventure genre. Harriet's not exactly someone you would find in a Clive Cussler novel."

"At least you read," I laughed when he got up from the table. "And I like Clive Cussler novels. I've read them all. Where are you going?"

"To get dessert."

He returned a few minutes later with two black-and-white parfaits topped with hot fudge and whipped cream served in small, old-fashioned parfait glasses. "I hope you're not too grand, Duchess, to allow me to remind you of your humble past." He set the glasses on the table.

Laughing, I exclaimed, "You remembered. We used to get these at Bricker's Ice Cream Palace. I think it was one of only a few places our parents let us go at that age."

"Yeah. We went there on a regular basis," he said and dipped his iced-tea spoon into the fudge sauce and vanilla ice-cream. I was polite and did the same, but I used to dig the long spoon Mr. Bricker supplied to the bottom for the chocolate ice cream first, dragging it upward making a mess."

"At least this is a mini version. I don't think I could eat one like Mr. Bricker served, especially not after the coq au vin and rolls. You have an excellent chef."

"Thanks. I'll tell him."

"This is nice," I said, before taking another bite of vanilla ice cream, making sure it was coated in fudge sauce, first. We ate the rest of our parfaits in silence and then Beck stood up, took my hand, and led me to the bedroom. The antique sleigh bed against the west wall was almost waving at me.

"Uh, Beckham?" We hadn't reached that level in our relationship…yet.

"No, ummm," he flushed. "I wanted to show you something I found. He led me to a section of the east wall, slid aside a panel, and exposed steps.

"Just like at Fielding House," I said in wonder.

"You're not the only one who has a house with a secret passage and history attached to it."

"Where does this lead?" I asked before following him down the first few steps. The bedroom's ceiling fixture cast enough light to guide us a short distance. I held onto his hand and picked my way down as we descended into darkness. "Don't you have a light on your phone?" I asked.

He shushed me. "I know the way," he whispered. "Be quiet and keep hold of my hand and use your other hand on the railing. Step when I step and keep your head down. This is another way downstairs. You couldn't see this area earlier. There's a hidden panel on both sides of the back stairwell, and we're behind one of them right now. He switched on his phone's light, so I could see the narrow, low-ceilinged space as we walked. "The kitchen closet blocks the other entrance to the stairs, and like I said, they go on to the attic".

We stopped on a landing where he shut off the light before whispering. "Take a look." Beck's breath was warm in my ear as we crouched under the ceiling next to a wall.

I found myself looking through two small holes into one of the dining rooms. Now I realized why a portrait was hanging just above the swinging door leading to the kitchen, and why the ceiling dropped suddenly. There was a hidden loft on one side, and I was looking through the eyes of one of those movable eyes paintings. Two dozen people were in the dining room just a few feet below me. Most were laughing, drinking, and eating Valentine's dinner. Heather and David were seated near the fireplace, but neither was speaking. Heather, who faced my direction, was staring at her plate so intensely that I wondered if something was wrong with her food.

Across the room, Betsy was there with her husband. I could hear her braying laugh over the crowd. Bianca was at a corner table near a front window with John Knoss, and Lucky Fine was at the next table with Duluth Hammond the nineteen-year-old Miss Pretty Pumpkin contestant he'd so admired. I turned and bumped into Beck. "God, they're all in the same room together! How can they stand it? The only missing ones are Steve and Shauna Taylor," I said in a low voice.

"Shhhh. They're in the other room. I saw them when I went down to pick up our dinner. Take my hand."

He turned and led me across the landing. "There's a peephole here that overlooks the kitchen."

When we went back upstairs, I turned on him, incredulous at what he'd shown me. "You *spy* on your employees and *guests*? That's illegal, Beck!"

"No. Jessie, no. I stumbled on this passage by accident. I was moving a piece of furniture and knocked a hole in the bedroom wall a couple of weeks ago. This house was built just before the Civil War. The Carters were pretty wealthy and had this space originally built to hide their valuables," he shared.

"I wondered about that obvious ceiling drop. I thought you had done that to make the interior more modern."

"Yeah, you're right, it does look that way. When I asked, the historical society knew all about the hidden passage, but Kismet never mentioned it. During the war, when the men were away fighting, the women would hide in there from bushwhackers. There's another hiding place above the other dining room, but it was closed off in the '50s renovation. The peepholes were to see if it was safe. The painting was added as a cover up. Kismet insisted it remain when I bought the place and not to disturb it, so I didn't. Unlike the Tardis on your famous pajamas, the inside of this place looks *smaller* than the outside."

"That's interesting. No wonder there were rumors about this house when we were growing up. Think of the tales it could tell. The places I've lived have had their share of stories, too."

"Did you see any ghosts? I know that girl asked you that at the reading, but tell me the truth, did you see any?"

"No, I may have felt some odd things. I'd be willing to bet there were some in the house in Cornwall. I never did like that place, other than the sea view."

"I'd like to see those passages in Fielding House," he murmured. "The place sounds incredible."

"Someday, perhaps. Jackson got lost in one. Liam had to rescue him," I said, settling back on the sofa while Beck moved the table and chairs where they belonged. "Jackson believes there is a dungeon somewhere under the house, left over from the castle days. It's possible, of course, but I'm not sure I want to know for certain."

We sat on the sofa watching the fire, telling stories, laughing about old times, and drinking brandy, until Beck suddenly leaned over and kissed me, not like the friendly pecks of late, but a real kiss - one that was passionate and lingering. Looking questioningly at me, he stood up and took my hand. We walked to the bedroom. This time it was not to look at the wall panel but to visit the sleigh bed. Maybe it was the brandy, the nostalgia, the talk of my life in England, loneliness, my missing Will and my family, or all of it, but Beck and I became more than friends a short time later.

Chapter Twenty-Five

"You can spend the night," Beck said, watching me pull on my sweater.

"I'd rather go home," I replied. "I don't want anyone seeing me leave later. I'm already the talk of the town." How could I tell him that this was an emotional time for me? Beck was the first man I'd slept with since Will, and I was very unsure of my feelings about it. It almost felt like I was betraying my husband.

He acquiesced and at nearly 2:00 a.m., walked me downstairs, out the front door, and onto the front porch where a magical scene awaited. The lampposts' lanterns cast pools of gold in the snow that spread out before us. Limbs creaked, making the still-falling snow sparkle and dance from the fairy lights that were wound along bare branches. A slight rushing sound of the creek could be heard below us.

"I can drive you home," Beck offered.

"Thanks, but the snow's not deep and there doesn't seem to be any ice," I replied. "I think it just started a short time ago, and it's not that far to my house. I'll be all right. I'm used to inclement weather."

"Just be sure to call me when you get home."

In the center of the footbridge, he stopped, pulled me to him, and started to give me a lingering kiss, but we broke apart when we heard voices.

"Where are they?" I whispered.

"I don't know. Sound travels over water."

"But at this hour and in this cold? Who would be out at 2:00 a.m. in the snow?" I whispered.

"We are," he said quietly. "Let's wait here a moment."

So we stood there, wrapped in each other's arms to, well, let's be honest, keep warm at this point. The sound of a shout and splash made us both jump, causing me to slip on the bridge's sandy-snow mix. Before I sank to the floor, I caught sight of something being carried by the water. It didn't look like a limb.

"Are you hurt?" Beck asked helping me up.

"No," I said, brushing my hands down my backside, but there's something in the water. Go look on the other side of the bridge," I cried.

"In the twinkling lights, a man could be seen riding the current face-up out from under the bridge. Beck walked as swiftly as he could to the end, calling out, "9-1-1, and find something warm to wrap him in," before he disappeared down the slippery slope to the creek.

"Beck?" He was gone, and then I heard another splash. Pulling out my phone, I called for help, and then hurried as best I could across the road to my car. There were a couple of blankets in the backseat that I'd been meaning to take to a charity shop in town.

"He's alive," Beck said when I joined him. "It's John Knoss, Jessie." He began wrapping John in the blankets.

The air felt very cold all of a sudden. The wind blowing through the trees had an eerie, high-pitched, wailing sound for a couple of minutes, and the fairy lights swung, throwing odd patterns of light. I shivered, but then looked at Beck who was minus his jacket. I could see it was dry and under John's head. Beck was soaked from pulling John from the creek.

"Beck, take my coat."

"It's okay. You keep it. As soon as the police arrive, I'll go upstairs and change clothes. Shouldn't be long," he said, teeth chattering. I handed him my scarf and he wrapped it around his neck.

"I'll get my car and we can try to get him in there while we wait," I offered. "We need to keep you both warm." I wrapped my arms around him.

"No, We shouldn't move him. I think his arm is broken, and there may be other injuries. Probably hit a rock or snagged a limb when he went around the bend. One trouser leg is torn."

The ambulance arrived with flashing lights – no siren. Right after, the police showed up. Beck and I went inside the restaurant to wait for an officer. I sent Beck upstairs to take a shower and change into warm, dry clothes. Still wearing my coat, I sat at a table in the dining room sipping a cup of tea. A few minutes later a police officer joined me.

"Oh, it's you," he said, a surprised look on his face. "I'm Officer Pincera, Ms, Your..." he hesitated at what to call me.

"Jessica," I said. "Would you like a cup of tea or coffee?"

"Coffee, sure. Thanks." He rubbed his gloved hands together.

"Come with me into the kitchen. It's warmer in there." I grabbed a mug, filled it with water and stuck it in the microwave to heat. "The coffee's instant, I'm afraid. I don't know how to work these fancy machines."

"Instant's fine with me. Freezing out there. Where's Mr. Hailey?"

"He's upstairs changing clothes. He went into the water. How *is* Mr. Knoss?"

"He'll survive, but we'll know more after the E.R. doctor takes a closer look at him," the young officer said.

"He must have fallen." I handed him the mug of coffee.

"Or maybe he was pushed," Beck offered, coming through the door, drying his damp hair with a towel.

"Why do you say that?" Officer Pincera asked after taking a sip of the coffee.

"Only that moments before, we heard voices that sounded to me like women, so it was a surprise to discover John in the water," Beck told him as he accepted a mug of coffee.

"Have any idea where they were?"

"Upstream, I guess, but that's about it."

"I mean how far."

"No idea."

"What about the iron bridge?" I suggested. "It would have been slippery by now. You can't sand it because it's a mesh deck, at least that's the way I remember it. Could he have been crossing it, slipped, and fallen under the railing?"

"Why do you think he'd be on that bridge?" Pincera questioned.

"I haven't been up there in years, but I understand that area has been turned into a small park," I answered.

"And what were you two doing out at that time?"

Beck and I looked at each other. We had to tell the truth.

"I was walking Jessica to her car. We'd had supper and she was just leaving."

"At 2:00 a.m.?"

"Yes," Beck and I said in unison.

The officer nodded his head in understanding. "Mr. Hailey, it's common knowledge that your wife has been having an affair with Mr. Knoss," he stated." Is there any bad blood between you and Mr. Knoss?"

"No. John was once a good friend. Bianca and I have been separated for two years, and John's daughter is a close friend of my daughter Jordan. In fact, Bianca signed the divorce papers on Valentine's Day."

"Just yesterday?"

"Yes."

"What made her decide to sign then?"

"I have no idea. A Valentine's gift to me or to herself?"

"Was this a fault divorce?"

"No. Separation-based."

"Mutual?"

"Yes. What are you getting at?"

"Just trying to piece together what happened tonight. You both need to come to the station, make statements, and sign them," Officer Pincera said, getting up. "I need to get back out there. We're searching the area."

"To the station?" I asked.

"Preferable."

"Would you give me a moment to freshen-up, please?" I asked.

"Of course. Thanks for the coffee." The officer got up and left Beck and me in the kitchen.

"I just need to use the restroom. I'll use the one down here," I said, heading for the kitchen door.

"Jessie, wait a second. I need to tell you this."

"What? I really do need to go, Beck. You had time to wash and, well…" I didn't hear what he was going to say because I was already to the hallway entrance.

He caught up to me. "Just a second." He reached inside the fresh, down-filled jacket he was carrying and pulled out something gold and sparkly, dangling it in front of me.

"For me? Oh, no. I don't want any gifts."

Beck turned red. "I found this in John's inside jacket pocket after I dragged him from the water. I'd unzipped his jacket to check him and saw a part of a gold chain hanging out. Take a look."

"It's lovely," I said taking in the heart-shaped gold and diamond pendant hanging from a gold chain. "I think it's 18 karat."

"Look on the back."

"I can't read it, Beck. I need my readers. Just a minute." I dug around in my handbag, found them, and studied the back of the pendant. The word 'Memories' was etched in silver. "Who was this for?"

"I don't know." Beck took the pendant from me and turned it over and over in his hands. "This doesn't sound like a sentiment for a daughter, so Bianca or Betsy, maybe."

"You've got to give this to the police," I said, opening the restroom's door. "Now it's got both our fingerprints on it."

"I know, and I am. I'm going to warm up the truck."

When I stepped out of the restroom, Beck was gone. I picked up a tablecloth from the floor, opened the closet to toss it out of the way, and jumped back in alarm, dropping the cloth on the floor. Standing in front of me, her back pressed against the shelves in the small closet, stood Bianca Hailey, her blonde hair a mess, her face pale, and her eyes wild.

"Jessie, don't scream," she said. "I'm not here to hurt anyone."

I had to sit down. Having no chair at the ready, I chose the third step on the staircase. When my heart stopped racing, I asked, "You gave me such a fright. Bianca, what are you doing in here?" Although I knew it was too early for the news about John to be out, I asked anyway for something to say. The look in her eyes surprised me. She *knew*.

"You were one of the voices Beck and I heard," I stated. "Were you with John when he fell in the creek?"

"I need help. Get Beck," she said, ignoring my question. "He's the only one who can help me."

"I don't know about that, Bianca," Beck's deep voice rang out. "Jessie, are you okay?"

"Jessie, Jessie. It's always been Jessie for you. Little nerdy Jessie, but she got your goat when you dumped her. Look at her now. She's a duchess," Bianca sniped. "Trying to win her back now that she's rich?"

"Bianca, this is not the time for your petty comments. What's going on? What are you even doing here? Your lover is in the hospital. You should be with him."

"Beck, she may be in shock." I stood up, took off my coat, and tried to drape it over her shoulders, but she shrugged it off.

"My lover? My fiancé as of Valentine's dinner, but I'm not in *shock* now! I'm angry! And that pendant you were talking about? I don't know who it's for, but it wasn't for me. Look!" She held out her hand. There on the third finger of her left-hand was a diamond ring – a large, round stone set between two smaller ones.

"You're engaged!" I cried.

"Yes. If John was giving me anything tonight, it was this ring, not some pendant with - what did you say was on it – *Memories*. I didn't even know it was John you pulled out of the creek, until I heard you all talking. I didn't see anyone except…" She closed her eyes and grimaced.

"You were hiding in the closet the whole time we were here?" Beck asked, not even addressing the engagement.

"Not the whole time, just when Pincera showed up. I had to hide somewhere."

"Did you push John into the water?" I asked, horrified.

"No, like I said, I didn't know John was even out there, yet. And even if I did, why would I push him in the creek? We'd just gotten engaged, but I *might* have been tempted if I'd known he was giving someone else a pendant. All that to-do at the restaurant tonight with the engagement! I didn't know he was seeing someone else, and now everyone's going to think he was cheating on me. *Me!*"

"You don't know he was cheating. The pendant could have been for you, or maybe for Allison. You're in shock," I said again.

"No!" she shouted at me. "Stay out of this. It has nothing to do with you, *Your Grace*, unless you're the one John's involved with."

"That's enough, Bianca. What happened to John?" Beck snapped.

No response as she glared at her ex-husband.

"You need to go to the police station and tell them what you know. Jessie and I are on our way there. We'll just tell them we found you hiding in the house. It may look bad for you if they determine John had help going in the water. You know it's been snowing and there will be tracks wherever you and John were."

"Beck, please, for Jordan," Bianca begged. "I wasn't alone, but I wasn't with John. I was with…Betsy. We were at the park not far from the bridge. I got a valentine with the message to meet John there between 1:30 and 2:00. When Betsy showed up, I assumed she was playing a prank on me because John and I got engaged, until we heard a cry and a splash and then…."

"The iron bridge?" I asked.

"Well what other bridge is around here, besides the one outside the restaurant. Of course, the iron bridge. I guess John was on it at one point but *I* wasn't."

"So you, Betsy, and John were out there?" I asked in disbelief. "In this weather? What were you doing?"

"Why are you part of this?" she snapped at me. "Beck, please, for Jordan. I can't say anything."

I saw him hesitate and I butted right in, "If you didn't do anything wrong, you have nothing to fear."

"I don't know about *that*," she said.

"Bianca, tell it to the police. You need to leave. In fact, we're all leaving. Us to the police station and you either to the police station or to the hospital. John needs you."

"No, if that pendant means anything, it seems he really doesn't, but I'll go for the sake of appearances and after that, I'll go to the police."

"You have to tell the police you were there," Beck told her as we walked to the staff entrance in back. "I knew you were here or somewhere nearby when I went to warm up the truck a few minutes ago. I saw your car. The police will have seen it, too."

On the way to the police station, Beck said, "You know, it's going to get out that you were here until 2:00 a.m., Jessie."

"And *I* told you that I wanted to go home so no one would see me in the morning. Turns out I should have stayed and avoided all of this," I said, laughing nervously. "It doesn't matter now, because John Knoss could have died! That water was freezing, and if he hit his head on one of the rocks...," I stopped talking and fought to control my trembling as I flashbacked to Will's accident.

Although I didn't see the body – Alistair wouldn't let me – I knew that Will's broken body had been washed far up on a beach a day after the sailing accident. It had been found by a couple of tourists who had ventured out after the previous day's storm to see the waves still coming in.

"The police need the pendant. I should have given it to Officer Pincera when he was there," Beck muttered, his voice bringing me out of the pit where I'd momentarily descended.

"Bianca was right. They had just gotten engaged. Why would he give her a pendant with that word on it? Maybe it was for Betsy. She didn't mention where Betsy was after they heard the splash, and we didn't see her anywhere around," I said.

"I'm going to try to see John at the hospital later today. Hopefully, he'll shed some light on things."

Chapter Twenty-Six

It was 4:30 in the morning when Beck dropped me off. He'd offered to come in, but all I wanted was a shower and sleep. It had been an evening of emotional ups and downs. At the police station, we'd gone over our stories, separately, and signed our statements. Beck confessed he'd found a pendant in John's pocket and turned it over. We both mentioned Bianca and said she was distraught, presumably over John's condition. It was up to her to talk to the police about the hows and whys she was in The Old House Restaurant's hall closet and what she knew. Anything we said was merely speculation, and she hadn't told us much.

Violet greeted me at the door. Picking her up, I wearily climbed the stairs, deposited her on my bed and headed for the bathroom. By 5:00 a.m. I was asleep, but that didn't last long. The despised ringing of my landline phone startled me awake. It was 9:00 a.m. and the caller was Heather.

"Oh my God! What happened to John Knoss?" she screeched in my ear. "David and I had dinner at the restaurant last night. John and Bianca were there, looking pretty cozy, and then John got down on one knee and proposed! Why on earth were they celebrating Valentine's Day at Beck's place, and why did John choose to propose *there*! I can't believe it! He's *marrying* her? I mean, proposing to your girlfriend at her soon-to-be ex-husband's restaurant and in front of your own ex-wife? Ta*cky*! "

"I didn't see it," I replied, yawning.

"Well, maybe not, but it's all over town that you and Beck found John, and at two in the morning! I can't believe you spent the *night* with him! And you can't deny it this time, Jessie. Did Bianca know that you were going to be there?"

"Heather," I said in a sleepy voice, "Please, just stop with the questions. I'm exhausted. I've had about four hours sleep." Violet, hearing my voice bounded into my room and leaped on my bed, meowing loudly for her late breakfast.

"Is that your cat, or is Beck there with you?"

"What? No! I can't talk about this. I was at the police station until nearly 4:30 this morning. Frankly, I don't see how it's all over town this quickly."

"Well, gossip flies when it's good," she said, "and this is *good*. People have police radios, and police have spouses who talk. I heard Gatsby Gregson was on the scene, but it must have been after you went to the police station. You know, Gatsby's wife is my third cousin on my mother's side," she rattled.

I wanted to scream at her to stop talking, but I didn't have the energy. All I could manage was to tell her that Bianca had signed the divorce papers yesterday, so at least that would end speculations of me with a married man.

"Has Beck been accused of anything?" she asked, suddenly serious. "Oh, I know he wouldn't have done anything, but the divorce, the proposal, and the accident -or whatever it was- came at the same time, so it might look suspicious, since he was her husband for years."

"Done what? Why would Beck be accused? *No one* has been accused of anything. Let the police figure this out. I don't think they know for certain how John ended up in the creek."

"My cousin said Gatsby told her that John was on the iron bridge and went through a damaged section. That bridge has a mesh deck, and it was snowing and windy when he was there, so it would have been slick. John could easily have fallen and slid into the water, accidentally, I mean. And," she paused either to catch her breath, or for dramatic effect, "David and I noticed he was drinking last night. What kind of fool goes out on a night like that and onto that old bridge?"

"Uh-huh," I murmured, switching the phone to my other ear and wondering how to get her to stop talking.

"Well, who wouldn't drink if they had to put up with Bianca, but he *proposed* to her! No accounting for taste! Disgusting!"

"Ummm, Heather, I need to…"

Ignoring my attempt to end the conversation, she continued, "Anyway, I saw Steve and Shauna there. She was wearing one of those skin-tight 'naked' dresses and spike heels in *that* weather…"

"Heather, STOP!" I cried. "Thanks for waking me up, now my cat's wanting breakfast and I'll have to get up. We'll talk when I have time to gather my thoughts. And, please, do not spread stories about Beck and me." I disconnected without saying goodbye. I liked Heather, but she gossiped too much.

In a surly mood, I threw on my robe and slippers. Trudging downstairs I fed the cat and put the kettle on. A few minutes later, I was sipping tea and looking out the window. The sun was shining and dead grass was already showing through an inch or so of snow that was left. At 10:30, Aunt Jane-Ann rang, but I wasn't ready for her two-cents. Carrying my tea upstairs, I set the cup and phone on the nightstand. Before I could even pull the duvet over me, I heard my phone ping. A text. I couldn't catch a break this morning, but at least the text was from Liam.

Hiya, Mum. Happy Late Valentine's Day! Got your message. Sorry I didn't ring yesterday. Out with a new girl. Bethany Bowman. Met her at a party a week ago.

Liam sounded cheerful. I texted back everything was fine. No sense letting the children know about last night, but I suspected Allison or Jordan would get in touch with Aisling sooner or later. Now that I was fully awake, I got up, tidied the kitchen, and then spent the rest of the time lazing on the sofa and watching television until Beck rang in the middle of the afternoon. His call, I gladly answered.

"Hey," he said. "How are you?"

"At the moment, tired," I replied, stifling a yawn. "Heather woke me at 9:00 this morning wanting information and telling me what she had heard. It was difficult going back to sleep after that. Any news about John?"

"A little, but first, your car is still in the parking lot across from the restaurant."

"Oh, that's right. I have Aisling's. I'll get mine as soon as I can."

"I'll come get you later, so you can pick it up."

"All right. "Did you talk to Bianca this morning? I hope she went to the police station with any information," I said.

"Yes, she did."

"So, she admitted to being one of the women arguing?"

"She had to. The police found Betsy hiding behind a bush in the park and she told them she was with Bianca."

"So was *she* on the bridge with John?"

"Neither one admits to that, but both women went there allegedly to meet him. Bianca, as you know, left her car at the restaurant and walked to the park, thinking John would drive her home."

"Quite foolish to walk the trail alone at night."

"Yeah, I agree, but Bianca takes chances all the time. Betsy's somewhat cautious; however, she still went to meet John at the park."

"At 2:00 a.m.? Was it about the pendant?"

"Hold on, Miss Marple, give me a chance here. This is what I know. Bianca and John arrived separately at the restaurant. I was covering the front until my hostess got back from the restroom. I saw Bianca enter alone, and I seated her. This morning, Bianca said she was to meet him at her house a little later that night for a private celebration, except when she got home after dinner, there was a red envelope on her door with a valentine from John. It included a note asking her to meet him at the park with the iron bridge instead. Apparently, they were into…um…*games*."

"Didn't need to know *that* part, Beck."

"It explains why she was out at the time," he said. "Turns out, Betsy got a similar valentine, but her message said he needed to talk to her privately about Allison and Bianca, otherwise she wouldn't have shown up. Peter knew she was going, so she felt safe."

"I understand that, but at 2:00 a.m. in a deserted park."

"Let me finish. Bianca and Betsy were pranksters in school. When they both showed up, they thought the other was pulling a prank and got into an argument. Bianca said she thought Betsy was getting back at her after the public proposal."

"It had to have been awkward for Betsy, and for you."

"Whatever. It is what it is. The gist is that they weren't paying attention to their surroundings until they heard a cry followed by a splash, so they turned and walked closer to the creekbank. Bianca said all they saw from the lamplights closest to the bridge on each end, was another person slowly walking away. Betsy called out and the person who was wearing heavy clothes turned and sang a nursery song in a reedy voice. The women were too startled to do anything but stare. After the person stepped off the bridge, Bianca said they heard high-pitched laughter, and then silence. She could just make out that the person headed north on the trail."

"Oh, Beck," I cried. "They heard someone call out and then the splash. They didn't check to see if anyone was in the water and didn't even call for help?"

"The women were afraid because they never saw John. They thought there was a crazy person on the loose in the park and ran for their lives. Bianca had a key to the restaurant. She wanted to hide somewhere safe and talk to me, but you and Officer Pincera were there, so she hid, hoping you would both leave."

"She could have talked to the officer and let him know what happened."

"I really think she was in shock, although she didn't admit to that. She was scared."

"What did the person sing?"

"Something that almost sounded like *London Bridge is Falling Down*."

I felt a sudden chill run down my spine. "Remember when I told you how I got the name of my first series?"

"Yeah. It was after the reunion and we were talking about Jasmine Hall being an astrophysicist."

"Yes, that's right. In my first book in *The Celestial Cat* mystery, *The Bridges of Cassiopeia*, a couple of characters are pushed off bridges around the small town of Cassiopeia Falls. I got the town's name from stargazing, but the idea about the bridges stemmed from those around Hilly Dale. In the story, the killer sang verses of *London Bridge* after pushing the victims into the water. The verses had to do with how the bridges were built. I used a swinging one and an *iron one*. The latter was based on the one in the park."

"Jessie, I know you have an *excellent* imagination, but no one killed John. Bianca said he told her that he fell and the lower iron bar gave way."

"It's been a long time since I was there. If I remember correctly, it's a truss bridge and there are only two bars running along the sides with scattered triangular units, which is exactly what I used in my book. John wasn't killed, but he *could* have died from drowning. He was wearing a winter jacket that could have dragged him under if he'd been a weaker man, or he could have hit his head on a rock when he went around the bend just north of the restaurant, or he could have died from hypothermia if we hadn't been nearby."

"That's a lot of 'could haves', but…"

"You said Betsy and Bianca liked to play pranks in school. You can't automatically rule them out just because one's your ex-wife and the other an old friend."

"They wouldn't pull something like this, and why would they? Betsy divorced John years ago and Bianca's going to *marry* him, plus they were together when John went in the water."

"All right. Isn't it possible that someone's intention was not to kill John but to torment him for some reason? Perhaps a prank that went wrong. Maybe Betsy *was* involved and hired someone to scare Bianca and John. That's not unheard of. There are television shows devoted to pranking others. Betsy was there when he and Bianca got engaged. If not her then, maybe John has some enemies who wanted to scare him, or maybe it was just an accident."

"John *has* upset a few people in town, and he hasn't always been on the up-and-up, so I guess it's possible, but it seems childish."

"*You* suggested to Officer Pincera that John was pushed into the water. Why? And why was he on the bridge in the first place where he could have easily slipped?"

"I don't know." Beck sounded annoyed with me. "I'm going to see John in a few minutes. Do you want to come? I could pick you up and you could get your car after we see him."

"No. I'm not up to it today," I replied testily. Excellent imagination! In other instances, that would have been a compliment, but not in this one. Beck was discounting my input. "You go on and let me know what you find out."

"Okay. And, Jessie, we had a nice time last night, let's not spoil *that* part with trying to solve a murder that wasn't even committed. It's all fine. John's going to be okay. Maybe it *was* a prank gone wrong and Betsy or John himself was behind it. Perhaps the other person who was supposedly with him got scared when John hit the water. The police will figure it out. Only those involved have the answers. You're not one of the characters in your books who solves crimes the police can't, and we aren't sure a crime was actually committed. I'll let you know if John sheds light on anything."

Needing to take my mind off what had happened last night – and not just poor John Knoss – I checked my email and followed up with my media accounts. Everything looked all right today, except my fan page was full of ugly comments by 'Krazy for Keasden' that were posted this afternoon. I didn't want to ban anyone, but this might be a first. My fans were taking the poster to task, but it was disruptive for what was usually a genial place.

After a frustrating hour trying to come up with an idea for the new *Harriet Donovan* book my publisher wanted quickly, I shut down the computer, leaned my chin on my cupped hands, closed my eyes, and tried to figure out how to manage everything, but flashbacks of the previous night with Beck interfered with my thought process.

Sleeping with Beck had been nice. I knew Will would want me to be happy with someone else, and had the situation been reversed, I would have wanted that for him, but I had no idea what my feelings for Beck were. I'd only been in Hilly Dale a short time and Beck and I hadn't spent a lot of it together. Was I using him to help me cope with all the stress? The fact that we had found his ex-wife's new fiancé injured and half-frozen in the creek by Beck's restaurant, followed by my encounter with Bianca gave me pause. I didn't want to be part of a scandal, particularly when I was being called 'The Duchess of Hillbilly Dale' and made to look like I was ridiculing my hometown.

After preparing a light lunch, I took it to the office, and closed the door to prevent Violet from entering while I enjoyed my meal in peace. As soon as I sat down, the call I dreaded came for the second time today. I had to get it over with.

My aunt read me the riot act for 'getting caught spending the night with Beckham Hailey *at his house*.' I wanted to ask her if she thought it would have been better had we been at that run-down motel with the little cottages just outside of town, but instead I took a bite of my turkey and let her harangue me. I didn't have the energy to fight with her. It was none of her business, but then she *had* to bring up John Knoss.

"What on earth happened with John? Everyone says he was drunk and fell off the bridge. Why on earth was he out there at that time of the night?" A second later she answered her own question with a dig at me, "Well, I suppose anything's possible since you were with Beckham at 2:00 a.m.! And Bianca Hailey was there too. Don't you go around acting like her, Jessica. I don't know how you lived your life in England, but this is NOT how the Jensons and Whitley's acted, and it was not how you were reared."

Reared. Another word I disliked. It made no sense and sounded like you had been rear-ended in an accident.

After taking a sip of water, I shifted in my great-grandfather Jenson's banker's chair, looked at the framed photos of my parents that were atop my great-grandfather Whitley's barrister bookcase, and finally answered. "I couldn't say. I don't know how any of you acted when you were younger."

"Jessica Carola Jen - whatever your name is now - that's an awful thing to say. The Jensons and the Whitleys were pillars of this community, and you know it. Don't you go sully our reputation."

Funny she was not thinking of her own late husband who did plenty of sullying. I had a feeling he was more than a gambler. You couldn't tell me with a wife like my aunt that he didn't have a little something-on-the-side waiting in the wings.

"This is such an embarrassment, Jessica. You should have called me first thing this morning to warn me, like you did when your secret life in England came out. At least I was able to save face and say I'd known all along. When everyone called this morning and began talking, I was in shock. I had to say that I knew you had been dating Beckham, a *married man*, for a couple of months. That was bad enough, but for you to be caught canoodling with him on a bridge in the middle-of-the night and then get mixed up in his wife's drama, that was just too much. I don't think I can show my face."

Oh, I bet she could. She'd be the center of attention. "Who is this 'everyone' you talk about?"

"What? Oh, Margo Hunter was the first to call, and then, of course, all the book club members called, except Betsy. She was part of it, and let me tell you, that's mortifying for the club, but *you've* become an issue for the garden club. They want to rescind your invitation to join. They've never done that in all the years I've been a member. The shame, Jessica. The shame!"

I bit into a sour pickle. Fitting

The shame. I was reminded of my mother-in-law and sister-in-law after I brought Aisling home from school in Switzerland a year early. They'd said the same thing.

"Are you there, Jessica?"

I swallowed the bite. "Yes, and I really don't see how this is so embarrassing for *you*. I'm the one who was 'caught,' with Beckham, not you. And as for your book club and your garden club's gossiping…"

"They don't gossip. They were concerned about me. And whether you think so or not, having lived *your* life over *there*, I have to live in this town. Whatever you do affects me here. The shame of having your invitation rescinded…and over your dalliance with a married man and then mixed-up in some scandal involving his wife and John Knoss!" she said again. "One of my friends asked if you, Beck, John and his fiancé were *swinging* together! I nearly died!

"Of course not! That's offensive, Aunt Jane-Ann. I was never going to join, if that's any consolation."

"It's not. That would have been another embarrassment. NO ONE turns down an invitation to the Hilly Dale Garden Club. Those invitations are not handed out willy-nilly." And on it went …*Blah, blah, blah.*

"Aunt Jane-Ann," I interrupted, fed up with her attitude, "perhaps you should step down off your self-absorbed high-horse and think about Jordan Hailey and Allison Knoss for a change. *They* are the innocents caught up in this mess. Now, I want to finish my meal and go to bed. I'm exhausted. Goodbye."

Hmmmm. As I set the phone back in its charger, an idea formed in my mind about the two girls. I'd mention it to Beck the next time I saw him. It might have been 6:30 p.m., but as soon as I reached my room, I fell into bed.

Chapter Twenty-Seven

Jackson Barker, ever-prompt, arrived at 8:30 a couple of days later to go with me to Walmart. Because my car was small and I liked to stock up to reduce the number of trips I made, Jackson and I often scheduled our Walmart runs together.

"Of course I heard all about what happened," he said after I joined him in his black SUV. "How are you doing?"

"To tell you the truth, I'm exasperated. Has Hilly Dale always been this nosy, or is it just because I was young when I lived here, or is it because *I'm* different now? We have scandals in Hearthestone Vale. There have been affairs among our set of associates and friends. The latter are usually tabloid fodder and may or may not be correct, but I've never seen anything like what goes on in Hilly Dale."

"A microcosm of small-town America? Boredom? That's all I have to offer. I moved here to teach after you left, At first when I arrived from Boston, I was talked about. Oh, nothing like you, but I was, well, different. For a while, people tried to fix me up with this or that eligible woman, but eventually they got the message and now they accept me, leaving me alone in that area. It's none of their business anyway. I don't care about *their* personal lives. If I meet someone, I meet someone. If I don't, well, that's how it goes and I'll be content. Your mother never bothered me about anything, which is why we became great friends."

"My mother always worried about you. She wanted you to be happy." I studied Jackson's neat, trim appearance and thought about his charming mannerisms. He deserved someone special, but that wasn't going to happen in a place like Hilly Dale. He'd already made his preferences clear and they went against the grain for some.

"I am happy...in my way. Hilly Dale is peaceful enough, with just a touch of drama every now-and-then to keep things interesting, and I love my house. After The Old House Restaurant, mine is the oldest restored property in town." Jackson lived in another pre-Civil War era house south of the restaurant. It was a simple two-story white-painted plank and river rock home with a wide front porch and tin roof. The entire property was surrounded by a low rock wall.

"Just think," Jackson continued, "if Beckham hadn't jumped in to save John, that poor man's body would have floated past my house. I doubt John would have been alive at that point. The water had to be freezing."

"I don't think he was floating. John was wearing a winter jacket, so he was fortunate to break the surface. I think he was floundering and happened to end up face-up riding the current when he got close to the footbridge. He had a broken arm, and I don't know what all else was wrong. On another note, you wouldn't have been up at that time to see him," I said.

"You're right. I'm an early-to-bed, early-to-rise individual. It's the teacher in me. I've always been up before dawn for as long as I can remember. I'm more productive at that time. I'm in bed by 8:30, but I always make time for reading."

"What is it this time?" I asked as we drove along.

"Thomas Wolfe's *You Can't Go Home Again*."

"I didn't read it in uni., but I was drawn to the title when I saw it in the bookcase at home. It's on my nightstand in the 'to read' pile. I'm starting to think the title is apropos."

"I have to see a thing a thousand times before I see it once," Jackson burst out. The man seemed to have a quote for everything, much like my mother had, and he was a walking encyclopedia on history as I'd discovered when we were in England.

"What's that?" I asked, sitting up straight in the vehicle. "What did you say?"

"It's a quote I like from the novel." Jackson turned off the main road and headed along Rush Street. The local Walmart was visible just ahead. "If you would read it…"

"I've been working on my own novels. I've got two going at once and now the publisher is asking me to stop those and is pushing for a new *Harriet Donovan*. There's something about that quote though…" my voice trailed off.

"Pardon?"

"Oh, nothing. It just reminded me how we can notice someone or something every day, and yet all it takes is *one* thing to happen before you see whatever it is you are meant to see for what it truly is."

"Sort of like 'you can't see the forest for the trees?'"

"Something like that, but not quite."

"Are you talking about you and Beckham?" Jackson steered into a parking space and shut off the SUV's engine. "I know you two were close as kids, but after what happened the other night and your…ummm…how do I put this delicately…your shag-fest, are you upping the relationship ante?"

"What? Shag-fest? Jackson!" I cried. "That's NOT putting it delicately. And no, that's not exactly what I'm talking about. I'm referring to life in Hilly Dale in general." I opened the door and got out.

"Now, Jessica, you know I'm not judging you," Jackson said, joining me in the parking lot. "I certainly couldn't, even if I wanted to, but this is a small town. You have to remember that."

"A small town where a *number* of people are engaging in shag-fests it seems."

"But not everyone here is famous. You're both a well-known author and, more importantly, a duchess, and a wealthy one at that. It's news. It's probably the biggest news that has, and will ever, come out of Hilly Dale, Arkansas. You've surpassed Lucky Fine in terms of interest right now."

I grabbed a couple of sanitizing wipes from the dispenser. "Here, let me get your shopping cart," I said, tugging on the front of one of the large ones.

"Thanks." The shopping cart was stuck and he helped me tug it loose. After that, he yanked on another one which came hurtling toward us. We wiped down the handlebars and baskets.

"At least I've learned to use 'cart' instead of 'trolley,' I've caught myself switching between American and British expressions, and speech patterns. Will said it was part of my charm. I had the same trouble when dining my first few years in England. I used the American zig-zag method with knife-and-fork. Switching the fork to the other hand after cutting, I mean. One of my flatmates teased me by saying I was arsing about with my fork when we were on a mini-break in York."

Jackson guffawed. "Arsing about with a fork in York! Now, *that* would make for an excellent limerick line."

I paused from wiping my cart, looked at Jackson, and replied." Yes, I suppose a risqué one. "It took me a while to stop arsing, and now I'm back in Hilly Dale and am trying to zig-zag again. just so I won't embarrass my aunt. She'd think I was shoveling my food, otherwise."

"You have a new skill, Jessica. You're bi-fork or ambiforkstrious."

"Jackson!"

"I was coming up with a limerick. I'll recite it when I've completed it."

"Please don't," I begged before pushing my cart past the greeter.

Walmart wasn't crowded at this hour and we shopped with ease. I was just examining the poultry offerings when Jackson grabbed my arm, causing me to drop the package of tenderloins into the case.

"What if it was a set-up?" he said quietly.

"What? I imagine they set the poultry selections…"

"No, Jessica, don't be a dolt. I'm talking about the other night."

I reached in the case again, picked up the tenderloins, and placed them in the basket. "The other night?" I started to push the cart toward the dairy case, but Jackson stopped me.

Looking around to see if anyone was within earshot and seeing no one nearby, he said, "Think about it. There's Beckham and you standing on the restaurant's bridge. There's Bianca and Betsy on the creekbank, and there's John apparently on the iron bridge, supposedly with someone. You're all conveniently placed, but for what reason?"

"Aren't you Jessica Keasden that author and duchess?" a young woman wearing a zipped Hilly Dale Hillbillies hoodie over a pair of faded jeans asked shyly. She was pushing a cart with a young child sitting in the main basket.

"Yes, I am," I replied, becoming used to this now.

"Could I have your autograph?" She pulled a worn paperback from her handbag. It was one of the early *Harriet Donovan* novels.

"Of course." I took the novel and the pen she handed me and asked for her name. I scrawled *To Ellie, Jessica Keasden* on the title page.

The girl thanked me and then said, "Can you sign it with your real name? Your duchess name?"

"I'm sorry, but I can't do that."

"Her Grace does not sign autographs, young lady," Jackson said in an imperious tone. "It's simply not done."

The woman looked askance at me. "I'm sorry," I told her. "He is correct, and anyway, Jessica Keasden wrote the book, so that's how I have to sign it. I don't think my publisher would want me to sign it any other way." I highly doubted Joe Fornot would mind at all. In fact, he'd probably be delighted. More publicity.

"Could I get a selfie then?"

"Not today, Ellie. This is my private time."

"Oh, I understand. Thank you. I love your books. My mother is in the local book club. You might know her. Adelaide Turnfell?"

"I'm sure I met her when I did a reading several months ago."

"Oh, I know you did. She said it was wonderful. Thanks." She smiled and maneuvered her cart past ours.

"Does that happen a lot?" Jackson asked.

"In Hilly Dale. The fact is, though, I haven't been out since the news broke about my title, except for the other night, and look what happened then! I didn't want to venture out today because of the John Knoss incident, but it was a necessity. I was low on toilet paper and out of cat food!"

"Violet's meals must prevail. Happy to be your bodyguard, Your Grace," he bowed his head to me right there at the poultry case. "No one's looking," he said, "and, remember, it's our private joke."

"My aunt says everyone is talking about me in some manner or other, and she's unhappy about that."

"Don't worry about your aunt. Jane-Ann *enjoys* the attention you've brought her. It's added excitement to her life and given her a purpose – a purpose to indulge in self-righteousness and, at the same time, be connected to someone important, and I know you're going to say you are not important, but in Hilly Dale, you are. Now, back to what we were talking about. What do you think about the incident being a set-up?"

"I think we should wait and discuss this in the car. That young woman's mother is a member of my aunt's book club, and you already know what that means." Seeing his quizzical expression, I said, "Betsy Potter Franklin is a member and is part of the John Knoss incident."

"Do you think the girl was a...a spy for the Hilly Dale Book Club?" Jackson's brown eyes widened in mock horror.

"Jackson, be serious. You were a few minutes ago. Let's get on with the shopping before we attract any more autograph seekers or the inquisitive." I pushed my cart to the cheese case where I selected a couple of shredded varieties.

"You really should shred your own," Jackson instructed. "Better flavor and better quality."

After we'd loaded everything in the SUV and pulled out of the parking lot, I broached the topic of Jackson's theory. "Why do you think it was a set-up?"

"Well, my friend Josie Deacon works at the hospital and said that John, once he regained his senses, began talking about someone on the bridge with him."

"Yes, Beck told me the next day that Bianca mentioned it."

"Well, then, what are the odds that John's ex-wife, along with his new fiancée whose ex-husband and *that* man's new girlfriend are all in the same vicinity at the same time of John's accident? And I might add it was snowing, cold, and in the early morning following what is generally considered to be an almost-guaranteed night of passion. We know why you and Beckham were in the vicinity, but why was *Betsy* there. She should have been at home in bed with her husband, not at a park with her ex-husband and his fiancée? And why were John and Bianca even out there? Generally speaking, a newly engaged couple aren't going to run around in the middle of the night. Something is wrong with this picture. Are the police even looking at Betsy?"

"I don't know, but I do understand that Betsy and Bianca were lured there. Just for the record, I'm not Beck's girlfriend, and I know how that sounds, Jackson. It sounds like a shag-fest, but I'm afraid it was a mistake, and…" I hesitated, afraid of revealing too much, even to a close friend.

"And what?"

"Nothing."

"Well, John apparently kept mentioning a pendant to Josie and wondering where it was. I assume the police have it," he said, before turning onto my street.

I wanted his opinion on the pendant, so I told him what it said.

"You're kidding!" he cried, after turning into my driveway. He pulled to the back, waited for the gate to open, shut off the vehicle's engine, and then sat there staring straight ahead. "Do you know who the pendant was for?"

"No," I said, opening the passenger door. "My guess is Betsy, since John and Bianca had just gotten engaged, or maybe Allison. Open the back so I can get my groceries, please."

"Betsy again," he murmured.

As we carried the bags into the kitchen, I told Jackson about how Betsy and Bianca were lured by valentines that were allegedly sent by John, and about what the mysterious person on the bridge did after John hit the water.

"Jessica, this really has the makings of a set-up, and, if true, that person singing after John went into the water is creepy. Did you hear the song while you were out there with Beckham?"

"No. I heard a breathy, high-pitched wailing sound when I first saw what looked like a person in the water, but then Beck and I were focused on a rescue. Had we the time to listen, we might have recognized it as a song, I suppose. We heard voices earlier but couldn't understand them. The cry and splash were quite audible. The water was up from the rains, but it was still a drop to the creek, and the current slightly faster than usual. The iron bridge is just about five-hundred yards upstream, but there is that slight bend not far after it which means we couldn't have seen anything, or even judged *exactly* from where the voices came, so…"

"Hmmmm. Makes it look even more convenient that you were there on Beckham's footbridge at the time all of this happened," Jackson interrupted. "I don't think John was meant to die – there are easier ways to accomplish that. No, he was either *helped* into the water or it was an accident, and they all panicked. Maybe it was a warning? I'm not one to gossip, but John Knoss is not the man most think he is. I've always found him shady."

"I've heard that from a couple of people now. I don't know enough about him to comment on his personal or professional lives."

"What was the person singing?" Jackson asked. "Do you know?"

I told him what Beck had said. "As it happens, the person was singing *iron bars will bend and break.*"

"How do you know those lyrics? Most people don't bother with anything after the first verse."

I explained about my first book and the plot. "And the iron bar gave way, which is why John fell in the water, I understand."

"Interesting. Did you even stop to think that *you* might play a part in this?"

"Don't you think you should take your own groceries home?" I asked, putting my frozen food into the freezer.

"It's too cold for anything to thaw, and it's a cloudy day. You're avoiding the issue."

"No, I don't think I'm involved in this at all. I have no real connection to Bianca, Betsy, or John."

"Well, you do, in a way. You went to school with Bianca, Betsy…and Beckham. Don't you think it's strange that the person sang that song that was used in your book?"

"It's a nursery song. Most people know it," I said quickly.

"But like I said, most people don't bother learning all the lyrics."

"Jackson," I shook my head. "Maybe that person bothered to learn them. I imagine it has to do with some personal grudge, or just a prank gone wrong. Beck said John and Bianca were into 'games,' and I've heard that Betsy and Bianca were pranksters in school."

"Games?" Jackson cringed. "Too much information." After handing me the tomatoes, he shrugged and continued. "I suppose I'd better be on my way. Consider what I said and talk to Beckham. No matter how far-fetched an idea might seem, tell the police."

I turned, faced Jackson, and sighed. "To tell you the truth, I *have* had some misgivings about the song and my first novel," I admitted, "but I don't want to think about it, and, besides, it's just one theory. There is something else that's troubling me." I told him about finding Bianca in the linen closet.

"In the closet? Hiding?"

"That's what it looked like. She was looking for Beck to get her out of a mess, knew the police and I were there, and was waiting for us to leave so she could talk to him. Unfortunately, I opened the door to put away a tablecloth that was on the floor while Beck went outside for a minute."

"Maybe she isn't over Beck and has been using John to make Beck jealous."

"I doubt that. Bianca and John had just gotten engaged hours earlier at the restaurant."

"True, but at Beck's restaurant? That not only shows a lack of class, but it's also odd. On the other hand, it's Bianca we're talking about and she's not known for her class. It's not her first affair, I've heard."

I didn't ask how he knew. Jackson had, however, managed to make me re-examine connections between my book and what happened. That John could have died had we not been there was horrifying, and I said so.

"But the point is, he *didn't*. Bianca and Betsy were there, albeit some distance away. You and Beckham were in the right place at the right time to see John go past if something went wrong, or at least someone was counting on that and knew Beckham would rescue John. The two of you had to be under surveillance, meaning everything was timed somehow." The horror I felt must have shown on my face because Jackson hurriedly added, "or maybe it was just a lucky break for John that you two were there."

"I hope so," I replied. "I'd hate to think we were being watched."

"You need to be careful. If that person *assisted* John into the water, then you don't know what he's capable of doing." Jackson offered to stay with me and bring his dog.

"I'm leaving for a book tour soon." Seeing the shock on his face, I said, "Yes, my agent and publisher want to capitalize on the whole duchess thing. It's all out there now, so I finally agreed. It will get me out of here for a while. If you would keep an eye on the house for me, I'd appreciate it."

"Anything for you, Duchess."

Chapter Twenty-Eight

Beck arrived at my house not long after the restaurant closed. He gave me a quick kiss and sank onto the living room sofa, patting the seat next to him. Before joining him, I poured us both a glass of Malbec.

"I know it's late but it was the only time I could stop by," he began after accepting the wine. "Since the John Knoss mess, the restaurant's been busier than usual. Curiosity-seekers, newshounds, and just the local nosy bunch all wandering over my property and the parts of the park where the incident occurred, taking selfies and snapping photos. I've had to put a 'No Stopping' sign on my footbridge! Thank goodness the iron bridge has been cordoned-off, but there's always some idiot who tries to cross the barricade."

"Did you find out anything?" I asked as I reached for the tray of cheese and crackers on the coffee table and offered it to Beck.

"Gatsby Gregson has been dogging this story since that night. He showed up at the restaurant for lunch today, but his main reason was to interview me." Beck took a slice of gouda and placed it on a cracker.

"You talked to him?" I placed the tray back on the coffee table and helped myself to a cracker.

"Well," Beck said, with a twinkle in his eyes, "I did agree to an information trade, but in the end, I had little to offer. I told him what he already knew and just one or two things he didn't – nothing important. He tried to press me on some things, but I suddenly had something that needed doing in the kitchen." He winked at me. "I comped his lunch, so I imagine he was happy. He had the check and could claim it on expenses, too."

"I've had several people stop at my gate today. A news channel van parked in my drive and someone rang the buzzer, but I didn't answer it. I have nothing to add. Anything I told them would be speculation. I don't want to be misquoted or have something taken out of context, making it appear that I've confirmed anything or, worse, pointed a finger at someone. I called the police and within minutes, an officer arrived and told the van's driver to move on."

"Gatsby was desperate enough for a story from me that he went first with the information. Duluth Hammond's mother was brought in for questioning. Dolly dated John for a while, but he left her for Betsy. Old Hank Douglas who has worked at Fitzpatrick's automotive shop for forty years was interrogated at length. Seems he and John had words at Cajun Daisy's over some expensive repair last year that Fitzpatrick's had to eat. I don't know how that was uncovered, or why it had any bearing on what happened the other night, except Hank doesn't live far from the park, but the man's in his sixties! Tommy was also questioned about some things, and so was Kismet Carter. Both of them had to do with real estate matters in which John was involved."

"They're grasping at straws. Tommy and Hank wouldn't fit with the pendant, I don't think. Kismet and Dolly might."

"That's where Mary-Helen Higginbotham came in. She had an affair with John and caused the breakup of his marriage to Betsy, and she's been in psychiatric care before – nervous breakdown a couple of years ago. Currently, she's the prime suspect. Gatsby said she had "spurned lover" written all over her, plus the police haven't been able to verify her alibi yet. Tommy and Kismet were each other's alibi, so that also looks iffy."

"I hate to think that people are forced to keep a minute-by-minute account of their time. Who can? Anyway, it was 2:00 in the morning. Most people are sleeping then. Gatsby should be called 'Gabby' the way he shares things."

"He thought I'd give him 'the low-down' as he called it, but after all of that, I had little to add except I was brought in for more questioning."

"You're not saying that the police suspect you had something to do with it! You saved John's life!"

"No, but I did handle the pendant and didn't tell them right away. They're covering their bases. Bianca has been having an affair with John for a couple of years, but I am only recently her ex-husband, so…"

"There isn't any way you could have been involved." I walked over to the fireplace, picked up a poker, and bent to stir up the fire. "I was with you, and the police haven't questioned me again, and I touched the pendant."

"You have no connection to John. I do. The townspeople are chalking John's…er…accident up to him being drunk, but his server doesn't recall that being the case, at least at the restaurant. He brought them a bottle of champagne to celebrate, but John only had a couple of glasses, and so did Bianca."

Picking up immediately on Beck's hesitation over the word 'accident,' I stood up quickly, placed the fireplace tool into its cast-iron stand, and turned to look at him. "Are you saying it might have been a deliberate action? I know you suggested to Officer Pincera that John might have been pushed, but I didn't realize you were serious."

Beck scrunched his shoulders, released them, and rotated his neck before answering. "John tends to walk the line, legally and morally, so it's not far-fetched that someone was upset with him. I talked to John in the hospital before he was released this morning. He wanted to thank me for saving his life. He said he slipped and slid against the railing which gave way. He backed Bianca's story that there was another person on the bridge and said that Betsy had been to see him yesterday and told him she went to the police and confirmed what Bianca had said."

"Did he tell you who it was?"

"No, All he said was that he had to meet someone, which pretty much flies the prank theory out the window."

"It must have been someone important…or someone he feared. You don't go wandering around on a slick bridge in freezing weather, otherwise." I told him Jackson's theory.

He maintains it was an accident and his fault, but even if it was, I think Jackson's right about a set-up. The question is why." Beck took a long sip of wine.

"Did he mention the pendant? Jackson said his friend Josie who is John's night nurse said he was rambling about it."

"Nothing said to me. He has to know who was on the bridge, but he's not saying. Maybe he's protecting someone? Maybe his family or either the person who was with him."

"How is Allison?" I asked while refilling our wine glasses.

"Jordan said she's worried, but she also told me Bianca and Betsy are talking a little. If anything, this may end the estrangement between the two. They have to present a united front, if only for their daughters, now that the girls will be stepsisters. By the way, I had to tell Jordan about us."

"It's quite all right, and it's better coming from you, rather than seeing it in the news or hearing it from her friends." I took a sip of wine before continuing, "Jackson said I should talk to you about something else." I told him about the ugly comments on my fan page and shared that I'd had an email from my media manager, Rebecca Caerphilly, asking to delete the messages.

"What's the poster's name?"

"I don't know anything other than 'Krazy for Keasden' but the person has been posting positive things for years. The only thing that has changed is my being a duchess. The posts are all targeted toward that. I'm going on my first book tour for over a week, so Rebecca was worried about this person showing up at one of the engagements. The tour's been announced on my pages."

"I'd let the posts stand. If the person decides posting isn't enough, you'll have evidence. I'm glad you're going on the book tour but be careful. I'll keep an eye out here for you," Beck said, pulling me against his shoulder.

I allowed myself to relax for a few minutes, and then remembered why I'd invited him over. Pulling away and sitting up quickly, I opened my mouth to share my idea. Beck gave me a look of resignation.

"Jessie, if you don't want to continue whatever's happening between us, just say so. Don't lead me on."

"It's not that," I replied, at least I wasn't sure that it was. "Before we got sidetracked, I asked you here tonight to discuss an idea I had. It involves Jordan and Allison." I explained that I wanted to treat the girls to a trip to England over their spring break. "It would get them away from this mess and Aisling doesn't start at St. Andrews until the following term. She would love to show them around." I stopped speaking. Beck was staring at me, his blue eyes narrowed. I couldn't tell what he was thinking.

"It's a good idea for the girls to get away," he finally said, "but I'd want to pay for Jordan's flight and…"

"No, it's a gift, Beck. Please accept it. I can afford to do this."

"Are you saying I can't?"

"No, but you have the restaurant costs and Jordan's expenses, and despite what you said about Bianca not wanting anything from the divorce since she was marrying John, that may not be the case now. She was upset about him having that pendant in his pocket. I assume she doesn't know who it was for and John isn't saying."

"Who knows with Bianca, but, Jessie, your gift is too much. Let me pay for something. I wouldn't feel right about it."

"All right. You can pay for her meals and entertainment – they aren't inexpensive over there, especially when you consider the dollar against the pound. I'll take care of all transportation and any place they stay that's not free. Is that a deal?"

"Agreed. Thanks. The girls don't deserve being mixed-up in this."

"I'm happy to do it for them, and for Aisling. She'll be so excited. Thank you," I said before calling it a night.

At the front door, Beck wrapped his arms around me and kissed me. "If I didn't have to be at the restaurant early and you didn't have a book tour to prepare for…" he hinted.

"I know, but perhaps when I get back and everything settles down, we can have more time together. Good night," I said, giving him a quick kiss.

***

Since our last phone conversation, Aunt Jane-Ann had been quiet. I was sure she found it all horrifying or embarrassing, or else like Jackson said, she was enjoying being close to the notoriety that seemed to follow me in Hilly Dale. I dreaded it, but I rang her to let her know about my upcoming book tour. She thought it was a good idea that I got out of Hilly Dale for a while to let things settle. Of course she let me know that she'd heard that Jordan and Allison were going to spend Spring Break in England.

"You could have sent me along with them. I'd like to get out of this embarrassing situation. Really, Jessica, sometimes I think you don't care what happens to me here. And you're part of this mess! Tell me, are you and Beckham still sneaking off together?"

"I rang you to let you know that I'd be out-of-town for a week or so, not to discuss my personal life." I gave her the dates of the tour and ended with, "Good afternoon, Aunt Jane-Ann," and turned off my phone. I'd glimpsed a softer side of my aunt when she admitted she knew all about her husband's gambling and had done her best to hide it. I'd felt sorry for her then, but good grief, the woman could be so exasperating!

Chapter Twenty-Nine

"Now, do you have everything?" Heather asked before she drove me to Little Rock. I was headed to Chicago to start the first leg of my book tour that would also take me to Kansas City, St. Louis, Nashville, Memphis and finally back to Little Rock. I'd balked at taking a longer tour my first time out. This one was going to be hectic; I was heavily scheduled.

"Yes, I think so. I can get anything I've forgotten along the way," I replied while buckling my seatbelt. "Thank you for driving. I wish you would let me pay for the petrol."

"Oh, it's my pleasure, Jessie. That's what friends are for," she said as she backed her Lexus out of my driveway. "I was glad to get away from school. I never take a day off, but I've got a good sub."

"Well, I've never done a tour before. I'm a tad nervous."

"I'd never imagine you to be nervous about anything. You seem so together, and you always have. I can't understand why Beck ever let you go."

"We were kids. People change."

"Yes, they do," she said wistfully. "Well, at least you're back together now."

"Back together? What do you mean by that?"

"I'd just assumed since you and he slept together…"

"I don't know what Beck and I are, and now with all this drama in Hilly Dale with John, Bianca, and Betsy, and my outing as a duchess, who knows where this will lead."

"Oh, John Knoss is a player. I'm surprised he didn't come after you, especially after your title became known. He ran around on Betsy for years, but I guess she either didn't know or didn't care. He's rich, but he's really no prize, if you ask me. Some women seem to think he's great. He's been with Betsy AND Bianca, and who knows who else in town. I'm surprised he didn't get in trouble before now. He's stepped on lots of toes, and visited lots of bedrooms, or so I've heard. And Beckham saved him. He *saved* the man who took his wife away. What a coincidence you were nearby to help."

"We were there at the right time, and I'm so glad we were."

"Yes, you certainly were. Without you two, John could have died that night." She took the eastbound exit off the highway and drove onto the interstate.

"The police questioned Mary-Helen Higginbotham," I replied.

"Yeah, she had an affair with John years ago. Betsy got an anonymous tip that John was cheating on her and had been seen at that run-down motel just outside of town, so there she went to check it out. She didn't catch them in the act like I caught Steve and Shauna, but she arrived in time to see John and Mary-Helen leaving the motel room. Betsy filed for divorce shortly after that. She got a little money in the settlement, along with the building that houses her gift shop, but that's about it. John still had to pay alimony. Child support too, because Allison was a minor. He's paying for Allison's education."

Leave it to Heather to know all the details except what happened in that motel room, and for that, I was thankful. "The one I feel sorry for is Allison."

"It's really generous of you to send her and Jordan to visit Aisling." Seeing my surprised glance, "Yes, everyone knows. Betsy has been telling the whole town. She's just thrilled. You know, it makes her look good, and like you two are best friends, but it also makes everyone question your relationship with Beck. You two took up together pretty quickly."

"It's reassuring to know that the Hilly Dale grapevine is working well and this is providing entertainment for 'everyone,'" I sniped. Really, it was as if they had a town crier. I thought about that for a moment. Perhaps they did, and it was Heather.

"You know what I wonder? I wonder if John's mishap on the bridge had something to do with Bianca's engagement to John. Maybe Betsy was upset about it. He *had* been her husband first, and he is Allison's father. Maybe that's why she and Bianca were arguing by the creekbank."

"No one knows but John," I replied.

"And that other person that was supposedly on the bridge. I heard that Beck and Bianca had a troubled marriage for years and John was the breaking point for Beck. If you hadn't been with him, Beck might have been arrested by now."

"Heather, how can you say something like that! Beck wouldn't hurt John!" I cried, appalled at her suggestion. "I'd rather not talk about this or about Beck's marriage, but I don't believe John actually broke it up."

"Really? I always thought he did. John and Beck were friends, you know, and the two couples ran around together for some time. Betsy and Bianca were competitive in school. Remember when Bianca got Homecoming Queen and Betsy didn't? They didn't speak for weeks. Betsy could have lured them both out to the park, pushed John off the bridge and blackmailed Bianca, so she'll stay quiet. They were such good friends, so she's bound to know something juicy on her. I willing to bet that Bianca won't stay with John after this, or if she does, it's only for his money."

"You've been reading too many of my novels," I said, laughing, but stopped suddenly as a sobering thought hit me. Bianca was frightened of someone, but I couldn't believe it was Betsy. "Peter and Betsy seem happy together, and Betsy divorced John some time ago. It was probably one of John's business deals gone wrong."

"Maybe 'seems' is the operative word. You never know what happens at home. You left Hilly Dale, so you wouldn't know anything about anyone. I know these people because I ended up staying. My parents couldn't afford to send me anywhere, and it didn't help that I was stuck with a baby and needed my parents' help while I worked. I'm just grateful I got to go to college when Acer was three."

"You worked hard and that's admirable. You're in a wonderful profession, and you're giving children a good start in life."

"That's true. I like my job. Don't get me wrong, Hilly Dale College is a great school, and David is on the faculty, but it's no Cambridge. To tell you the truth, Tim Hayes and his board are pricing the place out of reach for some of our local kids. I wish Acer could have gone to college. Maybe he wouldn't have gotten into so much trouble. You know he's in the penitentiary for drugs and assault, and other things."

"Oh, Heather. I didn't know. You never mention him, so I didn't want to pry."

"It's okay. Everyone knows. I'm surprised Beck or your Aunt Jane-Ann didn't tell you."

"My aunt said something about Nick Nethermeyer and you. She also said your son had gotten into trouble when he was younger, but she didn't say what sort. I'm so sorry."

"It was pretty bad. He beat the crap out of a guy during a drug deal gone wrong, but his buddy killed the other guy with them. Because he helped cover it up, Acer got an additional charge as an accessory. He's in for a while. I worry some about his nine-year-old son. The boy's mother isn't great. She was a slut he got involved with just out of high school. She's been married at least three times since."

"Do you see your grandson?"

"I've seen him three times in nine years, but I visit Acer a few times a year. It's awful to see him there, but he's resigned to it."

I didn't know what to say, so the rest of the way we talked about the tour, except the times Heather bragged about her daughter. Her greatest wish was that Krista would pledge the top sorority when the time came for her to go to the University of Arkansas. "Of course, she won't have a title or anything like Aisling, but I want her to pledge a sorority. I didn't have the chance to go there or do that." Heather turned up the music. "Ooooh, I love this song."

Cowboy Casanova by Carrie Underwood blasted my ears. He wasn't a cowboy, but John Knoss was definitely Hilly Dale's version of a Casanova. Well, him and Lucky Fine.

"Text me your details, and I'll pick you up. Send photos of the book tour," she called out the window as I made my way into the terminal. I was glad to leave Hilly Dale and its drama behind, at least for a week or so.

***

Since I didn't have a specific book to promote on the tour, people were buying from both series, but *Harriet Donovan* had the edge, for obvious reasons. I'd convinced my agent and publisher that billing me as a duchess would detract and reminded them that many people today thought 'Lord' was the great poet Tennyson's middle name, failing to notice there was a comma after his first. I also pointed out that it would be incorrect to use my title with my pen name.

Meggie, a young woman Dil Daly sent along with me was a blessing. I had to hit the ground running, but thanks to her, I managed to get through the question-and-answer sessions at two bookstores in the Chicago area, and an interview with a local magazine. The second day of meet-and-greets, signings, and an interview with *The Chicago Tribune*, I felt more confident. At 7:30, I was in my room at *The Viceroy* getting dressed for a dinner and reception. I'd just zipped up my long-sleeved, dark-brown, wool dress with the cream paisley vines pattern, when I had a text from Beck asking me to call him.

"I have news. Are you sitting down?" he asked.

"I'm finishing dressing for a dinner. Let me put you on speaker phone," I said, setting my phone on the bureau. "The dinner is being hosted by a women's club. I'm afraid I've been asked to speak. I'm a writer, and yet I had trouble crafting a speech on short notice. I'm better at questions and answers."

"You're at your best when evading questions."

"We spoke this morning, and I don't have a lot of time to talk right now," I said, attaching my dangling topaz and citrine earrings. "I have to be downstairs in twenty-five minutes."

"They've arrested someone for the attempted murder of John Knoss."

"Attempted murder? Wasn't it an accident? Mary-Helen?"

"You're full of questions. They brought in Tommy Fitzpatrick."

"What? I gasped, dropping the matching necklace to the floor. "Tommy? There's got to be a mistake. I can't imagine why he would be involved in some assignation on a bridge in the middle of a freezing night. And out there singing? What are they thinking?"

"Well, he was a tenor in the school choir."

"That's hardly a reason to suspect him. They need probable cause," I told him, while stooping to pick up the necklace. That made me think of the pendant with 'Memories' on the back. "Were they romantically involved?"

"Nooooo. When Tommy's wife became ill, he needed to raise some cash and was planning to sell one of his family's two automotive shops. John, knowing Tommy had inherited land north of the college, made him an offer so Tommy could keep his shops and not have to pay taxes on the land he wasn't using. It sounded like a good deal. At the time, Tommy and his wife had a kid in university and another about to graduate high school. Insurance was only covering so much of his wife's treatment. Tommy was in such a state that he didn't get an appraisal or seek advice first. John was his friend and Tommy desperately needed cash. It was a low-ball offer. A month later, John turned around and sold the land to the college for over a million dollars. That was more than Tommy's two shops were worth. Tommy had to sell one of his shops later on. Not long after that, he publicly accused John of swindling him and said he'd get his comeuppance one day. It isn't unreasonable that Tommy felt that way. John's on the Hilly Dale College Board of Directors. He and Timothy Hayes, the college president, are friends."

"Beck, Tommy didn't get an appraisal and that's his fault. I'm sure he knows that. I hardly think he would have waited all this time to exact his revenge. He doesn't strike me as someone who would do that anyway. If you had said it was Mary-Helen, I might have gone along with you."

"Well, Tommy lives about a quarter-mile upstream from the bridge and his alibi with Kismet didn't hold up, since she, too, had some issues with John in the past over the Carter place I eventually bought. I wanted to let you know before your aunt gave her take on it."

I stepped into my dark-brown heels. "My aunt wouldn't call me about something like that," I said, as I fastened the topaz and citrine necklace. "I apologize, but I have to meet Meggie Milson now. She's my assistant on this tour. Please keep me updated. I can't imagine Tommy would do something like this. I'll speak with you later." I switched off the phone, dropped it in my handbag, grabbed my camel-hair coat, and hurried to the elevator.

Chapter Thirty

The rest of the tour flew by. Meggie declared it a success after St. Louis four days ago. "You're wise to read an excerpt from your upcoming series and mixing up what you read from the other ones. I mean, instead of just reading *Harriet Donovan* like Dil wanted. See, you've got a knack for promoting," she praised

"I don't know about that," I said, as we arrived in Memphis. This last leg is tough." I'd done two signings, an interview, and attended a prominent book club meeting in Nashville yesterday, and the book-signing this morning had run overtime, causing us to miss our flight. With the next one delayed, due to the weather, Meggie had hired a car, but it had taken us nearly five hours – thank you, weather - to reach Memphis where we'd barely had time to check in at *The Peabody,* see the famous ducks march back upstairs, and make it to the large bookstore where my reading and signing was being held from 7:00-9:00. Afterwards, Meggie and I had enjoyed a late celebratory dinner.

At the end of the meal, I received a call from Beck, which I let go to voicemail. After I got back to my room, showered, and readied for bed, I got a text from him asking me to get in touch. It was late, so instead of calling him, I crawled into bed and turned off the lamp. Whatever he wanted could wait until morning. Fifteen minutes later, just as I was dozing off, I heard the annoying ping of an arriving text. Sighing, I reached over and picked up the phone. It was *another* text from Beck, but this one was marked *URGENT. That* got my attention. Had something happened to my aunt, my house, Jackson, Violet?

"Beck, it's awfully late and I'm tired. Is everything all right?" I asked when he answered.

"Are you out somewhere?" There was tension in his voice. "You didn't answer my call or the other text."

"No. I was at dinner when your call came through. I'm lying in bed trying to go to sleep. It's nearly midnight, and we're leaving for Little Rock at 7:30. We just spoke yesterday. Has something happened?" I rushed through my list of possibilities with him.

"None of those, so don't worry. They've arrested someone for the attempted murder of John Knoss."

I drew out a long 'yes.' Had he forgotten he'd said the exact same thing not long ago? "Tommy was arrested, but I just don't believe he did it. Did he confess? Is that why you're calling?"

"No. Tommy wasn't involved. I'm calling about…"

"See, I told you he couldn't have done it. It's not in his nature," I interrupted. "He…"

"Jessica, if you will stop talking, I'll tell you what I can, but first you need to know that Heather won't be picking you up at the book signing tomorrow. I'll be doing that."

"Oh, I'm sorry to hear that. I mean, not that you're picking me up, but because she was looking forward to attending. I had planned to surprise her with lunch in Little Rock to thank her. She wouldn't accept any money for driving me."

"Jessica, stop talking! Listen to me. Heather's the one who's been arrested."

"Heather! That's ridiculous. I'm beginning to doubt the competence of the Hilly Dale Police Department and the Sheriff's Department. First Tommy and now Heather, and look at those other people they brought in, and even YOU. They questioned *you* a couple of times and you *rescued* John! Who is next? Aunt Jane-Ann?" I cried, outraged.

"I'm sorry, but it's true," he said quietly.

"Rubbish! She didn't associate with John and what she knew about him, she didn't like."

"Did she tell you that?"

"Yes! We're friends. In fact she told me on the drive to Little Rock about him."

I could hear the sound a person makes when taking a deep breath, puffing out cheeks, and exhaling. "She, uh, isn't your friend, Jessie, not really. I'm sorry. She used you. She used me, and she used John. From what I understand, what happened to John was apparently the result of a meeting that went very wrong, very fast, and Heather flipped. They had something going on for a while."

I sat up and leaned against the headboard. This was crazy talk. An affair with John? Heather who had been a friend since elementary and who had stuck by me all the way through school arrested for attempted murder? Our lives, like others I had known in Hilly Dale, had gone in different directions, but not this – not this different.

"She contacted me when I moved back. She wanted to renew our friendship. I don't believe this."

"Maybe she did want to be friends, at first, but more likely she wanted to keep an eye on you and see what you could do for her."

"This is absurd. She invited me places; she drove me to Little Rock for the tour and was planning to pick me up."

"Well, she put up a good front for you."

"I don't understand."

"She's another one who plays a good game, Jessie. Remember those Stephen King movies, or any horror movie for that matter, where some kid wreaks havoc on certain *students* for real or imagined slights?"

"Beck, what you're implying is ridiculous. This isn't one of those films. Heather isn't a teenager. She's forty-eight now. This is Hilly Dale, Arkansas, and Heather is a first-grade teacher married to a well-respected professor. John didn't even go to *school* with us!"

"You're smart. Does the phrase 'Two Bitches and a Bastard' mean anything to you?"

I scrunched back down and laid my head on the pillows, putting my free hand to my forehead. "Beck, I…"

"It's okay. I acted like a bastard to you back then. Bianca and Betsy behaved like bitches. I get it. We were stupid teenagers. High school was everything to a lot of kids. Most like us, moved on, but Heather didn't."

"Heather was bullied in school. Do you remember what the boys called her? They called her Heather *Hilly* Dale because she developed very early."

"Ah, yes," he mused. "It was just locker room talk."

"But *she* felt self-conscious, and it didn't help that Bianca, Betsy, and their friends teased her and called her rude names. You know they bullied a lot of people. I came up with 'The Three Bs,' by the way," I admitted, cringing a little at the memory. "It was to make us all laugh – like a private joke."

"Yeah, I figured it was your doing. Bianca and Betsy referred to you and others in worse ways. Your description of the three of us was much cleverer."

"Thanks," I replied. "How *kind* of you to say so."

Beck laughed for a second and then turned serious again. "Anyway, Betsy and I met for breakfast this morning to talk about the girls' trip. She told me Heather's been holding a grudge against the 'Three Bs,' and she also agreed that Heather set us up. She said she should have realized something was wrong at the time, and she confirmed the valentine she received, purportedly from John, mentioned something about Allison."

"I'd go out anytime and anywhere if I feared there was something up with one of my children, so I can see where she'd show up, no matter the weather or time."

"Yeah, so would I. Anyway, we deduced that you may not have *originally* been part of the plan, but we're willing to bet when John proposed to Bianca, and you and I sort of, well, made-up, it threw a monkey-wrench into whatever Heather had been planning for some time. What happened on the bridge was likely a spur-of-the-moment thing due to her jealousy and hatred."

"Beck, I'm having trouble processing all of this." I turned on my side and with my free hand pulled the covers up. "How did the police find out it was Heather?"

"Betsy said John was forced into it by Heather herself. She showed up last night at his house drunk saying she'd left David and was moving in with him. She refused to accept that John was marrying Bianca, despite the fact that she had seen John propose in my restaurant."

I remembered seeing Heather's face when I looked through the peephole on Valentine's evening. She'd looked unhappy – angry even. Other than that, she and David seemed happy together when I'd seen them out and about, which is what I told Beck.

"David might have been, but it was all an act for Heather, which became frighteningly clear when she showed up at John's. Bianca was there to discuss their future together. When Heather saw Bianca, she pulled a knife and began ranting about high school and how Bianca, Betsy, and I had somehow ruined her life. At one point, she began slashing the knife through the air, laughing and saying that her revenge didn't play out like she hoped, but this was better than nothing, because she'd at least have taken John from Bianca. Betsy nearly cried when she told me Heather bragged about taking John away from her and being the one who tipped her off about Mary-Helen."

"That must have been awful to witness."

"It was. Heather was drunk, but she was also having a breakdown. You're lucky she didn't have one when she drove you to Little Rock. The thought of *that* scares me. "

"Was Bianca injured?"

"Thankfully, no. John tried to calm Heather while Bianca called the police. Frighteningly, Heather broke away from John and threw the knife at

Bianca, but it went straight into the wall, missing her by several feet. By the way, the pendant was actually for Heather. John apparently told Bianca it was for Betsy. It was supposed to be John's parting gift to Heather. That idiot tried to give it to her just before she threw the knife. That's what set her off again."

"My God!" I cried. "How did Betsy know all of this?" I suddenly felt sorry for Bianca and Betsy regarding their lives with John.

"Betsy's husband. He owns the newspaper here, remember? Gatsby Gregson is his top reporter. He's been on this case from the start but had just started looking into the high school angle."

"He has informants everywhere."

"Don't I know it. I should have realized something was wrong when Heather seemed to know a lot about the case when she called me just hours after we found John. She passed it off as being from her cousin who happens to be Gatsby's wife, and she knew a lot about John too."

I lay there in silence until Beck asked, "Jessie, have you fallen asleep?"

"What? Oh…no. I'm just trying to figure all of this out. It's doing my head in."

"Yeah," he said. "Heather's a bitter, jealous woman, and it seems she was willing to take things way too far. John wasn't *protecting* the person on the bridge; he was scared after what happened."

"So he didn't accidentally crash through the iron bar when he fell?"

"Well, he slipped and fell all right, but he'd just told Heather it was over and that he loved Bianca. When he tried to get up the bar moved and he asked Heather to help him, but instead, she leaned down and pushed him through and into the water. I think it was a spur-of-the-moment thing and she snapped after that."

"Remember when I told you the plot of my first book *The Bridges of Cassiopeia*? You thought my speculation was a result of my creative imagination. After that I didn't want to say that the killer was a woman in the story. I didn't think you or the police would believe me. I was afraid I'd be considered a person with an overactive imagination. Worse, I would be seen as an author promoting my book!"

"You can't be *sure* your story was why she concocted the scene on the bridge. You didn't have the spurned lover go to someone's house in the middle of the night and throw a knife at her rival, did you?"

"No, the character was killing those she thought had wronged her in some way, though."

"I don't know Heather all that well. Can you see her setting something up?" He asked, yawning.

His yawn was contagious. "Yes. She's got a malicious streak. Remember what she did with that dining room table that had belonged in Steve Taylor's family for a century?"

"Who hasn't heard that tale. It's been one of Heather's biggest bids for attention."

"The point is, that her action was vindictive back then, so maybe she did set us up, or at least you, Betsy, and Bianca, and I was a bonus for some reason. When I think about it, and the way Heather was in school, I see it. She wanted to wreak havoc in 'The Three B's' personal and professional lives, and she did. Betsy and Bianca might have been drawn to the park as witnesses to John's 'secret' meeting, but since they didn't pay attention, she had to do something drastic."

"Plausible, go on. Let's hear what a mystery writer has to say."

"Amusing, Beck. I don't think she wanted John to die. I believe she knew we were on the footbridge – maybe she heard *us*. Remember, we heard two women arguing. If she knew we were there, she'd figure you would rescue him, or in the worst-case scenario be accused of drowning him. In fact, she mentioned that when we were driving to Little Rock. Whatever happened, you, Bianca, Betsy and I would be drawn into a scandal. I just don't understand why I was involved."

"Maybe things didn't go the way she hoped with you as a 'friend.'" Beck yawned again. "Okay, it's late. We both need to get some sleep. I'm looking forward to seeing Jessica Keasden in action. The reading at the library was nice, but here I'll get to see people buying your book."

After I gave him the itinerary, I switched off the phone and drifted into an uneasy sleep filled with iron bridges, snow, nursery songs, and Beck.

Chapter Thirty-One

"Wow! That was a crowd." Beck exclaimed as we loaded my things into his truck. He turned to Meggie, "Nice to meet you, and thanks for taking care of Jessica."

"My pleasure," she replied. "Jessica, this was a wonderful tour. Dil and Mr. Fornot are so pleased with it that they want to have another as soon as possible. Are you up for it?"

"Maybe in a few months. I'm working on more than one book right now, and if they want them finished…"

"Got it," she said. "We're all so happy that you've come out…ummm… that your title has been revealed and you're willing to be more involved in the promotions, I mean."

"Oh, I thought the mysterious Jessica Keasden was a pretty good gimmick," Beck said, winking. "Ready to go, my lady?"

I rolled my eyes at Meggie, who laughed. We said our goodbyes at the large chain bookstore in Little Rock at 1:00. Meggie took the hired car to the airport and Beck and I pulled out of the parking lot, headed for Interstate 40.

We'd been driving in silence for a while, until Beck said, "Tommy figured it was Heather, you know. He told me when I went to see him the day after he was arrested."

"*You* went to see him?"

"Yeah. I bailed him out. We talked for a while. How did you think I knew about 'The Three Bs?'"

"Tommy?"

"Yeah, and he asked me to warn you, but because Heather was your friend, I didn't think you would believe me without actual proof."

"I probably wouldn't have."

"So, how are you feeling about things today."

I leaned back and closed my eyes. "Shocked mainly, but right now tired." When I opened my eyes again, we were more than halfway to Hilly Dale.

"Welcome back. You must have had a nice sleep," Beck said, "although I never guessed you could snore like that."

I gave him a dirty look.

Beck glanced at me before turning his eyes back to the interstate. "You must not have slept much last night. I'm sorry, but I had to let you know I was picking you up, and I knew you would ask me why. I wanted to give you as much info as I could before we got home. The whole town is going to be talking about it by now."

"I imagine it will. Was Hilly Dale always like this? Rife with scandals, affairs, greed, and deception?"

"Probably, but we were too young to notice then. I've seen it since I moved back. The goings-on here, as you know, have affected my life."

"Yes, they have, and now mine. Perhaps it *was* always this way and I'm just seeing it for the first time."

"You were an eighteen-year-old girl when you left. That's what the problem is, but if you hadn't come back, we wouldn't have had a chance to straighten everything out."

"I know. I'm happy about that." I stretched my legs as far as I could.

"Are you hungry? There's a *Cracker Barrel* a few miles ahead."

"I'd like to go home. This has been a very long week."

"That long? It was nine days, Jessie."

"I lost track of time," I said, and closed my eyes again.

"You've been quiet for a while." Beck's voice startled me out of a daydream.

"I hopped aboard the nostalgia train," I replied.

"Ah, so I should be flattered then?"

"Not really. I was considering a timeline."

"That's charming, Jessie. Glad you think so highly of our time together."

I had a comeback ready, but then I realized from the tone of his voice that he was teasing. "Very funny," I answered. "I *was* thinking about you, though. Everything changed in my little group of friends in seventh grade."

"Why was that?"

"You," I said, looking over at him. "You arrived from the 'big city' of Little Rock and changed the dynamics of the group."

Like many teen girls with their first boyfriend, I spent most of my free time with Beck, leaving me little extra for friends. My friends were still my friends, but they, too, had forged their own relationships and friendships through clubs. Heather had hung back from doing that, other than dating Gopher Getts in ninth grade.

After Beck and I broke up, I was back with my old friends, and later added my new boyfriend, Josh. Heather was still in the group, but she seemed more negative, particularly after her boyfriend dumped her. I never knew what happened. She wouldn't say.

We took the highway that led to Hilly Dale and began the climb and eventual descent into town. "So, are you saying I'm responsible for Heather's meltdown?" Beck took a curve too fast for my liking.

"Careful, please," I cried. "No, of course not. She has a mental health issue. I'm saying you were the catalyst for my group's change in seventh grade, but Heather's attitude stayed the same throughout her life. She just learned to hide it."

Beck took another curve a bit fast. "Hey, slow down, please."

"Sorry. I was thinking."

"Think about not driving us off the side of the hill."

"I am. I was considering what you said about me being the reason for Heather's actions."

"I didn't say that exactly. I said *catalyst* for change, and it didn't have anything to do with Heather. Pay attention!" I cried, watching the edge of the road as we wound our way to Hilly Dale after crossing the bridge over Tarnation River at a fairly high rate of speed. "You seem to be in a great hurry to get home."

"Aren't you? You told me you wanted to come straight home when I asked about eating."

"Yes, but I'd like to get there in one piece, please."

A short time later, the green sign with white lettering announced we were entering the city limits of Hilly Dale. This part of the drive was beautiful, but hilly and curvy. The houses here were large, newer, and had gorgeous views of the river to the south and the hills beyond. In a few minutes, we turned onto Rush Street, passing fast-food restaurants, a strip mall, and Walmart.

"Look, why don't you stop by the restaurant for dinner later? We haven't seen each other in some time, and when we have the talk has been about John. I'd like to have a nice, romantic dinner, and just relax tonight. Besides, you won't have to prepare anything to eat."

I was tired from the tour but agreed. As we started for my neighborhood, I reminded Beck, "Don't forget to stop at Dr. Longstead's clinic! I have to pick up Violet. She'll hate me forever if I leave her there another night."

We arrived at my front gate thirty minutes later. Slinging my tote bag over my shoulder and holding my handbag, I waited on the driveway while Beck dragged my suitcase from the truck and then hauled out a cat carrier with a cranky Violet inside. When we entered the kitchen, he set the bag and the carrier on the floor. Refusing his offer of help, I told him I'd see him later.

I dropped the tote and handbag onto a kitchen chair and opened the carrier's door. Violet refused to come out, so I lugged my suitcase to my bedroom, and started unpacking. A few minutes later, loud meows came from the kitchen. In this case, they sounded more like NOW, NOW, NOW. Violet had emerged and wanted a meal. I fed her, took my tote bag, and went back upstairs to take a long, hot bath in the clawfoot tub I rarely used. Afterwards I spent time with Violet who seemed to have forgiven me.

When I'd finished dressing, it was a little before 7:00. I texted Beck. At 7:15, he replied, asking me to come by at 8:00 and to use the front entrance. I was dropping and almost canceled, but I didn't want to do that to him, especially after he picked me up in Little Rock. Violet followed me around as I tossed clothes in the wash and checked messages until it was time to leave. When I picked up the keys and headed for the back door, she mewed like a kitten.

"I'll be back. I love you. I'm not leaving you all night, baby," I crooned in the voice I hoped no one ever heard me use.

A short time later, I walked into the restaurant and up to the hostess. "I'm here to see Mr. Hailey," I told the cute girl.

"Oh, yeah. You're that duchess everyone's talking about and you're the one that helped Mr. Hailey save that man who fell in the creek, right?" She picked up a menu.

"I am." Thanks to Gatsby Gregson, my private life was now public. That man had dug into every detail of my life, as well as my late-husband's family, and he'd gone right ahead with his column in the *Hilly Dale Gazette*. The society columnist wrote about my clothes and the cost of everything I wore, and any social engagements I attended, or anywhere I went. The latter was slim pickings, but it was like living in a fishbowl. I wondered how celebrities managed it.

"Follow me," the hostess said. Surprised, we passed through the entrance to the dining room to the right of the stairs where I'd first lunched with Heather. Although the room was crowded with diners, there was still a cozy feel with the red velvet curtains drawn and a fire burning in the hearth. I glanced at the dropped ceiling and smiled, remembering the pleasant part of the night I'd learned what was up there.

Beck, who was seated at a corner table, stood as the hostess and I approached. It appeared he and I were going to have our romantic dinner amidst the good citizens of Hilly Dale. Details would, of course, be in the next edition of the *Hilly Dale Gazette*, and that made me wish I'd dressed a tad better.

"I decided it was time to really bring things out in the open," he said, pulling out my chair. "Give the citizens something else to talk about."

***

A few evenings later, Beck and I sat on the sofa in his apartment discussing the wrap-up of recent events. Beck's ploy to stop people talking about our connection to Heather and start talking about the two of us dining together hadn't worked. Her meltdown and John Knoss were all people talked about these days. Beck was right, John wasn't a decent man. He hadn't even offered Tommy Fitzpatrick an apology for not coming forward when he was arrested.

I took a sip of Cabernet before reaching into my handbag and drawing out a plain white envelope with my name on it. David James had delivered it to me earlier in the day. He said Heather had given it to him when he visited her in the hospital two or three days ago, she had asked him to give it to me. He apologized profusely for not doing it right then. I felt so sad for him when he admitted he was having a difficult time accepting the true character of the woman he loved. I waited to read the letter when Beck and I were together.

So, the author had a big secret, and now it's out. You lied to your fans, to your own family, and you lied to your friends in Hilly Dale. We're just a bunch of stupid hicks to you and your fancy friends. You made jokes about your hometown. I hope it makes you feel good about yourself to know you're going to be just as despised as I have been. You sneered at your hometown, and now people will sneer at you, just like they have done with me all my life.

You betrayed me. You betrayed all of us who were tormented by Betsy, Bianca, Beck, and those others in school. You went back to Beck as soon as you arrived in Hilly Dale, but you wouldn't even tell me the truth about that!

Because of you, Duchess, I had to change MY plans. Beck was going to be MINE. My goal would have been complete then. Why didn't you take the hint and take up with Tommy Fitzpatrick?

I didn't plan to knock John off the bridge after he slipped, but he was breaking it off with me, so I had to do something. I wanted those bitches to know it was ME and be afraid, but I couldn't. At least they were scared, and I have the satisfaction that I ruined Betsy's marriage and destroyed Bianca's relationship, and in the process destroyed their friendship. And you and Beck got caught. That was the icing on the cake. I saw your car when David and I left the restaurant that night, and then I heard you and Beck outside. I knew he'd rescue John. That's who he is. The perfect Beck. Those other two didn't even bother to help John when he fell.

You, Duchess, spoiled my plans to have Beck. You are two-faced, a liar, a hypocrite, and a fake, and I hope your books fail. At least I've done my part to help THAT along.

-'Krazy for Keasden'

I sat there for a moment, stunned. What a hateful letter, but it settled the question of whether she was really my friend and it solved the fan page and social media poster's identity. My renewed friendship with Beck, my success and real life, and John's engagement to Bianca pushed her over the edge. I wondered if it would have been as bad if I hadn't returned to Hilly Dale. Maybe she wouldn't have lured those three to the bridge that night and John wouldn't have been in a life-and-death situation. I said as much to Beck.

Putting his arm around me, Beck said comfortingly. "What happened is not your fault. She's unbalanced and rambling. No remorse at all. She would have done something else, Jessie. Look how she went after Bianca later. The good thing is that she didn't kill anyone. John's alive, Bianca's unharmed, and so are we. The right person was arrested."

I gave him a sad smile and handed him the letter. "You give it to the police for me. I don't think I can. Heather needs good mental health care, and I'd like to see she gets it, Beck. We were friends, once."

Beck nodded and put the letter on the coffee table.

"Poor David James. He looked so pitiful when he stopped by the house this morning. He wouldn't even come inside. My heart breaks for that man," I said softly. "She used him."

"She used a lot of people. You know, David and Heather married quickly. He was new in town. Heather had a... reputation. He wouldn't have heard about her, and I didn't want to tell you right away either. You wouldn't have believed me."

"You're right. I wouldn't have. I believe in giving people chances. My aunt tried to warn me," I admitted, "but I assumed she was just being her typical judgmental self."

"Not in this case. Heather's 'dated' quite a few local men, and always for a purpose. That's common knowledge among the locals and is why she's never been accepted in clubs and organizations. John's a catch, but he also uses people. As Tommy Fitzpatrick said about John the other day, 'the user finally got used.'"

"That's an awful thing to say about someone. As far as Heather is concerned, I never wanted to be her competition. I only wanted a friend that wasn't connected to my parents. I wanted to forge my own way here."

"She never stood a chance with me, even if you never returned to Hilly Dale. I want you to know that."

Beck rubbed the back of my neck. "You know, Heather's a pretty good actress," he said. "If she hadn't been so hurt-filled all through school, she could have found her popularity through the theater club." He shook his head. "What a waste."

I rested my head on his shoulder. "Instead, she allowed her desire to be somebody control her. Maybe if she had left Hilly Dale, she would have forgotten all the hurts – imagined and real - she'd experienced."

"I'll say this much, in you, she found both a new audience and someone she thought she could use to her advantage, either to boost her up the social ladder, or to further her – and I can't believe I'm saying this – revenge."

"It's still a lot to take in." I said, lifting my head and scooting over.

"Why don't you stay here tonight? It's late and we hardly see each other these days. You've got a deadline to meet and I'm short-handed at the restaurant and working overtime. We haven't had much quality time together."

I looked into his eyes and almost succumbed. "I know, but I'd like to go home tonight, Beck. There's a lot to think about. Shall we have dinner at my house or Cajun Daisy's this week. I promise that we will spend quality time together soon."

We passed over the rock footbridge, on the way to my car, neither of us looking down at the water. The creek had taken on a different meaning for us now.

Chapter Thirty-Two

After I'd collected my thoughts, I spoke to each of my children about what had happened. I didn't think any of this would be in the international papers, but I wanted them to know. Aisling took the opportunity to thank me for providing a holiday for Jordan and Allison. She'd heard from both of them yesterday. "Despite what happened, they are over the moon about their trip! I wish they could leave earlier than next week and stay longer," she exclaimed. "Is it all right if we stay in London for a few days and then go to Fielding House? Liam said he'll bring some friends for a house party."

"You'll need to talk to Alistair about any house parties. See what he has going on."

"He doesn't mind. Cecilia is fine with it, and *no one* is telling her mother a thing about what happened in Hilly Dale. Cecilia's instructions. She was horrified that all that hillbilly business came out and your title was exposed. She blames herself."

"I'm fine, Aisling. Please don't worry. While on the subject of horrifying matters, don't frighten the girls with ghost stories, and don't let Liam do that. They've had a shock. Make the visit fun and relaxing for them. If you want to use the house in Broadway or even the one in Cornwall, clear it with Alistair."

"I'm showing them a good time, not sending them into seclusion," Aisling smarted-off.

"Good point," I said, laughing.

Beck and I had kept a discreet distance until the John, Heather, and Bianca drama faded a bit and then began seeing each other occasionally. I had a lot to think about, but I spent most of my time finishing the second book in the *Secrets of Snowdonia* series before returning to work on *Stars and Spikes Forever*, the book in *The Celestial Cat* series I'd started when I moved here and had worked on occasionally since. I'd asked my publisher to push back the *Harriet Donovan* one he had immediately wanted when my title became known. He reluctantly agreed, but only if I'd write something in the next one that had to do with my husband's family – maybe a legend.

For a brief moment, I considered visiting Heather at the jail, but Jackson pointed out that it would be more for my benefit than hers. He also reminded me that I was on the radar already in Hilly Dale for this or that reason, and of course, the state papers had picked up the story of the *Vengeful, Voluptuous Vixen*, linking my name to Heather– thank you, Gatsby Gregson – as one of her friends.

"Why give Gregson more fodder," Jackson advised

According to Aunt Jane-Ann, who, as usual, put her two-cents in about my 'shenanigans with Beckham Hailey' causing her once-again to defend the good names of Jenson and Whitley, David James was still a mess. Not only had he learned of his wife's affair and attempted attack on Bianca Hailey, but it came out that Heather had mashed up a strong sleeping pill in the dessert she gave David, making it easy for her to leave the house after their Valentine's evening together. Although nothing was his fault, he was ashamed. It took a lot of courage for him to stop by my house and deliver that letter.

After seeing how much their attitudes in school had affected Heather, Bianca and Betsy made an effort to make peace with me, but I suspect it had more to do with the holiday I was providing for their daughters. I couldn't have cared less about being friends with these two. Until they proved otherwise, I still felt they were cows way down deep, but for the sakes of Allison and Jordan, I accepted their apologies and invited them to tea at my home. I pulled out all the stops – sterling silver, fine china, and crystal, and even had the bakery re-create the High Tea menu from the reading I'd done at the library earlier in the year. My polite but cool impression somehow put them in their place, and I had to admit that gave me a great deal of satisfaction.

Bianca dumped John immediately but kept the engagement ring. Without a man, I suspected she would make a play for Beck in the near future, seeing as how her name was now associated with John and Heather. Betsy was doing just fine. She'd been through the John Knoss experience. Though shocked about his involvement with Heather and the role she played in her own divorce, Betsy no doubt thought Bianca got what she deserved for dating her ex-husband; however, it appeared they were trying to repair their friendship. The enemy of my enemy is my friend, and all that rot.

As for me, I had made a decision. A week later, right after Jordan and Allison left for England, I leaned against Beck as we swung back and forth on the green porch swing in the early spring evening. "Beck," I said, sitting up and looking at him in the glow of the porch light, "I...I...need to tell you something."

Beck took my face in his hands and looked straight into my eyes, "You're leaving," he said softly. "You're moving back to England."

"How did you know?"

He removed his hands from my face and shrugged. "I guess I've always known but didn't want to face it. You've been away too long. I hoped you would be happy here, but you aren't. It's not you," he said in a flat voice. "When I've looked at you when you didn't know that I was, I saw it. It's in your eyes. It's in your tone of voice."

"I tried, Beck. I wanted to fit in."

"No, you didn't, Jessie, not really. You only *thought* you wanted to live here. My friends told me you wouldn't stay, but I didn't listen. All you were doing when you moved here was running away from your life in England, but you ran straight into your past, didn't you."

I started to object, but he was right. I *hadn't* wanted to be part of Hilly Dale; I'd wanted to escape memories of Will and England. When I arrived in Hilly Dale, I reveled in the fact that everything seemed different. The house and its belongings were mine, but I soon realized they were all part of my childhood, and I was no longer a child.

After a couple of months, everywhere I looked were memories of my parents and my grandparents, and there were the expectations of people like my aunt which frustrated me. I was not my mother, and I could never hope to be. She wouldn't have wanted me to live her life. She would want me to live *mine,* but I didn't know exactly what that was anymore. I had carried on in Hilly Dale, trying to make it work, but it hadn't.

As time passed, I learned that the citizens of Hilly Dale didn't want *me.* They didn't want Jessica Jenson Fielding-Smythe. People wanted Jessica Keasden, and later those like Timothy Hayes wanted to be affiliated with Carola, Duchess of Hearthe because they thought it would help them in some way. Worse, there were people wanting my money, even before they knew I had a title, and after that, I was besieged by requests and dubbed selfish when I refused a number of them. I was deemed a snob because I didn't want to join clubs and organizations in which I had no interest, while there were others who *did* want to be part of them who were excluded. I was just someone to be used as a means to an end. Heather had shown me that in a brutal way.

The truth was that I felt suffocated in Hilly Dale, but oddly while in England, despite the restrictions when I married Will, I realized that I felt freer than I ever had in my life. It was as if I was meant to live in my adopted country. I'd been trying to find my place in the world after Will died and my children became able to care for themselves. There were times I didn't know exactly who I was, but one thing was for certain, I wasn't Jessie Jenson from Hilly Dale, Arkansas any longer.

I must have been quiet for some time because Beck asked, "What are you thinking, Jessie?"

I told him and added, "I care for you a great deal, but my life is in England. My family is there, and they've been telling me to come home since I arrived in Hilly Dale. When Aisling stayed behind it hurt, but now that Alistair and Cecilia have informed me that they are expecting a baby, it's clear that I shouldn't be here. I want to see my grandchildren grow up."

"I understand that, but you stayed, even when Aisling didn't. You shouldn't have come back here, Jessie. I mean not long enough to settle in and start up something."

"Perhaps I shouldn't have, but I did. I've done a lot of thinking over the past few days. I *was* escaping when I moved here, but I realized that I was also seeking closure in Hilly Dale. I know where I belong now, Beck. I'm sorry."

"Why? You basically said Hilly Dale was somewhere you had to see and be a part of to know what you wanted. So, I'm *closure*?"

"God, NO. You were unexpected! You are a good part of Hilly Dale. You said it yourself. I don't belong here anymore. I'm British now. I know that. I've lived there longer than I have in the States. I'm renouncing my American citizenship when I return – no more dual citizenship for me. It's time I make a choice."

"You're what? You know, I love you, Jessie, but..." Beck began and stood up. "God, I feel so stupid! I should have listened to my friends. I might have *felt* you weren't going to stay, but you *knew* you weren't, at least deep down you knew it. Why did you allow this whatever we have to start up when you were considering leaving America behind? You could have sold this house and left, but you stayed. Why? Why did you sleep with me those times? Were you just using me as part of your *escape*?"

"Until I moved here, I didn't know what I wanted," I said honestly, but the truth was, I couldn't answer his other questions because I didn't know for sure. Perhaps I did sleep with him to exorcise Will's ghost and help me move on, but I doubted it. I just knew I wasn't ready to settle down with him, at least not yet, and definitely not in Hilly Dale. I didn't want Bianca or Betsy or my aunt or anyone else interfering, gossiping about our relationship, or speculating. I *wanted* to be with my family. It wasn't a mistake coming to Hilly Dale; it was a mistake allowing myself to get mixed-up with Beck again. It wasn't good for either of us. This wasn't going to end well.

"And you still don't know," he said, walking toward the steps. "Were you using me?" he asked again.

"What? If you want to play that game, I could ask you the same thing. Why did you pursue me when you *felt* I would leave and your friends told you I would? Was it to sleep with me? Something you wanted to do but never got to when we were younger?"

"God, Jessie. No. I guess it was because when I saw you at Walmart, I wanted to be part of your life again. I was hoping against hope you *would* decide to stay, but since you're being so *blunt*, are you leaving because you would lose your title if you married someone else? Is your fancy life that important to you?" Beck asked, now standing at the foot of the steps. "Yeah, I did my research. I know I don't have a title, but I'm not broke, and I don't have to live in Hilly Dale. I've lived other places, you know."

"Do you think I'm that much of a....I can't even say the word…" I knew he was hurt by what I'd said, but this was mean. "I'm not Bianca who wanted you for your status in school, dumped you, and then miraculously found you after you made a fortune in New York, and then took up with her friend's ex-husband." I snapped. "Goodnight, Beck." I got up and headed for the front door.

Immediately regretting my words, I turned to apologize, but Beck cut me off before I could. "I don't know what to think of you," he called out as he made his way down the sidewalk. "Buzz me out the gate, *Your Grace*."

"All right," I replied before I shut the door. Was I proud of my behavior and what I said? No, but I didn't think Beck would say the things he did. Our emotions ran deep. We allowed them to get in the way of what I'd hoped would be a rational discussion. Couldn't he have understood? He had a daughter, friends and some other family in Hilly Dale and the surrounding area. I didn't, except for Aunt Jane-Ann. Couldn't I have expressed myself better? I supposed old hurts and misunderstandings did run deep.

Chapter Thirty-Three

I didn't hear from Beck the next day, but I shouldn't have expected it after the words we'd exchanged. On to the next person.

"What brings you to my door this morning, Jessica?" my aunt asked when I appeared unannounced. "You really should have called. I'm on my way to my garden club and then the book club tonight. I daresay you don't want to attend either of those."

"No, thank you for your kind invitation, though." Without being asked, I took a seat on the sofa.

"Don't be smart, Jessica. It's unbecoming. I would have thought your life elsewhere would have taught you things. I watch those British television shows sometimes."

I wasn't smarting off; I was serious. "Life does not always imitate art. I need to tell you something. When I'd finished what I'd come to say, I got up to leave. "I hope you understand. I don't want to keep you from your clubs."

"So, you come to Hilly Dale, enroll your daughter in college, live here a bit, disrupt lives, and then decide you don't like it here, and move off because Hilly Dale is just not grand enough for someone like you. And I've learned that you are actually a citizen over there! That's the *gist* of that flowery speech you gave. Oh, don't think the entire town doesn't know you have been sleeping with Beckham Hailey, and that you paid for his daughter's trip to England – her and that Knoss girl." Aunt Jane-Ann sniped.

Trying to maintain a semblance of the poise I'd tossed to the wind last night, I replied, "You're right. I found I no longer fit in, but it's not that I find myself better than anyone. Hilly Dale was always like it is now, in the sense of drama and such, but I didn't see it. I was too young. I'm an adult now and I see it in a different light. You can't understand because you've never lived anywhere but here. You don't know what it feels like to be gone and return many years later when most of your friends have either moved away, or else you've been gone out of their lives for so long they don't think of you, and if they do, it's because you're a..." I stopped for a moment. "It can be very lonely moving back."

"I tried to get you interested in my clubs."

"That's true, but I don't enjoy gardening, and I'm too busy with my writing to commit to a book club."

"Well, you are certainly different. You never did like it here, even when you were a child. You were always the odd one, Jessica. You only took interests in books, languages, and writing. Nothing especially social."

"What do you expect? My mother was an English professor, and you were a librarian for a number of years."

"Nevertheless, you didn't try to fit in back then, and you became friends with that girl who turned out to be a lunatic."

"How was I to know she would grow up to have some serious mental health problems."

"I tried to warn you about her, but I would have thought you would have been able to pick up on something. Well, you've made a name for yourself in this town. Friends with a crazy person, sleeping with a married man, insulting people with that horrible Hillbilly Dale business, and just trouncing our fine town, and now our country by giving up your citizenship. I don't know how I'll be able to live with the embarrassment."

Oh, I was sure she would find a way! Why did she make it so difficult to even like her. My mother loved her as a sister but liking her was another thing.

"Yes, you did try to warn me, and I didn't listen. That's on me, but as to the other things you mentioned, I suppose you won't mind that I'm leaving the country," I said, getting up and walking out. There were so many things I could have said to her, but I felt sorry for a woman who was so concerned with her standing in the town.

Jackson had a completely different attitude when I joined him at Cajun Daisy's for lunch.

"I've wondered why you waited so long. And I'll have someone to visit when I go to England!"

"You are welcome any time. Have I really made a mess of things in Hilly Dale? I've been told I haven't made an effort to fit in by two people now. I suppose someone will blame me for Heather's breakdown next." I told him about the letter.

"Well, that mystery's solved, and it's time you forgot about things in Hilly Dale. Why should you have to fit in? You have to be you. Your life is in England, regardless if you have a title or not. People expected you to be the same as you were when you left here. Of course you're different and have had trouble finding a niche for yourself. Yes, you can do your writing anywhere, but you're living in your childhood home, lovely though it is, and among all those things that belonged to your family. You're busy with work which means you still haven't managed to sort through things and have a sale."

"I know," I replied taking a bite of chicken.

"Townspeople have been driving you crazy for this or that. I know you haven't talked about it in a while, but I hear stories. you get to live with the consequences of the choices you make in a small town. Someone's always going to be 'put out' with you."

"Thank you. I needed to hear that."

"Now, how did Beckham take the news?"

"Not well," I said, and shared what happened.

"It's not surprising. You and Beckham went through an intense time recently. It brought you closer together, and perhaps things moved too fast. He'll be all right. Beckham just needs time. In the meantime, I'll help you sort through things and get ready for your move. When do you plan on leaving?"

"Four weeks should just about do it. Did I tell you that I'm going to be a grandmother?"

"NO!" Jackson shouted.

"Alistair and Cecilia told me. It's early days. I do want to talk with you about something I've been working on in secret. I am definitely going to need your help to oversee things."

"I need a project, Jessica. I'm bored since I retired."

For the next month, I spent my time working and sorting through things in the house. Jackson and I worked on my other project, so my days were full. I often worked late into the night on my manuscripts. Beck had kept his distance. I saw him once in Walmart and he nodded politely before pushing his cart on by. Betsy had, surprisingly, contacted me with an idea that fit with my project, and when I mentioned her to Jackson, he thought we should join forces. I had misjudged her. She had definitely changed from the girl I knew in high school. We reminisced about our early childhood when we were once friends. She and Bianca had made up a bit, but Bianca was planning a move from Hilly Dale.

It was a week before my movers arrived when I invited Aunt Jane-Ann to come by the house. "Well, it certainly looks like you've gone over everything, Jessica," she said looking around at a pile of boxes stacked in the foyer. "I understood you were getting rid of all you could in a sale. When is it? You know I told you during football season is a bad time. And you don't have a For Sale sign up, not that many people will be able to afford this house with all the changes you've made with the fence and alarms, and who knows what else. I'd try Dolen's Realty, if I were you. It's the best Hilly Dale has to offer. All the important people use them."

"That's just it. I'm not using an estate agent. I'm not selling the house."

"What? It's going to sit here empty?"

"That depends on you."

"What do you mean? I have no control over this house."

"Not yet."

For once, my aunt looked dumbfounded. "What do you…mean?" she asked again, looking around the foyer.

"I'm giving you the house and everything that I'm not taking back to England. They are all yours."

"You're giving this house to me?" she confirmed, looking at me like I was crazy.

"The deed will be transferred to your name. After that, you can live here or sell it, whatever you choose, but there's a wonderful back garden and rooms for hosting your clubs in style. There's a bedroom and a full bath downstairs, so you won't have to climb stairs all the time."

"I can't afford the upkeep. You should know that." She looked into the formal living room and then back at me.

"It's all arranged. I'm putting a certain amount of money in the bank, but I'd advise you to seek assistance from a financial advisor to budget. And, you can either rent or sell your house."

"I don't know what to say."

"Just say 'thank you.' That's enough for me."

My aunt left the house in a stupor. I hoped she'd be able to drive home. I was also leaving one car for Jordan and another for Allison Knoss.

***

I was emotional the day the movers arrived. I took one more look through the house, stopping in the turret room to gaze at the site of Hilly Dale spreading out below the hill where my street ran. There were the churches' steeples and spires. I could glimpse a section of the downtown, which with the money I'd left would be somewhat revitalized under the supervision of Jackson Barker and Betsy Franklin. I asked that the donor remain anonymous. I would always be connected to Hilly Dale, and this was my parting gift. The town contained my roots, like it or not, but that didn't mean they couldn't spread and grow elsewhere, even across the sea. I had deep roots in England now.

After putting Violet in her travel crate, I set the alarm, and walked out the front door into the late April sunshine. The fuchsia azaleas were blooming along the porch's edge. I'd half-expected to see Beck waiting for me at the gate to say goodbye, but he was not there. I'd texted him that I was leaving and wished him well, but there was nothing in reply. A clean break, I supposed.

Alistair hired a private jet for me, and this time, I didn't argue. It was easier with Violet along. I settled back in the comfortable seat for the long flight to England. I was going home.

Epilogue

Summer, One Year Later...

My flight landed at Heathrow early one summer morning. Although I'd made the crossing a few times in the past year for business, this time there was no car waiting to take me to my destination. I had decided to rent a car in order to pick up my daughter who was spending her spring break at a friend's house in Bibury. From there, we would go on to Fielding House.

The Cotswolds were beautiful, and on a day like today - partly sunny and not too warm - I knew there would be lots of tourists and was thankful my daughter was not staying in the town itself. Using GPS, I set it for the less-traveled roads and ended up veering onto country lanes where I avoided most traffic issues, other than the occasional horse and rider, and escaped the dreaded roundabouts. It was longer, but I enjoyed a less-hectic drive.

By the time I reached Haver Manor, a seventeenth-century house situated down a narrow lane, the sky had darkened and it had just started to rain. "That's all I needed today," I grumbled. About an hour later, the rain stopped and the sun was trying to peek out. A good sign.

I hadn't seen my daughter for a while since she began attending university. She liked it far better than Hilly Dale College. We drove along talking about this and that, as parents and children do, revealing some things, hinting at others, and completely hiding some of the most important topics, but that was mainly her doing. Of course, I'd been guilty of hiding things from her, too.

The fall-out from the John Knoss and Heather James mess had hit me hard. It had taken nearly a year for me to get my life back together. The move had definitely helped me gain perspective, but it hadn't been easy. I still thought of the burgeoning relationship I'd lost. I'd acted foolishly and selfishly toward the one person I didn't want to lose. Later, I couldn't understand how the both of us would give up so easily without at least trying to make it work After I left Hilly Dale, I'd wanted to make amends and offer friendship, but I didn't know how, given the way we left things. We hadn't even said goodbye.

"You missed the turn! What's the matter with you?" my daughter cried, as I sped past the turn-off to Fielding House.

What *was* the matter with me? I'd been thinking of my crazy idea, that's what, instead of paying attention. I drove ahead until I saw a place where I could maneuver the car and turn around. God, I was glad I'd rented a small car.

"Hey, I'm sorry. I was just thinking."

"Yeah, I know what about," she said.

The imposing portcullis set into the old stone gatehouse was open, which surprised me. I shifted gears and drove up the hill and then I saw it – Fielding House – waiting for me at the end of a short drive lined with evergreen shrubbery. The closer we got the more nervous I became. I didn't know why. This was what I wanted. The large three-story stone house in the traditional 'E' shape seemed daunting as I pulled up to the front entrance. My daughter hopped out of the car and made a beeline to the front door. I started to follow suit but paused for a moment looking up at the grand country house.

"Hurry up. Don't wait on the staff. They work so hard."

"I'm glad to see you don't expect others to cater to you," I replied, getting out and closing the car door. "You must have learned a lot at the university."

The front door opened and a young woman appeared and ran to greet us.

"Aisling!" my daughter cried. "See, I told you he'd come. He just needed some encouragement. Where's your mother?"

"She went for a walk."

"A walk? You said she be here by this time." And then it hit me. "Didn't she know I was coming?" I asked with what I was sure was accompanied by a horrified expression. When I'd finally made up my mind to talk to Jessie, I had wanted to do it in person. It was my understanding that she had agreed to it.

Both girls began laughing. "No," Aisling said. "Mum doesn't live here, at least not much of the time. She lives in Lilac House in the Cotswolds. I told her Alistair wanted her to come to Fielding House to go over some business, and to see her grandson, of course. How was your flight from New York?"

"Oh, he said it was fine," Jordan answered.

"Girls!" I cried, exasperated. "You *didn't* tell her." This was definitely not good. After Jessie left Hilly Dale, I'd driven past the white Victorian numerous times, just to make sure things were okay, of course. Her aunt had moved in and, from what I understood was overjoyed with owning the house. Jackson had eventually told me that Jessie was behind the downtown revitalization plan. I figured she was. I didn't know anyone who could give ten-million dollars for something like that, and I suspected everyone else knew too, the way the grapevine in that town worked, but I stayed quiet.

The one I felt the worst for was Allison Knoss. She'd stayed on at Hilly Dale College, but finally transferred to the University of Arkansas. Her father moved back to California. As for my ex-wife Bianca, she was in Montana and living with a rancher. Jackson told me a few months back that David James had found a position somewhere far from Hilly Dale. I didn't know what college, but I think he just took anything to get away. Heather was in a psychiatric hospital still undergoing treatment. She was improving, and there was hope in a couple of years she'd be released, but there was a petition circulating that she not be allowed back in Hilly Dale.

As for Jessie, I'd thought about contacting her over the past year. In fact, when she had a book signing in New York City several months ago, I'd taken off work early and gone to the bookstore fully intending to walk in and see her, but when I peered in the window at her sitting there, her face shining with happiness as she spoke with a fan, I couldn't go in. There were many times I'd wanted to call her to let her know I'd left Hilly Dale and moved back to New York where I was working for an investment company – a company that had a branch in London as it happened – I couldn't. I'd managed to convince my boss that I'd be the perfect one to act as a liaison between the NYC and London offices, because my daughter was going to school in England. Oh, she wasn't going to St. Andrews like Aisling was, but she was getting a good education and it got her out of Hilly Dale. It hadn't been easy for either of us there after last year's drama.

"Please come in," Aisling said. "Ceci and Alistair are upstairs with William Charles. He's my nephew, Mr. Hailey! And Liam's going to be here for dinner, Jordan." I caught the wink Aisling threw at my daughter. I knew Jordan was dating someone, but Liam?

As I walked through the Great Hall with its black-and-white tiled floors, and its pictures of Elizabeth I and other monarchs, it suddenly hit me. This really was Jessie's life – a stately home saturated in history and tradition. It was a place that had entertained kings and queens. I'd seen the photos and read the information about Fielding House that was available online, but I didn't really believe it, even when Jessie had shown me her personal photos, but this *was* real. I was here, and I was ready to run for the hills. This was more than I bargained for and way out-of-my league. How could anyone, including me, have expected Jessie to fit the Hilly Dale norm if they could see this place. A butler was hovering nearby talking with Aisling and Jordan. My daughter left them and walked over to me.

"Dad, she's at the lake by her favorite place." I stood there staring at the minstrel's gallery – at least I knew what it was. Jessie had shown me a picture of this room and told me. "Dad!" Jordan cried again, "What are you waiting for? Go get her."

Jordan propelled me toward the doorway where Aisling was standing. "This way, Mr. Hailey. It won't be dark for a little while, and if you're there longer, Mum knows the way back by heart."

We walked past an impressive staircase and exited out a glass-paned door into a courtyard between the two wings. Aisling pointed out a narrow path through the trees ahead. After leaving the house behind, I started walking down hill until the ground leveled. As I rounded a bend, I saw a bell tower in the distance, and soon I was passing through the graveyard, walking beside very old gravestones, some chipped, cracked, or leaning. An old church appeared on a peninsula that jutted into the lake. I soldiered on until I saw a woman wearing jeans and a loose, blue-and-white checked shirt facing the water. Her streaked light-brown hair was down and moving gently in the breeze. I stumbled on loose rocks along the path near the church, alerting her to my presence. She turned and faced me.

"Beckham?" she asked, an incredulous look on her beautiful face.

"Yes, I, uh..." I couldn't speak as I cautiously approached her.

"Beck," she said softly and reached out her hand to clasp mine. We stood there watching the sunset, neither of us speaking, until she suddenly turned to me, looked into my eyes, and asked, "Did you hear that?"

I heard nothing but the lake's small waves lapping against the cliff.

"Shhh," she said, pressing her fingers to my lips, and then I heard it. The dull tones of an old bell rang out, but that didn't make sense. The bell in that tower would have needed at least one person to pull the rope. Puzzled, I looked at Jessie. Her face was radiant in the glow of the sunset.

"It's Will," she said so quietly I had to lean closer to hear her. "This was our special place, and now he's sending a message that it's time for me to get on with my life and be happy."

"With me?" I asked.

"I hope so," she replied.

"I'm willing to give it another shot. After all I didn't travel to Fielding House for nothing," I said, trying to lighten the mood.

"I'm not the same girl I was growing up in Hilly Dale, Arkansas," she warned, "You know that now."

"Don't worry. I'm not a nostalgia nut. I'm all for new beginnings."

"The sun will be all the way down behind the hills soon. We had better make our way back."

Hand-in-hand, we walked through the graveyard toward Fielding House where her noble family and my daughter awaited us. I didn't know if I could handle a transatlantic romance, but Jessica Carola Jenson Fielding-Smythe, Duchess of Hearthe, writer of novels, and the love of my life, was worth the effort.

The End

Thank you for reading *The Duchess of Hillbilly Dale*.

Other books by Jennifer Cadgwith

The Face Age